MERRY MURDER

MERRY MURDER

The best Christmas mysteries from John D. MacDonald, Anthony Boucher, John Mortimer, Sir Arthur Conan Doyle and 18 more masters of mystery

Edited by Cynthia Manson

SEAFARER BOOKS • NEW YORK

SEAFARER BOOKS
a Division of Penguin Books USA Inc.
375 Hudson Street, New York, New York 10014

Published by Seafarer Books, a division of Penguin Books USA Inc.

First Seafarer Printing, October 1994

The stories in this book were selected from *Mystery for Christmas, Murder for Christmas*, and *Murder Under the Mistletoe*, which were originally published by Signet, an imprint of Dutton/Signet.

Complete text of *Mystery for Christmas* Copyright © 1990 by Davis Publications, Inc.
Complete text of *Murder for Christmas* Copyright © 1991 by Davis Publications, Inc.
Complete text of *Murder Under the Mistletoe* Copyright © 1992 by
Bantam Doubleday Dell Direct, Inc.
Abridgment Copyright © 1994 by Bantam Doubleday Dell Direct, Inc.
All rights reserved.

Pages 435–436 constitute an extension of this copyright page.

ISBN 0-8289-0883-4
Printed in the United States of America
10 9 8 7 6 5 4 3 2 1

Contents

Rumpole and the Spirit of Christmas
JOHN MORTIMER   1

Supper with Miss Shivers
PETER LOVESEY   14

The Adventure of the Blue Carbuncle
SIR ARTHUR CONAN DOYLE   25

A Matter of Life and Death
GEORGES SIMENON   47

I Saw Mommy Killing Santa Claus
GEORGE BAXT   109

Dead on Christmas Street
JOHN D. MACDONALD   118

The Christmas Bear
HERBERT RESNICOW   135

Mystery for Christmas
ANTHONY BOUCHER   151

On Christmas Day in the Morning
MARGERY ALLINGHAM   168

Santa Claus Beat
REX STOUT   179

Who Killed Father Christmas?
PATRICIA MOYES   184

'Twixt the Cup and the Lip
JULIAN SYMONS   195

Auggie Wren's Christmas Story
PAUL AUSTER   225

Murder at Christmas
C. M. CHAN   233

Father Crumlish Celebrates Christmas
ALICE SCANLAN REACH   280

The Plot Against Santa Claus
JAMES POWELL   300

Christmas Cop
THOMAS LARRY ADCOCK   324

But Once a Year ... Thank God!
JOYCE PORTER   337

Christmas Party
MARTIN WERNER   358

Kelso's Christmas
MALCOLM MCCLINTICK   367

The Spy and the Christmas Cipher
EDWARD D. HOCH   383

The Carol Singers
JOSEPHINE BELL   400

MERRY MURDER

RUMPOLE AND THE SPIRIT OF CHRISTMAS

BY JOHN MORTIMER

I realized that Christmas was upon us when I saw a sprig of holly over the list of prisoners hung on the wall of the cells under the Old Bailey.

I pulled out a new box of small cigars and found its opening obstructed by a tinseled band on which a scarlet-faced Santa was seen hurrying a sleigh full of carcinoma-packed goodies to the Rejoicing World. I lit one as the lethargic screw, with a complexion the color of faded Bronco, regretfully left his doorstep sandwich and mug of sweet tea to unlock the gate.

"Good morning, Mr. Rumpole. Come to visit a customer?"

"Happy Christmas, officer," I said as cheerfully as possible. "Is Mr. Timson at home?"

"Well, I don't believe he's slipped down to his little place in the country."

Such were the pleasantries that were exchanged between us legal hacks and discontented screws; jokes that no doubt have changed little since the turnkeys unlocked the door at Newgate to let in a pessimistic advocate, or the cells under the Coliseum were opened to admit the unwelcome news of the Imperial thumbs-down.

*   *   *

1

"My mum wants me home for Christmas."

Which Christmas? It would have been an unreasonable remark and I refrained from it. Instead, I said, "All things are possible."

As I sat in the interviewing room, an Old Bailey hack of some considerable experience, looking through my brief and inadvertently using my waistcoat as an ashtray, I hoped I wasn't on another loser. I had had a run of bad luck during that autumn season, and young Edward Timson was part of that huge south London family whose criminal activities provided such welcome grist to the Rumpole mill. The charge in the seventeen-year-old Eddie's case was nothing less than wilful murder.

"We're in with a chance, though, Mr. Rumpole, ain't we?"

Like all his family, young Timson was a confirmed optimist. And yet, of course, the merest outsider in the Grand National, the hundred-to-one shot, is in with a chance, and nothing is more like going round the course at Aintree than living through a murder trial. In this particular case, a fanatical prosecutor named Wrigglesworth, known to me as the Mad Monk, was to represent Beechers, and Mr. Justice Vosper, a bright but wintry-hearted judge who always felt it his duty to lead for the prosecution, was to play the part of a particularly menacing fence at the Canal Turn.

"A chance. Well, yes, of course you've got a chance, if they can't establish common purpose, and no one knows which of you bright lads had the weapon."

No doubt the time had come for a brief glance at the prosecution case, not an entirely cheering prospect. Eddie, also known as "Turpin" Timson, lived in a kind of decaying barracks, a sort of highrise Lubianka, known as Keir Hardie Court, somewhere in south London, together with his parents, his various brothers, and his thirteen-year-old sister, Noreen. This particular branch of the Timson family lived on the thirteenth floor. Below them, on the twelfth, lived the large clan of the O'Dowds. The war between the Timsons and the O'Dowds began, it seems, with the casting of the Nativity play at the local comprehensive school.

Christmas comes earlier each year and the school show was planned about September. When Bridget O'Dowd was chosen to play the lead in the face of strong competition from Noreen Timson, an incident occurred comparable in historical importance to the assassination of an obscure Austrian archduke at Sarejevo. Noreen Timson announced in the playground that Bridget O'Dowd was a spotty little tart unsuited to play any role of which the most notable characteristic was virginity.

Hearing this, Bridget O'Dowd kicked Noreen Timson behind the anthracite bunkers. Within a few days, war was declared between the Timson and O'Dowd children, and a present of lit fireworks was posted through the O'Dowd front door. On what is known as the "night in question," reinforcements of O'Dowds and Timsons arrived in old bangers from a number of south London addresses and battle was joined on the stone staircase, a bleak terrain of peeling walls scrawled with graffiti, blowing empty Coca-cola tins and torn newspapers. The weapons seemed to have been articles in general domestic use, such as bread knives, carving knives, broom handles, and a heavy screwdriver. At the end of the day it appeared that the upstairs flat had repelled the invaders, and Kevin O'Dowd lay on the stairs. Having been stabbed with a slender and pointed blade, he was in a condition to become known as "the deceased" in the case of the Queen against Edward Timson. I made an application for bail for my client which was refused, but a speedy trial was ordered.

So even as Bridget O'Dowd was giving her Virgin Mary at the comprehensive, the rest of the family was waiting to give evidence against Eddie Timson in that home of British drama, Number One Court at the Old Bailey.

"I never had no cutter, Mr. Rumpole. Straight up, I never had one," the defendant told me in the cells. He was an appealing-looking lad with soft brown eyes, who had already won the heart of the highly susceptible lady who wrote his social inquiry report. ("Although the charge is a serious one, this is a young man who might respond well to a period of probation." I could imagine the steely contempt in Mr. Justice Vosper's eye when he read that.)

"Well, tell me, Edward. Who had?"

"I never seen no cutters on no one, honest I didn't. We wasn't none of us tooled up, Mr. Rumpole."

"Come on, Eddie. Someone must have been. They say even young Noreen was brandishing a potato peeler."

"Not me, honest."

"What about your sword?"

There was one part of the prosecution evidence that I found particularly distasteful. It was agreed that on the previous Sunday morning, Eddie "Turpin" Timson had appeared on the stairs of Keir Hardie Court and flourished what appeared to be an antique cavalry saber at the assembled O'Dowds, who were just popping out to Mass.

"Me sword I bought up the Portobello? I didn't have that there, honest."

"The prosecution can't introduce evidence about the sword. It was an entirely different occasion." Mr. Barnard, my instructing solicitor who fancied himself as an infallible lawyer, spoke with a confidence which I couldn't feel. He, after all, wouldn't have to stand up on his hind legs and argue the legal toss with Mr. Justice Vosper.

"It rather depends on who's prosecuting us. I mean, if it's some fairly reasonable fellow—"

"I think," Mr. Barnard reminded me, shattering my faint optimism and ensuring that we were all in for a very rough Christmas indeed, "I think it's Mr. Wrigglesworth. Will he try to introduce the sword?"

I looked at "Turpin" Timson with a kind of pity. "If it is the Mad Monk, he undoubtedly will."

When I went into Court, Basil Wrigglesworth was standing with his shoulders hunched up round his large, red ears, his gown dropped to his elbows, his bony wrists protruding from the sleeves of his frayed jacket, his wig pushed back, and his huge hands joined on his lectern in what seemed to be an attitude of devoted prayer. A lump of cotton wool clung to his chin where he had cut himself shaving. Although well into his sixties, he preserved a look of boyish clumsiness. He appeared, as he always did when about to prosecute on a charge carrying a major punishment, radiantly happy.

"Ah, Rumpole," he said, lifting his eyes from the police verbals as though they were his breviary. "Are you defending *as usual*?"

"Yes, Wrigglesworth. And you're prosecuting *as usual*?" It wasn't much of a riposte but it was all I could think of at the time.

"Of course, I don't defend. One doesn't like to call witnesses who may not be telling the truth."

"You must have a few unhappy moments then, calling certain members of the Constabulary."

"I can honestly tell you, Rumpole—" his curiously innocent blue eyes looked at me with a sort of pain, as though I had questioned the doctrine of the immaculate conception "—I have never called a dishonest policeman."

"Yours must be a singularly simple faith, Wrigglesworth."

"As for the Detective Inspector in this case," counsel for the prosecution went on, "I've known Wainwright for years. In fact, this is his last trial before he retires. He could no more invent a verbal against a defendant than fly."

Any more on that tack, I thought, and we should soon be debating how many angels could dance on the point of a pin.

"Look here, Wrigglesworth. That evidence about my client having a sword: it's quite irrelevent. I'm sure you'd agree."

"Why is it irrelevant?" Wrigglesworth frowned.

"Because the murder clearly wasn't done with an antique cavalry saber. It was done with a small, thin blade."

"If he's a man who carries weapons, why isn't that relevant?"

"A man? Why do you call him a man? He's a child. A boy of seventeen!"

"Man enough to commit a serious crime."

"*If* he did."

"If he didn't, he'd hardly be in the dock."

"That's the difference between us, Wrigglesworth," I told him. "I believe in the presumption of innocence. You believe in original sin. Look here, old darling." I tried to give the Mad Monk a smile of friendship and became conscious of the fact that it looked, no doubt, like an ingratiating sneer. "Give us a chance. You won't introduce the evidence of the sword, will you?"

"Why ever not?"

"Well," I told him, "the Timsons are an industrious family of criminals. They work hard, they never go on strike. If it weren't for people like the Timsons, you and I would be out of a job."

"They sound in great need of prosecution and punishment. Why shouldn't I tell the jury about your client's sword? Can you give me one good reason?"

"Yes," I said, as convincingly as possible.

"What is it?" He peered at me, I thought, unfairly.

"Well, after all," I said, doing my best, "it is Christmas."

It would be idle to pretend that the first day in Court went well, although Wrigglesworth restrained himself from mentioning the sword in his opening speech, and told me that he was considering whether or not to call evidence about it the next day. I cross-examined a few members of the clan O'Dowd on the presence of lethal articles in the hands of the attacking force. The evidence about this varied, and weapons came and went in the hands of the inhabitants of Number Twelve as the witnesses were blown hither and thither in the winds of Rumpole's cross-examination. An interested observer from one of the other flats spoke of having seen a machete.

"Could that terrible weapon have been in the hands of Mr. Kevin O'Dowd, the deceased in this case?"

"I don't think so."

"But can you rule out the possibility?"

"No, I can't rule it out," the witness admitted, to my temporary delight.

"You can never rule out the possibility of anything in this world, Mr. Rumpole. But he doesn't think so. You have your answer."

Mr. Justice Vosper, in a voice like a splintering iceberg, gave me this unwelcome Christmas present. The case wasn't going well, but at least, by the end of the first day, the Mad Monk had kept out all mention of the sword. The next day he was to call young Bridget O'Dowd, fresh from her triumph in the Nativity play.

"I say, Rumpole, I'd be *so* grateful for a little help."

I was in Pommeroy's Wine Bar, drowning the sorrows of the day in my usual bottle of the cheapest Chateau Fleet Street (made from grapes which, judging from the bouquet, might have been not so much trodden as kicked to death by sturdy peasants in gum boots) when I looked up to see Wrigglesworth, dressed in an old mackintosh, doing business with Jack Pommeroy at the sales counter. When I crossed to him, he was not buying the jumbo-sized bottle of ginger beer which I imagined might be his celebratory Christmas tipple, but a tempting and respectably aged bottle of Chateau Pichon Longueville.

"What can I do for you, Wrigglesworth?"

"Well, as you know, Rumpole, I live in Croydon."

"Happiness is given to few of us on this earth," I said piously.

"And the Anglican Sisters of St. Agnes, Croydon, are anxious to buy a present for their Bishop," Wrigglesworth explained. "A dozen bottles for Christmas. They've asked my advice, Rumpole. I know so little about wine. You wouldn't care to try this for me? I mean, if you're not especially busy."

"I should be hurrying home to dinner." My wife, Hilda (She Who Must Be Obeyed), was laying on rissoles and frozen peas, washed down by my last bottle of Pommeroy's extremely ordinary. "However, as it's Christmas, I don't mind helping you out, Wrigglesworth."

The Mad Monk was clearly quite unused to wine. As we sampled the claret together, I saw the chance of getting him to commit himself on the vital question of the evidence of the sword, as well as absorbing an unusually decent bottle. After the Pichon Longueville I was kind enough to help him by sampling a Boyd-Cantenac and then I said, "Excellent, this. But of course the Bishop might be a burgundy man. The nuns might care to invest in a decent Macon."

"Shall we try a bottle?" Wrigglesworth suggested. "I'd be grateful for your advice."

"I'll do my best to help you, my old darling. And while we're on the subject, that ridiculous bit of evidence about young Timson and the sword—"

"I remember you saying I shouldn't bring that out because it's Christmas."

"Exactly." Jack Pommeroy had uncorked the Macon and it was mingling with the claret to produce a feeling of peace and goodwill towards men. Wrigglesworth frowned, as though trying to absorb an obscure point of theology.

"I don't quite see the relevance of Christmas to the question of your man Timson threatening his neighbors with a sword."

"Surely, Wrigglesworth—" I knew my prosecutor well "—you're of a religious disposition?" The Mad Monk was the product of some bleak northern Catholic boarding school. He lived alone, and no doubt wore a hair shirt under his black waistcoat and was vowed to celibacy. The fact that he had his nose deep into a glass of burgundy at the moment was due to the benign influence of Rumpole.

"I'm a Christian, yes."

"Then practice a little Christian tolerance."

"Tolerance towards evil?"

"Evil?" I asked. "What do you mean, evil?"

"Couldn't that be your trouble, Rumpole? That you really don't recognize evil when you see it."

"I suppose," I said, "evil might be locking up a seventeen-year-old during Her Majesty's pleasure, when Her Majesty may very probably forget all about him, banging him up with a couple of hard and violent cases and their own chamber-pots for twenty-two hours a day, so he won't come out till he's a real, genuine, middle-aged murderer."

"I did hear the Reverend Mother say—" Wrigglesworth was gazing vacantly at the empty Macon bottle "—that the Bishop likes his glass of port."

"Then in the spirit of Christmas tolerance I'll help you to sample some of Pommeroy's Light and Tawny."

A little later, Wrigglesworth held up his port glass in a reverent sort of fashion.

"You're suggesting, are you, that I should make some special concession in this case because it's Christmastime?"

"Look here, old darling." I absorbed half my glass, relishing the gentle fruitiness and the slight tang of wood. "If you spent your whole life in that highrise hell-hole called Keir Hardie Court, if you had no fat prosecutions to occupy your attention and no prospect of any job at all, if you had no sort of occupation except war with the O'Dowds—"

"My own flat isn't particularly comfortable. I don't know a great deal about *your* home life, Rumpole, but you don't seem to be in a tearing hurry to experience it."

"Touché, Wrigglesworth, my old darling." I ordered us a couple of refills of Pommeroy's port to further postpone the encounter with She Who Must Be Obeyed and her rissoles.

"But we don't have to fight to the death on the staircase," Wrigglesworth pointed out.

"We don't have to fight at all, Wrigglesworth."

"As your client did."

"As my client *may* have done. Remember the presumption of innocence."

"This is rather funny, this is." The prosecutor pulled back his lips to reveal strong, yellowish teeth and laughed appreciatively. "You know why your man Timson is called 'Turpin'?"

"No." I drank port uneasily, fearing an unwelcome revelation.

"Because he's always fighting with that sword of his. He's called after Dick Turpin, you see, who's always dueling on television. Do you watch television, Rumpole?"

"Hardly at all."

"I watch a great deal of television, as I'm alone rather a lot." Wrigglesworth referred to the box as though it were a sort of penance, like fasting or flagellation. "Detective

Inspector Wainwright told me about your client. Rather amusing, I thought it was. He's retiring this Christmas."

"My client?"

"No. D.I. Wainwright. Do you think we should settle on this port for the Bishop? Or would you like to try a glass of something else?"

"Christmas," I told Wrigglesworth severely as we sampled the Cockburn, "is not just a material, pagan celebration. It's not just an occasion for absorbing superior vintages, old darling. It must be a time when you try to do good, spiritual good to our enemies."

"To your client, you mean?"

"And to me."

"To you, Rumpole?"

"For God's sake, Wrigglesworth!" I was conscious of the fact that my appeal was growing desperate. "I've had six losers in a row down the Old Bailey. Can't I be included in any Christmas spirit that's going around?"

"You mean, at Christmas especially it is more blessed to give than to receive?"

"I mean exactly that." I was glad that he seemed, at last, to be following my drift.

"And you think I might give this case to someone, like a Christmas present?"

"If you care to put it that way, yes."

"I do not care to put it in *exactly* that way." He turned his pale-blue eyes on me with what I thought was genuine sympathy. "But I shall try and do the case of R. *v.* Timson in the way most appropriate to the greatest feast of the Christian year. It is a time, I quite agree, for the giving of presents."

When they finally threw us out of Pommeroy's, and after we had considered the possibility of buying the Bishop brandy in the Cock Tavern, and even beer in the Devereux, I let my instinct, like an aged horse, carry me on to the Underground and home to Gloucester Road, and there discovered the rissoles like some traces of a vanished civilization, fossilized in the oven. She Who Must Be Obeyed was already in bed, feigning sleep. When I climbed in beside her, she opened a hostile eye.

"You're drunk, Rumpole!" she said. "What on earth have you been doing?"

"I've been having a legal discussion," I told her, "on the subject of the admissibility of certain evidence. Vital, from my client's point of view. And, just for a change, Hilda, I think I've won."

"Well, you'd better try and get some sleep." And she added with a sort of satisfaction, "I'm sure you'll be feeling quite terrible in the morning."

As with all the grimmer predictions of She Who Must Be Obeyed, this one turned out to be true. I sat in the Court the next day with the wig feeling like a lead weight on the brain and the stiff collar sawing the neck like a blunt execution. My mouth tasted of matured birdcage and from a long way off I heard Wrigglesworth say to Bridget O'Dowd, who stood looking particularly saintly and virginal in the witness box, "About a week before this, did you see the defendant, Edward Timson, on your staircase flourishing any sort of weapon?"

It is no exaggeration to say that I felt deeply shocked and considerably betrayed. After his promise to me, Wrigglesworth had turned his back on the spirit of the great Christmas festival. He came not to bring peace but a sword.

I clambered with some difficulty to my feet. After my forensic efforts of the evening before, I was scarcely in the mood for a legal argument. Mr. Justice Vosper looked up in surprise and greeted me in his usual chilly fashion.

"Yes, Mr. Rumpole. Do you object to this evidence?"

Of course I object, I wanted to say. It's inhuman, unnecessary, unmerciful, and likely to lead to my losing another case. Also, it's clearly contrary to a solemn and binding contract entered into after a number of glasses of the Bishop's putative port. All I seemed to manage was a strangled, "Yes."

"I suppose Mr. Wrigglesworth would say—" Vosper, J., was, as ever, anxious to supply any argument that might not yet have occurred to the prosecution "—that it is evidence of 'system.' "

"System?" I heard my voice faintly and from a long way off. "It may be, I suppose. But the Court has a discretion to omit evidence which may be irrelevant and purely prejudicial."

"I feel sure Mr. Wrigglesworth has considered the matter most carefully and that he would not lead this evidence unless he considered it entirely relevant."

I looked at the Mad Monk on the seat beside me. He was smiling at me with a mixture of hearty cheerfulness and supreme pity, as though I were sinking rapidly and he had come to administer supreme unction. I made a few ill-chosen remarks to the Court, but I was in no condition, that morning, to enter into a complicated legal argument on the admissibility of evidence.

It wasn't long before Bridget O'Dowd had told a deeply disapproving jury all about Eddie "Turpin" Timson's sword. "A man," the judge said later in his summing up about young Edward, "clearly prepared to attack with cold steel whenever it suited him."

When the trial was over, I called in for refreshment at my favorite watering hole and there, to my surprise, was my opponent Wrigglesworth, sharing an expensive-looking bottle with Detective Inspector Wainwright, the officer in charge of the case. I stood at the bar, absorbing a consoling glass of Pommeroy's ordinary, when the D.I. came up to the bar for cigarettes. He gave me a friendly and maddeningly sympathetic smile.

"Sorry about that, sir. Still, win a few, lose a few. Isn't that it?"

"In my case lately, it's been win a few, lose a lot!"

"You couldn't have this one, sir. You see, Mr. Wrigglesworth had promised it to me."

"He had *what*?"

"Well, I'm retiring, as you know. And Mr. Wrigglesworth promised me faithfully that my last case would be a win. He promised me that, in a manner of speaking, as a Christmas present. Great man is our Mr. Wrigglesworth, sir, for the spirit of Christmas."

I looked across at the Mad Monk and a terrible suspicion entered my head. What was all that about a present for the Bishop? I searched my memory and I could find no trace of our having, in fact, bought wine for any sort of cleric. And was Wrigglesworth as inexperienced as he would have had me believe in the art of selecting claret?

As I watched him pour and sniff a glass from his superior bottle and hold it critically to the light, a horrible suspicion crossed my mind. Had the whole evening's events been nothing but a deception, a sinister attempt to nobble Rumpole, to present him with such a stupendous hangover that he would stumble in his legal argument? Was it all in aid of D.I. Wainwright's Christmas present?

I looked at Wrigglesworth, and it would be no exaggeration to say the mind boggled. He was, of course, perfectly right about me. I just didn't recognize evil when I saw it.

SUPPER WITH MISS SHIVERS

BY PETER LOVESEY

The door was stuck. Something inside was stopping it from opening, and Fran was numb with cold. School had broken up for Christmas that afternoon—"Lord dismiss us with Thy blessing"—and the jubilant kids had given her a blinding headache. She'd wobbled on her bike through the London traffic, two carriers filled with books suspended from the handlebars. She'd endured exhaust fumes and maniac motorists, and now she couldn't get into her own flat. She cursed, let the bike rest against her hip, and attacked the door with both hands.

"It was quite scary, actually," she told Jim when he got in later. "I mean, the door opened perfectly well when we left this morning. We could have been burgled. Or it could have been a body lying in the hall."

Jim, who worked as a systems analyst, didn't have the kind of imagination that expected bodies behind doors. "So what was it—the doormat?"

"Get knotted. It was a great bundle of Christmas cards wedged under the door. Look at them. I blame you for this, James Palmer."

"Me?"

Now that she was over the headache and warm again, she enjoyed poking gentle fun at Jim. "Putting our address

14

book on your computer and running the envelopes through the printer. This is the result. We're going to be up to our eyeballs in cards. I don't know how many you sent, but we've heard from the plumber, the dentist, the television repairman, and the people who moved us in, apart from family and friends. You must have gone straight through the address book. I won't even ask how many stamps you used."

"What an idiot," Jim admitted. "I forgot to use the sorting function."

"I left some for you to open."

"I bet you've opened all the ones with checks inside," said Jim. "I'd rather eat first."

"I'm slightly mystified by one," said Fran. "Do you remember sending to someone called Miss Shivers?"

"No. I'll check if you like. Curious name."

"It means nothing to me, but she's invited us to a meal."

Fran handed him the card—one of those desolate, old-fashioned snow scenes of someone dragging home a log. Inside, under the printed greetings, was the signature *E. Shivers (Miss)* followed by *Please make my Christmas— come for supper seven next Sunday, 23rd.* In the corner was an address label.

"Never heard of her," said Jim. "Must be a mistake."

"Maybe she sends her cards by computer," said Fran, and added, before he waded in, "I don't think it's a mistake, Jim. She named us on the envelope. I'd like to go."

"For crying out loud—Didmarsh is miles away. Berkshire or somewhere. We're far too busy."

"Thanks to your computer, we've got time in hand," Fran told him with a smile.

The moment she'd seen the invitation, she'd known she would accept. Three or four times in her life she'd felt a similar impulse and each time she had been right. She didn't think of herself as psychic or telepathic, but sometimes she felt guided by some force that couldn't be explained scientifically. A good force, she was certain. It had convinced her that she should marry no one else but Jim, and after three years together she had no doubts. Their love was unshakable. And because he loved her, he would

take her to supper with Miss Shivers. He wouldn't understand *why* she was so keen to go, but he would see that
she was in earnest, and that would be enough. . .

"By the way, I checked the computer," he told her in
front of the destinations board on Paddington Station next
Sunday. "We definitely didn't send a card to anyone
called Shivers."

"Makes it all the more exciting, doesn't it?" Fran said,
squeezing his arm.

Jim was the first man she had trusted. Trust was her top
requirement of the opposite sex. It didn't matter that he
wasn't particularly tall and that his nose came to a point.
He was loyal. And didn't Clint Eastwood have a pointed
nose?

She'd learned from her mother's three disastrous mar-
riages to be ultra-wary of men. The first—Fran's father,
Harry—had started the rot. He'd died in a train crash just
a few days before Fran was born. You'd think he couldn't
be blamed for that, but he could. Fran's mother had been
admitted to hospital with complications in the eighth
month, and Harry, the rat, had found someone else within
a week. On the night of the crash he'd been in London
with his mistress, buying her expensive clothes. He'd even
lied to his pregnant wife, stuck in hospital, about working overtime.

For years Fran's mother had fended off the questions
any child asks about a father she has never seen, telling
Fran to forget him and love her stepfather instead. Stepfather the First had turned into a violent alcoholic. The divorce had taken nine years to achieve. Stepfather the
Second—a Finn called Bengt (Fran called him Bent)—had
treated their Wimbledon terraced house as if it were a
sauna, insisting on communal baths and parading naked
around the place. When Fran was reaching puberty, there
were terrible rows because she wanted privacy. Her
mother had sided with Bengt until one terrible night when
he'd crept into Fran's bedroom and groped her. Bengt
walked out of their lives the next day, but, incredibly to
Fran, a lot of the blame seemed to be heaped on her, and
her relationship with her mother had been damaged for-

ever. At forty-three, her mother, deeply depressed, had taken a fatal overdose.

The hurts and horrors of those years had not disappeared, but marriage to Jim had provided a fresh start. Fran nestled against him in the carriage and he fingered a strand of her dark hair. It was supposed to be an Intercity train, but B.R. were using old rolling-stock for some of the Christmas period and Fran and Jim had this compartment to themselves.

"Did you let this Shivers woman know we're coming?"

She nodded. "I phoned. She's over the moon that I answered. She's going to meet us at the station."

"What's it all about, then?"

"She didn't say, and I didn't ask."

"You didn't? Why not, for God's sake?"

"It's a mystery trip—a Christmas mystery. I'd rather keep it that way."

"Sometimes, Fran, you leave me speechless."

"Kiss me instead, then."

A whistle blew somewhere and the line of taxis beside the platform appeared to be moving forward. Fran saw no more of the illusion because Jim had put his lips to hers.

Somewhere beyond Westbourne Park Station, they noticed how foggy the late afternoon had become. After days of mild, damp weather, a proper December chill had set in. The heating in the carriage was working only in fits and starts and Fran was beginning to wish she'd worn trousers instead of opting decorously for her corduroy skirt and boots.

"Do you think it's warmer farther up the train?"

"Want me to look?"

Jim slid aside the door. Before starting along the corridor, he joked, "If I'm not back in half an hour, send for Miss Marple."

"No need," said Fran. "I'll find you in the bar and mine's a hot cuppa."

She pressed herself into the warm space Jim had left in the corner and rubbed a spy-hole in the condensation. There wasn't anything to spy. She shivered and wondered if she'd been right to trust her hunch and come on this trip. It was more than a hunch, she told herself. It was intuition.

It wasn't long before she heard the door pulled back. She expected to see Jim, or perhaps the man who checked the tickets. Instead, there was a fellow about her own age, twenty-five, with a pink carrier bag containing something about the size of a box file. "Do you mind?" he asked. "The heating's given up altogether next door."

Fran gave a shrug. "I've got my doubts about the whole carriage."

He took the corner seat by the door and placed the bag beside him. Fran took stock of him rapidly, hoping Jim would soon return. She didn't feel threatened, but she wasn't used to these old-fashioned compartments. She rarely used the trains these days except the tube occasionally.

She decided the young man must have kitted himself in an Oxfam shop. He had a dark-blue car coat, black trousers with flares, and crepe-soled ankle boots. Around his neck was one of those striped scarves that college students wore in the sixties, one end slung over his left shoulder. And his thick, dark hair matched the image. Fran guessed he was unemployed. She wondered if he was going to ask her for money.

But he said, "Been up to town for the day?"

"I live there." She added quickly, "With my husband. He'll be back presently."

"I'm married, too," he said, and there was a chink of amusement in his eyes that Fran found reassuring. "I'm up from the country, smelling the wellies and cowdung. Don't care much for London. It's crazy in Bond Street this time of year."

"Bond Street?" repeated Fran. She hadn't got him down as a big spender.

"This once," he explained. "It's special, this Christmas. We're expecting our first, my wife and I."

"Congratulations."

He smiled. A self-conscious smile. "My wife, Pearlie—that's my name for her—Pearlie made all her own maternity clothes, but she's really looking forward to being slim again. She calls herself the frump with a lump. After the baby arrives, I want her to have something glamorous, really special. She deserves it. I've been putting money aside for months. Do you want to see what I got? I found it in Elaine Ducharme."

"I don't know it."

"It's a very posh shop. I found the advert in some fashion magazine." He had already taken the box from the carrier and was unwrapping the pink ribbon.

"You'd better not. It's gift-wrapped."

"Tell me what you think," he insisted, as he raised the lid, parted the tissue, and lifted out the gift for his wife. It was a nightdress, the sort of nightdress, Fran privately reflected, that men misguidedly buy for the women they adore. Pale-blue, in fine silk, styled in the empire line, gathered at the bodice, with masses of lace interwoven with yellow ribbons. Gorgeous to look at and hopelessly impractical to wash and use again. Not even comfortable to sleep in. His wife, she guessed, would wear it once and pack it away with her wedding veil and her love letters.

"It's exquisite."

"I'm glad I showed it to you." He started to replace it clumsily in the box.

"Let me," said Fran, leaning across to take it from him. The silk was irresistible. "I know she'll love it."

"It's not so much the gift," he said as if he sensed her thoughts. "It's what lies behind it. Pearlie would tell you I'm useless at romantic speeches. You should have seen me blushing in that shop. Frilly knickers on every side. The girls there had a right game with me, holding these nighties against themselves and asking what I thought."

Fran felt privileged. She doubted if Pearlie would ever be told of the gauntlet her young husband had run to acquire the nightdress. She warmed to him. He was fun in a way that Jim couldn't be. Not that she felt disloyal to Jim, but this guy was devoted to his Pearlie, and that made him easy to relax with. She talked to him some more, telling him about the teaching and some of the sweet things the kids had said at the end of the term.

"They value you," he said. "They should."

She reddened and said, "It's about time my husband came back." Switching the conversation away from herself, she told the story of the mysterious invitation from Miss Shivers.

"You're doing the right thing," he said. "Believe me, you are."

Suddenly uneasy for no reason she could name, Fran said, "I'd better look for my husband. He said I'd find him in the bar."

"Take care, then."

As she progressed along the corridor, rocked by the speeding train, she debated with herself whether to tell Jim about the young man. It would be difficult without risking upsetting him. Still, there was no cause really.

The next carriage was of the standard Intercity type. Teetering toward her along the center aisle was Jim, bearing two beakers of tea, fortunately capped with lids. He'd queued for ten minutes, he said. And he'd found two spare seats.

They claimed the places and sipped the tea. Fran decided to tell Jim what had happened. "While you were getting these," she began—and then stopped, for the carriage was plunged into darkness.

Often on a long train journey, there are unexplained breaks in the power supply. Normally, Fran wouldn't have been troubled. This time, she had a horrible sense of disaster, a vision of the carriage rearing up, thrusting her sideways. The sides seemed to buckle, shattered glass rained on her, and people were shrieking. Choking fumes. Searing pain in her legs. Dimly, she discerned a pair of legs to her right, dressed in dark trousers. Boots with crepe soles. And blood. A pool of blood.

"You've spilt tea all over your skirt!" Jim said.

The lights came on again, and the carriage was just as it had been. People were reading the evening paper as if nothing at all had occurred. But Fran had crushed the beaker in her hand—no wonder her legs had smarted.

The thickness of the corduroy skirt had prevented her from being badly scalded. She mopped it with a tissue. "I don't know what's wrong with me—I had a nightmare, except that I wasn't asleep. Where are we?"

"We went through Reading twenty minutes ago. I'd say we're almost there. Are you going to be okay?"

Over the public-address system came the announcement that the next station stop would be Didmarsh Halt.

So far as they could tell in the thick mist, they were the only people to leave the train at Didmarsh.

Miss Shivers was in the booking hall, a gaunt-faced, tense woman of about fifty, with cropped silver hair and red-framed glasses. Her hand was cold, but she shook Fran's firmly and lingered before letting it go.

She drove them in an old Maxi Estate to a cottage set back from the road not more than five minutes from the station. Christmas-tree lights were visible through the leaded window. The smell of roast turkey wafted from the door when she opened it. Jim handed across the bottle of wine he had thoughtfully brought.

"We're wondering how you heard of us."

"Yes, I'm sure you are," the woman answered, addressing herself more to Fran than Jim. "My name is Edith. I was your mother's best friend for ten years, but we fell out over a misunderstanding. You see, Fran, I loved your father."

Fran stiffened and turned to Jim. "I don't think we should stay."

"Please," said the woman, and she sounded close to desperation, "we did nothing wrong. I have something on my conscience, but it isn't adultery, whatever you were led to believe."

They consented to stay and eat the meal. Conversation was strained, but the food was superb. And when at last they sat in front of the fire sipping coffee, Edith Shivers explained why she had invited them. "As I said, I loved your father Harry. A crush, we called it in those days when it wasn't mutual. He was kind to me, took me out, kissed me sometimes, but that was all. He really loved your mother. Adored her."

"You've got to be kidding," said Fran grimly.

"No, your mother was mistaken. Tragically mistaken. I know what she believed, and nothing I could say or do would shake her. I tried writing, phoning, calling personally. She shut me out of her life completely."

"That much I can accept," said Fran. "She never mentioned you to me."

"Did she never talk about the train crash—the night your father was killed, just down the line from here?"

"Just once. After that it was a closed book. He betrayed her dreadfully. She was pregnant, expecting me It was traumatic. She hardly ever mentioned my father after that. She didn't even keep a photograph."

Miss Shivers put out her hand and pressed it over Fran's. "My dear, for both their sakes I want you to know the truth. Thirty-seven people died in that crash, twenty-five years ago this very evening. Your mother was shocked to learn that he was on the train, because he'd said nothing whatsoever to her about it. He'd told her he was working late. She read about the crash without supposing for a moment that Harry was one of the dead. When she was given the news, just a day or two before you were born, the grief was worse because he'd lied to her. Then she learned that I'd been a passenger on the same train, as indeed I had, and escaped unhurt. Fran, that was chance— pure chance. I happened to work in the City. My name was published in the press, and your mother saw it and came to a totally wrong conclusion."

"That my father and you—"

"Yes. And that wasn't all. Some days after the accident, Harry's personal effects were returned to her, and in the pocket of his jacket they found a receipt from a Bond Street shop for a nightdress."

"Elaine Ducharme," said Fran in a flat voice.

"You *know*?"

"Yes."

"The shop was very famous. They went out of business in 1969. You see—"

"He'd bought it for her," said Fran, "as a surprise."

Edith Shivers withdrew her hand from Fran's and put it to her mouth. "Then you know about me?"

"No."

Their hostess drew herself up in her chair. "I must tell you. Quite by chance on that night twenty-five years ago, I saw him getting on the train. I still loved him and he was alone, so I walked along the corridor and joined him. He was carrying a bag containing the nightdress. In the course of the journey he showed it to me, not realizing that it wounded me to see how much he loved her still. He told me how he'd gone into the shop—"

"Yes," said Fran expressionlessly. "And after Reading, the train crashed."

"He was killed instantly. The side of the carriage crushed him. But I was flung clear—bruised, cut in the forehead, but really unhurt. I could see that Harry was dead. Amazingly, the box with the nightdress wasn't damaged." Miss Shivers stared into the fire. "I coveted it. I told myself if I left it, someone would pick it up and steal it. Instead, I did. *I* stole it. And it's been on my conscience ever since."

Fran had listened in a trancelike way, thinking all the time about her meeting in the train.

Miss Shivers was saying, "If you hate me for what I did, I understand. You see, your mother assumed that Harry bought the nightdress for me. Whatever I said to the contrary, she wouldn't have believed me."

"Probably not," said Fran. "What happened to it?"

Miss Shivers got up and crossed the room to a sideboard, opened a drawer, and withdrew a box—the box Fran had handled only an hour or two previously. "I never wore it. It was never meant for me. I want you to have it, Fran. He would have wished that."

Fran's hands trembled as she opened the box and laid aside the tissue. She stroked the silk. She thought of what had happened, how she hadn't for a moment suspected that she had seen a ghost. She refused to think of him as that. She rejoiced in the miracle that she had met her own father, who had died before she was born—

met him in the prime of his young life, when he was her own age.

Still holding the box, she got up and kissed Edith Shivers on the forehead. "My parents are at peace now, I'm sure of it. This is a wonderful Christmas present," she said.

THE ADVENTURE OF THE BLUE CARBUNCLE

BY SIR ARTHUR CONAN DOYLE

I had called upon my friend Sherlock Holmes upon the second morning after Christmas, with the intention of wishing him the compliments of the season. He was lounging upon the sofa in a purple dressing-gown, a pipe-rack within his reach upon the right, and a pile of crumpled morning papers, evidently newly studied, near at hand. Beside the couch was a wooden chair, and on the angle of the back hung a very seedy and disreputable hard-felt hat, much the worse for wear, and cracked in several places. A lens and a forceps lying upon the seat of the chair suggested that the hat had been suspended in this manner for the purpose of examination.

"You are engaged," said I; "perhaps I interrupt you."

"Not at all. I am glad to have a friend with whom I can discuss my results. The matter is a perfectly trivial one"— he jerked his thumb in the direction of the old hat—"but there are points in connection with it which are not entirely devoid of interest and even of instruction."

I seated myself in his armchair and warmed my hands before his crackling fire, for a sharp frost had set in, and the windows were thick with the ice crystals. "I suppose,"

I remarked, "that, homely as it looks, this thing has some deadly story linked on to it—that it is the clue which will guide you in the solution of some mystery and the punishment of some crime."

"No, no. No crime," said Sherlock Holmes, laughing. "Only one of those whimsical little incidents which will happen when you have four million human beings all jostling each other within the space of a few square miles. Amid the action and reaction of so dense a swarm of humanity, every possible combination of events may be expected to take place, and many a little problem will be presented which may be striking and bizarre without being criminal. We have already had experience of such."

"So much so," I remarked, "that of the last six cases which I have added to my notes, three have been entirely free of any legal crime."

"Precisely. You allude to my attempt to recover the Irene Adler papers, to the singular case of Miss Mary Sutherland, and to the adventure of the man with the twisted lip. Well, I have no doubt that this small matter will fall into the same innocent category. You know Peterson, the commissionaire?"

"Yes."

"It is to him that this trophy belongs."

"It is his hat."

"No, no; he found it. Its owner is unknown. I beg that you will look upon it not as a battered billycock but as an intellectual problem. And, first, as to how it came here. It arrived upon Christmas morning, in company with a good fat goose, which is, I have no doubt, roasting at this moment in front of Peterson's fire. The facts are these: about four o'clock on Christmas morning, Peterson, who, as you know, is a very honest fellow, was returning from some small jollification and was making his way homeward down Tottenham Court Road. In front of him he saw, in the gaslight, a tallish man, walking with a slight stagger, and carrying a white goose slung over his shoulder. As he reached the corner of Goodge Street, a row broke out between this stranger and a little knot of roughs. One of the latter knocked off the man's hat, on which he raised his stick to defend himself, and swinging it over his head, smashed the shop window behind him. Peterson had rushed forward to protect the stranger from his assailants; but the man, shocked at having broken the window, and seeing an official-looking person in uniform rushing towards him, dropped his goose, took to his heels, and vanished amid the labyrinth of small streets which lie at the back of Tottenham Court Road. The roughs had also fled at the appearance of Peterson, so that he was left in possession of the field of battle, and also of the spoils of victory in the shape of this battered hat and a most unimpeachable Christmas goose."

"Which surely he restored to their owner?"

"My dear fellow, there lies the problem. It is true that 'For Mrs. Henry Baker' was printed upon a small card which was tied to the bird's left leg, and it is also true that the initials 'H.B.' are legible upon the lining of this hat; but as there are some thousands of Bakers, and some hundreds of Henry Bakers in this city of ours, it is not easy to restore lost property to any of them."

"What, then, did Peterson do?"

"He brought round both hat and goose to me on Christmas morning, knowing that even the smallest problems are of interest to me. The goose we retained until this morning, when there were signs that, in spite of the slight frost, it would be well that it should be eaten without unnecessary delay. Its finder has carried it off, therefore, to fulfil the ultimate destiny of a goose, while I continue to retain the hat of the unknown gentleman who lost his Christmas dinner."

"Did he not advertise?"

"No."

"Then, what clue could you have as to his identity?"

"Only as much as we can deduce."

"From his hat?"

"Precisely."

"But you are joking. What can you gather from this old battered felt?"

"Here is my lens. You know my methods. What can you

gather yourself as to the individuality of the man who has worn this article?"

I took the tattered object in my hands and turned it over rather ruefully. It was a very ordinary black hat of the usual round shape, hard and much the worse for wear. The lining had been of red silk, but was a good deal discoloured. There was no maker's name; but, as Holmes had remarked, the initials "H.B." were scrawled upon one side. It was pierced in the brim for a hat-securer, but the elastic was missing. For the rest, it was cracked, exceedingly dusty, and spotted in several places, although there seemed to have been some attempt to hide the discoloured patches by smearing them with ink.

"I can see nothing," said I, handing it back to my friend.

"On the contrary, Watson, you can see everything. You fail, however, to reason from what you see. You are too timid in drawing your inferences."

"Then, pray tell me what it is that you can infer from this hat?"

He picked it up and gazed at it in the peculiar introspective fashion which was characteristic of him. "It is perhaps less suggestive than it might have been," he remarked, "and yet there are a few inferences which are very distinct, and a few others which represent at least a strong balance of probability. That the man was highly intellectual is of course obvious upon the face of it, and also that he was fairly well-to-do within the last three years, although he has now fallen upon evil days. He had foresight, but has less now than formerly, pointing to a moral retrogression, which, when taken with the decline of his fortunes, seems to indicate some evil influence, probably drink, at work upon him. This may account also for the obvious fact that his wife has ceased to love him."

"My dear Holmes!"

"He has, however, retained some degree of self-respect," he continued, disregarding my remonstrance. "He is a man who leads a sendentary life, goes out little, is out of training entirely, is middle-aged, has grizzled hair which he has had cut within the last few days, and which he anoints with lime-cream. These are the more patent facts which are to be deduced from his hat. Also, by the way, that it is extremely improbable that he has gas laid on in his house."

"You are certainly joking, Holmes."

"Not in the least. Is it possible that even now, when I give you these results, you are unable to see how they are attained?"

"I have no doubt that I am very stupid, but I must confess that I am unable to follow you. For example, how did you deduce that this man was intellectual?"

For answer Holmes clapped the hat upon his head. It came right over the forehead and settled upon the bridge of his nose. "It is a question of cubic capacity," said he; "a man with so large a brain must have something in it."

"The decline of his fortunes, then?"

"This hat is three years old. These flat brims curled at the edge came in then. It is a hat of the very best quality. Look at the band of ribbed silk and the excellent lining. If this man could afford to buy so expensive a hat three years ago, and has had no hat since, then he has assuredly gone down in the world."

"Well, that is clear enough, certainly. But how about the foresight and the moral retrogression?"

Sherlock Holmes laughed. "Here is the foresight," said he, putting his finger upon the little disc and loop of the hat-securer. "They are never sold upon hats. If this man ordered one, it is a sign of a certain amount of foresight, since he went out of his way to take this precaution against the wind. But since we see that he has broken the elastic and has not troubled to replace it, it is obvious that he has less foresight now than formerly, which is a distinct proof of a weakening nature. On the other hand, he has endeavored to conceal some of these stains upon the felt by daubing them with ink, which is a sign that he has not entirely lost his self-respect."

"Your reasoning is certainly plausible."

"The further points, that he is middle-aged, that his hair is grizzled, that it has been recently cut, and that he uses lime-cream, are all to be gathered from a close examination of the lower part of the lining. The lens discloses a

large number of hair-ends, clean cut by the scissors of the
barber. They all appear to be adhesive, and there is a
distinct odour of lime-cream. This dust, you will observe,
is not the gritty, gray dust of the street but the fluffy brown
dust of the house, showing that it has been hung up indoors most of the time; while the marks of moisture upon
the inside are proof positive that the wearer perspired very
freely, and could therefore, hardly be in the best of
training."

"But his wife—you said that she had ceased to love
him."

"This hat has not been brushed for weeks. When I see
you, my dear Watson, with a week's accumulation of dust
upon your hat, and when your wife allows you to go out
in such a state, I shall fear that you also have been unfortunate enough to lose your wife's affection."

"But he might be a bachelor."

"Nay, he was bringing home the goose as a peace-
offering to his wife. Remember the card upon the bird's
leg."

"You have an answer to everything. But how on earth
do you deduce that the gas is not laid on in his house?"

"One tallow stain, or even two, might come by chance;
but when I see no less than five, I think that there can be
little doubt that the individual must be brought into frequent contact with burning tallow—walks upstairs at night
probably with his hat in one hand and a gutterlng candle
in the other. Anyhow, he never got tallow-stains from a
gas jet. Are you satisfied?"

"Well, it is very ingenious," said I, laughing; "but since,
as you said just now, there has been no crime committed,
and no harm done save the loss of a goose, all this seems
to be rather a waste of energy."

Sherlock Holmes had opened his mouth to reply, when
the door flew open, and Peterson, the commissionaire,
rushed into the apartment with flushed cheeks and the face
of a man who is dazed with astonishment.

"The goose, Mr. Holmes! The goose, sir!" he gasped.

"Eh? What of it, then? Has it returned to life and
flapped off through the kitchen window?" Holmes twisted

himself round upon the sofa to get a fairer view of the man's excited face.

"See here, sir! See what my wife found in its crop!" He held out his hand and displayed upon the center of the palm a brilliantly scintillating blue stone, rather smaller than a bean in size, but of such purity and radiance that it twinkled like an electric point in the dark hollow of his hand.

Sherlock Holmes sat up with a whistle. "By Jove, Peterson!" said he, "this is treasure trove indeed. I suppose you know what you have got?"

"A diamond, sir? A precious stone. It cuts into glass as though it were putty."

"It's more than a precious stone. It is *the* precious stone."

"Not the Countess of Morcar's blue carbuncle!" I ejaculated.

"Precisely so. I ought to know its size and shape, seeing that I have read the advertisement about it in *The Times* every day lately. It is absolutely unique, and its value can only be conjectured, but the reward offered of one thousand pounds is certainly not within a twentieth part of the market price."

"A thousand pounds! Great Lord of mercy!" The commissionaire plumped down into a chair and stared from one to the other of us.

"That is the reward, and I have reason to know that there are sentimental considerations in the background which would induce the Countess to part with half her fortune if she could but recover the gem."

"It was lost, if I remember aright, at the Hotel Cosmopolitan," I remarked.

"Precisely so, on December 22nd, just five days ago. John Horner, a plumber, was accused of having abstracted it from the lady's jewel-case. The evidence against him was so strong that the case has been referred to the Assizes. I have some account of the matter here, I believe." He rummaged amid his newspapers, glancing over the dates, until at last he smoothed one out, doubled it over, and read the following paragraph:

"Hotel Cosmopolitan Jewel Robbery. John Horner, 26, plumber, was brought up upon the charge of having upon the 22d inst., abstracted from the jewel-case of the Countess of Morcar the valuable gem known as the blue carbuncle. James Ryder, upper-attendant at the hotel, gave his evidence to the effect that he had shown Horner up to the dressing-room of the Countess of Morcar upon the day of the robbery in order that he might solder the second bar of the grate, which was loose. He had remained with Horner some little time, but had finally been called away. On returning, he found that Horner had disappeared, that the bureau had been forced open, and that the small morocco casket in which, as it afterwards transpired, the Countess was accustomed to keep her jewel, was lying empty upon the dressing-table. Ryder instantly gave the alarm, and Horner was arrested the same evening; but the stone could not be found either upon his person or in his rooms. Catherine Cusack, maid to the Countess, deposed to having heard Ryder's cry of dismay on discovering the robbery, and to having rushed into the room, where she found matters as described by the last witness. Inspector Bradstreet, B division, gave evidence as to the arrest of Horner, who struggled frantically, and protested his innocence in the strongest terms. Evidence of a previous conviction for robbery having been given against the prisoner, the magistrate refused to deal summarily with the offence, but referred it to the Assizes. Horner, who had shown signs of intense emotion during the proceedings, fainted away at the conclusion and was carried out of the court.

"Hum! So much for the police-court," said Holmes thoughtfully, tossing aside the paper. "The question for us now to solve is the sequence of events leading from a rifled jewel-case at one end to the crop of a goose in Tottenham Court Road at the other. You see, Watson, our little deductions have suddenly assumed a much more important and less innocent aspect. Here is the stone; the stone came from the goose, and the goose came from Mr. Henry Baker, the gentleman with the bad hat and all the other characteristics with which I have bored you. So now we must set ourselves very seriously to finding this gentleman and ascertaining what part he has played in this little mystery. To do this, we must try the simplest means first, and these lie undoubtedly in an advertisement in all the evening papers. If this fails, I shall have recourse to other methods."

"What will you say?"

"Give me a pencil and that slip of paper. Now, then:

"Found at the corner of Goodge Street, a goose and a black felt hat. Mr. Henry Baker can have the same by applying at 6:30 this evening at 221B Baker Street.

That is clear and concise."

"Very. But will he see it?"

"Well, he is sure to keep an eye on the papers, since, to a poor man, the loss was a heavy one. He was clearly so scared by his mischance in breaking the window and by the approach of Peterson that he thought of nothing but flight, but since then he must have bitterly regretted the impulse which caused him to drop his bird. Then, again, the introduction of his name will cause him to see it, for everyone who knows him will direct his attention to it. Here you are, Peterson, run down to the advertising agency and have this put in the evening papers."

"In which sir?"

"Oh, in the *Globe, Star, Pall Mall, St. James's, Evening News Standard, Echo,* and any others that occur to you."

"Very well, sir. And this stone?"

"Ah, yes, I shall keep the stone. Thank you. And, I say, Peterson, just buy a goose on your way back and leave it here with me, for we must have one to give to this gentleman in place of the one which your family is now devouring."

When the commissionaire had gone, Holmes took up the stone and held it against the light. "It's a bonny thing," said he. "Just see how it glints and sparkles. Of course it is a nucleus and focus of crime. Every good stone is. They are the devil's pet baits. In the larger and older jewels every facet may stand for a bloody deed. This stone is not yet twenty years old. It was found in the banks of the

Amoy River in southern China and is remarkable in having every characteristic of the carbuncle, save that it is blue in shade instead of ruby red. In spite of its youth, it has already a sinister history. There have been two murders, a vitriol-throwing, a suicide, and several robberies brought about for the sake of this forty-grain weight of crystallized charcoal. Who would think that so pretty a toy would be a purveyor to the gallows and the prison? I'll lock it up in my strong box now and drop a line to the Countess to say that we have it."

"Do you think that this man Horner is innocent?"

"I cannot tell."

"Well, then, do you imagine that this other one, Henry Baker, had anything to do with the matter?"

"It is, I think, much more likely that Henry Baker is an absolutely innocent man, who had no idea that the bird which he was carrying was of considerably more value than if it were made of solid gold. That, however, I shall determine by a very simple test if we have an answer to our advertisement."

"And you can do nothing until then?"

"Nothing."

"In that case I shall continue my professional round. But I shall come back in the evening at the hour you have mentioned, for I should like to see the solution of so tangled a business."

"Very glad to see you. I dine at seven. There is a woodcock, I believe. By the way, in view of recent occurrences, perhaps I ought to ask Mrs. Hudson to examine its crop."

I had been delayed at a case, and it was a little after half-past six when I found myself in Baker Street once more. As I approached the house I saw a tall man in a Scotch bonnet with a coat which was buttoned up to his chin waiting outside in the bright semicircle which was thrown from the fanlight. Just as I arrived the door was opened, and we were shown up together to Holmes's room.

"Mr. Henry Baker, I believe," said he, rising from his armchair and greeting his visitor with the easy air of geniality which he could so readily assume. "Pray take this chair by the fire, Mr. Baker. It is a cold night, and I observe that your circulation is more adapted for summer than for winter. Ah, Watson, you have just come at the right time. Is that your hat, Mr. Baker?"

"Yes, sir, that is undoubtedly my hat."

He was a large man with rounded shoulders, a massive head, and a broad, intelligent face, sloping down to a pointed beard of grizzled brown. A touch of red in nose and cheeks, with a slight tremor of his extended hand, recalled Holmes's surmise as to his habits. His rusty black frock-coat was buttoned right up in front, with the collar turned up, and his lank wrists protruded from his sleeves without a sign of cuff or shirt. He spoke in a slow staccato fashion, choosing his words with care, and gave the impression generally of a man of learning and letters who had had ill-usage at the hands of fortune.

"We have retained these things for some days," said Holmes, "because we expected to see an advertisement from you giving your address. I am at a loss to know now why you did not advertise."

Our visitor gave a rather shamefaced laugh. "Shillings have not been plentiful with me as they once were," he remarked. "I had no doubt that the gang of roughs who assaulted me had carried off both my hat and the bird. I did not care to spend more money in a hopeless attempt at recovering them."

"Very naturally. By the way, about the bird, we were compelled to eat it."

"To eat it!" Our visitor half rose from his chair in his excitement.

"Yes, it would have been of no use to anyone had we not done so. But I presume that this other goose upon the sideboard, which is about the same weight and perfectly fresh, will answer your purpose equally well?"

"Oh, certainly, certainly," answered Mr. Baker with a sigh of relief.

"Of course, we still have the feathers, legs, crop, and so on of your own bird, so if you wish—"

The man burst into a hearty laugh. "They might be useful to me as relics of my adventure," said he, "but beyond that I can hardly see what use the *disjecta membra* of my late acquaintance are going to be to me. No, sir, I think that, with your permission, I will confine my attentions to the excellent bird which I perceive upon the sideboard."

Sherlock Holmes glanced sharply across at me with a slight shrug of his shoulders.

"There is your hat, then, and there your bird," said he. "By the way, would it bore you to tell me where you got the other one from? I am somewhat of a fowl fancier, and I have seldom seen a better grown goose."

"Certainly, sir," said Baker, who had risen and tucked his newly gained property under his arm. "There are a few of us who frequent the Alpha Inn, near the Museum—we are to be found in the Museum itself during the day, you understand. This year our good host, Windigate by name, instituted a goose club, by which, on consideration for some few pence every week, we were each to receive a bird at Christmas. My pence were duly paid, and the rest is familiar to you. I am much indebted to you, sir, for a Scotch bonnet is fitted neither to my years nor my gravity." With a comical pomposity of manner he bowed solemnly to both of us and strode off upon his way.

"So much for Mr. Henry Baker," said Holmes when he had closed the door behind him. "It is quite certain that he knows nothing whatever about the matter. Are you hungry, Watson?"

"Not particularly."

"Then I suggest that we turn our dinner into a supper and follow up this clue while it is still hot."

"By all means."

It was a bitter night, so we drew on our ulsters and wrapped cravats about our throats. Outside, the stars were shining coldly in a cloudless sky, and the breath of the passers-by blew out into smoke like so many pistol shots. Our footfalls rang out crisply and loudly as we swung through the doctors' quarter, Wimpole Street, Harley Street and so through Wigmore Street into Oxford Street. In a quarter of an hour we were in Bloomsbury at the Alpha Inn, which is a small public-house at the corner of one of the streets which runs down into Holborn. Holmes pushed open the door of the private bar and ordered two glasses of beer from the ruddy-faced, white-aproned landlord.

"Your beer should be excellent if it is as good as your geese," said he.

"My geese!" The man seemed surprised.

"Yes. I was speaking only half an hour ago to Mr. Henry Baker, who was a member of your goose club."

"Ah! yes, I see. But you see, sir, them's not *our* geese."

"Indeed! Whose, then?"

"Well, I got the two dozen from a salesman in Covent Garden."

"Indeed? I know some of them. Which was it?"

"Breckinridge is his name."

"Ah! I don't know him. Well, here's your good health, landlord, and prosperity to your house. Good-night.

"Now for Mr. Breckinridge," he continued, buttoning up his coat as we came out into the frosty air. "Remember, Watson, that though we have so homely a thing as a goose at one end of this chain, we have at the other a man who will certainly get seven years' penal servitude unless we can establish his innocence. It is possible that our inquiry may but confirm his guilt; but, in any case, we have a line of investigation which has been missed by the police, and which a singular chance has placed in our hands. Let us follow it out to the bitter end. Faces to the south, then, and quick march!"

We passed across Holborn, down Endell Street, and so through a zigzag of slums to Covent Garden Market. One of the largest stalls bore the name of Breckinridge upon it, and the proprietor, a horsy-looking man, with a sharp face and trim side-whiskers, was helping a boy to put up the shutters.

"Good-evening. It's a cold night," said Holmes.

The salesman nodded and shot a questioning glance at my companion.

"Sold out of geese, I see," continued Holmes, pointing at the bare slabs of marble.

"Let you have five hundred to-morrow morning."

"That's no good."

"Well, there are some on the stall with the gas-flare."

"Ah, but I was recommended to you."

"Who by?"

"The landlord of the Alpha."

"Oh, yes; I sent him a couple of dozen."

"Fine birds they were, too. Now where did you get them from?"

To my surprise the question provoked a burst of anger from the salesman.

"Now, then, mister," said he, with his head cocked and his arms akimbo, "what are you driving at? Let's have it straight, now."

"It is straight enough. I should like to know who sold you the geese which you supplied to the Alpha."

"Well, then, I shan't tell you. So now!"

"Oh, it is a matter of no importance; but I don't know why you should be so warm over such a trifle."

"Warm! You'd be as warm, maybe, if you were as pestered as I am. When I pay good money for a good article there should be an end of the business; but it's 'Where are the geese?' and 'Who did you sell the geese to?' and 'What will you take for the geese?' One would think they were the only geese in the world, to hear the fuss that is made over them."

"Well, I have no connection with any other people who have been making inquiries," said Holmes carelessly. "If you won't tell us the bet is off, that is all. But I'm always ready to back my opinion on a matter of fowls, and I have a fiver on it that the bird I ate is country bred."

"Well, then, you've lost your fiver, for it's town bred," snapped the salesman.

"It's nothing of the kind."

"I say it is."

"I don't believe it."

"D'you think you know more about fowls than I, who have handled them ever since I was a nipper? I tell you, all those birds that went to the Alpha were town bred."

"You'll never persuade me to believe that."

"Will you bet, then?"

"It's merely taking your money, for I know that I am

right. But I'll have a sovereign on with you, just to teach you not to be obstinate."

The salesman chuckled grimly. "Bring me the books, Bill," said he.

The small boy brought round a small thin volume and a great greasy-backed one, laying them out together beneath the hanging lamp.

"Now then, Mr. Cocksure," said the salesman, "I thought that I was out of geese, but before I finish you'll find that there is still one left in my shop. You see this little book?"

"Well?"

"That's the list of the folk from whom I buy. D'you see? Well, then, here on this page are the country folk, and the numbers after their names are where their accounts are in the big ledger. Now, then! You see this other page in red ink? Well, that is a list of my town suppliers. Now, look at that third name. Just read it out to me."

" 'Mrs. Oakshott, 117, Brixton Road—249,' " read Holmes.

"Quite so. Now turn that up in the ledger."

Holmes turned to the page indicated. "Here you are, 'Mrs. Oakshott, 117 Brixton Road, egg and poultry supplier.' "

"Now, then, what's the last entry?"

" 'December 22d. Twenty-four geese at 7s. 6d.' "

"Quite so. There you are. And underneath?"

" 'Sold to Mr. Windigate of the Alpha, at 12s.' "

"What have you to say now?"

Sherlock Holmes looked deeply chagrined. He drew a sovereign from his pocket and threw it down upon the slab, turning away with the air of a man whose disgust is too deep for words. A few yards off he stopped under a lamp-post and laughed in the hearty, noiseless fashion which was peculiar to him.

"When you see a man with whiskers of that cut and the 'Pink 'un' protruding out of his pocket, you can always draw him by a bet," said he. "I daresay that if I had put £100 down in front of him, that man would not have given me such complete information as was drawn from him by the idea that he was doing me on a wager. Well, Watson, we are, I fancy, nearing the end of our quest, and the only point which remains to be determined is whether we should go on to this Mrs. Oakshott to-night, or whether we should reserve it for to-morrow. It is clear from what that surly fellow said that there are others besides ourselves who are anxious about the matter, and I should—"

His remarks were suddenly cut short by a loud hubbub which broke out from the stall which we had just left. Turning round we saw a little rat-faced fellow standing in the centre of the circle of yellow light which was thrown by the swinging lamp, while Breckinridge, the salesman, framed in the door of his stall, was shaking his fists fiercely at the cringing figure.

"I've had enough of you and your geese," he shouted. "I wish you were all at the devil together. If you come pestering me any more with your silly talk I'll set the dog at you. You bring Mrs. Oakshott here and I'll answer her, but what have you to do with it? Did I buy the geese off you?"

"No; but one of them was mine all the same," whined the little man.

"Well, then, ask Mrs. Oakshott for it."

"She told me to ask you."

"Well, you can ask the King of Proosia, for all I care. I've had enough of it. Get out of this!" He rushed fiercely forward, and the inquirer flitted away into the darkness.

"Ha! this may save us a visit to Brixton Road," whispered Holmes. "Come with me, and we will see what is to be made of this fellow." Striding through the scattered knots of people who lounged round the flaring stalls, my companion speedily overtook the little man and touched him upon the shoulder. He sprang round, and I could see in the gas-light that every vestige of colour had been driven from his face.

"Who are you, then? What do you want?" he asked in a quavering voice.

"You will excuse me," said Holmes blandly, "but I could not help overhearing the questions which you put to the salesman just now. I think that I could be of assistance to you."

"You? Who are you? How could you know anything of the matter?"

"My name is Sherlock Holmes. It is my business to know what other people don't know."

"But you can know nothing of this?"

"Excuse me, I know everything of it. You are endeavoring to trace some geese which were sold by Mrs. Oakshott, of Brixton Road, to a salesman named Breckinridge, by him in turn to Mr. Windigate, of the Alpha, and by him to his club, of which Mr. Henry Baker is a member."

"Oh, sir, you are the very man whom I have longed to meet," cried the little fellow with outstretched hands and quivering fingers. "I can hardly explain to you how interested I am in this matter."

Sherlock Holmes hailed a four-wheeler which was passing. "In that case we had better discuss it in a cosy room rather than in this wind-swept market-place," said he. "But pray tell me, before we go further, who it is that I have the pleasure of assisting."

The man hesitated for an instant. "My name is John Robinson," he answered with a sidelong glance.

"No, no; the real name," said Holmes sweetly. "It is always awkward doing business with an alias."

A flush sprang to the white cheeks of the stranger. "Well, then," said he, "my real name is James Ryder."

"Precisely so. Head attendant at the Hotel Cosmopolitan. Pray step into the cab, and I shall soon be able to tell you everything which you would wish to know."

The little man stood glancing from one to the other of us with half-frightened, half-hopeful eyes, as one who is not sure whether he is on the verge of a windfall or of a catastrophe. Then he stepped into the cab, and in half an hour we were back in the sitting-room at Baker Street. Nothing had been said during our drive, but the high, thin breathing of our new companion, and the claspings and unclaspings of his hands, spoke of the nervous tension within him.

"Here we are!" said Holmes cheerily as we filed into

the room. "The fire looks very seasonable in this weather. You look cold, Mr. Ryder. Pray take the basket-chair. I will just put on my slippers before we settle this little matter of yours. Now, then! You want to know what became of those geese?"

"Yes, sir."

"Or rather, I fancy, of that goose. It was one bird, I imagine, in which you were interested—white, with a black bar across the tail."

Ryder quivered with emotion. "Oh, sir," he cried, "can you tell me where it went to?"

"It came here."

"Here?"

"Yes, and a most remarkable bird it proved. I don't wonder that you should take an interest in it. It laid an egg after it was dead—the bonniest, brightest little blue egg that ever was seen. I have it here in my museum."

Our visitor staggered to his feet and clutched the mantelpiece with his right hand. Holmes unlocked his strongbox and held up the blue carbuncle, which shone out like a star, with a cold, brilliant, many-pointed radiance. Ryder stood glaring with a drawn face, uncertain whether to claim or to disown it.

"The game's up, Ryder," said Holmes quietly. "Hold up, man, or you'll be into the fire! Give him an arm back into his chair, Watson. He's not got blood enough to go in for felony with impunity. Give him a dash of brandy. So! Now he looks a little more human. What a shrimp it is, to be sure!"

For a moment he had staggered and nearly fallen, but the brandy brought a tinge of colour into his cheeks, and he sat staring with frightened eyes at his accuser.

"I have almost every link in my hands, and all the proofs which I could possibly need, so there is little which you need tell me. Still, that little may as well be cleared up to make the case complete. You had heard, Ryder, of this blue stone of the Countess of Morcar's?"

"It was Catherine Cusack who told me of it," said he in a crackling voice.

"I see—her ladyship's waiting-maid. Well, the temptation of sudden wealth so easily acquired was too much for you, as it has been for better men before you; but you were not very scrupulous in the means you used. It seems to me, Ryder, that there is the making of a very pretty villain in you. You knew that this man Horner, the plumber, had been concerned in some such matter before, and that suspicion would rest the more readily upon him. What did you do, then? You made some small job in my lady's room—you and your confederate Cusack—and you managed that he should be the man sent for. Then, when he had left, you rifled the jewel-case, raised the alarm, and had this unfortunate man arrested. You then—"

Ryder threw himself down suddenly upon the rug and clutched at my companion's knee. "For God's sake, have mercy!" he shrieked. "Think of my father! of my mother! It would break their hearts. I never went wrong before! I never will again. I swear it. I'll swear it on a Bible. Oh, don't bring it into court! For Christ's sake, don't!"

"Get back into your chair!" said Holmes sternly. "It is very well to cringe and crawl now, but you thought little enough of this poor Horner in the dock for a crime of which he knew nothing."

"I will fly, Mr. Holmes. I will leave the country, sir. Then the charge against him will break down."

"Hum! We will talk about that. And now let us hear a true account of the next act. How came the stone into the goose, and how came the goose into the open market? Tell us the truth, for there lies your only hope of safety."

Ryder passed his tongue over his parched lips. "I will tell you it just as it happened, sir," said he. "When Horner had been arrested, it seemed to me that it would be best for me to get away with the stone at once, for I did not know at what moment the police might not take it into their heads to search me and my room. There was no place about the hotel where it would be safe. I went out, as if on some commission, and I made for my sister's house. She had married a man named Oakshott, and lived in Brixton Road, where she fattened fowls for the market. All the way there every man I met seemed to me to be a policeman or a detective; and, for all that it was a cold

night, the sweat was pouring down my face before I came
to the Brixton Road. My sister asked me what was the
matter, and why I was so pale; but I told her that I had
been upset by the jewel robbery at the hotel. Then I went
into the back yard and smoked a pipe, and wondered what
it would be best to do.

"I had a friend once called Maudsley, who went to the
bad, and has just been serving his time in Pentonville. One
day he had met me, and fell into talk about the ways of
thieves, and how they could get rid of what they stole. I
knew that he would be true to me, for I knew one or two
things about him; so I made up my mind to go right on
to Kilburn, where he lived, and take him into my confidence. He would show me how to turn the stone into
money. But how to get to him in safety? I thought of the
agonies I had gone through in coming from the hotel. I
might at any moment be seized and searched, and there
would be the stone in my waistcoat pocket. I was leaning
against the wall at the time and looking at the geese which
were waddling about round my feet, and suddenly an idea
came into my head which showed me how I could beat
the best detective that ever lived.

"My sister had told me some weeks before that I might
have the pick of her geese for a Christmas present, and I
knew that she was always as good as her word. I would
take my goose now, and in it I would carry my stone to
Kilburn. There was a little shed in the yard, and behind
this I drove one of the birds—a fine big one, white, with
a barred tail. I caught it, and, prying its bill open, I thrust
the stone down its throat as far as my finger could reach.
The bird gave a gulp, and I felt the stone pass along its
gullet and down into its crop. But the creature flapped and
struggled, and out came my sister to know what was the
matter. As I turned to speak to her the brute broke loose
and fluttered off among the others.

" 'Whatever were you doing with that bird, Jem?' says
she.

" 'Well,' said I, 'you said you'd give me one for Christmas, and I was feeling which was the fattest.'

" 'Oh,' says she, 'we've set yours aside for you—Jem's

bird, we call it. It's the big white one over yonder. There's twenty-six of them, which makes one for you, and one for us, and two dozen for the market.'

" 'Thank you, Maggie,' says I; 'but if it is all the same to you, I'd rather have that one I was handling just now.'

" 'The other is a good three pound heavier,' said she, 'and we fattened it expressly for you.'

" 'Never mind. I'll have the other, and I'll take it now,' said I.

" 'Oh, just as you like,' said she, a little huffed. 'Which is it you want, then?'

" 'That white one with the barred tail, right in the middle of the flock.'

" 'Oh, very well. Kill it and take it with you.'

"Well, I did what she said, Mr. Holmes, and I carried the bird all the way to Kilburn. I told my pal what I had done, for he was a man that it was easy to tell a thing like that to. He laughed until he choked, and we got a knife and opened the goose. My heart turned to water, for there was no sign of the stone, and I knew that some terrible mistake had occurred. I left the bird, rushed back to my sister's, and hurried into the back yard. There was not a bird to be seen there.

" 'Where are they all, Maggie?' I cried.

" 'Gone to the dealer's, Jem.'

" 'Which dealer's?'

" 'Breckinridge, of Covent Garden.'

" 'But was there another with a barred tail?' I asked, 'the same as the one I chose?'

" 'Yes, Jem; there were two barred-tailed ones, and I could never tell them apart.'

"Well, then, of course I saw it all, and I ran off as hard as my feet would carry me to this man Breckinridge; but he had sold the lot at once, and not one word would he tell me as to where they had gone. You heard him yourselves to-night. Well, he has always answered me like that. My sister thinks that I am going mad. Sometimes I think that I am myself. And now—and now I am myself a branded thief, without ever having touched the wealth for which I sold my character. God help me! God help me!"

He burst into convulsive sobbing, with his face buried in his hands.

There was a long silence, broken only by his heavy breathing, and by the measured tapping of Sherlock Holmes's finger-tips upon the edge of the table. Then my friend rose and threw open the door.

"Get out!" said he.

"What, sir! Oh, Heaven bless you!"

"No more words. Get out!"

And no more words were needed. There was a rush, a clatter upon the stairs, the bang of a door, and the crisp rattle of running footfalls from the street.

"After all, Watson," said Holmes, reaching up his hand for his clay pipe, "I am not retained by the police to supply their deficiencies. If Horner were in danger it would be another thing; but this fellow will not appear against him, and the case must collapse. I suppose that I am committing a felony, but it is just possible that I am saving a soul. This fellow will not go wrong again; he is too terribly frightened. Send him to jail now, and you make him a jail-bird for life. Besides, it is the season of forgiveness. Chance has put in our way a most singular and whimsical problem, and its solution is its own reward. If you will have the goodness to touch the bell, Doctor, we will begin another investigation, in which, also, a bird will be the chief feature."

A MATTER OF LIFE
AND DEATH

BY GEORGES SIMENON

"At home we always used to go to Midnight Mass. I can't remember a Christmas when we missed it, though it meant a good half hour's drive from the farm to the village."

The speaker, Sommer, was making some coffee on a little electric stove.

"There were five of us," he went on. "Five boys, that is. The winters were colder in those days. Sometimes we had to go by sledge."

Lecœur, on the switchboard, had taken off his earphones to listen. "In what part of the country was that?"

"Lorraine."

"The winters in Lorraine were no colder thirty or forty years ago than they are now—only, of course, in those days the peasant had no cars. How many times did you go to Midnight Mass by sledge?"

"Couldn't say, exactly."

"Three times? Twice? Perhaps no more than once. Only it made a great impression on you, as you were a child."

"Anyhow, when we got back, we'd all have black pudding, and I'm not exaggerating when I tell you I've never had anything like it since. I don't know what my mother used to put in them, but her *boudins* were quite different from anyone else's. My wife's tried, but it wasn't the same thing, though she had the exact recipe from my eldest sister—at least, my sister swore it was."

He walked over to one of the huge, uncurtained windows, through which was nothing but blackness, and scratched the pane with a fingernail.

"Hallo, there's frost forming. That again reminds me of when I was little. The water used to freeze in our rooms and we'd have to break the ice in the morning when we wanted to wash."

"People didn't have central heating in those days," answered Lecœur coolly.

There were three of them on night duty. *Les nuiteux,* they were called. They had been in that vast room since eleven o'clock, and now, at six on that Christmas morning, all three were looking a bit jaded. Three or four empty bottles were lying about, with the remains of the sandwiches they had brought with them.

A lamp no bigger than an aspirin tablet lit up on one of the walls. Its position told Lecœur at once where the call came from.

"Thirteenth Arrondissement, Croulebarbe," he murmured, replacing his earphones. He seized a plug and pushed it into a hole.

"Croulebarbe? Your car's been called out—what for?"

"A call from the Boulevard Masséna. Two drunks fighting."

Lecœur carefully made a little cross in one of the columns of his notebook.

"How are you getting on down your way?"

"There are only four of us here. Two are playing dominoes."

"Had any *boudin* tonight?"

"No. Why?"

"Never mind. I must ring off now. There's a call from the Sixteenth."

A gigantic map of Paris was drawn on the wall in front of him and on it each police station was represented by a little lamp. As soon as anything happened anywhere, a lamp would light up and Lecœur would plug into the appropriate socket.

"Chaillot? Hallo! Your car's out?"

In front of each police station throughout the twenty arrondissements of Paris, one or more cars stood waiting, ready to dash off the moment an alarm was raised.

"What with?"

"Veronal."

That would be a woman. It was the third suicide that night, the second in the smart district of Passy.

Another little cross was entered in the appropriate column of Lecœur's notebook. Mambret, the third member of the watch, was sitting at a desk filling out forms.

"Hallo! Odéon? What's going on? Oh, a car stolen."

That was for Mambret, who took down the particulars, then phoned them through to Piedbœuf in the room above. Piedbœuf, the teleprinter operator, had such a resounding voice that the others could hear it through the ceiling. This was the forty-eighth car whose details he had circulated that night.

An ordinary night, in fact—for them. Not so for the world outside. For this was the great night, *la nuit de Noël*. Not only was there the Midnight Mass, but all the theaters and cinemas were crammed, and at the big stores, which stayed open till twelve, a crowd of people jostled each other in a last-minute scramble to finish off their Christmas shopping.

Indoors were family gatherings feasting on roast turkey and perhaps also on *boudins* made, like the ones Sommer had been talking about, from a secret recipe handed down from mother to daughter.

There were children sleeping restlessly while their parents crept about playing the part of Santa Claus, arranging the presents they would find on waking.

At the restaurants and cabarets every table had been booked at least a week in advance. In the Salvation Army barge on the Seine, tramps and paupers queued up for an extra special.

Sommer had a wife and five children. Piedbœuf, the teleprinter operator upstairs, was a father of one week's standing. Without the frost on the windowpanes, they wouldn't have known it was freezing outside, In that vast, dingy room they were in a world apart, surrounded on all sides by the empty offices of the Préfecture de Police, which stood facing the Palais de Justice. It wasn't till the following day that those offices would once again be teeming with people in search of passport visas, driving licenses, and permits of every description.

In the courtyard below, cars stood waiting for emergency calls, the men of the flying squad dozing on the seats. Nothing, however, had happened that night of sufficient importance to justify their being called out. You could see that from the little crosses in Lecœur's notebook. He didn't bother to count them, but he could tell at a glance that there were something like two hundred in the drunks' column.

No doubt there'd have been a lot more if it hadn't been that this was a night for indulgence. In most cases the police were able to persuade those who had had too much to go home and keep out of trouble. Those arrested were the ones in whom drink raised the devil, those who smashed windows or molested other people.

Two hundred of that sort—a handful of women among them—were now out of harm's way, sleeping heavily on the wooden benches in the lockups.

There'd been five knifings. Two near the Porte d'Italie. Three in the remoter part of Montmartre, not in the Montmartre of the Moulin Rouge and the Lapin Agile but in the Zone, beyond where the Fortifs used to be, whose population included over 100,000 Arabs living in huts made of old packing cases and roofing-felt.

A few children had been lost in the exodus from the churches, but they were soon returned to their anxious parents.

"Hallo! Chaillot? How's your veronal case getting on?"

She wasn't dead. Of course not! Few went as far as that. Suicide is all very well as a gesture—indeed, it can be a very effective one. But there's no need to go and kill yourself!

"Talking of *boudin*," said Mambret, who was smoking an enormous meerschaum pipe, "that reminds me of—"

They were never to know what he was reminded of. There were steps in the corridor, then the handle of the door was turned. All three looked round at once, wondering who could be coming to see them at ten past six in the morning.

"*Salut!*" said the man who entered, throwing his hat down on a chair.

"Whatever brings you here, Janvier?"

It was a detective of the Brigade des Homicides, who walked straight to the stove to warm his hands.

"I got pretty bored sitting all by myself and I thought I might as well come over here. After all, if the killer's going to do his stuff I'd hear about it quicker here than anywhere."

He, too, had been on duty all night, but round the corner, in the Police Judiciaire.

"You don't mind, do you?" he asked, picking up the coffeepot. "There's a bitter wind blowing."

It had made his ears red.

"I don't suppose we'll hear till eight, probably later," said Lecœur.

For the last fifteen years, he had spent his nights in that room, sitting at the switchboard, keeping an eye on the big map with the little lamps. He knew half the police in Paris by name, or, at any rate, those who did night duty. Of many he knew even their private affairs, as, when things were quiet, he would have long chats with them over the telephone to pass the time away. "Oh, it's you, Dumas. How are things at home?"

But though there were many whose voices were familiar, there were hardly any of them he knew by sight.

Nor was his acquaintance confined to the police. He was on equally familiar terms with many of the hospitals.

"Hallo! Bichat? What about the chap who was brought in half an hour ago? Is he dead yet?"

He was dead, and another little cross went into the notebook. The latter was, in its unpretentious way, quite a mine of information. If you asked Lecœur how many mur-

ders in the last twelve months had been done for the sake
of money, he'd give the answer in a moment—sixty-seven.

"How many murders committed by foreigners?"

"Forty-two."

You could go on like that for hours without being able
to trip him up. And yet he trotted out his figures without
a trace of swank. It was his hobby, that was all

For he wasn't obliged to make those crosses. It was his
own idea. Like the chats over the telephone lines, they
helped to pass the time away, and the result gave him
much the same satisfaction that others derive from a collection of stamps.

He was unmarried. Few knew where he lived or what
sort of a life he led outside that room. It was difficult to
picture him anywhere else, even to think of him walking
along the street like an ordinary person. He turned to
Janvier to say: "For your cases, we generally have to wait
till people are up and about. It's when a concierge goes
up with the post or when a maid takes her mistress's
breakfast into the bedroom that things like that come to
light."

He claimed no special merit in knowing a thing like that.
It was just a fact. A bit earlier in summer, of course, and
later in winter. On Christmas Day probably later still, as
a considerable part of the population hadn't gotten to bed
until two or even later, to say nothing of their having to
sleep off a good many glasses of champagne.

Before then, still more water would have gone under
the bridge—a few more stolen cars, a few belated drunks.

"Hallo! Saint-Gervais?"

His Paris was not the one known to the rest of us—the
Eiffel Tower, the Louvre, the Opéra—but one of somber,
massive buildings with a police car waiting under the blue
lamp and the bicycles of the *agents cyclistes* leaning against
the wall.

"The chief is convinced the chap'll have another go tonight," said Janvier. "It's just the night for people of that
sort. Seems to excite them."

No name was mentioned, for none was known. Nor
could he be described as the man in the fawn raincoat or

the man in the grey hat, since no one had ever seen him.
For a while the papers had referred to him as Monsieur
Dimanche, as his first three murders had been on Sunday,
but since then five others had been on weekdays, at the
rate of about one a week, though not quite regularly.

"It's because of him you've been on all night, is it?"
asked Mambret.

Janvier wasn't the only one. All over Paris extra men
were on duty, watching or waiting.

"You'll see," put in Sommer, "when you do get him
you'll find he's only a loony."

"Loony or not, he's killed eight people," sighed Janvier,
sipping his coffee. "Look, Lecœur—there's one of your
lamps burning."

"Hallo! Your car's out? What's that? Just a moment."

They could see Lecœur hesitate, not knowing in which
column to put a cross. There was one for hangings, one
for those who jumped out of the window, another for—

"Here, listen to this. On the Pont d'Austerlitz, a chap
climbed up onto the parapet. He had his legs tied together
and a cord round his neck with the end made fast to a
lamppost, and as he threw himself over he fired a shot
into his head!"

"Taking no risks, what? And which column does that
one go into?"

"There's one for neurasthenics. We may as well call it
that."

Those who hadn't been to Midnight Mass were now on
their way to early service. With hands thrust deep in their
pockets and drops on the ends of their noses, they walked
bent forward into the cutting wind, which seemed to blow
up a fine, icy dust from the pavements. It would soon be
time for the children to be waking up, jumping out of bed,
and gathering barefoot around lighted Christmas trees.

"But it's not at all sure the fellow's mad. In fact, the
experts say that if he was he'd always do it the same way.
If it was a knife, then it would always be a knife."

"What did he use this time?"

"A hammer."

"And the time before?"

"A dagger."

"What makes you think it's the same chap?"

"First of all, the fact that there've been eight murders in quick succession. You don't get eight new murderers cropping up in Paris all at once." Belonging to the Police Judiciaire, Janvier had, of course, heard the subject discussed at length. "Besides, there's a sort of family likeness between them all. The victims are invariably solitary people, people who live alone, without any family or friends."

Sommer looked at Lecœur, whom he could never forgive for not being a family man. Not only had he five children himself, but a sixth was already on the way. "You'd better look out, Lecœur—you see the kind of thing it leads to!"

"Then, not one of the crimes has been committed in one of the wealthier districts."

"Yet he steals, doesn't he?"

"He does, but not much. The little hoards hidden under the mattress—that's his mark. He doesn't break in. In fact, apart from the murder and the money missing, he leaves no trace at all."

Another lamp burning. A stolen car found abandoned in a little side street near the Place des Ternes.

"All the same, I can't help laughing over the people who had to walk home."

Another hour or more and they would be relieved, except Lecœur, who had promised to do the first day shift as well so that his opposite number could join in a family Christmas party somewhere near Rouen.

It was a thing he often did, so much so that he had come to be regarded as an ever-ready substitute for anybody who wanted a day off.

"I say, Lecœur, do you think you could look out for me on Friday?"

At first the request was proffered with a suitable excuse—a sick mother, a funeral, or a First Communion, and he was generally rewarded with a bottle of wine. But now it was taken for granted and treated quite casually.

To tell the truth, had it been possible, Lecœur would

have been only too glad to spend his whole life in that
room, snatching a few hours' sleep on a camp bed and
picnicking as best he could with the aid of the little electric
stove. It was a funny thing—although he was as careful as
any of the others about his personal appearance, and much
more so than Sommer, who always looked a bit tousled,
there was something a bit drab about him which betrayed
the bachelor.

He wore strong glasses, which gave him big, globular
eyes, and it came as a surprise to everyone when he took
them off to wipe them with the bit of chamois leather he
always carried about to see the transformation. Without
them, his eyes were gentle, rather shy, and inclined to look
away quickly when anyone looked his way.

"Hallo! Javel?"

Another lamp. One near the Quai de Javel in the 15th
Arrondissement, a district full of factories.

"Votre car est sorti?"

"We don't know yet what it is. Someone's broken the
glass of the alarm in the Rue Leblanc."

"Wasn't there a message?"

"No. We've sent our car to investigate. I'll ring you
again later."

Scattered here and there all over Paris are red-painted
telephone pillars standing by the curb, and you have only
to break the glass to be in direct telephone communication
with the nearest police station. Had a passerby broken the
glass accidentally? It looked like it, for a couple of minutes
later Javel rang up again.

"Hallo! Central? Our car's just got back. Nobody about.
The whole district seems quiet as the grave. All the same,
we've sent out a patrol."

How was Lecœur to classify that one? Unwilling to
admit defeat, he put a little cross in the column on the
extreme right headed "Miscellaneous."

"Is there any coffee left?" he asked.

"I'll make some more."

The same lamp lit up again, barely ten minutes after the
first call.

"Javel? What's it this time?"

"Same again. Another glass broken."

"Nothing said?"

"Not a word. Must be some practical joker. Thinks it funny to keep us on the hop. When we catch him he'll find out whether it's funny or not!"

"Which one was it?"

"The one on the Pont Mirabeau."

"Seems to walk pretty quickly, your practical joker!"

There was indeed quite a good stretch between the two pillars.

So far, nobody was taking it very seriously. False alarms were not uncommon. Some people took advantage of these handy instruments to express their feelings about the police. *"Mort aux flics!"* was the favorite phrase.

With his feet on a radiator, Janvier was just dozing off when he heard Lecœur telephoning again. He half opened his eyes, saw which lamp was on, and muttered sleepily, "There he is again."

He was right. A glass broken at the top of the Avenue de Versailles.

"Silly ass," he grunted, settling down again.

It wouldn't be really light until half past seven or even eight. Sometimes they could hear a vague sound of church bells, but that was in another world. The wretched men of the flying squad waiting in the cars below must be half frozen.

"Talking of *boudin*—"

"What *boudin*?" murmured Janvier, whose cheeks were flushed with sleep.

"The one my mother used to—"

"Hallo! What? You're not going to tell me someone's smashed the glass of one of your telephone pillars? Really? It must be the same chap. We've already had two reported from the Fifteenth. Yes, they tried to nab him but couldn't find a soul about. Gets about pretty fast, doesn't he? He crossed the river by the Pont Mirabeau. Seems to be heading in this direction. Yes, you may as well have a try."

Another little cross. By half past seven, with only half

an hour of the night watch to go, there were five crosses in the Miscellaneous column.

Mad or sane, the person was a good walker. Perhaps the cold wind had something to do with it. It wasn't the weather for sauntering along.

For a time it had looked as though he was keeping to the right bank of the Seine, then he had sheered off into the wealthy Auteuil district, breaking a glass in the Rue la Fontaine.

"He's only five minutes' walk from the Bois de Boulogne," Lecœur had said. "If he once gets there, they'll never pick him up."

But the fellow had turned round and made for the quays again, breaking a glass in the Rue Berton, just around the corner from the Quai de Passy.

The first calls had come from the poorer quarters of Grenelle, but the man had only to cross the river to find himself in entirely different surroundings—quiet, spacious, and deserted streets, where his footfalls must have rung out clearly on the frosty pavements.

Sixth call. Skirting the Place du Trocadéro, he was in the Rue de Longchamp.

"The chap seems to think he's on a paper chase," remarked Mambret. "Only he uses broken glass instead of paper."

Other calls came in in quick succession. Another stolen car, a revolver-shot in the Rue de Flandres, whose victim swore he didn't know who fired it, though he'd been seen all through the night drinking in company with another man.

"Hallo! Here's Javel again. Hallo! Javel? It can't be your practical joker this time: he must be somewhere near the Champs Elysées by now. Oh, yes. He's still at it. Well, what's your trouble? What? Spell it, will you? Rue Michat. Yes, I've got it. Between the Rue Lecourbe and the Boulevard Felix Faure. By the viaduct—yes, I know. Number 17. Who reported it? The concierge? She's just been up, I suppose. Oh, shut up, will you! No, I wasn't speaking to you. It's Sommer here, who can't stop talking about a *boudin* he ate thirty years ago!"

Sommer broke off and listened to the man on the switchboard.

"What were you saying? A shabby seven-story block of flats. Yes—"

There were plenty of buildings like that in the district, buildings that weren't really old, but of such poor construction that they were already dilapidated. Buildings that as often as not thrust themselves up bleakly in the middle of a bit of wasteland, towering over the little shacks and hovels around them, their blind walls plastered with advertisements.

"You say she heard someone running downstairs and then a door slam. The door of the house, I suppose. On which floor is the flat? The *entresol*. Which way does it face? Onto an inner courtyard— Just a moment, there's a call coming in from the Eighth. That must be our friend of the telephone pillars."

Lecœur asked the new caller to wait, then came back to Javel.

"An old woman, you say. Madame Fayet. Worked as charwoman. Dead? A blunt instrument. Is the doctor there? You're sure she's dead? What about her money? I suppose she had some tucked away somewhere. Right. Call me back. Or I'll ring you."

He turned to the detective, who was now sleeping soundly.

"Janvier! Hey, Janvier! This is for you."

"What? What is it?"

"The killer."

"Where?"

"Near the Rue Lecourbe. Here's the address. This time he's done in an old charwoman, a Madame Fayet."

Janvier put on his overcoat, looked round for his hat, and gulped down the remains of the coffee in his cup.

"Who's dealing with it?"

"Gonesse, of the Fifteenth."

"Ring up the P.J., will you, and tell them I've gone there."

A minute or two later, Lecœur was able to add another little cross to the six that were already in the column.

Someone has smashed the glass of the pillar in the Avenue d'Iéna only one hundred and fifty yards from the Arc de Triomphe.

"Among the broken glass they found a handkerchief flecked with blood. It was a child's handkerchief."

"Has it got initials?"

"No. It's a blue-check handkerchief, rather dirty. The chap must have wrapped it round his knuckles for breaking the glass."

There were steps in the corridor. The day shift coming to take over. They looked very clean and close-shaven and the cold wind had whipped the blood into their cheeks.

"Happy Christmas!"

Sommer closed the tin in which he brought his sandwiches. Mambret knocked out his pipe. Only Lecœur remained in his seat, since there was no relief for him.

The fat Godin had been the first to arrive, promptly changing his jacket for the grey-linen coat in which he always worked, then putting some water on to boil for his grog. All through the winter he suffered from one never-ending cold which he combated, or perhaps nourished, by one hot grog after another.

"Hallo! Yes, I'm still here. I'm doing a shift for Potier, who's gone down to his family in Normandy. Yes. I want to hear all about it. Most particularly. Janvier's gone, but I'll pass it on to the P.J. An invalid, you say? What invalid?"

One had to be patient on that job, as people always talked about their cases as though everyone else was in the picture.

"A low building behind, right. Not in the Rue Michat, then? Rue Vasco de Gama. Yes, yes. I know. The little house with a garden behind some railings. Only I didn't know he was an invalid. Right. He doesn't sleep much. Saw a young boy climbing up a drainpipe? How old? He couldn't say? Of course not, in the dark. How did he know it was a boy, then? Listen, ring me up again, will you? Oh, you're going off. Who's relieving you? Jules? Right. Well, ask him to keep me informed."

"What's going on?" asked Godin.

"An old woman who's been done in. Down by the Rue Lecourbe."

"Who did it?"

"There's an invalid opposite who says he saw a small boy climbing up a drainpipe and along the top of a wall."

"You mean to say it was a boy who killed the old woman?"

"We don't know yet."

No one was very interested. After all, murders were an everyday matter to these people. The lights were still on in the room, as it was still only a bleak, dull daylight that found its way through the frosty window panes. One of the new watch went and scratched a bit of the frost away. It was instinctive. A childish memory perhaps, like Sommer's *boudin*.

The latter had gone home. So had Mambret. The newcomers settled down to their work, turning over the papers on their desks.

A car stolen from the Square la Bruyère.

Lecœur looked pensively at his seven crosses. Then, with a sigh, he got up and stood gazing at the immense street plan on the wall.

"Brushing up on your Paris?"

"I think I know it pretty well already. Something's just struck me. There's a chap wandering about smashing the glass of telephone pillars. Seven in the last hour and a half. He hasn't been going in a straight line but zigzagging—first this way, then that."

"Perhaps he doesn't know Paris."

"Or knows it only too well! Not once has he ventured within sight of a police station. If he'd gone straight, he'd have passed two or three. What's more, he's skirted all the main crossroads where there'd be likely to be a man on duty." Lecœur pointed them out. "The only risk he took was in crossing the Pont Mirabeau, but if he wanted to cross the river he'd have run that risk at any of the bridges."

"I expect he's drunk," said Godin, sipping his rum.

"What I want to know is why he's stopped."

"Perhaps he's got home."

"A man who's down by the Quai de Javel at half past six in the morning isn't likely to live near the Etoile."

"Seems to interest you a lot."

"It's got me scared!"

"Go on."

It was strange to see the worried expression on Lecœur's face. He was notorious for his calmness and his most dramatic nights were coolly summarized by the little crosses in his notebook.

"Hallo! Javel? Is that Jules? Lecœur speaking. Look here, Jules, behind the flats in the Rue Michat is the little house where the invalid lives. Well, now, on one side of it is an apartment house, a red-brick building with a grocer's shop on the ground floor. You know it?

"Good. Has anything happened there? Nothing reported. No, we've heard nothing here. All the same, I can't explain why, but I think you ought to inquire."

He was hot all at once. He stubbed out a half finished cigarette.

"Hallo! Ternes? Any alarms gone off in your neighborhood? Nothing. Only drunks? Is the *patrouille cycliste* out? Just leaving? Ask them to keep their eyes open for a young boy looking tired and very likely bleeding from the right hand. Lost? Not exactly that. I can't explain now."

His eyes went back to the street plan on the wall, in which no light went on for a good ten minutes, and then only for an accidental death in the Eighteenth Arrondissement, right up at the top of Montmartre, caused by an escape of gas.

Outside, in the cold streets of Paris, dark figures were hurrying home from the churches . . .

One of the sharpest impressions Andre Lecœur retained of his infancy was one of immobility. His world at that period was a large kitchen in Orleans, on the outskirts of the town. He must have spent his winters there, too, but he remembered it best flooded with sunlight, with the door wide open onto a little garden where hens clucked incessantly and rabbits nibbled lettuce leaves behind the wire netting of their hutches. But, if the door was open, its passage was barred to him by a little gate which his father had made one Sunday for that express purpose.

On weekdays, at half past eight, his father went off on his bicycle to the gas works at the other end of the town. His mother did the housework, doing the same things in the same order every day. Before making the beds, she put the bedclothes over the windowsill for an hour to air.

At ten o'clock, a little bell would ring in the street. That was the greengrocer, with his barrow, passing on his daily round. Twice a week at eleven, a bearded doctor came to see his little brother, who was constantly ill. Andre hardly ever saw the latter, as he wasn't allowed into his room.

That was all, or so it seemed in retrospect. He had just time to play a bit and drink his milk, and there was his father home again for the midday meal.

If nothing had happened at home, lots had happened to him. He had been to read the meters in any number of houses and chatted with all sorts of people, about whom he would talk during dinner.

As for the afternoon, it slipped away quicker still, perhaps because he was made to sleep during the first part of it.

For his mother, apparently, the time passed just as quickly. Often had he heard her say with a sigh: "There, I've no sooner washed up after one meal than it's time to start making another!"

Perhaps it wasn't so very different now. Here in the Préfecture de Police the nights seemed long enough at the time, but at the end they seemed to have slipped by in no time, with nothing to show for them except for these columns of the little crosses in his notebook.

A few more lamps lit up. A few more incidents reported, including a collision between a car and a bus in the Rue de Clignancourt, and then once again it was Javel on the line.

It wasn't Jules, however, but Gonesse, the detective who'd been to the scene of the crime. While there he had received Lecœur's message suggesting something might have happened in the other house in the Rue Vasco de Gama. He had been to see.

"Is that you, Lecœur?" There was a queer note in his voice. Either irritation or suspicion.

"Look here, what made you think of that house? Do you know the old woman, Madame Fayet?"

"I've never seen her, but I know all about her."

What had finally come to pass that Christmas morning was something that Andre Lecœur had foreseen and perhaps dreaded for more than ten years. Again and again, as he stared at the huge plan of Paris, with its little lamps, he had said to himself, "It's only a question of time. Sooner or later, it'll be something that's happened to someone I know."

There'd been many a near miss, an accident in his own street or a crime in a house nearby. But, like thunder, it had approached only to recede once again into the distance.

This time it was a direct hit.

"Have you seen the concierge?" he asked. He could imagine the puzzled look on the detective's face as he went on: "Is the boy at home?"

And Gonesse muttered, "Oh? So you know him, too?"

"He's my nephew. Weren't you told his name was Lecœur?"

"Yes, but—"

"Never mind about that. Tell me what's happened."

"The boy's not there."

"What about his father?"

"He got home just after seven."

"As usual. He does night work, too."

"The concierge heard him go up to his flat—on the third floor at the back of the house."

"I know it."

"He came running down a minute or two later in a great state. To use her expression, he seemed out of his wits."

"The boy had disappeared?"

"Yes. His father wanted to know if she'd seen him leave the house. She hadn't. Then he asked if a telegram had been delivered."

"Was there a telegram?"

"No. Can you make head or tail of it? Since you're one

of the family, you might be able to help us. Could you get someone to relieve you and come round here?"

"It wouldn't do any good. Where's Janvier?"

"In the old woman's room. The men of the Identité Judiciaire have already got to work. The first thing they found were some child's fingerprints on the handle of the door. Come on—jump into a taxi and come round."

"No. In any case, there's no one to take my place."

That was true enough up to a point. All the same, if he'd really got to work on the telephone he'd have found someone all right. The truth was he didn't want to go and didn't think it would do any good if he did.

"Listen, Gonesse, I've got to find that boy, and I can do it better from here than anywhere. You understand, don't you? Tell Janvier I'm staying here. And tell him old Madame Fayet had plenty of money, probably hidden away somewhere in the room."

A little feverish, Lecœur stuck his plug into one socket after another, calling up the various police stations of the Eighth Arrondissement.

"Keep a lookout for a boy of ten, rather poorly dressed. Keep all telephone pillars under observation."

His two fellow-watchkeepers looked at him with curiosity.

"Do you think it was the boy who did the job?"

Lecœur didn't bother to answer. The next moment he was through to the teleprinter room, where they also dealt with radio messages.

"Justin? Oh, you're on, are you? Here's something special. Will you send out a call to all cars on patrol anywhere near the Etoile to keep a lookout for—"

Once again the description of the boy, Francois Lecœur.

"No. I've no idea in which direction he'll be making. All I can tell you is that he seems to keep well clear of police stations, and as far as possible from any place where there's likely to be anyone on traffic duty."

He knew his brother's flat in the Rue Vasco de Gama. Two rather dark rooms and a tiny kitchen. The boy slept there alone while his father was at work. From the windows you could see the back of the house in the Rue

Michat, across a courtyard generally hung with washing. On some of the windowsills were pots of geraniums, and through the windows, many of which were uncurtained, you could catch glimpses of a miscellaneous assortment of humanity.

As a matter of fact, there, too, the windowpanes ought to be covered with frost. He stored that idea up in a corner of his mind. It might be important.

"You think it's a boy who's been smashing the alarm glasses?"

"It was a child's handkerchief they found," said Lecœur curtly. He didn't want to be drawn into a discussion. He sat mutely at the switchboard, wondering what to do next.

In the Rue Michat, things seemed to be moving fast. The next time he got through it was to learn that a doctor was there as well as an examining magistrate who had most likely been dragged from his bed.

What help could Lecœur have given them? But if he wasn't there, he could see the place almost as clearly as those that were, the dismal houses and the grimy viaduct of the Métro which cut right across the landscape.

Nothing but poor people in that neighborhood. The younger generation's one hope was to escape from it. The middle-aged already doubted whether they ever would, while the old ones had already accepted their fate and tried to make the best of it.

He rang Javel once again.

"Is Gonesse still there?"

"He's writing up his report. Shall I call him?"

"Yes, please. Hallo, Gonesse, Lecœur speaking. Sorry to bother you, but did you go up to my brother's flat? Had the boy's bed been slept in? It had? Good. That makes it look a bit better. Another thing: were there any parcels there? Yes, parcels, Christmas presents. What? A small square radio. Hadn't been unpacked. Naturally. Anything else? A chicken, a *boudin,* a Saint-Honoré. I suppose Janvier's not with you? Still on the spot. Right. Has he rung up the P.J.? Good."

He was surprised to see it was already half past nine. It

was no use now expecting anything from the neighborhood of the Etoile. If the boy had gone on walking as he had been earlier, he could be pretty well anywhere by this time.

"Hallo! Police Judiciaire? Is Inspector Saillard there?"

He was another whom the murder had dragged from his fireside. How many people were there whose Christmas was going to be spoiled by it?

"Excuse my troubling you, Monsieur le Commissaire. It's about that young boy, Francois Lecœur."

"Do you know anything? Is he a relation of yours?"

"He's my brother's son. And it looks as if he may well be the person who's been smashing the glasses of the telephone pillars. Seven of them. I don't know whether they've had time to tell you about that. What I wanted to ask was whether I might put out a general call?"

"Could you nip over to see me?"

"There's no one here to take my place."

"Right. I'll come over myself. Meanwhile you can send out the call."

Lecœur kept calm, though his hand shook slightly as he plugged in once again to the room above.

"Justin? Lecœur again. Appel General. Yes. It's the same boy. Francois Lecœur. Ten and a half, rather tall for his age, thin. I don't know what he's wearing, probably a khaki jumper made from American battle-dress. No, no cap. He's always bare-headed, with plenty of hair flopping over his forehead. Perhaps it would be as well to send out a description of his father, too. That's not so easy. You know me, don't you? Well, Olivier Lecœur is rather like a paler version of me. He has a timid look about him and physically he's not robust. The sort that's never in the middle of the pavement but always dodging out of other people's way. He walks a bit queerly, owing to a wound he got in the first war. No, I haven't the least idea where they might be going, only I don't think they're together. To my mind, the boy is probably in danger. I can't explain why—it would take too long. Get the descriptions out as quickly as possible, will you? And let me know if there's any response."

*   *   *

By the time Lecœur had finished telephoning, Inspector
Saillard was there, having only had to come round the
corner from the Quai des Orfèvres. He was an imposing
figure of a man, particularly in his bulky overcoat. With a
comprehensive wave of the hand, he greeted the three
men on watch, then, seizing a chair as though it were a
wisp of straw, he swung it round towards him and sat down
heavily. "The boy?" he inquired, looking keenly at
Lecœur.

"I can't understand why he's stopped calling us up."

"Calling us up?"

"Attracting our attention, anyway."

"But why should he attract our attention and then not
say anything?"

"Supposing he was followed. Or was following
someone."

"I see what you mean. Look here, Lecœur, is your
brother in financial straits?"

"He's a poor man, yes."

"Is that all?"

"He lost his job three months ago."

"What job?"

"He was linotype operator at *La Presse* in the Rue du
Croissant. He was on the night shift. He always did night
work. Runs in the family."

"How did he come to lose his job?"

"I suppose he fell out with somebody."

"Is that a failing of his?"

They were interrupted by an incoming call from the
Eighteenth to say that a boy selling branches of holly had
been picked up in the Rue Lepic. It turned out, however,
to be a little Pole who couldn't speak any French.

"You were asking if my brother was in the habit of
quarreling with people. I hardly know what to answer. He
was never strong. Pretty well all his childhood he was ill
on and off. He hardly ever went to school. But he read a
great deal alone in his room."

"Is he married?"

"His wife died two years after they were married, leaving him with a baby ten months old."

"Did he bring it up himself?"

"Entirely. I can see him now bathing the little chap, changing his diapers, and warming the milk for his bottle."

"That doesn't explain why he quarrels with people."

Admittedly. But it was difficult to put it into words.

"Soured?"

"Not exactly. The thing is—"

"What?"

"That he's never lived like other people. Perhaps Olivier isn't really very intelligent. Perhaps, from reading so much, he knows too much about some things and too little about others."

"Do you think him capable of killing the old woman?"

The Inspector puffed at his pipe. They could hear the people in the room above walking about. The two other men fiddled with their papers, pretending not to listen.

"She was his mother-in-law," sighed Lecœur. "You'd have found it out anyhow, sooner or later."

"They didn't hit it off?"

"She hated him."

"Why?"

"She considered him responsible for her daughter's death. It seems she could have been saved if the operation had been done in time. It wasn't my brother's fault. The people at the hospital refused to take her in. Some silly question of her papers not being in order. All the same, Madame Fayet held to it that Olivier was to blame."

"Did they see each other?"

"Not unless they passed each other in the street, and then they never spoke."

"Did the boy know?"

"That she was his grandmother? I don't think so."

"You think his father never told him?"

Never for more than a second or two did Lecœur's eyes leave the plan of Paris, but, besides being Christmas, it was the quiet time of the day, and the little lamps lit up rarely. Two or three street accidents, a lady's handbag snatched in the Métro, a suitcase pinched at the Gare de L'Est.

No sign of the boy. It was surprising considering how few people were about. In the poor quarters a few little children played on the pavements with their new toys, but on the whole the day was lived indoors. Nearly all the shops were shuttered and the cafes and the little bars were almost empty.

For a moment, the town came to life a bit when the church bells started pealing and families in their Sunday best hurried to High Mass. But soon the streets were quiet again, though haunted here and there by the vague rumble of an organ or a sudden gust of singing.

The thought of churches gave Lecœur an idea. Might not the boy have tucked himself away in one of them? Would the police think of looking there? He spoke to Inspector Saillard about it and then got through to Justin for the third time.

"The churches. Ask them to have a look at the congregations. They'll be doing the stations, of course—that's most important."

He took off his glasses for a moment, showing eyelids that were red, probably from lack of sleep.

"Hallo! Yes. The Inspector's here. Hold on."

He held the receiver to Saillard. "It's Janvier."

The bitter wind was still driving through the streets. The light was harsh and bleak, though here and there among the closely packed clouds was a yellowy streak which could be taken as a faint promise of sunshine to come.

When the Inspector put down the receiver, he muttered, "Dr. Paul says the crime was committed between five and half past six this morning. The old woman wasn't killed by the first blow. Apparently she was in bed when she heard a noise and got up and faced the intruder. Indeed, it looks as though she tried to defend herself with the only weapon that came to hand—a shoe."

"Have they found the weapon she was killed with?"

"No. It might have been a hammer. More likely a bit of lead piping or something of that sort."

"Have they found her money?"

"Only her purse, with some small change in it and her identity card. Tell me, Lecœur, did you know she was a money-lender?"

"Yes. I knew."

"And didn't you tell me your brother's been out of work for three months?"

"He has."

"The concierge didn't know."

"Neither did the boy. It was for his sake he kept it dark."

The Inspector crossed and uncrossed his legs. He was uncomfortable. He glanced at the other two men who couldn't help hearing everything, then turned with a puzzled look to stare at Lecœur.

"Do you realize what all this is pointing to?"

"I do."

"You've thought of it yourself?"

"No."

"Because he's your brother?"

"No."

"How long is it that this killer's been at work? Nine weeks, isn't it?"

Without haste, Lecœur studied the columns of his notebook.

"Yes. Just over nine weeks. The first was on the twentieth of October, in the Epinettes district."

"You say your brother didn't tell his son he was out of a job. Do you mean to say he went on leaving home in the evening just as though he was going to work?"

"Yes. He couldn't face the idea of telling him. You see—it's difficult to explain. He was completely wrapped up in the boy. He was all he had to live for. He cooked and scrubbed for him, tucked him up in bed before going off, and woke him up in the morning."

"That doesn't explain why he couldn't tell him."

"He couldn't bear the thought of appearing to the kid as a failure, a man nobody wanted and who had doors slammed in his face."

"But what did he do with himself all night?"

"Odd jobs. When he could get them. For a fortnight, he

was employed as night watchman in a factory in Billan-
court, but that was only while the regular man was ill.
Often he got a few hours' work washing down cars in one
of the big garages. When that failed, he'd sometimes lend
a hand at the market unloading vegetables. When he had
one of his bouts—"

"Bouts of what?"

"Asthma. He had them from time to time. Then he'd
lie down in a station waiting room. Once he spent a whole
night here, chatting with me."

"Suppose the boy woke up early this morning and saw
his father at Madame Fayet's?"

"There was frost on the windows."

"There wouldn't be if the window was open. Lots of
people sleep with their windows open even in the cold-
est weather."

"It wasn't the case with my brother. He was always a
chilly person. And he was much too poor to waste
warmth."

"As far as his window was concerned, the boy had only
to scratch away the frost with his fingernail. When I was
a boy—"

"Yes. So did I. The thing is to find out whether the old
woman's window was open."

"It was, and the light was switched on."

"I wonder where Francois can have got to."

"The boy?"

It was surprising and a little disconcerting the way he
kept all the time reverting to him. The situation was certainly embarrassing, and somehow made all the more so
by the calm way in which Andre Lecœur gave the Inspector the most damaging details about his brother.

"When he came in this morning," began Saillard again,
"he was carrying a number of parcels. You realize—"

"It's Christmas."

"Yes. But he'd have needed quite a bit of money to buy
a chicken, a cake, and that new radio. Has he borrowed
any from you lately?"

"Not for a month. I haven't seen him for a month. I
wish I had. I'd have told him that I was getting a radio

for Francois myself. I've got it here. Downstairs, that is, in the cloakroom. I was going to take it straight round as soon as I was relieved."

"Would Madame Fayet have consented to lend him money?"

"It's unlikely. She was a queer lot. She must have had quite enough money to live on, yet she still went out to work, charring from morning to evening. Often she lent money to the people she worked for. At exorbitant interest, of course. All the neighborhood knew about it, and people always came to her when they needed something to tide them over till the end of the month."

Still embarrassed, the Inspector rose to his feet. "I'm going to have a look," he said.

"At Madame Fayet's?"

"There and in the Rue Vasco de Gama. If you get any news, let me know, will you?"

"You won't find any telephone there, but I can get a message to you through the Javel police station."

The Inspector's footsteps had hardly died away before the telephone bell rang. No lamp had lit up on the wall. This was an outside call, coming from the Gare d'Austerlitz.

"Lecœur? Station police speaking. We've got him."

"Who?"

"The man whose description was circulated. Lecœur. Same as you. Olivier Lecœur. No doubt about it, I've seen his identity card."

"Hold on, will you?"

Lecœur dashed out of the room and down the stairs just in time to catch the Inspector as he was getting into one of the cars belonging to the Prefecture.

"Inspector! The Gare d'Austerlitz is on the phone. They've found my brother."

Saillard was a stout man and he went up the stairs puffing and blowing. He took the receiver himself.

"Hallo! Yes. Where was he? What was he doing? What? No, there's no point in your questioning him now. You're sure he didn't know? Right. Go on looking out. It's quite possible. As for him, send him here straightaway. At the Prefecture, yes."

He hesitated for a second and glanced at Lecœur before saying finally, "Yes. Send someone with him. We can't take any risks."

The Inspector filled his pipe and lit it before explaining, and when he spoke he looked at nobody in particular.

"He was picked up after he'd been wandering about the station for over an hour. He seemed very jumpy. Said he was waiting there to meet his son, from whom he'd received a message."

"Did they tell him about the murder?"

"Yes. He appeared to be staggered by the news and terrified. I asked them to bring him along." Rather diffidently he added: "I asked them to bring him here. Considering your relationship, I didn't want you to think—"

Lecœur had been in that room since eleven o'clock the night before. It was rather like his early years when he spent his days in his mother's kitchen. Around him was an unchanging world. There were the little lamps, of course, that kept going on and off, but that's what they always did. They were part and parcel of the immutability of the place. Time flowed by without anyone noticing it.

Yet, outside, Paris was celebrating Christmas. Thousands of people had been to Midnight Mass, thousands more had spent the night roistering, and those who hadn't known where to draw the line had sobered down in the police station and were now being called upon to explain things they couldn't remember doing.

What had his brother Olivier been doing all through the night? An old woman had been found dead. A boy started before dawn on a breathless race through the streets, breaking the glass of the telephone pillars as he passed them, having wrapped his handkerchief round his fist.

And what was Olivier waiting for at the Gare d'Austerlitz, sometimes in the overheated waiting rooms, sometimes on the windswept platforms, too nervous to settle down in any one place for long?

Less than ten minutes elapsed, just time enough for Godin, whose nose really was running, to make himself another glass of hot grog.

"Can I offer you one, Monsieur le Commissaire?"

"No, thanks."

Looking more embarrassed than ever, Saillard leaned over towards Lecœur to say in an undertone, "Would you like us to question him in another room?"

No. Lecœur wasn't going to leave his post for anything. He wanted to stay there, with his little lamps and his switchboard. Was it that he was thinking more of the boy than of his brother?

Olivier came in with a detective on either side, but they had spared him the handcuffs. He looked dreadful, like a bad photograph faded with age. At once he turned to Andre. "Where's Francois?"

"We don't know. We're hunting for him."

"Where?"

Andre Lecœur pointed to his plan of Paris and his switchboard of a thousand lines. "Everywhere."

The two detectives had already been sent away.

"Sit down," said the Inspector. "I believe you've been told of Madame Fayet's death."

Olivier didn't wear spectacles, but he had the same pale and rather fugitive eyes as his brother had when he took his glasses off. He glanced at the Inspector, by whom he didn't seem the least overawed, then turned back to Andre. "He left a note for me," he said, delving into one of the pockets of his grubby mackintosh. "Here. See if you can understand."

He held out a bit of paper torn out of a schoolboy's exercise book. The writing wasn't any too good. It didn't look as though Francois was the best of pupils. He had used an indelible pencil, wetting the end in his mouth, so that his lips were very likely stained with it.

"Uncle Gedeon arrives this morning Gare d'Austerlitz. Come as soon as you can and meet us there. Love. Bib."

Without a word, Andre Lecœur passed it on to the Inspector, who turned it over and over with his thick fingers. "What's Bib stand for?"

"It's his nickname. A baby name. I never use it when other people are about. It comes from *biberon*. When I used to give him his bottle—" He spoke in a toneless voice. He seemed to be in a fog and was probably only dimly conscious of where he was.

"Who's Uncle Gedeon?"

"There isn't any such person."

Did he realize he was talking to the head of the Brigade des Homicides, who was at the moment investigating a murder?

It was his brother who came to the rescue, explaining, "As a matter of fact, we had an Uncle Gedeon but he's been dead for some years. He was one of my mother's brothers who emigrated to America as a young man."

Olivier looked at his brother as much as to say: What's the point of going into that?

"We got into the habit, in the family, of speaking— jocularly, of course—of our rich American uncle and of the fortune he'd leave us one day."

"Was he rich?"

"We didn't know. We never heard from him except for a postcard once a year, signed Gedeon. Wishing us a happy New Year."

"He died?"

"When Francois was four."

"Really, Andre, do you think it's any use—"

"Let me go on. The Inspector wants to know everything. My brother carried on the family tradition, talking to his son about our Uncle Gedeon, who had become by now quite a legendary figure. He provided a theme for bedtime stories, and all sorts of adventures were attributed to him. Naturally he was fabulously rich, and when one day he came back to France—"

"I understand. He died out there?"

"In a hospital in Cleveland. It was then we found out he had been really a porter in a restaurant. It would have been too cruel to tell the boy that, so the legend went on."

"Did he believe in it?"

It was Olivier who answered. "My brother thought he didn't, that he'd guessed the truth but wasn't going to spoil the game. But I always maintained the contrary and I'm still practically certain he took it all in. He was like that. Long after his schoolfellows had stopped believing in Father Christmas, he still went on."

Talking about his son brought him back to life, transfigured him.

"But as for this note he left, I don't know what to make of it. I asked the concierge if a telegram had come. For a moment I thought Andre might have played us a practical joke, but I soon dismissed the idea. It isn't much of a joke to get a boy dashing off to a station on a freezing night. Naturally I dashed off to the Gare d'Austerlitz as fast as I could. There I hunted high and low, then wandered about, waiting anxiously for him to turn up. Andre, you're sure he hasn't been—"

He looked at the street plan on the wall and at the switchboard. He knew very well that every accident was reported.

"He hasn't been run over," said Andre. "At about eight o'clock he was near the Etoile, but we've completely lost track of him since then."

"Near the Etoile? How do you know?"

"It's rather a long story, but it boils down to this—that a whole series of alarms were set off by someone smashing the glass. They followed a circuitous route from your place to the Arc de Triomphe. At the foot of the last one, they found a blue-check handerchief, a boy's handkerchief, among the broken glass."

"He has handkerchiefs like that."

"From eight o'clock onward, not a sign of him."

"Then I'd better get back to the station. He's certain to go there, if he told me to meet him there."

He was surprised at the sudden silence with which his last words were greeted. He looked from one to the other, perplexed, then anxious.

"What is it?"

His brother looked down at the floor. Inspector Saillard cleared his throat, hesitated, then asked, "Did you go to see your mother-in-law last night?"

Perhaps, as his brother had suggested, Olivier was rather

lacking in intelligence. It took a long time for the words to sink in. You could follow their progress in his features.

He had been gazing rather blankly at the Inspector. Suddenly he swung around on his brother, his cheeks red, his eyes flashing. "Andre, you dare to suggest that I—"

Without the slightest transition, his indignation faded away. He leaned forward in his chair, took his head in his two hands, and burst into a fit of raucous weeping.

Ill at ease, Inspector Saillard looked at Andre Lecœur, surprised at the latter's calmness, and a little shocked, perhaps, by what he may well have taken for heartlessness. Perhaps Saillard had never had a brother of his own. Andre had known his since childhood. It wasn't the first time he had seen Olivier break down. Not by any means. And this time he was almost pleased, as it might have been a great deal worse. What he had dreaded was the moment of indignation, and he was relieved that it had passed so quickly. Had he continued on that tack, he'd have ended by putting everyone's back up, which would have done him no good at all.

Wasn't that how he'd lost one job after another? For weeks, for months, he would go meekly about his work, toeing the line and swallowing what he felt to be humiliations, till all at once he could hold no more, and for some trifle—a chance word, a smile, a harmless contradiction—he would flare up unexpectedly and make a nuisance of himself to everybody.

What do we do now? The Inspector's eyes were asking.

Andre Lecœur's eyes answered, Wait.

It didn't last very long. The emotional crisis waned, started again, then petered out altogether. Olivier shot a sulky look at the Inspector, then hid his face again.

Finally, with an air of bitter resignation, he sat up, and with even a touch of pride said: "Fire away. I'll answer."

"At what time last night did you go to Madame Fayet's? Wait a moment. First of all, when did you leave your flat?"

"At eight o'clock, as usual, after Francois was in bed."

"Nothing exceptional happened?"

"No. We'd had supper together. Then he'd helped me to wash up."

"Did you talk about Christmas?"

"Yes. I told him he'd be getting a surprise."

"The table radio. Was he expecting one?"

"He'd been longing for one for some time. You see, he doesn't play with the other boys in the street. Practically all his free time he spends at home."

"Did it ever occur to you that the boy might know you'd lost your job at the *Presse*? Did he ever ring you up there?"

"Never. When I'm at work, he's asleep."

"Could anyone have told him?"

"No one knew. Not in the neighborhood, that is."

"Is he observant?"

"Very. He notices everything."

"You saw him safely in bed and then you went off. Do you take anything with you—anything to eat, I mean?"

The Inspector suddenly thought of that, seeing Godin produce a ham sandwich. Olivier looked blankly at his empty hands.

"My tin."

"The tin in which you took your sandwiches?"

"Yes. I had it with me when I left. I'm sure of that. I can't think where I could have left it, unless it was at—"

"At Madame Fayet's?"

"Yes."

"Just a moment. Lecœur, get me Javel on the phone, will you? Hallo! Who's speaking? Is Janvier there? Good, ask him to speak to me. Hallo! Is that you, Janvier? Have you come across a tin box containing some sandwiches? Nothing of the sort. Really? All the same, I'd like you to make sure. Ring me back. It's important."

And, turning again to Olivier: "Was Francois actually sleeping when you left?"

"No. But he'd snuggled down in bed and soon would be. Outside, I wandered about for a bit. I walked down to the Seine and waited on the embankment."

"Waited? What for?"

"For Francois to be fast asleep. From his room you can see Madame Fayet's windows."

"So you'd made up your mind to go and see her."

"It was the only way. I hadn't a bean left."

"What about your brother?"

Olivier and Andre looked at each other.

"He'd already given me so much. I felt I couldn't ask him again."

"You rang at the house door, I suppose. At what time?"

"A little after nine. The concierge saw me. I made no attempt to hide—except from Francois."

"Had your mother-in-law gone to bed?"

"No. She was fully dressed when she opened her door. She said, 'Oh, it's you, you wretch!' "

"After that beginning, did you still think she'd lend you money?"

"I was sure of it."

"Why?"

"It was her business. Perhaps also for the pleasure of squeezing me if I didn't pay her back. She lent me ten thousand francs, but made me sign an I.O.U. for twenty thousand."

"How soon had you to pay her back?"

"In a fortnight's time."

"How could you hope to?"

"I don't know. Somehow. The thing that mattered was for the boy to have a good Christmas."

Andre Lecœur was tempted to butt in to explain to the puzzled Inspector, "You see! He's always been like that!"

"Did you get the money easily?"

"Oh, no. We were at it for a long time."

"How long?"

"Half an hour, I daresay, and during most of that time she was calling me names, telling me I was no good to anyone and had ruined her daughter's life before I finally killed her. I didn't answer her back. I wanted the money too badly."

"You didn't threaten her?"

Olivier reddened. "Not exactly. I said if she didn't let me have it I'd kill myself."

"Would you have done it?"

"I don't think so. At least, I don't know. I was fed up, worn out."

"And when you got the money?"

"I walked to the nearest Metro station, Lourmel, and took the underground to Palais Royal. There I went into the Grands Magasins du Louvre. The place was crowded, with queues at many of the counters."

"What time was it?"

"It was after eleven before I left the place. I was in no hurry. I had a good look around. I stood a long time watching a toy electric train."

Andre couldn't help smiling at the Inspector. "You didn't miss your sandwich tin?"

"No. I was thinking about Francois and his present."

"And with money in your pocket you banished all your cares!"

The Inspector hadn't known Olivier Lecœur since childhood, but he had sized him up all right. He had hit the nail on the head. When things were black, Olivier would go about with drooping shoulders and a hangdog air, but no sooner had he a thousand-franc note in his pocket than he'd feel on top of the world.

"To come back to Madame Fayet, you say you gave her a receipt. What did she do with it?"

"She slipped it into an old wallet she always carried about with her in a pocket somewhere under her skirt."

"So you knew about the wallet?"

"Yes. Everybody did."

The Inspector turned towards Andre.

"It hasn't been found!"

Then to Olivier: "You bought some things. In the Louvre?"

"No. I bought the little radio in the Rue Montmartre."

"In which shop?"

"I don't know the name. It's next door to a shoe shop."

"And the other things?"

"A little farther on."

"What time was it when you'd finished shopping?"

"Close on midnight. People were coming out of the theaters and movies and crowding into the restaurants. Some of them were rather noisy."

His brother at that time was already here at his switchboard.

"What did you do during the rest of the night?"

"At the corner of the Boulevard des Italiens, there's a movie that stays open all night."

"You'd been there before?"

Avoiding his brother's eye, Andre answered rather sheepishly: "Two or three times. After all, it costs no more than going into a cafe and you can stay there as long as you like. It's nice and warm. Some people go there regularly to sleep."

"When was it you decided to go to the movies?"

"As soon as I left Madame Fayet's."

Andre Lecœur was tempted to intervene once again to say to the Inspector: "You see, these people who are down and out are not so utterly miserable after all. If they were, they'd never stick it out. They've got a world of their own, in odd corners of which they can take refuge and even amuse themselves."

It was all so like Olivier! With a few notes in his pocket—and Heaven only knew how he was ever going to pay them back—with a few notes in his pocket, his trials were forgotten. He had only one thought: to give his boy a good Christmas. With that secured, he was ready to stand himself a little treat.

So while other families were gathered at table or knelt at Midnight Mass, Olivier went to the movies all by himself. It was the best he could do.

"When did you leave the movie?"

"A little before six."

"What was the film?"

"*Cœurs Ardents.* With a documentary on Eskimos."

"How many times did you see the program?"

"Twice right through, except for the news, which was just coming on again when I left."

Andre Lecœur knew that all this was going to be verified, if only as a matter of routine. It wasn't necessary, however. Diving into his pockets, Olivier produced the torn-off half of a movie ticket, then another ticket—a pink one. "Look at that. It's the Métro ticket I had coming home."

It bore the name of the station—Opéra—together with the date and the time.

Olivier had been telling the truth. He couldn't have been in Madame Fayet's flat any time between five and six-thirty.

There was a little spark of triumph in his eye, mixed with a touch of disdain. He seemed to be saying to them all, including his brother Andre: "Because I'm poor and unlucky I come under suspicion. I know—that's the way things are. I don't blame you."

And, funnily enough, it seemed as though all at once the room had grown colder. That was probably because, with Olivier Lecœur cleared of suspicion, everyone's thoughts reverted to the child. As though moved by one impulse, all eyes turned instinctively toward the huge plan on the wall.

Some time had elapsed since any of the lamps had lit up. Certainly it was a quiet morning. On any ordinary day there would be a street accident coming in every few minutes, particularly old women knocked down in the crowded thoroughfares of Montmartre and other overpopulated quarters.

Today the streets were almost empty—emptier than in August, when half Paris is away on holiday.

Half past eleven. For three and a half hours there'd been no sign of Francois Lecœur.

"Hallo! Yes, Saillard speaking. Is that Janvier? You say you couldn't find a tin anywhere? Except in her kitchen, of course. Now, look here, was it you who went through the old girl's clothes? Oh, Gonesse had already done it. There should have been an old wallet in a pocket under her skirt. You're sure there wasn't anything of that sort? That's what Gonesse told you, is it? What's that about the concierge? She saw someone go up a little after nine last night. I know. I know who it was. There were people coming in and out the best part of the night? Of course. I'd

like you to go back to the house in the Rue Vasco de
Gama. See what you can find out about the comings and
goings there, particularly on the third floor. Yes. I'll still
be here."

He turned back to the boy's father, who was now sitting
humbly in his chair, looking as intimidated as a patient in
a doctor's waiting room.

"You understand why I asked that, don't you? Does
Francois often wake up in the course of the night?"

"He's been known to get up in his sleep."

"Does he walk about?"

"No. Generally he doesn't even get right out of bed—
just sits up and calls out. It's always the same thing. He
thinks the house is on fire. His eyes are open, but I don't
think he sees anything. Then, little by little, he calms down
and with a deep sigh lies down again. The next day he
doesn't remember a thing."

"Is he always asleep when you get back in the
morning?"

"Not always. But if he isn't, he always pretends to be
so that I can wake him up as usual with a hug."

"The people in the house were probably making more
noise than usual last night. Who have you got in the
next flat?"

"A Czech who works at Renault's."

"Is he married?"

"I really don't know. There are so many people in the
house and they change so often we don't know much
about them. All I can tell you is that on Sundays other
Czechs come there and they sing a lot of their own songs."

"Janvier will tell us whether there was a party there last
night. If there was, they may well have awakened the boy.
Besides, children are apt to sleep more lightly when
they're excited about a present they're expecting. If he got
out of bed, he might easily have looked out of the window,
in which case he might have seen you at Madame Fayet's.
He didn't know she was his grandmother, did he?"

"No. He didn't like her. He sometimes passed her in the
street and he used to say she smelled like a squashed bug."

The boy would probably know what he was talking about. A house like his was no doubt infested with vermin.

"He'd have been surprised to see you with her?"

"Certainly."

"Did he know she lent money?"

"Everyone knew."

"Would there be anybody working at the *Presse* on a day like this?"

"There's always somebody there."

The Inspector asked Andre to ring them up.

"See if anyone's ever been round to ask for your brother."

Olivier looked uncomfortable, but when his brother reached for the telephone directory, he gave him the number. Both he and the Inspector stared at Andre while he got through.

"It's very important, Mademoiselle. It may even be a matter of life and death. Yes, please. See if you can find out. Ask everybody who's in the building now. What? Yes, I know it's Christmas Day. It's Christmas Day here, too, but we have to carry on just the same."

Between his teeth he muttered, "Silly little bitch!"

He could hear the linotypes clicking as he held the line, waiting for her answer.

"Yes. What? Three weeks ago. A young boy—"

Olivier went pale in the face. His eyes dropped, and during the rest of the conversation he stared obstinately at his hands.

"He didn't telephone? Came round himself. At what time? On a Thursday, you say. What did he want? Asked if Olivier Lecœur worked there? What? What was he told?"

Looking up, Olivier saw a flush spread over his brother's face before he banged down the receiver.

"Francois went there one Thursday afternoon. He must have suspected something. They told him you hadn't been working there for some time."

There was no point in repeating what he had heard. What they'd said to the boy was: "We chucked the old fool out weeks ago."

Perhaps not out of cruelty. They may not have thought it was the man's son they were speaking to.

"Do you begin to understand, Olivier?"

Did he realize that the situation was the reverse of what he had imagined? He had been going off at night, armed with his little box of sandwiches, keeping up an elaborate pretense. And in the end he had been the one to be taken in!

The boy had found him out. And wasn't it only fair to suppose that he had seen through the Uncle Gedeon story, too?

He hadn't said a word. He had simply fallen in with the game.

No one dared say anything for fear of saying too much, for fear of evoking images that would be heartrending.

A father and a son each lying to avoid hurting the other.

They had to look at it through the eyes of the child, with all childhood's tragic earnestness. His father kisses him good night and goes off to the job that doesn't really exist, saying: "Sleep well. There'll be a surprise for you in the morning."

A radio. It could only be that. And didn't he know that his father's pockets were empty? Did he try to go to sleep? Or did he get up as soon as his father had gone, to sit miserably staring out of the window obsessed by one thought? *His father had no money—yet he was going to buy him a radio!*

To the accompaniment, in all probability, of a full-throated Czech choir singing their national songs on the other side of the thin wall!

The Inspector sighed and knocked out his pipe on his heel.

"It looks as though he saw you at Madame Fayet's."

Olivier nodded.

"We'll check up on this, but it seems likely that, looking down from his window, he wouldn't see very far into the room."

"That's quite right."

"Could he have seen you leave the room?"

"No. The door's on the opposite side from the window."

"Do you remember going near the window?"

"At one time I was sitting on the windowsill."

"Was the window open then? We know it was later."

"It was open a few inches. I'm sure of that, because I moved away from it, as I felt an icy draught on my back. She lived with us for a while, just after our marriage, and I know she couldn't bear not to have her window open all the year round. You see, she'd been brought up in the country."

"So there'd be no frost on the panes. He'd certainly have seen you if he was looking."

A call. Lecœur thrust his contact plug into one of the sockets.

"Yes. What's that? A boy?"

The other two held their breath.

"Yes. Yes. What? Yes. Send out the *agents cyclistes*. Comb the whole neighborhood. I'll see about the station. How long ago was it? Half an hour? Couldn't he have let us know sooner?"

Without losing time over explanations, Lecœur plugged in to the Gare du Nord.

"Hallo! Gare du Nord! Who's speaking? Ah, Lambert. Listen, this is urgent. Have the station searched from end to end. Ask everybody if they've seen a boy of ten wandering about. What? Alone? He may be. Or he may be accompanied. We don't know. Let me know what you find out. Yes, of course. Grab him at once if you set eyes on him."

"Did you say accompanied?" asked Olivier anxiously.

"Why not? It's possible. Anything's possible. Of course, it may not be him. If it is, we're half an hour late. It was a small grocer in the Rue de Maubeuge whose shopfront is open onto the street. He saw a boy snatch a couple of oranges and make off. He didn't run after him. Only later, when a policeman passed, he thought he might as well mention it."

"Had your son any money?" asked the Inspector.

"Not a sou."

"Hasn't he got a money-box?"

"Yes. But I borrowed what was in it two days ago, saying that I didn't want to change a banknote."

A pathetic little confession, but what did things like that matter now?

"Don't you think it would be better if I went to the Gare du Nord myself?"

"I doubt if it would help, and we may need you here."

They were almost prisoners in that room. With its direct links with every nerve center of Paris, that was the place where any news would first arrive. Even in his room in the Police Judiciaire, the Inspector would be less well placed. He had thought of going back there, but now at last took off his overcoat, deciding to see the job through where he was.

"If he had no money, he couldn't take a bus or the Métro. Nor could he go into a cafe or use a public telephone. He probably hasn't had anything to eat since his supper last night."

"But what can he be doing?" exclaimed Olivier, becoming more and more nervous. "And why should he have sent me to the Gare d'Austerlitz?"

"Perhaps to help you get away," grunted Saillard.

"Get away? Me?"

"Listen. The boy knows you're down and out. Yet you're going to buy him a little radio. I'm not reproaching you. I'm just looking at the facts. He leans on the windowsill and sees you with the old woman he knows to be a money-lender. What does he conclude?"

"I see."

"That you've gone to her to borrow money. He may be touched by it, he may be saddened—we don't know. He goes back to bed and to sleep."

"You think so?"

"I'm pretty sure of it. Anyhow, we've no reason to think he left the house then."

"No. Of course not."

"Let's say he goes back to sleep, then. But he wakes up early, as children mostly do on Christmas Day. And the first thing he notices is the frost on the window. The first frost this winter, don't forget that. He wants to look at it, to touch it."

A faint smile flickered across Andre Lecœur's face. This massive Inspector hadn't forgotten what it was like to be a boy.

"He scratches a bit of it away with his nails. It won't be difficult to get confirmation, for once the frost is tampered with it can't form again in quite the same pattern. What does he notice then? That in the buildings opposite one window is lit up, and one only—the window of the room in which a few hours before he had seen his father. It's guesswork, of course, but I don't mind betting he saw the body, or part of it. If he'd merely seen a foot it would have been enough to startle him."

"You mean to say—" began Olivier, wide-eyed.

"That he thought you'd killed her. As I did myself—for a moment. And very likely not her only. Just think for a minute. The man who's been committing all these murders is a man, like you, who wanders about at night. His victims live in the poorer quarters of Paris, like Madame Fayet in the Rue Michat. Does the boy know anything of how you've been spending your nights since you lost your job? No. All that he has to go on is that he has seen you in the murdered woman's room. Would it be surprising if his imagination got to work?

"You said just now that you sat on the windowsill. Might it be there that you put down your box of sandwiches?"

"Now I come to think of it, yes. I'm practically sure."

"Then he saw it. And he's quite old enough to know what the police would think when they saw it lying there. Is your name on it?"

"Yes. Scratched on the lid."

"You see! He thought you'd be coming home as usual between seven and eight. The thing was to get you as quickly as possible out of the danger zone."

"You mean—by writing me that note?"

"Yes. He didn't know what to say. He couldn't refer to the murder without compromising you. Then he thought of Uncle Gedeon. Whether he believed in his existence or not doesn't matter. He knew you'd go to the Gare d'Austerlitz."

"But he's not yet eleven!"

"Boys of that age know a lot more than you think. Doesn't he read detective stories?"

"Yes."

"Of course he does. They all do. If they don't read them, they get them on the radio. Perhaps that's why he wanted a set of his own so badly."

"It's true."

"He couldn't stay in the flat to wait for you, for he had something more important to do. He had to get hold of that box. I suppose he knew the courtyard well. He'd played there, hadn't he?"

"At one time, yes. With the concierge's little girl."

"So he'd know about the rainwater pipes, may even have climbed up them for sport."

"Very well," said Olivier, suddenly calm, "let's say he gets into the room and takes the box. He wouldn't need to climb down the way he'd come. He could simply walk out of the flat and out of the house. You can open the house door from inside without knocking up the concierge. You say it was at about six o'clock, don't you?"

"I see what you're driving at," grunted the Inspector. "Even at a leisurely pace, it would hardly have taken him two hours to walk to the Gare d'Austerlitz. Yet he wasn't there."

Leaving them to thrash it out, Lecœur was busy telephoning.

"No news yet?"

And the man at the Gare du Nord answered, "Nothing so far. We've pounced on any number of boys, but none of them was Francois Lecœur."

Admittedly, any street boy could have pinched a couple of oranges and taken to his heels. The same couldn't be said for the broken glass of the telephone pillars, however. Andre Lecœur looked once again at the column with the seven crosses, as though some clue might suddenly emerge from them. He had never thought himself much cleverer than his brother. Where he scored was in patience and perseverance.

"If the box of sandwiches is ever found, it'll be at the bottom of the Seine near the Pont Mirabeau," he said.

Steps in the corridor. On an ordinary day they would not have been noticed, but in the stillness of a Christmas morning everyone listened.

It was an *agent cycliste*, who produced a bloodstained blue-check handkerchief, the one that had been found among the glass splinters at the seventh telephone pillar.

"That's his, all right," said the boy's father.

"He must have been followed," said the Inspector. "If he'd had time, he wouldn't merely have broken the glass. He'd have said something."

"Who by?" asked Olivier, who was the only one not to understand. "Who'd want to follow him?" he asked. "And why should he call the police?"

They hesitated to put him wise. In the end it was his brother who explained:

"When he went to the old woman's he thought you were the murderer. When he came away, he knew you weren't. He knew—"

"Knew what?"

"He knew who was. Do you understand now? He found out something, though we don't know what. He wants to tell us about it, but someone's stopping him."

"You mean?"

"I mean that Francois is after the murderer or the murderer is after him. One is following, one is followed—we don't know which. By the way, Inspector, is there a reward offered?"

"A handsome reward was offered after the third murder and it was doubled last week. It's been in all the papers."

"Then my guess," said Andre Lecœur, "is that it's the kid who's doing the following. Only in that case—"

It was twelve o'clock, four hours since they'd lost track of him. Unless, of course, it was he who had snaffled the oranges in the Rue Maubeuge.

Might not this be his great moment? Andre Lecœur had

read somewhere that even to the dullest and most un-
eventful lives such a moment comes sooner or later.

He had never had a particularly high opinion of himself
or of his abilities. When people asked him why he'd chosen
so dreary and monotonous a job rather than one in, say,
the Brigade des Homicides, he would answer: "I suppose
I'm lazy."

Sometimes he would add:

"I'm scared of being knocked about."

As a matter of fact, he was neither lazy nor a coward.
If he lacked anything it was brains.

He knew it. All he had learned at school had cost him
a great effort. The police exams that others took so easily
in their stride, he had only passed by dint of perseverance.

Was it a consciousness of his own shortcomings that had
kept him single? Possibly. It seemed to him that the sort
of woman he would want to marry would be his superior,
and he didn't relish the idea of playing second fiddle in
the home.

But he wasn't thinking of all this now. Indeed, if this
was his moment of greatness, it was stealing upon him
unawares.

Another team arrived, those of the second day shift
looking very fresh and well groomed in their Sunday
clothes. They had been celebrating Christmas with their
families, and they brought in with them, as it were, a whiff
of good viands and liqueurs.

Old Bedeau had taken his place at the switchboard, but
Lecœur made no move to go.

"I'll stay on a bit," he said simply.

Inspector Saillard had gone for a quick lunch at the
Brasserie Dauphine just around the corner, leaving strict
injunctions that he was to be fetched at once if anything
happened. Janvier was back at the Quai des Orfèvres, writing up his report.

If Lecœur was tired, he didn't notice it. He certainly
wasn't sleepy and couldn't bear the thought of going home
to bed. He had plenty of stamina. Once, when there were
riots in the Place de la Concorde, he had done thirty-six

hours nonstop, and on another occasion, during a general strike, they had all camped in the room for four days and nights.

His brother showed the strain more. He was getting jumpy again.

"I'm going," he announced suddenly.

"Where to?"

"To find Bib."

"Where?"

"I don't know exactly. I'll start round the Gare du Nord."

"How do you know it was Bib who stole the oranges? He may be at the other end of Paris. We might get news at any minute. You'd better stay."

"I can't stand this waiting."

He was nevertheless persuaded to. He was given a chair in a corner. He refused to lie down. His eyes were red with anxiety and fatigue. He sat fidgeting, looking rather as, when a boy, he had been put in the corner.

With more self-control, Andre forced himself to take some rest. Next to the big room was a little one with a wash-basin, where they hung their coats and which was provided with a couple of camp beds on which the *nuiteux* could lie down during a quiet hour.

He shut his eyes, but only for a moment. Then his hand felt for the little notebook which never left him, and lying on his back he began to turn over the pages.

There were nothing but crosses, columns and columns of tiny little crosses which, month after month, year after year, he had accumulated, Heaven knows why. Just to satisfy something inside him. After all, other people keep a diary—or the most meticulous household accounts, even when they don't need to economize at all.

Those crosses told the story of the night life of Paris.

"Some coffee, Lecœur?"

"Thanks."

Feeling rather out of touch where he was, he dragged his camp bed into the big room, placing it in a position from which he could see the wall-plan. There he sipped his coffee, after which he stretched himself out again, sometimes studying his notebook, sometimes lying with his eyes shut. Now and again he stole a glance at his brother, who sat hunched in his chair with drooping shoulders, the twitching of his long white fingers being the only sign of the torture he was enduring.

There were hundreds of men now, not only in Paris but in the suburbs, keeping their eyes skinned for the boy whose description had been circulated. Sometimes false hopes were raised, only to be dashed when the exact particulars were given.

Lecœur shut his eyes again, but opened them suddenly next moment, as though he had actually dozed off. He glanced at the clock, then looked round for the Inspector.

"Hasn't Saillard got back yet?" he asked, getting to his feet.

"I expect he's looked in at the Quai des Orfèvres."

Olivier stared at his brother, surprised to see him pacing up and down the room. The latter was so absorbed in his thoughts that he hardly noticed that the sun had broken through the clouds, bathing Paris on that Christmas afternoon in a glow of light more like that of spring.

While thinking, he listened, and it wasn't long before he heard Inspector Saillard's heavy tread outside.

"You'd better go and get some sandwiches," he said to his brother. "Get some for me, too."

"What kind?"

"Ham. Anything. Whatever you find."

Olivier went out, after a parting glance at the map, relieved, in spite of his anxiety, to be doing something.

The men of the afternoon shift knew little of what was afoot, except that the killer had done another job the previous night and that there was a general hunt for a small boy. For them, the case couldn't have the flavor it had for those who were involved. At the switchboard, Bedeau was doing a crossword with his earphones on his head, breaking off from time to time for the classic: "Hallo! Austerlitz. Your car's out."

A body fished out of the Seine. You couldn't have a Christmas without that!

*   *   *

"Could I have a word with you, Inspector?"

The camp bed was back in the cloakroom. It was there that Lecœur led the chief of the homicide squad.

"I hope you won't mind my butting in. I know it isn't for me to make suggestions. But, about the killer—"

He had his little notebook in his hand. He must have known its contents almost by heart.

"I've been doing a lot of thinking since this morning and—"

A little while ago, while he was lying down, it had seemed so clear, but now that he had to explain things, it was difficult to put them in logical order.

"It's like this. First of all, I noticed that all the murders were committed after two in the morning, most of them after three."

He could see by the look on the Inspector's face that he hadn't exactly scored a hit, and he hurried on:

"I've been looking up the time of other murders over the past three years. They were nearly always between ten in the evening and two in the morning."

Neither did that observation seem to make much impression. Why not take the bull by the horns and say straight out what was on his mind?

"Just now, looking at my brother, it occurred to me that the man you're looking for might be a man like him. As a matter of fact, I, too, for a moment wondered whether it wasn't him. Wait a moment—"

That was better. The look of polite boredom had gone from Saillard's face.

"If I'd had more experience in this sort of work I'd be able to explain myself better. But you'll see in a moment. A man who's killed eight people one after the other is, if not a madman, at any rate a man who's been thrown off his balance. He might have had a sudden shock. Take my brother, for instance. When he lost his job it upset him so much that he preferred to live in a tissue of lies rather than let his son—"

No. Put into words, it all sounded very clumsy.

"When a man suddenly loses everything he has in life—"

"He doesn't necessarily go mad."

"I'm not saying he's actually mad. But imagine a person so full of resentment that he considers himself justified in revenging himself on his fellow-men. I don't need to point out to you, Inspector, that other murderers always kill in much the same way. This one has used a hammer, a knife, a spanner, and one woman he strangled. And he's never been seen, never left a clue. Wherever he lives in Paris, he must have walked miles and miles at night when there was no transport available, sometimes, when the alarm had been given, with the police on the lookout, questioning everybody they found in the streets. How is it he avoided them?"

He was certain he was on the right track. If only Saillard would hear him out.

The Inspector sat on one of the camp beds. The cloak-room was small, and as Lecœur paced up and down in front of him he could do no more than three paces each way.

"This morning, for instance, assuming he was with the boy, he went halfway across Paris, keeping out of sight of every police station and every traffic point where there'd be a man on duty."

"You mean he knows the Fifteenth and Sixteenth Arrondissements by heart?"

"And not those only. At least two there, the Twelfth and the Twentieth, as he showed on previous occasions. He didn't choose his victims haphazardly. He knew they lived alone and could be done in without any great risk."

What a nuisance! There was his brother, saying: "Here are the sandwiches, Andre."

"Thanks. Go ahead, will you? Don't wait for me. I'll be with you in a moment."

He bundled Olivier back into his corner and returned to the cloakroom. He didn't want him to hear.

"If he's used a different weapon each time, it's because he knows it will puzzle us. He knows that murderers gener-ally have their own way and stick to it."

The Inspector had risen to his feet and was staring at Andre with a faraway look, as though he was following a train of thought of his own.

"You mean that he's—"

"That he's one of us—or has been. I can't get the idea out of my head."

He lowered his voice.

"Someone who's been up against it in the same sort of way as my brother. A discharged fireman might take to arson. It's happened two or three times. A policeman—"

"But why should he steal?"

"Wasn't my brother in need of money? This other chap may be like him in more ways than one. Supposing he, too, was a night worker and goes on pretending he's still in a job. That would explain why the crimes are committed so late. He has to be out all night. The first part of it is easy enough—the cafes and bars are open. Afterward, he's all alone with himself."

As though to himself, Saillard muttered: "There wouldn't be anybody in the personnel department on a day like this."

"Perhaps you could ring up the director at his home. He might remember . . ."

"Hallo! Can I speak to Monsieur Guillaume, please? He's not in? Where could I reach him? At his daughter's in Ateuil? Have you got the number?"

"Hallo! Monsieur Guillaume? Saillard speaking. I hope I'm not disturbing you too much. Oh, you'd finished, had you? Good. It's about the killer. Yes, there's been another one. No. Nothing definite. Only we have an idea that needs checking, and it's urgent. Don't be too surprised at my question.

"Has any member of the Paris police been sacked recently—say two or three months ago? I beg your pardon? Not a single one this year? I see."

Lecœur felt a sudden constriction around his heart, as though overwhelmed by a catastrophe, and threw a pathetic, despairing look at the wall-map. He had already given up and was surprised to hear his chief go on:

"As a matter of fact, it doesn't need to be as recent as

all that. It would be someone who had worked in various parts of Paris, including the Fifteenth and Sixteenth. Probably also the Twelfth and Twentieth. Seems to have done a good deal of night work. Also to have been embittered by his dismissal. What?"

The way Saillard pronounced that last word gave Lecœur renewed hope.

"Sergeant Loubet? Yes, I remember the name, though I never actually came across him. Three years ago! You wouldn't know where he lived, I suppose? Somewhere near Les Halles?"

Three years ago. No, it wouldn't do, and Lecœur's heart sank again. You could hardly expect a man to bottle up his resentments for three years and then suddenly start hitting back.

"Have you any idea what became of him? No, of course not. And it's not a good day for finding out."

He hung up and looked thoughtfully at Lecœur. When he spoke, it was as though he was addressing an equal.

"Did you hear? Sergeant Loubet. He was constantly getting into trouble and was shifted three or four times before being finally dismissed. Drink. That was his trouble. He took his dismissal very hard. Guillaume can't say for certain what has become of him, but he thinks he joined a private detective agency. If you'd like to have a try—"

Lecœur set to work. He had little hope of succeeding, but it was better to do something than sit watching for the little lamps in the street-plan. He began with the agencies of the most doubtful reputation, refusing to believe that a person such as Loubet would readily find a job with a reputable firm. Most of the offices were shut, and he had to ring up their proprietors at home.

"Don't know him. You'd better try Tisserand in the Boulevard Saint-Martin. He's the one who takes all the riffraff."

But Tisserand, a firm that specialized in shadowings, was no good, either.

"Don't speak to me of that good-for-nothing. It's a good two months or more since I chucked him out, in spite of his threatening to blackmail me. If he ever shows up at my office again, I'll throw him down the stairs."

"What sort of job did he have?"

"Night work. Watching blocks of flats."

"Did he drink much?"

"He wasn't often sober. I don't know how he managed it, but he always knew where to get free drinks. Blackmail again, I suppose."

"Can you give me his address?"

"Twenty-seven bis, Rue du Pas-de-la-Mule."

"Does he have a telephone?"

"Maybe. I don't know. I've never had the slightest desire to ring him up. Is that all? Can I go back to my game of bridge?"

The Inspector had already snatched up the telephone directory and was looking for Loubet's number. He rang up himself. There was now a tacit understanding between him and Lecœur. They shared the same hope, the same trembling eagerness, while Olivier, realizing that something important was going on, came and stood near them.

Without being invited, Andre did something he wouldn't have dreamed of doing that morning. He picked up the second earphone to listen in. The bell rang in the flat in the Rue du Pas-de-la-Mule. It rang for a long time, as though the place was deserted, and his anxiety was becoming acute when at last it stopped and a voice answered.

Thank Heaven! It was a woman's voice, an elderly one. "Is that you at last? Where are you?"

"Hallo! This isn't your husband here, Madame."

"Has he met with an accident?"

From the hopefulness of her tone, it sounded as though she had long been expecting one and wouldn't be sorry when it happened.

"It is Madame Loubet I'm speaking to, isn't it?"

"Who else would it be?"

"Your husband's not at home?"

"First of all, who are you?"

"Inspector Saillard."

"What do you want him for?"

The Inspector put his hand over the mouthpiece to say

to Lecœur: "Get through to Janvier. Tell him to dash round there as quick as he can."

"Didn't your husband come home this morning?"

"You ought to know! I thought the police knew everything!"

"Does it often happen?"

"That's his business, isn't it?"

No doubt she hated her drunkard of a husband, but now that he was threatened she was ready to stand up for him.

"I suppose you know he no longer belongs to the police force."

"Perhaps he found a cleaner job."

"When did he stop working for the Agence Argus?"

"What's that? What are you getting at?"

"I assure you, Madame, your husband was dismissed from the Agence Argus over two months ago."

"You're lying."

"Which means that for these last two months he's been going off to work every evening."

"Where else would he be going? To the Folies Bergère?"

"Have you any idea why he hasn't come back today? He hasn't telephoned, has he?"

She must have been afraid of saying the wrong thing, for she rang off without another word.

When the Inspector put his receiver down, he turned round to see Lecœur standing behind him, looking away. In a shaky voice, the latter said:

"Janvier's on his way now."

He was treated as an equal. He knew it wouldn't last, that tomorrow, sitting at his switchboard, he would be once more but a small cog in the huge wheel.

The others simply didn't count—not even his brother, whose timid eyes darted from one to the other uncomprehendingly, wondering why, if his boy's life was in danger, they talked so much instead of doing something.

Twice he had to pluck at Andre's sleeve to get a word in edgewise.

"Let me go and look for him myself," he begged.

What could he do? The hunt had widened now. A description of ex-Sergeant Loubet had been passed to all police stations and patrols.

It was no longer only a boy of ten who was being looked for, but also a man of fifty-eight, probably the worse for drink, dressed in a black overcoat with a velvet collar and an old grey-felt hat, a man who knew his Paris like the palm of his hand, and who was acquainted with the police.

Janvier had returned, looking fresher than the men there in spite of his night's vigil.

"She tried to slam the door in my face, but I'd taken the precaution of sticking my foot in. She doesn't know anything. She says he's been handing over his pay every month."

"That's why he had to steal. He didn't need big sums. In fact, he wouldn't have known what to do with them. What's she like?"

"Small and dark, with piercing eyes. Her hair's dyed a sort of blue. She must have eczema or something of the sort—she wears mittens."

"Did you get a photo of him?"

"There was one on the dining-room sideboard. She wouldn't give it to me, so I just took it."

A heavy-built, florid man, with bulging eyes, who in his youth had probably been the village beau and had conserved an air of stupid arrogance. The photograph was some years old. No doubt he looked quite different now.

"She didn't give you any idea where he was likely to be, did she?"

"As far as I could make out, except at night, when he was supposed to be at work, she kept him pretty well tied to her apron strings. I talked to the concierge, who told me he was scared stiff of his wife. Often she's seen him stagger home in the morning, then suddenly pull himself together when he went upstairs. He goes out shopping with his wife. In fact, he never goes out alone in the daytime. If she goes out when he's in bed, she locks him in."

"What do you think, Lecœur?"

"I'm wondering whether my nephew and he aren't together."

"What do you mean?"

"They weren't together at the beginning, or Loubet would have stopped the boy giving the alarm. There must have been some distance between them. One was following the other."

"Which way round?"

"When the kid climbed up the drainpipe, he thought his father was guilty. Otherwise, why should he have sent him off to the Gare d'Austerlitz, where no doubt he intended to join him after getting rid of the sandwich tin?"

"It looks like it."

"No, Andre. Francois could never have thought—"

"Leave this alone. You don't understand. At that time the crime had certainly been committed. Francois wouldn't have dreamed of burgling someone's flat for a tin box if it hadn't been that he'd seen the body."

"From his window," put in Janvier, "he could see most of the legs."

"What we don't know is whether the murderer was still there."

"I can't believe he was," said Saillard. "If he had been, he'd have kept out of sight, let the boy get into the room, and then done the same to him as he'd done to the old woman."

"Look here, Olivier. When you got home this morning, was the light on?"

"Yes."

"In the boy's room?"

"Yes. It was the first thing I noticed. It gave me a shock. I thought perhaps he was ill."

"So the murderer very likely saw it and feared his crime had had a witness. He certainly wouldn't have expected anyone to climb up the drainpipe. He must have rushed straight out of the house."

"And waited outside to see what would happen."

Guesswork! Yes. But that was all they could do. The important thing was to guess right. For that you had to put yourself in the other chap's place and think as he had thought. The rest was a matter of patrols, of the hundreds of policemen scattered all over Paris, and, lastly, of luck.

"Rather than go down the way he'd come, the boy must have left the house by the entrance in the Rue Michat."

"Just a moment, Inspector. By that time he probably knew that his father wasn't the murderer."

"Why?"

"Janvier said just now that Madame Fayet lost a lot of blood. If it had been his father, the blood would have had time to dry up more or less. It was some nine hours since Francois had seen him in the room. It was on leaving the house that he found out who had done it, whether it was Loubet or not. The latter wouldn't know whether the boy had seen him up in the room. Francois would have been scared and taken to his heels."

This time it was the boy's father who interrupted.

"No. Not if he knew there was a big reward offered. Not if he knew I'd lost my job. Not if he'd seen me go to the old woman to borrow some money."

The Inspector and Andre Lecœur exchanged glances. They had to admit Olivier was right, and it made them afraid.

No, it had to be pictured otherwise. A dark, deserted street in an outlying quarter of Paris two hours before dawn.

On the other hand, the ex-policeman, obsessed by his sense of grievance, who had just committed his ninth murder to revenge himself on the society that had spurned him, and perhaps still more to prove to himself he was still a man by defying the whole police force—indeed, the whole world.

Was he drunk again? On a night like that, when the bars were open long after their usual closing time, he had no doubt had more than ever. And in that dark, silent street, what did he see with his bulging drink-inflamed eyes? A young boy, the first person who had found him out, and who would now—

"I'd like to know whether he's got a gun on him," sighed the Inspector.

Janvier answered at once:

"I asked his wife. It seems he always carries one about. An automatic pistol, but it's not loaded."

"How can she know that?"

"Once or twice, when he was more than usually drunk, he rounded on her, threatening her with the gun. After that, she got hold of his ammunition and locked it up, telling him an unloaded pistol was quite enough to frighten people without his having to fire it."

Had those two really stalked each other through the streets of Paris? A strange sort of duel in which the man had the strength and the boy the speed?

The boy may well have been scared, but the man stood for something precious enough to push fear into the background: a fortune and the end of his father's worries and humiliations.

Having got so far, there wasn't a lot more to be said by the little group of people waiting in the Préfecture de Police. They sat gazing at the street-plan with a picture in their minds of a boy following a man, the boy no doubt keeping his distance. Everyone else was sleeping. There was no one in the streets who could be a help to the one or a menace to the other. Had Loubet produced his gun in an attempt to frighten the boy away?

When people woke up and began coming out into the streets, what would the boy do then? Would he rush up to the first person he met and start screaming "Murder"?

"Yes. It was Loubet who walked in front," said Saillard slowly.

"And it was I," put in Andre Lecœur, "who told the boy all about the pillar telephone system."

The little crosses came to life. What had at first been mysterious was now almost simple. But it was tragic.

The child was risking his skin to save his father. Tears were slowly trickling down the latter's face. He made no attempt to hide them.

He was in a strange place, surrounded by outlandish objects, and by people who talked to him as though he wasn't there, as though he was someone else. And his brother was among these people, a brother he could hardly recognize and whom he regarded with instinctive respect.

Even when they did speak, it wasn't necessary to say much. They understood each other. A word sufficed.

"Loubet couldn't go home, of course."

Andre Lecœur smiled suddenly as a thought struck him.

"It didn't occur to him that Francois hadn't a centime in his pocket. He could have escaped by diving into the Métro."

No. That wouldn't hold water. The boy had seen him and would give his description.

Place du Trocadéro, the Etoile. The time was passing. It was practically broad daylight. People were up and about. Why hadn't Francois called for help? Anyhow, with people in the streets it was no longer possible for Loubet to kill him.

The Inspector was deep in thought.

"For one reason or another," he murmured, "I think they're going about together now."

At the same moment, a lamp lit up on the wall. As though he knew it would be for him, Lecœur answered in place of Bedeau.

"Yes. I thought as much."

"It's about the two oranges. They found an Arab boy asleep in the third-class waiting room at the Gare du Nord. He still had the oranges in his pockets. He'd run away from home because his father had beaten him."

"Do you think Bib's dead?"

"If he was dead, Loubet would have gone home, as he would no longer have anything to fear."

So the struggle was still going on somewhere in this now sunny Paris in which families were sauntering along the boulevards taking the air.

It would be the fear of losing him in the crowd that had brought Francois close to his quarry. Why didn't he call for help? No doubt because Loubet had threatened him with his gun. "One word from you, my lad, and I'll empty this into your guts."

So each was pursuing his own goal: for the one to shake off the boy somehow, for the other to watch for the moment when the murderer was off his guard and give the alarm before he had time to shoot.

It was a matter of life and death.

"Loubet isn't likely to be in the center of the town, where policemen are too plentiful for his liking, to say nothing of the fact that many of them know him by sight."

Their most likely direction from the Etoile was towards Montmartre—not to the amusement quarter, but to the remoter and quieter parts.

It was half past two. Had they had anything to eat? Had Loubet, with his mind set on escape, been able to resist the temptation to drink?

"Monsieur le Commissaire—"

Andre Lecœur couldn't speak with the assurance he would have liked. He couldn't get rid of the feeling that he was an upstart, if not a usurper.

"I know there are thousands of little bars in Paris. But if we chose the more likely districts and put plenty of men on the job—"

Not only were all the men there roped in, but Saillard got through to the Police Judiciaire, where there were six men on duty, and set every one of them to work on six different telephone lines.

"Hallo! Is that the Bar des Amis? In the course of the day have you seen a middle-aged man accompanied by a boy of ten? The man's wearing a black overcoat and a—"

Again Lecœur made little crosses, not in his notebook this time, but in the telephone directory. There were ten pages of bars, some of them with the weirdest names.

A plan of Paris was spread out on a table all ready and it was in a little alley of ill-repute behind the Place Clichy that the Inspector was able to make the first mark in red chalk.

"Yes, there was a man of that description here about twelve o'clock. He drank three glasses of Calvados and ordered a glass of white wine for the boy. The boy didn't want to drink at first, but he did in the end and he wolfed a couple of eggs."

By the way Olivier Lecœur's face lit up, you might have thought he heard his boy's voice.

"You don't know which way they went?"

"Towards the Boulevard des Batignolles, I think. The man looked as though he'd already had one or two before he came in."

"Hallo! Zanzi-Bar? Have you at any time seen a—"

It became a refrain. As soon as one man had finished, the same words, or practically the same, were repeated by his neighbor.

Rue Damrémont. Montmartre again, only farther out this time. One-thirty. Loubet had broken a glass, his movements by this time being somewhat clumsy. The boy got up and made off in the direction of the lavatory, but when the man followed, he thought better of it and went back to his seat.

"Yes. The boy did look a bit frightened. As for the man, he was laughing and smirking as though he was enjoying a huge joke."

"Do you hear that, Olivier? Bib was still there at one-forty."

Andre Lecœur dared not say what was in his mind. The struggle was nearing its climax. Now that Loubet had really started drinking it was just a question of time. The only thing was: would the boy wait long enough?

It was all very well for Madame Loubet to say the gun wasn't loaded. The butt of an automatic was quite hard enough to crack a boy's skull.

His eyes wandered to his brother, and he had a vision of what Olivier might well have come to if his asthma hadn't prevented him drinking.

"Hallo! Yes. Where? Boulevard Ney?"

They had reached the outskirts of Paris. The ex-Sergeant seemed still to have his wits about him. Little by little, in easy stages, he was leading the boy to one of those outlying districts where there were still empty building sites and desolate spaces.

Three police cars were promptly switched to that neighborhood, as well as every available *agent cycliste* within reach. Even Janvier dashed off, taking the Inspector's little car, and it was all they could do to prevent Olivier from running after him.

"I tell you, you'd much better stay here. He may easily go off on a false trail, and then you won't know anything."

Nobody had time for making coffee. The men of the second day shift had not thoroughly warmed to the case. Everyone was strung up.

"Hallo! Yes. Orient Bar. What is it?"

It was Andre Lecœur who took the call. With the receiver to his ear, he rose to his feet, making queer signs that brought the whole room to a hush.

"What? Don't speak so close to the mouthpiece."

In the silence, the others could hear a high-pitched voice.

"It's for the police! Tell the police I've got him! The killer! Hallo? What? Is that Uncle Andre?"

The voice was lowered a tone to say shakily: "I tell you, I'll shoot, Uncle Andre."

Lecœur hardly knew to whom he handed the receiver. He dashed out of the room and up the stairs, almost breaking down the door of the room.

"Quick, all cars to the Orient Bar, Porte Clignancourt."

And without waiting to hear the message go out, he dashed back as fast as he'd come. At the door he stopped dead, struck by the calm that had suddenly descended on the room.

It was Saillard who held the receiver into which, in the thickest of Parisian dialects, a voice was saying:

"It's all right. Don't worry. I gave the chap a crack on the head with a bottle. Laid him out properly. God knows what he wanted to do to the kid. What's that? You want to speak to him? Here, little one, come here. And give me your popgun. I don't like those toys. Why, it isn't loaded."

Another voice. "Is that Uncle Andre?"

The Inspector looked round, and it was not to Andre but to Olivier that he handed the receiver.

"Uncle Andre. I got him."

"Bib! It's me."

"What are you doing there, Dad?"

"Nothing. Waiting to hear from you. It's been—"

"You can't think how bucked I am. Wait a moment, here's the police. They're just arriving."

Confused sounds. Voices, the shuffling of feet, the clink of glasses. Olivier Lecœur listened, standing there awkwardly, gazing at the wall-map which he did not see, his thoughts far away at the northern extremity of Paris, in a windswept boulevard.

"They're taking me with them."

Another voice. "Is that you, Chief? Janvier here."

One might have thought it was Olivier Lecœur who had been knocked on the head with a bottle by the way he held the receiver out, staring blankly in front of him.

"He's out, right out, Chief. They're lugging him away now. When the boy heard the telephone ringing, he decided it was his chance. He grabbed Loubet's gun from his pocket and made a dash for the phone. The proprietor here's a pretty tough nut. If it hadn't been for—"

A little lamp lit up in the plan of Paris.

"Hallo! Your car's gone out?"

"Someone's smashed the glass of the pillar telephone in the Place Clignancourt. Says there's a row going on in a bar. I'll ring up again when we know what's going on."

It wouldn't be necessary.

Nor was it necessary for Andre Lecœur to put a cross in his notebook under Miscellaneous.

—translated by Geoffrey Sainsbury

I SAW MOMMY KILLING SANTA CLAUS

BY GEORGE BAXT

We buried my mother yesterday, so I feel free to tell the truth. She lived to be ninety-three because, like the sainted, loyal son I chose to be, I didn't blab to the cops. I'm Oscar Leigh and my mother was Desiree Leigh. That's right—Desiree Leigh, inventor of the Desiree face cream that promised eternal youth to the young and rejuvenation to the aged. It was one of the great con games in the cosmetics industry. I suppose once this is published, it'll be the end of the Desiree cosmetics empire, but frankly, my dears, I don't give a damn. Desiree Cosmetics was bought by a Japanese combine four years ago, and my share (more than two billion) is safely salted away. I suppose I inherit Mom's billions, too, but what in heaven's name will I do with it all? Count it, I guess.

Desiree Leigh wasn't her real name. She was born Daisy Ray Letch, and who could go through life with a surname like Letch? For the past fourteen years she's been entertaining Alzheimer's and that was when I began to take an interest in her past. She was always very mysterious about her origins and equally arcane about the identity of my father. She said he was killed in North Africa back in 1943 and that his name was Clarence Kolb. I spent a lot of money tracing Clarence, until one night, in bed watching an old movie, the closing credits rolled and one of the character actors was named Clarence Kolb. I mentioned this to Mother the next morning at breakfast, but she said it was a coincidence and she and my father used to laugh about it.

She had no photos of my father, which I thought was strange. When they married a few months before the war, they settled in Brooklyn, in Coney Island. Surely they must have had their picture taken in one of the Coney Island fun galleries? But no, insisted Mother, they avoided the boardwalk and the amusement parks—they were too poor for such frivolities. How did Father make his living? He was a milkman, she said—his route was in Sheepshead Bay. She said he worked for the Borden Company. Well, let me tell you this; there is no record of a Clarence Kolb ever having been employed by the Borden Milk Company. It cost an ugly penny tracking that down.

Did Mom work, too, perhaps? "Oh, yes," she told me one night in Cannes where our yacht was berthed for a few days, "I worked right up until the day before you were born."

"What did you do?" We were on deck playing honeymoon bridge in the blazing sunlight so Mom could keep an eye on the first mate, with whom she was either having an affair or planning to have one.

"I worked in a laboratory." She said it so matter of factly while collecting a trick she shouldn't have collected that I didn't believe her. "You don't believe me." (She not only conned, stole, and lied, she was a mind-reader.) "Sure I believe you." I sounded as convincing as an East Berlin commissar assuring would-be emigrés they'd have their visas to freedom before sundown.*

"It was a privately owned laboratory," she said, sneaking a look at the first mate, who was sneaking a look at the second mate. "It was a couple of blocks from our apartment."

*Ed. note: A joyful note to anachronism—shortly after this story was written.

"What kind of a laboratory was it?" I asked, mindful that the second mate was sneaking a look at me.

"It was owned by a man named Desmond Tester. He fooled around with all kinds of formulas."

"Some sort of mad scientist?"

She chuckled as she cheated another trick in her favor. "I guess he *was* kind of mad in a way. He had a very brilliant mind. I learned a great deal from him."

"Is that where you originated the Desiree creams and lotions?"

"The seed was planted there."

"How long were you with this—"

"Desmond Tester. Let me see now. Your daddy went into the Army in February of '42. I didn't know I was pregnant then or he'd never have gone. On the other hand, I suppose if I *had* known, I would have kept it to myself so your dad could go and prove he was a hero and not just a common everyday milkman."

"I don't see anything wrong in delivering milk."

"There's nothing heroic about it, either. Where was I?"

"Taking my king of hearts, which you shouldn't be."

She ignored me and favored the first mate with a seductive smile, and I blushed when the second mate winked at me. "Anyway, I took time off to give birth to you and then I went right back to work for Professor Tester. A nice lady in the neighborhood looked after you. Let me think, what was her name? Oh, yes— Blanche Yurka."

"Isn't that the name of the actress who played Ma Barker in a gangster movie we saw on the late show?"

"I don't know, isn't it? That's my ten of clubs you're taking," she said sharply.

"I've captured it fair and square with the queen of clubs," I told her. "How come you never married again?"

"I guess I was too busy being a career woman. I was assisting Professor Tester in marketing some of his creams and lotions by then. I had such a hard time cracking the department stores."

"When did you come up with your own formulas?"

"That was after the professor met with his unfortunate death."

Unfortunate, indeed. I saw her kill him.

It was Christmas of 1950—in fact, it was Christmas Day. Mom was preparing to roast a turkey at the professor's house—our apartment was much too small for entertaining—and I remember almost everyone who was there. It was mostly kids from the neighborhood, the unfortunate ones whose families couldn't afford a proper Christmas dinner. There must have been about ten of them. Mother and the professor were the only adults, although Mom still insists there was a woman there named Laurette with whom the professor was having an affair. Mom says this woman was jealous of her because she thought Mom and the professor were having a little ding-dong of their own. (I've always suspected my mother of doing quite a bit of dinging and donging in the neighborhood when she couldn't meet a grocery bill or a butcher bill or satisfy the landlord or Mr. Kumbog, who owned the liquor store.)

Mom says it was Laurette who shot the professor in the heart and ran away (and was never heard of again, need I tell you?)—but I'm getting ahead of myself. It happened like this: Mom was in the kitchen stuffing the turkey when Professor Tester appeared in the doorway dressed in the Santa Claus suit. He had stuffed his stomach but still looked no more like Santa Claus than Monty Woolley did in *Life Begins at Eight-Thirty.*

"Daisy Ray, I have to talk to you," he said.

"Just let me finish stuffing this turkey and get it in the oven," she told him. "I'd like to feed the kids by around five o'clock when I'm sure they'll be tired of playing Post Office and Spin the Bottle and Doctor." I remember her asking me, "Sonny, have you been playing Doctor?"

"As often as I can," I replied with a smirk. And I still do. Now I'm a specialist.

"Daisy Ray, come with me to the laboratory," Tester insisted.

"Oh, really, Desmond," Mother said, "I don't understand your tone of voice."

"There are a lot of things going on around here that are hard to understand," the professor said ominously. "Daisy Ray!" He sounded uncannily like Captain Bligh summoning Mr. Christian.

I caught a very strange and very scary look on my mother's face. And then she did something I now realize should have made the professor realize that something unexpected and undesirable was about to befall him. She picked up her handbag, which was hanging by its strap on the back of a chair, and followed him out of the room. "Sonny, you stay here." Her voice sounded as though it was coming from that echo chamber I heard on the spooky radio show, *The Witch's Tale*.

"Yes, Mama."

I watched her follow Professor Tester out of the kitchen. I was frightened. I was terribly frightened. I had a premonition that something awful was going to happen, so I disobeyed her orders and tiptoed after them.

The laboratory was in the basement. I waited in the hall until I heard them reach the bottom of the stairs and head for the main testing room, then I tiptoed downstairs, praying the stairs wouldn't squeak and betray me. But I had nothing to worry about. They were having a shouting match that would have drowned out the exploding of an atom bomb.

The door to the testing room was slightly ajar and I could hear everything.

"What have you done with the formula?" he raged.

"I don't know what you're talking about." Mama was quite cool, subtly underplaying him. It was one of those rare occasions when I almost admired her.

"You damn well know what I'm talking about, you thief!"

"How dare you!" What a display of indignation—had she heard it, Norma Shearer would have died of envy.

"You stole the formula for my rejuvenating cream! You've formed a partnership with the Sibonay Group in Mexico!"

"You're hallucinating. You've been taking too many of your own drugs."

"I've got a friend at Sibonay—he's told me everything! I'm going to put you behind bars unless you give me back my formula!"

Although I didn't doubt for one moment that my mother had betrayed him, I still had to put my hand over my mouth to stifle a laugh. I mean, have you ever seen Santa Claus blowing his top? It's a scream in red and white.

"Don't you touch me! Don't you lay a hand on me!" Mother's handbag was open and she was fumbling for something in it. He slapped her hard across the face. Then I heard the *pop* and the professor was clutching at his chest. Through his fingers little streams of blood began to form. Mom was holding a tiny pearl-handled pistol in her hand, the kind Kay Francis used to carry around in a beaded bag. My God, I remember saying to myself, I just saw Mommy killing Santa Claus.

I turned tail and ran. I bolted up the stairs and into the front of the house, where the other kids who couldn't possibly have heard what had gone on in the basement were busy choosing up sides for a game called Kill the Hostess. I joined in and there wasn't a peep out of Mom for at least half an hour.

I began to wonder if maybe I had been hallucinating, if maybe I hadn't seen Mom slay the professor. I left the other kids and—out of curiosity and I suppose a little anxiety—I went to the kitchen.

You've got to hand it to Mom (you might as well, she'd take it anyway): the turkey was in the oven, roasting away. She had prepared the salad. Vegetables were simmering, timed to be ready when the turkey was finished roasting. She was topping a sweet-potato pie with little round marshmallows. She looked up when I came in and asked, "Enjoying yourself, Sonny?"

I couldn't resist asking her. "When is Santa Claus coming with his bag of presents for us?"

"Good Lord, when indeed! Now, where could Santa be, do you suppose?"

Dead as a doornail in the testing room, I should have responded, but instead I said, "Shucks, Mom, it beats me."

She thought for a moment and then said brightly, "I'll bet he's downstairs working on a new formula. Go down and tell him it's time he put in his appearance."

Can you top that? Sending her son into the basement to discover the body of the man she'd just assassinated?

Well, I dutifully discovered the body and started yelling my head off, deciding that was the wisest course under the circumstances. Mom and the kids came running. When they saw the body, the kids began shrieking, me shrieking the loudest so that maybe Mom would be proud of me, and Mom hurried and phoned the police.

What ensued after the police arrived was sheer genius on my mother's part. I don't remember the detective's name—by now he must be in that Big Squadroom in the Sky—but I'm sure if he was ever given an I.Q. test he must have ended up owing them about fifty points. Mom was saying hysterically, "Oh, my God, to think there was a murderer in the house while I was in the kitchen preparing our Christmas dinner and the children were in the parlor playing guessing games!" She carried the monologue for about ten minutes until the medical examiner came into the kitchen to tell the detective the professor had been done in by a bullet to the heart.

"Any sign of the weapon?" asked the detective.

"It's not *my* job to look for one," replied the examiner testily.

So others were dispatched to look for a weapon. Knowing Mom, it wouldn't be in her handbag, but where, I wondered, could she have stashed it? I stopped in mid-wonder when I heard her say, "It might have been Laurette."

"Who's she?" asked the detective.

Mom folded her hands, managing to look virtuous and sound scornful. "She was the professor's girl friend, if you know what I mean. He broke it off with her last week and she wasn't about to let him off so easy. She's been phoning and making threats, and this morning he told me she might be coming around to give him his Christmas present." She added darkly, "That Christmas present was called—*death!*"

"Did you see her here today?" the detective asked.

Mom said she hadn't. He asked us all if we'd seen a strange lady come into the house. I was tempted to tell him the only strange lady I saw come into the house was my mother, but I thought of that formula and how wealthy we'd become and I became a truly loving son.

"She could have come in by the cellar door," I volunteered.

It was the first time I saw my mother look at me with love and admiration. "It's on the other side of the house, and with all the noise we were making—"

"And I had the radio on in the kitchen, listening to the *Make Believe Ballroom*," was the fuel Mother added to the fire I had ignited. The arson was successful. The police finally left—without finding the weapon—taking the body with them, and Mom proceeded with Christmas dinner as though killing a man was an everyday occurrence.

The dinner was delicious, although some of us kids noted the turkey had a slightly strange taste to it.

"Turkey can be gamey," Mama trilled—and within the next six months she was on her way to becoming one of the most powerful names in the cosmetics industry.

I remained a bachelor. I worked alongside Mother and her associates and watched as, one by one over the years, she got rid of all of them. She destroyed the Sibonay people in Mexico by proving falsely and at great cost, that they were the front for a dope-running operation. She thought it would be fun if I could become a mayor of New York City, but a psychic told me to forget about it and go into junk bonds—which I did and suffered staggering losses. (The psychic died a mysterious death, which she obviously hadn't foretold herself.)

Year after year, Christmas after Christmas, I was sorely tempted to tell Mama I saw her kill Santa Claus. Year after year, Christmas after Christmas, I was aching to know where she had hidden the weapon.

And then I found out. It was Christmas Day fourteen years ago.

The doctors, after numerous tests, had assured me that Mom was showing signs of Alzheimer's. Such as when applying lipstick, she ended up covering her chin with rouge. And wearing three dresses at the same time. And filing her shoes and accessories in the deep freeze. It was sad, really, even for a murderess who deserved no mercy. Yet she insisted on cooking the Christmas dinner herself that year.

"It's going to be just like that Christmas Day when we had that wonderful dinner with the neighborhood kiddies," she said. "And Professor Tester dressed up as Santa Claus and brought in that big bag of games and toys. And he gave me the wonderful gift of the exclusive rights to the formula for the Desiree Rejuvenating Lotion."

There were twenty for dinner and, believe it or not, Mother cooked it impeccably. The servants were a bit nervous, but the guests were too drunk to notice. Then, while eating the turkey, Mother asked me across the table, "Does the turkey taste the same way it did way back when, Sonny?"

And then I remembered how the turkey had tasted that day forty years ago when Mama had said something about turkey sometimes tasting gamey. I looked at her and, ill or not, there was mockery in her eyes. It was then that I said to her, not knowing if she would understand what I meant: "Mama, I saw what you did."

There was a small smile on her face. Slowly her head began to bob up and down. "I had a feeling you did," she said. "But you haven't answered me. Does the turkey taste the same way it did then?"

I spoke the truth. "No, Mama, it doesn't. It's very good."

She was laughing like a madwoman. Everyone at the table looked embarrassed and there was nowhere for me to hide. "Is this a private joke between you and your mother?" the man at my right asked me. But I couldn't answer. Because my mother had reached across the table and shoved her hand into the turkey's cavity, obscenely pulling out gobs of stuffing and flinging it at me.

"Don't you know why the turkey tasted strange? Can't you guess why, Sonny? Can't you guess what I hid in the stuffing so those damn fool cops wouldn't find it? Can't you guess, Sonny? Can't you?"

DEAD ON CHRISTMAS STREET

BY JOHN D. MacDONALD

The police in the first prowl car on the scene got out a tarpaulin. A traffic policeman threw it over the body and herded the crowd back. They moved uneasily in the gray slush. Some of them looked up from time to time.

In the newspaper picture the window would be marked with a bold X. A dotted line would descend from the X to the spot where the covered body now lay. Some of the spectators, laden with tinsel- and evergreen-decorated packages, turned away, suppressing a nameless guilt.

But the curious stayed on. Across the street, in the window of a department store, a vast mechanical Santa rocked back and forth, slapping a mechanical hand against a padded thigh, roaring forever, "Whaw haw ho ho ho. Whaw haw ho ho ho." The slapping hand had worn the red plush from the padded thigh.

The ambulance arrived, with a brisk intern to make out the DOA. Sawdust was shoveled onto the sidewalk, then pushed off into the sewer drain. Wet snow fell into the city. And there was nothing else to see. The corner Santa, a leathery man with a pinched, blue nose, began to ring his hand bell again.

*   *   *

Daniel Fowler, one of the young Assistant District Attorneys, was at his desk when the call came through from Lieutenant Shinn of the Detective Squad. "Dan? This is Gil. You heard about the Garrity girl yet?"

For a moment the name meant nothing, and then suddenly he remembered: Loreen Garrity was the witness in the Sheridan City Loan Company case. She had made positive identification of two of the three kids who had tried to pull that holdup, and the case was on the calendar for February. Provided the kids didn't confess before it came up, Dan was going to prosecute. He had the Garrity girl's statement, and her promise to appear.

"What about her, Gil?" he asked.

"She took a high dive out of her office window—about an hour ago. Seventeen stories, and right into the Christmas rush. How come she didn't land on somebody, we'll never know. Connie Wyant is handling it. He remembered she figured in the loan-company deal, and he told me. Look, Dan. She was a big girl, and she tried hard not to go out that window. She was shoved. That's how come Connie has it. Nice Christmas present for him."

"Nice Christmas present for the lads who pushed over the loan company, too," Dan said grimly. "Without her there's no case. Tell Connie that. It ought to give him the right line."

Dan Fowler set aside the brief he was working on and walked down the hall. The District Attorney's secretary was at her desk. "Boss busy, Jane?"

She was a small girl with wide, gray eyes, a mass of dark hair, a soft mouth. She raised one eyebrow and looked at him speculatively. "I could be bribed, you know."

He looked around with exaggerated caution, went around her desk on tiptoe, bent and kissed her upraised lips. He smiled down at her. "People are beginning to talk," he whispered, not getting it as light as he meant it to be.

She tilted her head to one side, frowned, and said, "What is it, Dan?"

He sat on the corner of her desk and took her hands in his, and he told her about the big, dark-haired, swaggering

woman who had gone out the window. He knew Jane
would want to know. He had regretted bringing Jane in
on the case, but he had had the unhappy hunch that Garrity might sell out, if the offer was high enough. And so
he had enlisted Jane, depending on her intuition. He had
taken the two of them to lunch, and had invented an excuse to duck out and leave them alone.

Afterward, Jane had said, "I guess I don't really like
her, Dan. She was suspicious of me, of course, and she's
a terribly vital sort of person. But I would say that she'll
be willing to testify. And I don't think she'll sell out."

Now as he told her about the girl, he saw the sudden
tears of sympathy in her gray eyes. "Oh, Dan! How dreadful! You'd better tell the boss right away. That Vince Servius must have hired somebody to do it."

"Easy, lady," he said softly.

He touched her dark hair with his fingertips, smiled at
her, and crossed to the door of the inner office, opened it
and went in.

Jim Heglon, the District Attorney, was a narrow-faced
man with glasses that had heavy frames. He had a professional look, a dry wit, and a driving energy.

"Every time I see you, Dan, I have to conceal my annoyance," Heglon said. "You're going to cart away the best
secretary I ever had."

"Maybe I'll keep her working for a while. Keep her out
of trouble."

"Excellent! And speaking of trouble—"

"Does it show, Jim?" Dan sat on the arm of a heavy
leather chair which faced Heglon's desk. "I do have some.
Remember the Sheridan City Loan case?"

"Vaguely. Give me an outline."

"October. Five o'clock one afternoon, just as the loan
office was closing. Three punks tried to knock it over. Two
of them, Castrella and Kelly, are eighteen. The leader,
Johnny Servius, is nineteen. Johnny is Vince Servius's
kid brother.

"They went into the loan company wearing masks and
waving guns. The manager had more guts than sense. He
was loading the safe. He saw them and slammed the door

and spun the knob. They beat on him, but he convinced them it was a time lock, which it wasn't. They took fifteen dollars out of his pants, and four dollars from the girl behind the counter and took off.

"Right across the hall is the office of an accountant named Thomas Kistner. He'd already left. His secretary, Loreen Garrity, was closing up the office. She had the door open a crack. She saw the three kids come out of the loan company, taking their masks off. Fortunately, they didn't see her.

"She went to headquarters and looked at the gallery, and picked out Servius and Castrella. They were picked up. Kelly was with them, so they took him in, too. In the lineup the Garrity girl made a positive identification of Servius and Castrella again. The manager thought he could recognize Kelly's voice.

"Bail was set high, because we expected Vince Servius would get them out. Much to everybody's surprise, he's left them in there. The only thing he did was line up George Terrafierro to defend them, which makes it tough from our point of view, but not too tough—if we could put the Garrity girl on the stand. She was the type to make a good witness. Very positive sort of girl."

"Was? Past tense?"

"This afternoon she was pushed out the window of the office where she works. Seventeen stories above the sidewalk. Gil Shinn tells me that Connie Wyant has it definitely tagged as homicide."

"If Connie says it is, then it is. What would conviction have meant to the three lads?"

"Servius had one previous conviction—car theft; Castrella had one conviction for assault with a deadly weapon. Kelly is clean, Jim."

Heglon frowned. "Odd, isn't it? In this state, armed robbery has a mandatory sentence of seven to fifteen years for a first offense in that category. With the weight Vince can swing, his kid brother would do about five years. Murder seems a little extreme as a way of avoiding a five-year sentence."

"Perhaps, Jim, the answer is in the relationship between

Vince and the kid. There's quite a difference in ages. Vince must be nearly forty. He was in the big time early enough to give Johnny all the breaks. The kid has been thrown out of three good schools I know of. According to Vince, Johnny can do no wrong. Maybe that's why he left those three in jail awaiting trial—to keep them in the clear on this killing."

"It could be, Dan," Heglon said. "Go ahead with your investigation. And let me know."

Dan Fowler found out at the desk that Lieutenant Connie Wyant and Sergeant Levandowski were in the Interrogation Room. Dan sat down and waited.

After a few moments Connie waddled through the doorway and came over to him. He had bulging blue eyes and a dull expression.

Dan stood up, towering over the squat lieutenant. "Well, what's the picture, Connie?"

"No case against the kids, Gil says. Me, I wish it was just somebody thought it would be nice to jump out a window. But she grabbed the casing so hard, she broke her fingernails down to the quick.

"Marks you can see, in oak as hard as iron. Banged her head on the sill and left black hair on the rough edge of the casing. Lab matched it up. And one shoe up there, under the radiator. The radiator sits right in front of the window. Come listen to Kistner."

Dan followed him back to the Interrogation Room. Thomas Kistner sat at one side of the long table. A cigar lay dead on the glass ashtray near his elbow. As they opened the door, he glanced up quickly. He was a big, bloated man with an unhealthy grayish complexion and an important manner.

He said, "I was just telling the sergeant the tribulations of an accountant."

"We all got troubles," Connie said. "This is Mr. Fowler from the D.A.'s office, Kistner."

Mr. Kistner got up laboriously. "Happy to meet you, sir," he said. "Sorry that it has to be such an unpleasant occasion, however."

Connie sat down heavily. "Kistner, I want you to go through your story again. If it makes it easier, tell it to Mr. Fowler instead of me. He hasn't heard it before."

"I'll do anything in my power to help, Lieutenant," Kistner said firmly. He turned toward Dan. "I am out of my office a great deal. I do accounting on a contract basis for thirty-three small retail establishments. I visit them frequently.

"When Loreen came in this morning, she seemed nervous. I asked her what the trouble was, and she said that she felt quite sure somebody had been following her for the past week.

"She described him to me. Slim, middle height, pearl-gray felt hat, tan raglan topcoat, swarthy complexion. I told her that because she was the witness in a trial coming up, she should maybe report it to the police and ask for protection. She said she didn't like the idea of yelling for help. She was a very—ah—independent sort of girl."

"I got that impression," Dan said.

"I went out then and didn't think anything more about what she'd said. I spent most of the morning at Finch Pharmacy, on the north side. I had a sandwich there and then drove back to the office, later than usual. Nearly two.

"I came up to the seventeenth floor. Going down the corridor, I pass the Men's Room before I get to my office. I unlocked the door with my key and went in. I was in there maybe three minutes.

"I came out and a man brushes by me in the corridor. He had his collar up, and was pulling down on his hatbrim and walking fast. At the moment, you understand, it meant nothing to me.

"I went into the office. The window was wide open, and the snow was blowing in. No Loreen. I couldn't figure it. I thought she'd gone to the Ladies' Room and had left the window open for some crazy reason. I started to shut it, and then I heard all the screaming down in the street.

"I leaned out. I saw her, right under me, sprawled on the sidewalk. I recognized the cocoa-colored suit. A new suit, I think. I stood in a state of shock, I guess, and then suddenly I remembered about the man following her, and

I remembered the man in the hall—he had a gray hat and a tan topcoat, and I had the impression he was swarthy-faced.

"The first thing I did was call the police, naturally. While they were on the way, I called my wife. It just about broke her up. We were both fond of Loreen."

The big man smiled sadly. "And it seems to me I've been telling the story over and over again ever since. Oh, I don't mind, you understand. But it's a dreadful thing. The way I see it, when a person witnesses a crime, they ought to be given police protection until the trial is all over."

"We don't have that many cops," Connie said glumly. "How big was the man you saw in the corridor?"

"Medium size. A little on the thin side."

"How old?"

"I don't know. Twenty-five, forty-five. I couldn't see his face, and you understand I wasn't looking closely."

Connie turned toward Dan. "Nothing from the elevator boys about this guy. He probably took the stairs. The lobby is too busy for anybody to notice him coming through by way of the fire door. Did the Garrity girl ever lock herself in the office, Kistner?"

"I never knew of her doing that, Lieutenant."

Connie said, "Okay, so the guy could breeze in and clip her one. Then, from the way the rug was pulled up, he lugged her across to the window. She came to as he was trying to work her out the window, and she put up a battle. People in the office three stories underneath say she was screaming as she went by."

"How about the offices across the way?" Dan asked.

"It's a wide street, Dan, and they couldn't see through the snow. It started snowing hard about fifteen minutes before she was pushed out the window. I think the killer waited for that snow. It gave him a curtain to hide behind."

"Any chance that she marked the killer, Connie?" Dan asked.

"Doubt it. From the marks of her fingernails, he lifted her up and slid her feet out first, so her back was to him.

She grabbed the sill on each side. Her head hit the window sash. All he had to do was hold her shoulders, and bang her in the small of the back with his knee. Once her fanny slid off the sill, she couldn't hold on with her hands any longer. And from the looks of the doorknobs, he wore gloves."

Dan turned to Kistner. "What was her home situation? I tried to question her. She was pretty evasive."

Kistner shrugged. "Big family. She didn't get along with them. Seven girls, I think, and she was next to oldest. She moved out when she got her first job. She lived alone in a one-room apartment on Leeds Avenue, near the bridge."

"You know of any boy friend?" Connie asked.

"Nobody special. She used to go out a lot, but nobody special."

Connie rapped his knuckles on the edge of the table. "You ever make a pass at her, Kistner?"

The room was silent. Kistner stared at his dead cigar. "I don't want to lie to you, but I don't want any trouble at home, either. I got a boy in the Army, and I got a girl in her last year of high. But you work in a small office alone with a girl like Loreen, and it can get you.

"About six months ago I had to go to the state capital on a tax thing. I asked her to come along. She did. It was a damn fool thing to do. And it—didn't work out so good. We agreed to forget it ever happened.

"We were awkward around the office for a couple of weeks, and then I guess we sort of forgot. She was a good worker, and I was paying her well, so it was to both our advantages to be practical and not get emotional. I didn't have to tell you men this, but, like I said, I don't see any point in lying to the police. Hell, you might have found out some way, and that might make it look like I killed her or something."

"Thanks for leveling," Connie said expressionlessly. "We'll call you if we need you."

Kistner ceremoniously shook hands all around and left with obvious relief.

As soon as the door shut behind him, Connie said, "I'll buy it. A long time ago I learned you can't jail a guy for being a jerk. Funny how many honest people I meet I don't like at all, and how many thieves make good guys to knock over a beer with. How's your girl?"

Dan looked at his watch. "Dressing for dinner, and I should be, too," he said. "How are the steaks out at the Cat and Fiddle?"

Connie half closed his eyes. After a time he sighed. "Okay. That might be a good way to go at the guy. Phone me and give me the reaction if he does talk. If not, don't bother."

Jane was in holiday mood until Dan told her where they were headed. She said tartly, "I admit freely that I am a working girl. But do I get overtime for this?"

Dan said slowly, carefully, "Darling, you better understand, if you don't already, that there's one part of me I can't change. I can't shut the office door and forget the cases piled up in there. I have a nasty habit of carrying them around with me. So we go someplace else and I try like blazes to be gay, or we go to the Cat and Fiddle and get something off my mind."

She moved closer to him. "Dull old work horse," she said.

"Guilty."

"All right, now I'll confess," Jane said. "I was going to suggest we go out there later. I just got sore when you beat me to the draw."

He laughed, and at the next stop light he kissed her hurriedly.

The Cat and Fiddle was eight miles beyond the city line. At last Dan saw the green-and-blue neon sign, and he turned into the asphalt parking area. There were about forty other cars there.

They went from the check room into the low-ceilinged bar and lounge. The only sign of Christmas was a small silver tree on the bar; a tiny blue spot was focused on it.

They sat at the bar and ordered drinks. Several other couples were at the tables, talking in low voices. A pianist played softly in the dining room.

Dan took out a business card and wrote on it: *Only if you happen to have an opinion.*

He called the nearest bartender over. "Would you please see that Vince gets this?"

The man glanced at the name. "I'll see if Mr. Servius is in." He said something to the other bartender and left through a paneled door at the rear of the bar. He was back in less than a minute, smiling politely.

"Please go up the stair. Mr. Servius is in his office—the second door on the right."

"I'll wait here, Dan," Jane said.

"If you are Miss Raymer, Mr. Servius would like to have you join him, too," the bartender said.

Jane looked at Dan. He nodded and she slid off the stool.

As they went up the stairs, Jane said, "I seem to be known here."

"Notorious female. I suspect he wants a witness."

Vincent Servius was standing at a small corner bar mixing himself a drink when they entered. He turned and smiled. "Fowler, Miss Raymer. Nice of you to stop by. Can I mix you something?"

Dan refused politely, and they sat down.

Vince was a compact man with cropped, prematurely white hair, a sunlamp tan, and beautifully cut clothes. He had not been directly concerned with violence in many years. In that time he had eliminated most of the traces of the hoodlum.

The over-all impression he gave was that of the up-and-coming clubman. Golf lessons, voice lessons, plastic surgery, and a good tailor—these had all helped; but nothing had been able to destroy a certain aura of alertness, ruthlessness. He was a man you would never joke with. He had made his own laws, and he carried the awareness of his own ultimate authority around with him, as unmistakable as a loaded gun.

Vince went over to the fieldstone fireplace, drink in hand, and turned, resting his elbow on the mantel.

"Very clever, Fowler. 'Only if you happen to have an opinion.' I have an opinion. The kid is no good. That's my opinion. He's a cheap punk. I didn't admit that to myself until he tried to put the hook on that loan company. He was working for me at the time. I was trying to break him in here—buying foods.

"But now I'm through, Fowler. You can tell Jim Heglon that for me. Terrafierro will back it up. Ask him what I told him. I said, 'Defend the kid. Get him off if you can, and no hard feelings if you can't. If you get him off, I'm having him run out of town, out of the state. I don't want him around.' I told George that.

"Now there's this Garrity thing. It looks like I went out on a limb for the kid. Going out on limbs was yesterday, Fowler. Not today and not tomorrow. I was a sucker long enough."

He took out a crisp handkerchief and mopped his forehead. "I go right up in the air," he said. "I talk too loud."

"You can see how Heglon is thinking," Dan said quietly. "And the police, too."

"That's the hell of it. I swear I had nothing to do with it." He half smiled. "It would have helped if I'd had a tape recorder up here last month when the Garrity girl came to see what she could sell me."

Dan leaned forward. "She came here?"

"With bells on. Nothing coy about that kid. Pay off, Mr. Servius, and I'll change my identification of your brother."

"What part of last month?"

"Let me think. The tenth it was. Monday the tenth."

Jane said softly, "That's why I got the impression she wouldn't sell out, Dan. I had lunch with her later that same week. She had tried to and couldn't."

Vince took a sip of his drink. "She started with big money and worked her way down. I let her go ahead. Finally, after I'd had my laughs, I told her even one dollar was too much. I told her I wanted the kid sent up.

"She blew her top. For a couple of minutes I thought I might have to clip her to shut her up. But after a couple of drinks she quieted down. That gave me a chance to find out something that had been bothering me. It seemed too pat, kind of."

"What do you mean, Servius?" Dan asked.

"The set up was too neat, the way the door *happened* to be open a crack, and the way she *happened* to be working late, and the way she *happened* to see the kids come out.

"I couldn't get her to admit anything at first, because she was making a little play for me, but when I convinced her I wasn't having any, she let me in on what really happened. She was hanging around waiting for the manager of that loan outfit to quit work.

"They had a system. She'd wait in the accountant's office with the light out, watching his door. Then, when the manager left, she'd wait about five minutes and leave herself. That would give him time to get his car out of the parking lot. He'd pick her up at the corner. She said he was the super-cautious, married type. They just dated once in a while. I wasn't having any of that. Too rough for me, Fowler."

There was a long silence. Dan asked, "How about friends of your brother, Servius, or friends of Kelly and Castrella?"

Vince walked over and sat down, facing them. "One— Johnny didn't have a friend who'd bring a bucket of water if he was on fire. And two—I sent the word out."

"What does that mean?"

"I like things quiet in this end of the state. I didn't want anyone helping those three punks. Everybody got the word. So who would do anything? Now both of you please tell Heglon exactly what I said. Tell him to check with Terrafierro. Tell him to have the cops check their pigeons. Ask the kid himself. I paid him a little visit. Now, if you don't mind, I've got another appointment."

They had finished their steaks before Dan was able to get any line on Connie Wyant. On the third telephone call he was given a message. Lieutenant Wyant was waiting for Mr. Fowler at 311 Leeds Street, Apartment 6A, and would Mr. Fowler please bring Miss Raymer with him.

They drove back to the city. A department car was parked in front of the building. Sergeant Levandowski was half asleep behind the wheel. "Go right in. Ground floor in the back. 6A."

Connie greeted them gravely and listened without question to Dan's report of the conversation with Vince Servius. After Dan had finished, Connie nodded casually, as though it was of little importance, and said, "Miss Raymer, I'm not so good at this, so I thought maybe you could help. There's the Garrity girl's closet. Go through it and give me an estimate on the cost."

Jane went to the open closet. She began to examine the clothes. "Hey!" she exclaimed.

"What do you think?" Connie asked.

"If this suit cost a nickel under two hundred, I'll eat it. And look at this coat. Four hundred, anyway." She bent over and picked up a shoe. "For ages I've dreamed of owning a pair of these. Thirty-seven fifty, at least."

"Care to make an estimate on the total?" Connie asked her.

"Gosh, thousands. I don't know. There are nine dresses in there that must have cost at least a hundred apiece. Do you have to have it accurate?"

"That's close enough, thanks." He took a small blue bankbook out of his pocket and flipped it to Dan. Dan caught it and looked inside. Loreen Garrity had more than $1100 on hand. There had been large deposits and large withdrawals—nothing small.

Connie said, "I've been to see her family. They're good people. They didn't want to talk mean about the dead, so it took a little time. But I found out our Loreen was one for the angles—a chiseler—no conscience and less morals. A rough, tough cookie to get tied up with.

"From there, I went to see the Kistners. Every time the old lady would try to answer a question, Kistner'd jump in with all four feet. I finally had to have Levandowski take him downtown just to get him out of the way. Then the old lady talked.

"She had a lot to say about how lousy business is. How they're scrimping and scraping along, and how the girl couldn't have a new formal for the Christmas dance tomorrow night at the high school gym.

"Then I called up an accountant friend after I left her. I asked him how Kistner had been doing. He cussed out Kistner and said he'd been doing fine; in fact, he had stolen some nice retail accounts out from under the other boys in the same racket. So I came over here and it looked like this was where the profit was going. So I waited for you so I could make sure."

"What can you do about it?" Dan demanded, anger in his voice, anger at the big puffy man who hadn't wanted to lie to the police.

"I've been thinking. It's eleven o'clock. He's been sitting down there sweating. I've got to get my Christmas shopping done tomorrow, and the only way I'll ever get around to it is to break him fast."

Jane had been listening, wide-eyed. "They always forget some little thing, don't they?" she asked. "Or there is something they don't know about. Like a clock that is five minutes slow, or something. I mean, in the stories ..." Her voice trailed off uncertainly.

"Give her a badge, Connie," Dan said with amusement.

Connie rubbed his chin. "I might do that, Dan. I just might do that. Miss Raymer, you got a strong stomach? If so, maybe you get to watch your idea in operation."

It was nearly midnight, and Connie had left Dan and Jane alone in a small office at headquarters for nearly a half hour. He opened the door and stuck his head in. "Come on, people. Just don't say a word."

They went to the Interrogation Room. Kistner jumped up the moment they came in. Levandowski sat at the long table, looking bored.

Kistner said heatedly, "As you know, Lieutenant, I was perfectly willing to cooperate. But you are being high-handed. I demand to know why I was brought down here. I want to know why I can't phone a lawyer. You are exceeding your authority, and I—"

"Siddown!" Connie roared with all the power of his lungs.

Kistner's mouth worked silently. He sat down, shocked by the unexpected roar. A tired young man slouched in, sat at the table, flipped open a notebook, and placed three sharp pencils within easy reach.

Connie motioned Dan and Jane over toward chairs in a shadowed corner of the room. They sat side by side, and Jane held Dan's wrist, her nails sharp against his skin.

"Kistner, tell us again about how you came back to the office," Connie said.

Kistner replied in a tone of excruciating patience, as though talking to children, "I parked my car in my parking space in the lot behind the building. I used the back way into the lobby. I went up—"

"You went to the cigar counter."

"So I did! I had forgotten that. I went to the cigar counter. I bought three cigars and chatted with Barney. Then I took an elevator up."

"And talked to the elevator boy."

"I usually do. Is there a law?"

"No law, Kistner. Go on."

"And then I opened the Men's Room door with my key, and I was in there maybe three minutes. And then when I came out, the man I described brushed by me. I went to the office and found the window open. I was shutting it when I heard—"

"All this was at two o'clock, give or take a couple of minutes?"

"That's right, Lieutenant." Talking had restored Kistner's self-assurance.

Connie nodded to Levandowski. The sergeant got up lazily, walked to the door, and opened it. A burly, diffident young man came in. He wore khaki pants and a leather jacket.

"Sit down," Connie said casually. "What's your name?"

"Paul Hilbert, officer."

The tired young man was taking notes.

"What's your occupation?"

"I'm a plumber, officer. Central Plumbing, Incorporated."

"Did you get a call today from the Associated Bank Building?"

"Well, I didn't get the call, but I was sent out on the

job. I talked to the super, and he sent me up to the seventeenth floor. Sink drain clogged in the Men's Room."

"What time did you get there?"

"That's on my report, officer. Quarter after one."

"How long did it take you to finish the job?"

"About three o'clock."

"Did you leave the Men's Room at any time during that period?"

"No, I didn't."

"I suppose people tried to come in there?"

"Three or four. But I had all the water connections turned off, so I told them to go down to sixteen. The super had the door unlocked down there."

"Did you get a look at everybody who came in?"

"Sure, officer."

"You said three or four. Is one of them at this table?"

The shy young man looked around. He shook his head. "No, sir."

"Thanks, Hilbert. Wait outside. We'll want you to sign the statement when it's typed up."

Hilbert's footsteps sounded loud as he walked to the door. Everyone was watching Kistner. His face was still, and he seemed to be looking into a remote and alien future, as cold as the back of the moon.

Kistner said in a husky, barely audible voice. "A bad break. A stupid thing. Ten seconds it would have taken me to look in there. I had to establish the time. I talked to Barney. And to the elevator boy. They'd know when she fell. But I had to be some place else. Not in the office.

"You don't know how it was. She kept wanting more money. She wouldn't have anything to do with me, except when there was money. And I didn't have any more, finally.

"I guess I was crazy. I started to milk the accounts. That wasn't hard; the clients trust me. Take a little here and a little there. She found out. She wanted more and more. And that gave her a new angle. Give me more, or I'll tell.

"I thought it over. I kept thinking about her being a witness. All I had to do was make it look like she was killed to keep her from testifying. I don't care what you do to me. Now it's over, and I feel glad."

He gave Connie a long, wondering look. "Is that crazy? To feel glad it's over? Do other people feel that way?"

Connie asked Dan and Jane to wait in the small office. He came in ten minutes later; he looked tired. The plumber came in with him.

Connie said, "Me, I hate this business. I'm after him, and I bust him, and then I start bleeding for him. What the hell? Anyway, you get your badge, Miss Raymer."

"But wouldn't you have found out about the plumber anyway?" Jane asked.

Connie grinned ruefully at her. He jerked a thumb toward the plumber. "Meet Patrolman Hilbert. Doesn't know a pipe wrench from a faucet. We just took the chance that Kistner was too eager to toss the girl out the window—so eager he didn't make a quick check of the Men's Room. If he had, he could have laughed us under the table. As it is, I can get my Christmas shopping done tomorrow. Or is it today?"

Dan and Jane left headquarters. They walked down the street, arm in arm. There was holly, and a big tree in front of the courthouse, and a car went by with a lot of people in it singing about We Three Kings of Orient Are. Kistner was a stain, fading slowly.

They walked until it was entirely Christmas Eve, and they were entirely alone in the snow that began to fall again, making tiny perfect stars of lace that lingered in her dark hair.

THE CHRISTMAS BEAR

BY HERBERT RESNICOW

"Up there, Grandma," Debbie pointed, all excited, tugging at my skirt, "in the top row. Against the wall. See?" I'm not really her grandma, but at six and a half the idea of a great-grandmother is hard to understand. All her little friends have grandmothers, so she has a grandmother. When she's a little older, I'll tell her the whole story.

The firehouse was crowded this Friday night, not like the usual weekend where the volunteer firemen explain to their wives that they have to polish the old pumper and the second-hand ladder truck. They give the equipment a quick lick-and-a-promise and then sit down to an uninterrupted evening of pinochle. Not that there's all that much to do in Pitman anyway—we're over fifty miles from Pittsburgh, even if anyone could afford to pay city prices for what the big city offers—but still, a man's first thought has to be of his wife and family. Lord knows I've seen too much of the opposite in my own generation and all the pain and trouble it caused, and mine could've given lessons in devotion to this new generation that seems to be interested only in fun. What they call fun.

Still, they weren't all bad. Even Homer Curtis, who was the worst boy of his day, always full of mischief and very disrespectful, didn't turn out all that bad. That was after he got married, of course; not before. He was just voted fire chief and, to give him credit, this whole Rozovski affair was his idea, may God bless him.

Little Petrina Rozovski—she's only four years old and she's always been small for her age—her grandfather was shift foreman over my Jake in the mine while we were courting. We married young in those days because there was no future and you grabbed what happincss you could and that's how I came to be the youngest great-grandmother in the county, only sixty-seven, though that big horsefaced Mildred Ungaric keeps telling everybody I'm over seventy. Poor Petrina has to have a liver transplant, and soon. Real soon. You wouldn't believe what that costs, even if you could find the right liver in the first place. Seventy-five thousand dollars, and it could go to a lot more than that, depending. There isn't that much money in the whole county.

There was talk about going to the government—as if the government's got any way to just give money for things like this or to make somebody give her baby's liver to a poor little girl—or holding a raffle, or something, but none of the ideas was worth a tinker's dam. Then Homer, God bless him, had this inspiration. The volunteer firemen— they do it every year—collect toys for the poor children, which, these days, is half the town, to make sure every child gets *some* present for Christmas. And we all, even if we can't afford it, we all give something. Then one of them dresses up as Santa Claus and they all get on the ladder truck and, on Christmas Eve, they ride through the town giving out the presents. There's a box for everyone, so nobody knows who's getting a present, but the boxes for the families where the father is still working just have a candy bar in them or something like that. And for the littlest kids, they put Santa on top of the ladder and two guys turn the winch and lift him up to the roof as though he's going to go down the chimney and the kids' eyes get all round and everybody feels the way a kid should on Christmas Eve.

We had a town meeting to discuss the matter. "Raffles are no good," Homer declared, "because one person wins and everybody else loses. This year we're going to have an auction where everybody wins. Everybody who can will give a good toy—it can be used, but it's got to be good—in addition to what they give for the poor kids. Then the firemen will auction off those extra toys and the idea of that auction is to pay as *much* as possible instead of as little." That was sort of like the Indian potlatches they used to have around here that my grandfather told me about. Well, you can imagine the opposition to that one. But Homer overrode them all. Skinny as he is, when he stands up and raises his voice—he's the tallest man in town by far—he usually gets his way. Except with his wife, and that's as it should be. "Anyway," he pointed out, "it's a painless way of getting the donations Rozovski needs to get a liver transplant for Petrina."

Shorty Porter, who never backed water for anyone, told Homer, "Your brain ain't getting enough oxygen up there. Even if every family in town bought something for ten dollars on the average, with only twelve hundred families in town, we'd be short at least sixty-three thousand dollars, not to mention what it would cost for Irma Rozovski to stay in a motel near the hospital. And not everybody in town can pay more than what the present he bids on is worth. So you better figure on getting a lot less than twelve thousand, Homer, and what good that'll do, I fail to see." Levi Porter always had a good head for figures. One of these days we ought to make him mayor, if he could take the time off from busting his butt in his little back yard farm which, with his brood, he really can't.

"I never said," Homer replied, "that we were going to raise enough money this way to take care of the operation and everything. The beauty of my plan is . . . I figure we'll raise about four thousand. Right, Shorty?"

"That's about what I figured," Shorty admitted.

"We give the money to Hank and Irma and they take Petrina to New York. They take her to a TV station, to one of those news reporters who are always looking for ways to help people. We have a real problem here, a real emergency, and Petrina, with that sweet little face and her big brown eyes, once she appears on TV, her problems are over. If only ten percent of the people in the U.S. send in one cent each, that's all, just one cent, we'd get two hundred fifty thousand dollars. That would cover everything and leave plenty over to set up an office, right here in Pitman, for a clearing house for livers for all the poor little kids in that fix. And the publicity would remind some poor unfortunate mother that her child—children are dying in accidents every day and nobody knows who or where, healthy children—her child's liver could help save the life of a poor little girl."

Even Shorty had to admit it made sense. "And to top it all," Homer added, "if we do get enough money to set up a liver clearing house, we've brought a job to Pitman, for which I'd like to nominate Irma Rozovski, to make up for what she's gone through. And if it works out that way, maybe even two jobs, so Hank can have some work too." Well, that was the clincher. We all agreed and that's how it came about that I was standing in front of the display of the auction presents in the firehouse on the Friday night before Christmas week while Deborah was tugging and pointing at that funny-looking teddy bear, all excited, like I'd never seen her before.

Deborah's a sad little girl. Not that she doesn't have reason, what with her father running off just before the wedding and leaving Caroline in trouble; I never did like that Wesley Sladen in the first place. The Social Security doesn't give enough to support three on, and nobody around here's about to marry a girl going on twenty-nine with another mouth to feed, and I'm too old to earn much money, so Carrie's working as a waitress at the Highway Rest. But thanks to my Jake, we have a roof over our heads and we always will. My father was against my marrying him. I was born a Horvath, and my father wanted me to marry a nice Hungarian boy, not a damn foreigner, but I was of age and my mother was on my side and Jake and I got married in St. Anselms's and I wore a white gown, and I had a right to, not like it is today.

That was in '41 and before the year was out we were in the war. Jake volunteered and, not knowing I was pregnant, I didn't stop him. He was a good man, made sergeant, always sent every penny home. With me working in the factory, I even put a little away. After Marian was born, the foreman was nice enough to give me work to do at home on my sewing machine, so it was all right. Jake had taken out the full G.I. insurance and, when it happened, we got ten thousand dollars, which was a lot of money in those days. I bought the house, which cost almost two thousand dollars, and put the rest away for the bad times.

My daughter grew up to be a beautiful girl and she married a nice boy, John Brodzowski, but when Caroline was born, complications set in and Marian never made it out of the hospital. I took care of John and the baby for six months until John, who had been drinking, hit a tree going seventy. The police said it was an accident. I knew better but I kept my mouth shut because we needed the insurance.

So here we were, quiet little Deborah pulling at me and pointing at that teddy bear, all excited, and smiling for the first time I can remember. "That's what I want, Grandma," she begged. "He's my bear."

"You have a teddy bear," I told her. "We can't afford another one. I just brought you to the firehouse to look at all the nice things."

"He's not a teddy bear, Grandma, and I love him."

"But he's so funny looking," I objected. And he was, too. Black, sort of, but shining blueish when the light hit the right way, with very long hair. Ears bigger than a teddy bear's, and a longer snout. Not cute at all. Some white hairs at the chin and a big crescent-shaped white patch on his chest. And the eyes, not round little buttons, but slanted oval pieces of purple glass. I couldn't imagine what she saw in him. There was a tag, with #273 on it, around his neck. "Besides," I said, "I've only got eighteen dollars for all the presents, for everything. I'm sure they'll want at least ten dollars for him on account of it's for charity."

She began crying, quietly, not making a fuss; Deborah never did. Even at her age she understood, children do understand, that there were certain things that were not for us, but I could see her heart was broken and I didn't know what to do.

Just then the opening ceremonies started. Young Father Casimir, of St. Anselm's, gave the opening benediction, closing with "It is more blessed to give than to receive." I don't know how well that set with Irma Rozovski and the other poor people there, but he'll learn better when he gets older. Then Homer brought up Irma, with Petrina in her arms looking weaker and yellower than ever, to speak. "I just want to thank you all, all my friends and neighbors, for being so kind and . . ." Then she broke down and couldn't talk at all. Petrina didn't cry, she never cried, just looked sad and hung onto her mother. Then Homer came and led Irma away and said a few words I didn't even listen to. I knew what I had to do and I'd do it. Christmas is for the children, to make the children happy, that's the most important part. The children. I'd just explain to Carrie, when she got home, that I didn't get her anything this year and I didn't want her to get me anything. She'd understand.

I got hold of Homer in a corner and told him, "Look, Homer, for some reason Deborah's set on that teddy bear in the top row. Now all I've got is eighteen dollars, and I don't think you'd get anywhere near that much for it at the auction, but I don't want to take a chance on losing it and break Deborah's heart. I'm willing to give it all to you right now, if you'll sell it to me."

"Gee, I'd like to, Miz Sophie," he said, "but I can't. I have to go according to the rules. And if I did that for you, I'd have to do it for everybody, then with everybody picking their favorites, nobody would bid on anything and we couldn't raise the money for Petrina to go to New York."

"Come on, Homer, this ain't the first time you've broken some rules. Besides, I wouldn't tell anyone; I'd just take it off the shelf after everybody's left and no one would know the difference. It's an ugly looking teddy bear anyway."

"I'm real sorry, Mrs. Slowinski," he said, going all formal on me, "but I can't. Besides, there's no way to get it now. Those shelves, they're just boxes piled up with boards across them. You look at them crooked, and the whole thing'll fall down. There's no way to get to the top row until you've taken off the other rows. That's why the numbers start at the bottom."

"You're a damned fool, Homer, and I'm going to get that bear for Deborah anyway. I'm going to get him for a lot less than eighteen dollars too, so your stubbornness has cost the fund a lot of money and you ought to be ashamed of yourself."

We didn't go back to the firehouse until two days before Christmas Eve, Monday, when Carrie was off. Deborah had insisted on showing the bear to her mother to make sure we knew exactly which bear it was she wanted, but when we got there the bear was gone. Poor Deborah started crying, real loud this time, and even Carrie couldn't quiet her down. I picked her up and told her, swore to her, that I would get that bear back for her, but she just kept on sobbing.

I went right up to Homer to tell him off for selling the bear to somebody else instead of to me but before I could open my mouth, he said, "That wasn't right, Mrs. Slowinski, but as long as it's done, I won't make a fuss. Just give me the eighteen dollars and we'll forget about it."

That was like accusing me of stealing, and Milly Ungaric was standing near and she had that nasty smile on her face, so I knew who had stolen the bear. I ignored what Homer said and asked, "Who was on duty last night?" We don't have a fancy alarm system in Pitman; one of the firemen sleeps in the firehouse near the phone.

"Shorty Porter," Homer said, and I went right off.

I got hold of him on the side. "Levi, did you see anyone come in last night?" I asked. "I mean late."

"Only Miz Mildred," he said. "Just before I went to sleep."

Well, I knew it was her, but that wasn't what I meant. "I mean after you went to sleep. Did any noise wake you up?"

"When I sleep, Miz Sophie, only the phone bell wakes me up."

She must have come back later, the doors are never locked, and taken the bear. She's big enough, but how could she reach it? She couldn't climb over the shelves, everything would be knocked over. And she couldn't reach it from the floor. So how did she do it? Maybe it wasn't her, though I would have liked it to be. I went back to Homer. He was tall enough and had arms like a chimpanzee. "Homer," I said, "I'm going to forget what you said if you'll just do one thing. Stand in front of the toys and reach for the top shelf."

He got red, but he didn't blow. After a minute he said, sort of strangled, "I already thought of that. If I can't reach it by four feet, nobody can. Tell you what; give me seventeen dollars and explain how you did it, and I'll pay the other dollar out of my own pocket."

"You always were a stupid, nasty boy, Homer, and you always will be. Well, if you won't help me, I'll have to find out by myself, start at the beginning and trace who'd want to steal a funny-looking bear like that. Who donated the bear?"

"People just put toys in the boxes near the door. We pick out the ones for the auction and the ones for the Santa Claus boxes. No way of knowing who gave what."

I knew he wouldn't be any help, so I got Carrie and Debbie and went to the one man in town who might help me trace the bear, Mr. Wong. He doesn't have just a grocery, a *credit* grocery, thank God; he carries things you wouldn't even find in Pittsburgh. His kids were all grown, all famous scientists and doctors and professors, but he still stayed here, even after Mrs. Wong died. Mrs. Wong never spoke a word of English, but she understood everything. Used to be, her kids all came here for Chinese New Year—that's about a month after ours—and they'd have a big feast and bring the grandchildren. Funny how Mrs. Wong was able to raise six kids in real hard times, but none of her children has more than two. Now, on Chinese New Year, Mr. Wong closes the store for a week and goes to one of his kids. But he always comes back here.

"Look I have for you," he said, and gave Debbie a little snake on a stick, the kind where you turn it and the snake moves like it's real. She was still sniffling, but she smiled a little. The store was chock full of all kinds of Chinese things; little dragons and fat Buddhas with bobbing heads and candied ginger. I knew I was in the right place.

"Did you ever sell anyone a teddy bear?" I asked. "Not a regular teddy bear, but a black one with big purple eyes."

"No sell," he said. "Give."

"Okay." I had struck gold on the first try. "Who'd you give it to?"

"Nobody. Put in box in firehouse."

"You mean for the auction?"

"Petrina nice girl. Like Debbie. Very sick. Must help."

"But ..." Dead end. I'd have to find another way to trace the bear so I could find out who'd want to steal it. "All right, where'd you get the teddy bear?"

"Grandmother give me. Before I go U. S. Make good luck. Not teddy bear. Blue bear. From Kansu."

"You mean there's a bear that looks like this?"

"Oh yes. Chinese bear. Moon bear. Very danger. Strong. In Kansu."

"Your grandmother *made* it? For you?"

"Not *make,* make. Grandfather big hunter, kill bear. Moon bear very big good luck. Eat bear, get strong, very good. Have good luck in U.S."

"That bear is real bearskin?"

"Oh yes. Grandmother cut little piece for here," he put his hand under his chin, "and for here," he put his hand on his chest. "Make moon." He moved his hand in the crescent shape the bear had on its chest. "Why call moon bear."

"You had that since you were a little boy?" I was touched. "And you gave it for Petrina? Instead of your own grandchildren?"

"Own grandchildren want sportcar, computer, skateboard, not old Chinese bear."

Well, that was typical of all modern kids, not just Chinese, but it didn't get me any closer to finding out who had stolen the teddy bear, the moon bear. Deborah, though, was listening with wide eyes, no longer crying. But what was worse, that romantic story would make it all the harder on her if I didn't get that bear back. She went up to the counter and asked, "Did it come in?"

"Oh yes." He reached down and put a wooden lazy tongs on top of the counter.

"I got it for you, Grandma," Debbie said, "for your arthritis, so you don't have to bend down. I was going to save it for under the tree, but you looked so sad . . ."

God bless you, Deborah, I said in my heart, that's the answer. I put my fingers in the scissor grip and extended the tongs. They were only about three feet long, not long enough, and they were already beginning to bend under their own weight. No way anyone, not even Mildred Ungaric, could use them to steal the moon bear. Then I knew. For sure. I turned around and there it was, hanging on the top shelf. I turned back to Mr. Wong and said, casually, "What do you call that thing grocers use to get cans from the top shelf? The long stickhandle with the grippers at the end?"

"Don't know. In Chinese I say, 'Get can high shelf.' "

"Doesn't matter. Why did you steal the bear back? Decided to sell it to a museum or something?"

" 'No. Why I steal? If I want sell, I no give." He was puzzled, not insulted. "Somebody steal moon bear?"

He was right. But so was I. At least I knew *how* it was stolen. You didn't need a "get can high shelf." All the thief needed was a long thing with a hook on the end. Or a noose. Like a broomstick. Or a fishing rod. Anything that would reach from where you were standing to the top of the back row so you could get the bear without knocking over the shelves or the other toys. It had to be Mildred Ungaric; she might be mean, but she wasn't stupid. Any woman had enough long sticks in her kitchen, and enough string and hooks to make a bear-stealer, though she'd look awful funny walking down the street carrying one of those. But it didn't have to be that way. There was something in the firehouse that anyone could use, one of those long poles with the hooks on the end they break your windows with when you have a fire. All you'd have to do is get that hook under the string that held the number tag around the moon bear's neck and do it quietly enough not to wake Levi Porter. Which meant that anyone in town could have stolen the moon bear.

But who would? It would be like stealing from poor little Petrina herself. Mildred was mean, but even she wouldn't do that. Homer was nasty; maybe he accused me to cover up for himself. Mr. Wong might have changed his mind, in spite of what he said; you don't give away a sixty-year-old childhood memory like that without regrets. Levi Porter was in the best position to do it; there was only his word that he slept all through the night and he has eight kids he can hardly feed. Heck, anyone in town could have done it. All I knew was that I didn't.

So who stole the moon bear?

That night I made a special supper for Carrie, and Deborah served. There's nothing a waitress enjoys so much on her time off as being served. I know; there was a time I waitressed myself. After supper, Carrie put Deborah to bed and read to her, watched TV for a while, then got ready to turn in herself. There's really nothing for a young woman to do in Pitman unless she's the kind that runs around with the truckers that stop by, and Carrie wasn't that type. She had made one mistake, trusted one boy, but that could have happened to anybody. And she did what was right and was raising Deborah to be a pride to us all.

I stayed up and sat in my rocker, trying to think of who would steal that bear, but there was no way to find that out. At least it wasn't a kid, a little kid, who had done it; those firemen's poles are heavy. Of course it could have been a teenager, but what would a teenager want with a funny-looking little bear like that? There were plenty of better toys in the lower rows to tempt a teenager, toys that anyone could take in a second with no trouble at all. But none of them had been stolen. No, it wasn't a teenager; I was pretty sure of that.

Finally, I went to sleep. Or to bed, at least. I must have been awake for half the night and didn't come up with anything. But I did know one thing I had to do.

That night being the last night before Christmas Eve, they were going to hold the auction for Petrina in the fire house. I didn't want to get there too early; no point in making Deborah feel bad seeing all the other presents bought up and knowing she wasn't going to get her moon bear. But I did want her to know it wasn't just idle talk when I promised I'd get her bear back.

Debbie and I waited until the last toy was auctioned off and Porter announced the total. Four thousand, three hundred seventy-two dollars and fifty cents. More than we had expected and more than enough to send the Rozovskis to New York. Then I stood up and said, "I bid eighteen dollars, cash, for the little black bear, Number 273."

Homer looked embarrassed. "Please, Mrs. Slowinski, you know we don't have that bear any more."

"I just want to make sure, *Mr.* Curtis, that when I find that bear, it's mine. Mine and Deborah's. So you can just add eighteen dollars to your total, *Mr.* Porter, and when that bear turns up, it's mine." Now if anyone was seen with the bear, everybody'd know whose it was. And what's more, if the thief had a guilty conscience, he'd know where to return the bear.

That night I stayed in my rocking chair again, rocking and thinking, thinking and rocking. I was sure I was on the right track. Why would anyone want to take the moon bear? That had to be the way to find the thief; to figure out why anyone would take the bear. But as much as I rocked, much as I thought, I was stuck right there. Finally, after midnight, I gave up. There was no way to figure it out. Maybe if I slept on it . . . Only trouble was, tomorrow was Christmas Eve, and even if I figured out who took the bear, there was no way I could get it back in time to put it under the tree so Debbie would find it when she woke up Christmas morning. For all I knew, the bear was in Pittsburgh by now, or even back in China. Maybe I shouldn't have warned the thief by making such a fuss when I bought the missing bear.

Going to bed didn't help. I lay awake, thinking of everything that had happened, from the time we first stood behind the firetrucks and saw the bear, to the time in Mr. Wong's store when I figured out how the bear had been stolen. Then all of a sudden it was clear. I knew who had stolen the bear. That is I knew *how* it had been stolen and that told me *who* had stolen it which told me how, which ... What really happened was I knew it all, all at once. Of course, I didn't know *where* the bear was, not exactly, but I'd get to that eventually. One thing I had to remember was not to tell Deborah what I had figured out. Not that I was wrong—I *wasn't* wrong; everything fit too perfectly—but I might not be able to get the bear back. After all, how hard would it be to destroy the bear, to burn it or throw it in the dump, rather than go to jail?

The next morning Deborah woke me. "It's all right, Grandma," she said. "I didn't really want that old moon bear. I really wanted a wetting doll. Or a plain doll. So don't cry." I wasn't aware I was crying, but I guess I was. Whatever else I had done in my life, whatever else Carrie had done, to bring to life, to bring up such a sweet wonderful human being, a girl like this, one to be so proud of, that made up for everything. I only wished Jake could have been here with me to see her. And Wesley Sladen, the fool, to see what he'd missed.

I didn't say anything during breakfast—we always let Carrie sleep late because of her hours but right after we washed up, I dressed Deborah warmly. "We're going for a long walk," I told her. She took my hand and we started out.

I went to the garage where he worked and motioned Levi Porter to come out. He came, wiping his hands on a rag. Without hesitating, I told him what I had to tell him. "You stole the teddy bear. You swiveled the ladder on the ladder truck around, pointing in the right direction, and turned the winch until the ladder extended over the bear. Then you crawled out on the flat ladder and stole the bear. After you put everything back where it was before, you went to sleep."

Well, he didn't bat an eye, just nodded his head. "Yep, that's the way it was," he said, not even saying he was sorry. "I figured you knew something when you bought the missing bear. Nobody throws away eighteen dollars for nothing." Deborah just stared up at him, not understanding how a human being could do such a thing to her. She took my hand for comfort, keeping me between her and Shorty Porter.

"Well, that's *my* bear," I said. "I bought it for Deborah; she had her heart set on it." He wasn't a bit moved. "She loved that bear, Porter. You broke her heart."

"I'm sorry about that, Miz Sophie," he said, "I really didn't want to hurt anybody. I didn't know about Debbie when I stole the bear."

"Well, the least you could do is give it back. If you do, I might consider, just *consider,* not setting the law on you." I didn't really want to put a man with eight children in jail and, up till now, he'd been a pretty good citizen, but I wasn't about to show him that. "So you just go get it, *Mr.* Porter. Right now, and hop to it."

"Okay, Miz Sophie, but it ain't here. We'll have to drive over." He stuck his head in the shop and told Ed Mahaffey that he had to go someplace, be back soon, and we got in his pickup truck.

I wasn't paying attention to where we were going and when he stopped, my heart stopped too. Petrina was lying on the couch in the living room, clutching the moon bear to her skinny little chest. Irma was just standing there wondering what had brought us. "It's about the teddy bear," Levi Porter apologized. "It belongs to Debbie. I have to take it back."

We went over to the couch. "You see," he explained to me, "on opening night, Petrina fell in love with the bear. I wanted to get it for her, but I didn't have any money left. So I took it, figuring it wasn't really stealing; everything there was for Petrina anyway. If I'd knowed about Debbie, I would've worked out something else, maybe."

He leaned over the couch and gently, very gently, took the moon bear out of Petrina's hands. "I'm sorry, honey," he told the thin little girl, "it's really Debbie's. I'll get you a different bear soon." The sad little girl let the bear slip slowly out of her hands, not resisting, but not really letting go either. She said nothing, so used to hurt, so used to disappointment, so used to having everything slip away from her, but her soft dark eyes filled with tears as Shorty took the bear. I could have sworn that the moon bear's purple glass eyes looked full of pain, too.

Shorty put the bear gently into Debbie's arms and she cradled the bear closely to her. She put her face next to the bear's and kissed him and whispered something to him that I didn't catch, my hearing not being what it used to be. Then she went over to the couch and put the bear back into Petrina's hands. "He likes you better," she said. "He wants to stay with you. He loves you."

We stood there for a moment, all of us, silent. Petrina clutched the bear to her, tightly, lovingly, and almost smiled. Irma started crying and I might've too, a little. Shorty picked Deborah up and kissed her like she was his own. "You're blessed," he said to me. "From heaven."

He drove us home, and on the way back I asked Debbie what she said to the bear. "I was just telling him his name," she said innocently, "and he said it was exactly right."

"What is his name?" I asked.

"Oh, that was *my* name for him, Grandma. Petrina told him *her* name; he has a different name now," and that's all she would say about it.

I invited Shorty in but he couldn't stay; had to get back to the garage. If he took too long—well, there were plenty of good mechanics out of work. He promised he'd get Deborah another gift for Christmas, but he couldn't do it in time for tonight. I told him not to worry; I'd work out something.

When we got home, I got started making cookies with chocolate sprinkles, the kind Deborah likes. She helped me. After a while, when the first batch of cookies was baking, her cheeks powdered with flour and her pretty face turned away, she said, quietly, "It's all right not to get a present for Christmas. As long as you know somebody *wanted* to give it to you and spent all her money to get it."

My heart was so full I couldn't say anything for a while. Then I lifted her onto my lap and hugged her to my heart.

"Oh, Debbie my love, you'll understand when you're older, but you've just gotten the best Christmas present of all: the chance to make a little child happy."

I held her away and looked into her wise, innocent eyes and wondered if, maybe, she already understood that.

MYSTERY FOR CHRISTMAS

BY ANTHONY BOUCHER

That was why the Benson jewel robbery was solved—because Aram Melekian was too much for Mr. Quilter's temper.

His almost invisible eyebrows soared, and the scalp of his close-cropped head twitched angrily. "Damme!" said Mr. Quilter, and in that mild and archaic oath there was more compressed fury than in paragraphs of uncensored profanity. "So you, sir, are the untrammeled creative artist, and I am a drudging, hampering hack!"

Aram Melekian tilted his hat a trifle more jauntily. "That's the size of it, brother. And if you hamper this untrammeled opus any more, Metropolis Pictures is going to be sueing its youngest genius for breach of contract."

Mr. Quilter rose to his full lean height. "I've seen them come and go," he announced; "and there hasn't been a one of them, sir, who failed to learn something from me. What is so creative about pouring out the full vigor of your young life? The creative task is mine, molding that vigor, shaping it to some end."

"Go play with your blue pencil," Melekian suggested. "I've got a dream coming on."

151

"Because I have never produced anything myself, you young men jeer at me. You never see that your successful screen plays are more my effort than your inspiration." Mr. Quilter's thin frame was aquiver.

"Then what do you need us for?"

"What— Damme, sir, what indeed? Ha!" said Mr. Quilter loudly. "I'll show you. I'll pick the first man off the street that has life and a story in him. What more do you contribute? And through me he'll turn out a job that will sell. If I do this, sir, then will you consent to the revisions I've asked of you?"

"Go lay an egg," said Aram Melekian. "And I've no doubt you will."

Mr. Quilter stalked out of the studio with high dreams. He saw the horny-handed son of toil out of whom he had coaxed a masterpiece signing a contract with F.X. He saw a discomfited Armenian genius in the background busily devouring his own words. He saw himself freed of his own sense of frustration, proving at last that his was the significant part of writing.

He felt a bumping shock and the squealing of brakes. The next thing he saw was the asphalt paving.

Mr. Quilter rose to his feet undecided whether to curse the driver for knocking him down or bless him for stopping so miraculously short of danger. The young man in the brown suit was so disarmingly concerned that the latter choice was inevitable.

"I'm awfully sorry," the young man blurted. "Are you hurt? It's this bad wing of mine, I guess." His left arm was in a sling.

"Nothing at all, sir. My fault. I was preoccupied . . ."

They stood awkwardly for a moment, each striving for a phrase that was not mere politeness. Then they both spoke at once.

"You came out of that studio," the young man said. "Do you" (his tone was awed) "do you *work* there?"

And Mr. Quilter had spotted a sheaf of eight and a half by eleven paper protruding from the young man's pocket. "Are you a writer, sir? Is that a manuscript?"

The young man shuffled and came near blushing. "Naw. I'm not a writer. I'm a policeman. But I'm going to be a writer. This is a story I was trying to tell about what happened to me— But are you a writer? In *there*?"

Mr. Quilter's eyes were aglow under their invisible brows. "I, sir," he announced proudly, "am what makes writers tick. Are you interested?"

He was also, he might have added, what makes *detectives* tick. But he did not know that yet.

The Christmas trees were lighting up in front yards and in windows as Officer Tom Smith turned his rickety Model A onto the side street where Mr. Quilter lived. Hollywood is full of these quiet streets, where ordinary people live and move and have their being, and are happy or unhappy as chance wills, but both in a normal and unspectacular way. This is really Hollywood—the Hollywood that patronizes the twenty-cent fourth-run houses and crowds the stores on the Boulevard on Dollar Day.

To Mr. Quilter, saturated at the studio with the other Hollywood, this was always a relief. Kids were playing ball in the evening sun, radios were tuning in to Amos and Andy, and from the small houses came either the smell of cooking or the clatter of dish-washing.

And the Christmas trees, he knew, had been decorated not for the benefit of the photographers from the fan magazines, but because the children liked them and they looked warm and friendly from the street.

"Gosh, Mr. Quilter," Tom Smith was saying, "this is sure a swell break for me. You know, I'm a good copper. But to be honest I don't know as I'm very bright. And that's why I want to write, because maybe that way I can train myself to be and then I won't be a plain patrolman all my life. And besides, this writing, it kind of itches-like inside you."

"*Cacoëthes scribendi,*" observed Mr. Quilter, not unkindly. "You see, sir, you have hit, in your fumbling way, on one of the classic expressions for your condition."

"Now that's what I mean. You know what I mean even when I don't say it. Between us, Mr. Quilter ..."

Mr. Quilter, his long thin legs outdistancing even the policeman's, led the way into his bungalow and on down the hall to a room which at first glance contained nothing but thousands of books. Mr. Quilter waved at them. "Here, sir, is assembled every helpful fact that mortal need know. But I cannot breathe life into these dry bones. Books are not written from books. But I can provide bones, and correctly articulated, for the life which you, sir— But here is a chair. And a reading lamp. Now, sir, let me hear your story."

Tom Smith shifted uncomfortably on the chair. "The trouble is," he confessed, "it hasn't got an ending."

Mr. Quilter beamed. "When I have heard it, I shall demonstrate to you, sir, the one ending it inevitably must have."

"I sure hope you will, because it's got to have and I promised her it would have and— You know Beverly Benson?"

"Why, yes. I entered the industry at the beginning of talkies. She was still somewhat in evidence. But why ... ?"

"I was only a kid when she made *Sable Sin* and *Orchids at Breakfast* and all the rest, and I thought she was something pretty marvelous. There was a girl in our high school was supposed to look like her, and I used to think, 'Gee, if I could ever see the real Beverly Benson!' And last night I did."

"Hm. And this story, sir, is the result?"

"Yeah. And this too." He smiled wryly and indicated his wounded arm. "But I better read you the story." He cleared his throat loudly. "*The Red and Green Mystery*," he declaimed. "By Arden Van Arden."

"A pseudonym, sir?"

"Well, I sort of thought ... Tom Smith—that doesn't sound like a writer."

"Arden Van Arden, sir, doesn't sound like anything. But go on."

And Officer Tom Smith began his narrative:

THE RED AND GREEN MYSTERY

by ARDEN VAN ARDEN

It was a screwy party for the police to bust in on. Not that it was a raid or anything like that. God knows I've run into some bughouse parties that way, but I'm assigned to the jewelry squad now under Lieutenant Michaels, and when this call came in he took three other guys and me and we shot out to the big house in Laurel Canyon.

I wasn't paying much attention to where we were going and I wouldn't have known the place anyway, but I knew *her*, all right. She was standing in the doorway waiting for us. For just a minute it stumped me who she was, but then I knew. It was the eyes mostly. She'd changed a lot since *Sable Sin*, but you still couldn't miss the Beverly Benson eyes. The rest of her had got older (not older exactly either— you might maybe say richer) but the eyes were still the same. She had red hair. They didn't have technicolor when she was in pictures and I hadn't even known what color her hair was. It struck me funny seeing her like that—the way I'd been nuts about her when I was a kid and not even knowing what color her hair was.

She had on a funny dress—a little-girl kind of thing with a short skirt with flounces, I guess you call them. It looked familiar, but I couldn't make it. Not until I saw the mask that was lying in the hall, and then I knew. She was dressed like Minnie Mouse. It turned out later they all were—not like Minnie Mouse, but like all the characters in the cartoons. It was that kind of a party—a Disney Christmas party. There were studio drawings all over the walls, and there were little figures of extinct animals and winged ponies holding the lights on the Christmas tree.

She came right to the point. I could see Michaels liked that; some of these women throw a big act and it's an hour before you know what's been stolen. "It's my emeralds and rubies," she said. "They're gone. There are some other pieces missing too, but I don't so much care about them. The emeralds and the rubies are the important thing. You've got to find them."

"Necklaces?" Michaels asked.

"A necklace."

"Of emeralds *and* rubies?" Michaels knows his jewelry. His old man is in the business and tried to bring him up in it, but he joined the force. He knows a thing or two just the same, and his left eyebrow does tricks when he hears or sees something that isn't kosher. It was doing tricks now.

"I know that may sound strange, Lieutenant, but this is no time for discussing the esthetics of jewelry. It struck me once that it would be exciting to have red and green in one necklace, and I had it made. They're perfectly cut and matched, and it could never be duplicated."

Michaels didn't look happy. "You could drape it on a Christmas tree," he said. But Beverly Benson's Christmas tree was a cold white with the little animals holding blue lights.

Those Benson eyes were generally lovely and melting. Now they flashed. "Lieutenant, I summoned you to find my jewelry, not to criticize my taste. If I wanted a cultural opinion, I should hardly consult the police."

"You could do worse," Michaels said. "Now tell us all about it."

She took us into the library. The other men Michaels sent off to guard the exits, even if there wasn't much chance of the thief still sticking around. The Lieutenant told me once, when we were off duty, "Tom," he said, "you're the most useful man in my detail. Some of the others can think, and some of them can act; but there's not a damned one of them can just stand there and look so much like the Law." He's a little guy himself and kind of on the smooth and dapper side; so he keeps me with him to back him up, just standing there.

There wasn't much to what she told us. Just that she was giving this Disney Christmas party, like I said, and it was going along fine. Then late in the evening, when almost everybody had gone home, they got to talking about jewelry. She didn't know who started the talk that way, but there they were. And she told them about the emeralds and rubies.

"Then Fig—Philip Newton, you know—the photographer who does all those marvelous sand dunes and magnolia blossoms and things—" (her voice went all sort of tender when she mentioned him, and I could see Michaels taking it all in) "Fig said he didn't believe it. He felt the same way you do, Lieutenant, and I'm sure I can't see why. 'It's unworthy of you, darling,' he said. So I laughed and tried to tell him they were really beautiful—for they are, you know—and when he went on scoffing I said, 'All right, then, I'll show you.' So I went into the little dressing room where I keep my jewel box, and they weren't there. And that's all I know."

Then Michaels settled down to questions. When had she last seen the necklace? Was the lock forced? Had there been any prowlers around? What else was missing? And suchlike.

Beverly Benson answered impatiently, like she expected us to just go out there like that and grab the thief and say, "Here you are, lady." She had shown the necklace to another guest early in the party—he'd gone home long ago, but she gave us the name and address to check. No, the lock hadn't been forced. They hadn't seen anything suspicious, either. There were some small things missing, too—a couple of diamond rings, a star sapphire pendant, a pair of pearl earrings—but those didn't worry her so much. It was the emerald and ruby necklace that she wanted.

That left eyebrow went to work while Michaels thought about what she'd said. "If the lock wasn't forced, that lets out a chance prowler. It was somebody who knew you, who'd had a chance to lift your key or take an impression of it. Where'd you keep it?"

"The key? In my handbag usually. Tonight it was in a box on my dressing table."

Michaels sort of groaned. "And women wonder why jewels get stolen! Smith, get Ferguson and have him go over the box for prints. In the meantime, Miss Benson, give me a list of all your guests tonight. We'll take up the servants later. I'm warning you now it's a ten-to-one chance you'll ever see your Christmas tree ornament again unless a fence sings; but we'll do what we can. Then I'll deliver my famous little lecture on safes, and we'll pray for the future."

When I'd seen Ferguson, I waited for Michaels in the room where the guests were. There were only five left, and I didn't know who they were yet. They'd all taken off their masks; but they still had on their cartoon costumes. It felt screwy to sit there among them and think: This is serious, this is a felony, and look at those bright funny costumes.

Donald Duck was sitting by himself, with one hand resting on his long-billed mask while the other made steady grabs for the cigarette box beside him. His face looked familiar; I thought maybe I'd seen him in bits.

Three of them sat in a group: Mickey Mouse, Snow White, and Dopey. Snow White looked about fourteen at first, and it took you a while to realize she was a woman and a swell one at that. She was a little brunette, slender and cool-looking—a simple real kind of person that didn't seem to belong in a Hollywood crowd. Mickey Mouse was a hefty blond guy about as tall as I am and built like a tackle that could hold any line; but his face didn't go with his body. It was shrewd-like, and what they call sensitive. Dopey looked just that—a nice guy and not too bright.

Then over in another corner was a Little Pig. I don't know do they have names, but this was the one that wears a sailor suit and plays the fiddle. He had bushy hair sticking out from under the sailor cap and long skillful-looking hands stretched in front of him. The fiddle was beside him, but he didn't touch it. He was passed out—dead to the world, close as I could judge.

He and Donald were silent, but the group of three talked a little.

"I guess it didn't work," Dopey said.

"You couldn't help that, Harvey." Snow White's voice was just like I expected—not like Snow White's in the picture, but deep and smooth, like a stream that's running in the shade with moss on its banks. "Even an agent can't cast people."

"You're a swell guy, Madison," Mickey Mouse said.

"You tried, and thanks. But if it's no go, hell, it's just no go. It's up to her."

"Miss Benson is surely more valuable to your career." The running stream was ice cold.

Now maybe I haven't got anything else that'd make me a good detective, but I do have curiosity, and here's where I saw a way to satisfy it. I spoke to all of them and I said, "I'd better take down some information while we're waiting for the Lieutenant." I started on Donald Duck. "Name?"

"Daniel Wappingham." The voice was English. I could tell that much. I don't have such a good ear for stuff like that, but I thought maybe it wasn't the best English.

"Occupation?"

"Actor."

And I took down the address and the rest of it. Then I turned to the drunk and shook him. He woke up part way but he didn't hear what I was saying. He just threw his head back and said loudly, "Waltzes! Ha!" and went under again. His voice was gutteral—some kind of German, I guessed. I let it go at that and went over to the three.

Dopey's name was Harvey Madison; occupation, actor's representative—tenpercenter to you. Mickey Mouse was Philip Newton; occupation, photographer. (That was the guy Beverly Benson mentioned, the one she sounded that-away about.) And Snow White was Jane Newton.

"Any relation?" I asked.

"Yes and no," she said, so soft I could hardly hear her.

"Mrs. Newton," Mickey Mouse stated, "was once my wife." And the silence was so strong you could taste it.

I got it then. The two of them sitting there, remembering all the little things of their life together, being close to each other and yet somehow held apart. And on Christmas, too, when you remember things. There was still something between them even if they didn't admit it themselves. But Beverly Benson seemed to have a piece of the man, and where did Dopey fit in?

It sort of worried me. They looked like swell people—people that belonged together. But it was my job to worry about the necklace and not about people's troubles. I was glad Michaels came in just then.

He was being polite at the moment, explaining to Beverly Benson how Ferguson hadn't got anywhere with the prints and how the jewels were probably miles away by now. "But we'll do what we can," he said. "We'll talk to these people and find out what's possible. I doubt, however, if you'll ever see that necklace again. It was insured, of course, Miss Benson?"

"Of course. So were the other things, and with them I don't mind. But this necklace I couldn't conceivably duplicate, Lieutenant."

Just then Michaels' eye lit on Donald Duck, and the eyebrow did tricks worth putting in a cartoon. "We'll take you one by one," he said. "You with the tail-feathers, we'll start with you. Come along, Smith."

Donald Duck grabbed a fresh cigarette, thought a minute, then reached out again for a handful. He whistled off key and followed us into the library.

"I gave all the material to your stooge here, Lieutenant," he began. "Name, Wappingham. Occupation, actor. Address——"

Michaels was getting so polite it had me bothered. "You won't mind, sir," he purred, "if I suggest a few corrections in your statement?"

Donald looked worried. "Don't you think I know my own name?"

"Possibly. But would you mind if I altered the statement to read: Name, Alfred Higgins. Occupation, jewel thief—conceivably reformed?"

The Duck wasn't so bad hit as you might have thought. He let out a pretty fair laugh and said, "So the fat's in the fire at last. But I'm glad you concede the possibility of my having reformed."

"The possibility, yes." Michaels underlined the word. "You admit you're Higgins?"

"Why not? You can't blame me for not telling you right off; it wouldn't look good when somebody had just been up to my old tricks. But now that you know—— And by the way, Lieutenant, just how do you know?"

"Some bright boy at Scotland Yard spotted you in an American picture. Sent your description and record out to us just in case you ever took up your career again."

"Considerate of him, wasn't it?"

But Michaels wasn't in a mood for bright chatter any longer. We got down to work. We stripped that duck costume off the actor and left him shivering while we went over it inch by inch. He didn't like it much.

At last Michaels let him get dressed again. "You came in your car?"

"Yes."

"You're going home in a taxi. We could hold you on suspicion, but I'd sooner play it this way."

"Now I understand," Donald said, "what they mean by the high-handed American police procedure." And he went back into the other room with us.

All the same that was a smart move of Michaels'. It meant that Wappingham-Higgins-Duck would either have to give up all hope of the jewels (he certainly didn't have them on him) or lead us straight to them, because of course I knew a tail would follow that taxi and camp on his doorstep all next week if need be.

Donald Duck said goodnight to his hostess and nodded to the other guests. Then he picked up his mask.

"Just a minute," Michaels said. "Let's have a look at that."

"At this?" he asked innocent-like and backed toward the French window. Then he was standing there with an automatic in his hand. It was little but damned nasty-looking. I never thought what a good holster that long bill would make.

"Stay where you are, gentlemen," he said calmly. "I'm leaving undisturbed, *if* you don't mind."

The room was frozen still. Beverly Benson and Snow White let out little gasps of terror. The drunk was still dead to the world. The other two men looked at us and did nothing. It was Donald's round.

Or would've been if I hadn't played football in high school. It was a crazy chance, but I took it. I was the closest to him, only his eyes were on Michaels. It was a good flying tackle and it brought him to the ground in a heap consisting mostly of me. The mask smashed as we rolled over on it and I saw bright glitters pouring out.

Ferguson and O'Hara were there by now. One of them picked up his gun and the other snapped on the handcuffs. I got to my feet and turned to Michaels and Beverly Benson. They began to say things both at once about what a swell thing I'd done and then I keeled over.

When I came to I was on a couch in a little dark room. I learned later it was the dressing room where the necklace had been stolen. Somebody was bathing my arm and sobbing.

I sort of half sat up and said, "Where am I?" I always thought it was just in stories people said that, but it was the first thing popped into my mind.

"You're all right," a cool voice told me. "It's only a flesh wound."

"And I didn't feel a thing. . . . You mean he winged me?"

"I guess that's what you call it. When I told the Lieutenant I was a nurse he said I could fix you up and they wouldn't need the ambulance. You're all right now." Her voice was shaky in the dark, but I knew it was Snow White.

"Well, anyways, that broke the case pretty quick."

"But it didn't." And she explained: Donald had been up to his old tricks, all right; but what he had hidden in his bill was the diamonds and the sapphire and the pearl earrings, only no emerald and ruby necklace. Beverly Benson was wild, and Michaels and our men were combing the house from top to bottom to see where he'd stashed it.

"There," she said. She finished the story and the bandaging at the same time. "Can you stand up all right now?"

I was still kind of punchy. Nothing else could excuse me for what I said next. But she was so sweet and tender and good I wanted to say something nice, so like a dumb jerk I up and said, "You'd make some man a grand wife."

That was what got her. She just went to pieces—dissolved, you might say. I'm not used to tears on the shoulder of my uniform, but what could I do? I didn't try to say anything—just patted her back and let her talk. And I learned all about it.

How she'd married Philip Newton back in '29 when he was a promising young architect and she was an heiress just out of finishing school. How the fortune she was heiress to went fooey like all the others and her father took the quick way out. How the architect business went all to hell with no building going on and just when things were worst she had a baby. And then how Philip started drinking, and finally— Well, anyways, there it was.

They'd both pulled themselves together now. She was making enough as a nurse to keep the kid (she was too proud to take alimony), and Philip was doing fine in this arty photographic line he'd taken up. A Newton photograph was The Thing to Have in the smart Hollywood set. But they couldn't come together again, not while he was such a success. If she went to him, he'd think she was begging; if he came to her, she'd think he was being noble. And Beverly Benson had set her cap for him.

Then this agent Harvey Madison (that's Dopey), who had known them both when, decided to try and fix things. He brought Snow White to this party; neither of them knew the other would be here. And it was a party and it was Christmas, and some of their happiest memories were Christmases together. I guess that's pretty much true of everybody. So she felt everything all over again, only—

"You don't know what it's done for me to tell you this. Please don't feel hurt; but in that uniform and everything you don't seem quite like a person. I can talk and feel free. And this has been hurting me all night and I had to say it."

I wanted to take the two of them and knock their heads together; only first off I had to find that emerald and ruby necklace. It isn't my job to heal broken hearts. I was feeling O.K. now, so we went back to the others.

Only they weren't there. There wasn't anybody in the room but only the drunk. I guessed where Mickey and Dopey were: stripped and being searched.

"Who's that?" I asked Snow White.

She looked at the Little Pig. "Poor fellow. He's been going through torture tonight too. That's Bela Strauss."

"Bella's a woman's name."

"He's part Hungarian." (I guess that might explain anything.) "He comes from Vienna. They brought him out here to write music for pictures because his name is Strauss. But he's a very serious composer—you know, like . . ." and she said some tongue twisters that didn't mean anything to me. "They think because his name is Strauss he can write all sorts of pretty dance tunes, and they won't let him write anything else. It's made him all twisted and unhappy, and he drinks too much."

"I can see that." I walked over and shook him. The sailor cap fell off. He stirred and looked up at me. I think it was the uniform that got him. He sat up sharp and said something in I guess German. Then he thought around a while and found some words in English.

"Why are you here? Why the po-lice?" It came out in little one-syllable lumps, like he had to hunt hard for each sound.

I told him. I tried to make it simple, but that wasn't easy. Snow White knew a little German, so she helped.

"Ach!" he sighed. "And I through it all slept!"

"That's one word for it," I said.

"But this thief of jewels—him I have seen."

It was a sweet job to get it out of him, but it boiled down to this: Where he passed out was on that same couch where they took me—right in the dressing-room. He came to once when he heard somebody in there, and he saw the person take something out of a box. Something red and green.

"Who was it?"

"The face, you understand, I do not see it. But the costume, yes. I see that clear. It was Mikki Maus." It sounded funny to hear something as American as Mickey Mouse in an accent like that.

It took Snow White a couple of seconds to realize who wore the Mickey Mouse outfit. Then she said "Philip" and fainted.

*   *   *

Officer Tom Smith laid down his manuscript. "That's all, Mr. Quilter."

"All, sir?"

"When Michaels came in, I told him. He figured Newton must've got away with the necklace and then the English crook made his try later and got the other stuff. They didn't find the necklace anywhere; but he must've pulled a fast one and stashed it away some place. With direct evidence like that, what can you do? They're holding him."

"And you chose, sir, not to end your story on that note of finality?"

"I couldn't, Mr. Quilter. I . . . I like that girl who was Snow White. I want to see the two of them together again and I'd sooner he was innocent. And besides, when we were leaving, Beverly Benson caught me alone. She said, 'I can't talk to your Lieutenant. He is *not* sympathetic. But you . . .' " Tom Smith almost blushed. "So she went on about how certain she was that Newton was innocent and begged me to help her prove it. So I promised."

"Hm," said Mr. Quilter. "Your problem, sir, is simple. You have good human values there in your story. Now we must round them out properly. And the solution is simple. We have two women in love with the hero, one highly sympathetic and the other less so; for the spectacle of a *passée* actress pursuing a new celebrity is not a pleasant one. This less sympathetic woman, to please the audience, must redeem herself with a gesture of self-immolation to secure the hero's happiness with the heroine. Therefore, sir, let her confess to the robbery."

"Confess to the . . . But Mr. Quilter, that makes a different story out of it. I'm trying to write as close as I can to what happened. And I promised—"

"Damme, sir, it's obvious. She did steal the necklace herself. She hasn't worked for years. She must need money. You mentioned insurance. The necklace was probably pawned long ago, and now she is trying to collect."

"But that won't work. It really was stolen. Somebody

saw it earlier in the evening, and the search didn't locate it. And believe me, that squad knows how to search."

"Fiddle-faddle, sir." Mr. Quilter's close-cropped scalp was beginning to twitch. "What was seen must have been a paste imitation. She could dissolve that readily in acid and dispose of it down the plumbing. And Wappingham's presence makes her plot doubly sure; she knew him for what he was, and invited him as a scapegoat."

Tom Smith squirmed. "I'd almost think you were right, Mr. Quilter. Only Bela Strauss did see Newton take the necklace."

Mr. Quilter laughed. "If that is all that perturbs you . . ." He rose to his feet. "Come with me, sir. One of my neighbors is a Viennese writer now acting as a reader in German for Metropolis. He is also new in this country; his cultural background is identical with Strauss's. Come. But first we must step down to the corner drugstore and purchase what I believe is termed a comic book."

Mr. Quilter, his eyes agleam, hardly apologized for their intrusion into the home of the Viennese writer. He simply pointed at a picture in the comic book and demanded, "Tell me, sir. What character is that?"

The bemused Viennese smiled. "Why, that is Mikki Maus."

Mr. Quilter's finger rested on a pert little drawing of Minnie.

Philip Newton sat in the cold jail cell, but he was oblivious of the cold. He was holding his wife's hands through the bars and she was saying, "I could come to you now, dear, where I couldn't before. Then you might have thought it was just because you were successful, but now I can tell you how much I love you and need you—need you even when you're in disgrace. . . ."

They were kissing through the bars when Michaels came with the good news. "She's admitted it, all right. It was just the way Smith reconstructed it. She'd destroyed the paste replica and was trying to use us to pull off an insurance frame. She cracked when we had Strauss point out a picture of what he called 'Mikki Maus.' So you're free again, Newton. How's that for a Christmas present?"

"I've got a better one, officer. We're getting married again."

"You wouldn't need a new wedding ring, would you?" Michaels asked with filial devotion. "Michaels, Fifth between Spring and Broadway—fine stock."

Mr. Quilter laid down the final draft of Tom Smith's story, complete now with ending, and fixed the officer with a reproachful gaze. "You omitted, sir, the explanation of why such a misunderstanding should arise."

Tom Smith shifted uncomfortably. "I'm afraid, Mr. Quilter, I couldn't remember all that straight."

"It is simple. The noun *Maus* in German is of feminine gender. Therefore a *Mikki Maus* is a female. The male, naturally, is a *Mikki Mäserich.* I recall a delightful Viennese song of some seasons ago, which we once employed as background music, wherein the singer declares that he and his beloved will be forever paired, *'wie die Mikki Mikki Mikki Mikki Mikki Maus und der Mikki Mäserich.'* "

"Gosh," said Tom Smith. "You know a lot of things."

Mr. Quilter allowed himself to beam. "Between us, sir, there should be little that we do not know."

"We sure make a swell team as a detective."

The beam faded. "As a detective? Damme, sir, do you think I cared about your robbery? I simply explained the inevitable denouement to this story.' "

"But she didn't confess and make a gesture. Michaels had to prove it on her."

"All the better, sir. That makes her mysterious and deep. A Bette Davis role. I think we will first try for a magazine sale on this. Studios are more impressed by matter already in print. Then I shall show it to F.X., and we shall watch the squirmings of that genius Aram Melekian."

Tom Smith looked out the window, frowning. They made a team, all right; but which way? He still itched to write, but the promotion Michaels had promised him sounded good, too. Were he and this strange lean old man a team for writing or for detection?

The friendly red and green lights of the neighborhood Christmas trees seemed an equally good omen either way.

ON CHRISTMAS DAY
IN THE MORNING

BY MARGERY ALLINGHAM

Sir Leo Persuivant, the Chief Constable, had been sitting in his comfortable study after a magnificent lunch and talking shyly of the sadness of Christmas while his guest, Mr. Albert Campion, most favored of his large house party, had been laughing at him gently.

It was true, the younger man had admitted, his pale eyes sleepy behind his horn-rimmed spectacles, that, however good the organization, the festival was never quite the same after one was middle-aged, but then only dear old Leo would expect it to be, and meanwhile, what a truly remarkable bird that had been!

But at that point the Superintendent had arrived with his grim little story and everything had seemed quite spoiled.

At the moment their visitor sat in a highbacked chair, against a paneled wall festooned with holly and tinsel, his round black eyes hard and preoccupied under his short gray hair. Superintendent Bussy was one of those lean and urgent countrymen who never quite lose their fondness for a genuine wonder. Despite years of experience and disillusion, the thing that simply can't have happened and yet indubitably *has* happened, retains a place in their cosmos. He was holding forth about one now. It had already

168

ruined his Christmas and had kept a great many other people out in the sleet all day; but nothing would induce him to leave it alone even for five minutes. The turkey sandwiches, which Sir Leo had insisted on ordering for him, were disappearing without him noticing them and the glass of scotch and soda stood untasted.

"You can see I had to come at once," he was saying for the third time. "I had to. I don't see what happened and that's a fact. It's a sort of miracle. Besides," he eyed them angrily, "fancy killing a poor old *postman* on Christmas morning! That's inhuman, isn't it? Unnatural."

Sir Leo nodded his white head. "Horrible," he agreed. "Now, let me get this clear. The man appears to have been run down at the Benham-Ashby crossroads . . ."

Bussy took a handful of cigarettes from the box at his side and arranged them in a cross on the table.

"Look," he said. "Here is the Ashby road with a slight bend in it, and here, running at right angles slap through the curve, is the Benham road. As you know as well as I do, Sir Leo, they're both good wide main thoroughfares, as roads go in these parts. This morning the Benham postman, old Fred Noakes, a bachelor thank God and a good chap, came along the Benham Road loaded down with Christmas mail."

"On a bicycle?" asked Campion.

"Naturally. On a bicycle. He called at the last farm before the crossroads and left just about 10 o'clock. We know that because he had a cup of tea there. Then his way led him over the crossing and on towards Benham proper."

He paused and looked up from his cigarettes.

"There was very little traffic early today, terrible weather all the time, and quite a bit of activity later; so we've got no skid marks to help us. Well, to resume: no one seems to have seen old Noakes, poor chap, until close on half an hour later. Then the Benham constable, who lives some 300 yards from the crossing and on the Benham road, came out of his house and walked down to his gate to see if the mail had come. He saw the postman at once, lying in the middle of the road across his machine. He was dead then."

"You suggest he'd been trying to carry on, do you?" put in Sir Leo.

"Yes. He was walking, pushing the bike, and had dropped in his tracks. There was a depressed fracture in the side of his skull where something—say, a car mirror—had struck him. I've got the doctor's report. I'll show you that later. Meanwhile there's something else."

Bussy's finger turned to his other line of cigarettes.

"Also, just about 10, there were a couple of fellows walking here on the *Ashby* road, just before the bend. They report that they were almost run down by a wildly driven car which came up behind them. It missed them and careered off out of their sight round the bend towards the crossing. But a few minutes later, half a mile farther on, on the other side of the crossroads, a police car met and succeeded in stopping the same car. There was a row and the driver, getting the wind up suddenly, started up again, skidded and smashed the car into the nearest telephone pole. The car turned out to be stolen and there were four half-full bottles of gin in the back. The two occupants were both fighting drunk and are now detained."

Mr. Campion took off his spectacles and blinked at the speaker.

"You suggest that there was a connection, do you?—that the postman and the gin drinkers met at the crossroads? Any signs on the car?"

Bussy shrugged his shoulders. "Our chaps are at work on that now," he said. "The second smash has complicated things a bit, but last time I 'phoned they were hopeful."

"But my dear fellow!" Sir Leo was puzzled. "If you can get expert evidence of a collision between the car and the postman, your worries are over. That is, of course, if the medical evidence permits the theory that the unfortunate fellow picked himself up and struggled the 300 yards towards the constable's house."

Bussy hesitated.

"There's the trouble," he admitted. "If that were all we'd be sitting pretty, but it's not and I'll tell you why. In that 300 yards of Benham Road, between the crossing and the spot where old Fred died, there is a stile which leads to a footpath. Down the footpath, the best part of a quarter of a mile over very rough going, there is one small cottage, and at that cottage letters were delivered this morning. The doctor says Noakes might have staggered the 300 yards up the road leaning on his bike, but he puts his foot down and says the other journey, over the stile and so on, would have been absolutely impossible. I've talked to the doctor. He's the best man in the world on the job and we won't shake him on that."

"All of which would argue," observed Mr. Campion brightly, "that the postman was hit by a car *after* he came back from the cottage—between the stile and the constable's house."

"That's what the constable thought." Bussy's black eyes were snapping. "As soon as he'd telephoned for help he slipped down to the cottage to see if Noakes had actually called there. When he found he had, he searched the road. He was mystified though because both he and his missus had been at their window for an hour watching for the mail and they hadn't seen a vehicle of any sort go by either way. If a car did hit the postman where he fell, it must have turned and gone back afterwards."

Leo frowned at him. "What about the other witnesses? Did they see any second car?"

"No." Bussy was getting to the heart of the matter and his face shone with honest wonder. "I made sure of that. Everybody sticks to it that there was no other car or cart about and a good job too, they say, considering the way the smashed-up car was being driven. As I see it, it's a proper mystery, a kind of not very nice miracle, and those two beauties are going to get away with murder on the strength of it. Whatever our fellows find on the car they'll never get past the doctor's testimony."

Mr. Campion got up sadly. The sleet was beating on the windows, and from inside the house came the more cheerful sound of tea cups. He nodded to Sir Leo.

"I fear we shall have to see that footpath before it gets too dark. In this weather, conditions may have changed by tomorrow."

Sir Leo sighed. " 'On Christmas day in the morning!' " he quoted bitterly. "Perhaps you're right."

They stopped their dreary journey at the Benham police station to pick up the constable. He proved to be a pleasant youngster with a face like one of the angel choir and boots like a fairy tale, but he had liked the postman and was anxious to serve as their guide.

They inspected the crossroads and the bend and the spot where the car had come to grief. By the time they reached the stile, the world was gray and freezing, and all trace of Christmas had vanished, leaving only the hopeless winter it had been invented to refute.

Mr. Campion negotiated the stile and Sir Leo followed him with some difficulty. It was an awkward climb, and the path below was narrow and slippery. It wound out into the mist before them, apparently without end.

The procession slid and scrambled on in silence for what seemed a mile, only to encounter a second stile and a plank bridge over a stream, followed by a brief area of what appeared to be simple bog. As he struggled out of it, Bussy pushed back his dripping hat and gazed at the constable.

"You're not having a game with us, I suppose?" he inquired.

"No, sir." The boy was all blush. "The little house is just here. You can't make it out because it's a bit low. There it is, sir. There."

He pointed to a hump in the near distance which they had all taken to be a haystack. Gradually it emerged as the roof of a hovel which squatted with its back towards them in the wet waste.

"Good Heavens!" Sir Leo regarded its desolation with dismay. "Does anybody really live there?"

"Oh, yes, sir. An old widow lady. Mrs. Fyson's the name."

"Alone?" He was aghast. "How old?"

"I don't rightly know, sir. Quite old. Over 75, must be."

Sir Leo stopped in his tracks and a silence fell on the

company. The scene was so forlorn, so unutterably quiet in its loneliness, that the world might have died.

It was Campion who broke the spell.

"Definitely no walk for a dying man," he said firmly. "Doctor's evidence completely convincing, don't you think? Now that we're here, perhaps we should drop in and see the householder."

Sir Leo shivered. "We can't *all* get in," he objected. "Perhaps the Superintendent . . ."

"No. You and I will go." Campion was obstinate. "Is that all right with you, Super?"

Bussy waved them on. "If you have to dig for us we shall be just about here," he said cheerfully. "I'm over my ankles now. What a place! Does anybody ever come here *except* the postman, Constable?"

Campion took Sir Leo's arm and led him firmly round to the front of the cottage. There was a yellow light in the single window on the ground floor and, as they slid up a narrow brick path to the very small door, Sir Leo hung back. His repugnance was as apparent as the cold.

"I hate this," he muttered. "Go on. Knock if you must."

Mr. Campion obeyed, stooping so that his head might miss the lintel. There was a movement inside, and at once the door was opened wide, so that he was startled by the rush of warmth from within.

A little old woman stood before him, peering up without astonishment. He was principally aware of bright eyes.

"Oh, dear," she said unexpectedly, and her voice was friendly. "You *are* damp. Come in." And then, looking past him at the skulking Sir Leo. "Two of you! Well, isn't that nice. Mind your poor heads."

The visit became a social occasion before they were well in the room. Her complete lack of surprise, coupled with the extreme lowness of the ceiling, gave her an advantage from which the interview never entirely recovered.

From the first she did her best to put them at ease.

"You'll have to sit down at once," she said, laughing as she waved them to two little chairs one on either side of the small black stove. "Most people have to. I'm all right, you see, because I'm not tall. This is my chair here. You must undo that," she went on touching Sir Leo's coat. "Otherwise you may take cold when you go out. It is so very chilly, isn't it? But so seasonable and that's always nice."

Afterwards it was Mr. Campion's belief that neither he nor Sir Leo had a word to say for themselves for the first five minutes. They were certainly seated and looking round the one downstairs room which the house contained before anything approaching a conversation took place.

It was not a sordid room, yet the walls were unpapered, the furniture old without being in any way antique, and the place could hardly have been called neat. But at the moment it was festive. There was holly over the two pictures and on the mantel above the stove, and a crowd of bright Christmas cards.

Their hostess sat between them, near the table. It was set for a small tea party and the oil lamp with the red and white frosted glass shade, which stood in the center of it, shed a comfortable light on her serene face.

She was a short, plump old person whose white hair was brushed tightly to her little round head. Her clothes were all knitted and of an assortment of colors, and with them she wore, most unsuitably, a maltése-silk lace collarette and a heavy gold chain. It was only when they noticed she was blushing that they realized she was shy.

"Oh," she exclaimed at last, making a move which put their dumbness to shame. "I quite forgot to say it before. A Merry Christmas to you! Isn't it wonderful how it keeps coming round? Very quickly, I'm afraid, but it is so nice when it does. It's such a *happy* time, isn't it?"

Sir Leo pulled himself together with an effort which was practically visible.

"I must apologize," he began. "This is an imposition on such a day. I . . ." But she smiled and silenced him again.

"Not at all," she said. "Oh, not at all. Visitors are a great treat. Not everybody braves my footpath in the winter."

"But some people do, of course?" ventured Mr. Campion.

"Of course." She shot him her shy smile. "Certainly

every week. They send down from the village every week and only this morning a young man, the policeman to be exact, came all the way over the fields to wish me the compliments of the season and to know if I'd got my post!"

"And you had!" Sir Leo glanced at the array of Christmas cards with relief. He was a kindly, sentimental, family man, with a horror of loneliness.

She nodded at the brave collection with deep affection. "It's lovely to see them all up there again, it's one of the real joys of Christmas, isn't it? Messages from people you love and who love you and all so *pretty,* too."

"Did you come down bright and early to meet the postman?" Sir Leo's question was disarmingly innocent, but she looked ashamed and dropped her eyes.

"I wasn't up! Wasn't it dreadful? I was late this morning. In fact, I was only just picking the letters off the mat there when the policeman called. He helped me gather them, the nice boy. There were such a lot. I lay lazily in bed this morning thinking of them instead of moving."

"Still, you heard them come." Sir Leo was very satisfied. "And you knew they were there."

"Oh, yes." She sounded content. "I knew they were there. May I offer you a cup of tea? I'm waiting for my party ... just a woman and her dear little boy; they won't be long. In fact, when I heard your knock I thought they were here already."

Sir Leo excused them, but not with any undue haste. He appeared to be enjoying himself. Meanwhile, Mr. Campion, who had risen to inspect the display on the mantel shelf more closely, helped her to move the kettle so that it should not boil too soon.

The Christmas cards were splendid. There were nearly 30 of them in all, and the envelopes which had contained them were packed in a neat bundle and tucked behind the clock, to add even more color to the whole.

In design, they were mostly conventional. There were wreaths and firesides, saints and angels, with a secondary line of gardens in unseasonable bloom and Scotch terriers in tamo'shanter caps. One magnificent card was entirely

in ivorine, with a cutout disclosing a coach and horses
surrounded by roses and forget-me-nots. The written messages were all warm and personal, all breathing affection
and friendliness and the out-spoken joy of the season:

The very best to you, Darling, from all at The Limes
To dear Auntie from Little Phil.
Love and Memories. Edith and Ted.
There is no wish like the old wish. Warm regards,
George.
For dearest Mother.
Cheerio. Lots of love. Just off. Writing. Take care of
yourself. Sonny.
For dear little Agnes with love from us all.

Mr. Campion stood before them far a long time but at
length he turned away. He had to stoop to avoid the beam
and yet he towered over the old woman who stood looking
up at him.

Something had happened. It had suddenly become very
still in the house. The gentle hissing of the kettle sounded
unnaturally loud. The recollection of its lonely remoteness
returned to chill the cosy room.

The old lady had lost her smile and there was wariness
in her eyes.

"Tell me." Campion spoke very gently. "What do you
do? Do you put them all down there on the mat in their
envelopes before you go to bed on Christmas Eve?"

While the point of his question and the enormity of it
was dawning up on Sir Leo, there was silence. It was
breathless and unbearable until old Mrs. Fyson pierced it
with a laugh of genuine naughtiness.

"Well," she said, "it does make it more fun!" She
glanced back at Sir Leo whose handsome face was growing
steadily more and more scarlet.

"Then ... ?" He was having difficulty with his voice.
"Then the postman did *not* call this morning, ma'am?"

She stood looking at him placidly, the flicker of the smile
still playing round her mouth.

"The postman never calls here except when he brings
something from the Government," she said pleasantly.
"Everybody gets letters from the Government nowadays,

don't they? But he doesn't call here with *personal* letters because, you see, I'm the last of us." She paused and frowned very faintly. It rippled like a shadow over the smoothness of her quiet, careless brow. "There's been so many wars," she said sadly.

"But, dear lady . . ." Sir Leo was completely overcome. There were tears in his eyes and his voice failed him.

She patted his arm to comfort him.

"My dear man," she said kindly. "Don't be distressed. It's not sad. It's Christmas. We all loved Christmas. They sent me their love at Christmas and you see *I've still got it.* At Christmas I remember them and they remember me . . . wherever they are." Her eyes strayed to the ivorine card with the coach on it. "I do sometimes wonder about poor George," she remarked seriously. "He was my husband's elder brother and he really did have quite a shocking life. But he once sent me that remarkable card and I kept it with the others. After all, we ought to be charitable, oughtn't we? At Christmas time . . ."

As the four men plodded back through the fields, Bussy was jubilant.

"That's done the trick," he said. "Cleared up the mystery and made it all plain sailing. We'll get those two crooks for doing in poor old Noakes. A real bit of luck that Mr. Campion was here," he added generously, as he squelched on through the mud. "The old girl was just cheering herself up and you fell for it, eh, Constable? Oh, don't worry, my boy. There's no harm done, and it's a thing that might have deceived anybody. Just let it be a lesson to you. I know how it happened. You didn't want to worry the old thing with the tale of a death on Christmas morning, so you took the sight of the Christmas cards as evidence and didn't go into it. As it turned out, you were wrong. That's life."

He thrust the young man on ahead of him and came over to Mr. Campion.

"What beats me is how you cottoned to it," he confided. "What gave you the idea?"

"I merely read it, I'm afraid." Mr. Campion sounded

apologetic. "All the envelopes were there, sticking out from behind the clock. The top one had a ha'penny stamp on it, so I looked at the postmark. It was 1914."

Bussy laughed "Given to you," he chuckled. "Still, I bet you had a job to believe your eyes."

"Ah." Mr. Campion's voice was thoughtful in the dusk. "That, Super, that was the really difficult bit."

Sir Leo, who had been striding in silence, was the last to climb up onto the road. He glanced anxiously towards the village for a moment or so, and presently touched Campion on the shoulder.

"Look there."

A woman was hurrying towards them and at her side, earnest and expectant, trotted a small, plump child. They scurried past and as they paused by the stile, and the woman lifted the boy onto the footpath, Sir Leo expelled a long sighing breath.

"So there was a party," he said simply. "Thank God for that. Do you know, Campion, all the way back here I've been wonderin'."

SANTA CLAUS BEAT

BY REX STOUT

"Christmas Eve," Art Hipple was thinking to himself, "would be a good time for the murder."

The thought was both timely and characteristic. It was 3 o'clock in the afternoon of December 24, and though the murder would have got an eager welcome from Art Hipple any day at all, his disdainful attitude toward the prolonged hurly-burly of Christmas sentiment and shopping made that the best possible date for it. He did not actually turn up his nose at Christmas, for that would have been un-American; but as a New York cop not yet out of his twenties who had recently been made a precinct dick and had hung his uniform in the back of the closet of his furnished room, it had to be made clear, especially to himself, that he was good and tough. A cynical slant on Christmas was therefore imperative.

His hope of running across a murder had begun back in the days when his assignment had been tagging illegally parked cars, and was merely practical and professional. His biggest ambition was promotion to Homicide, and the shortest cut would have been discovery of a corpse, followed by swift, brilliant, solo detection and capture of the culprit. It had not gone so far as becoming an obsession; as he strode down the sidewalk this December afternoon he was not sniffing for the scent of blood at each dingy entrance he passed; but when he reached the number he

179

had been given and turned to enter, his hand darted inside
his jacket to touch his gun.

None of the three people he found in the cluttered and
smelly little room one flight up seemed to need shooting.
Art identified himself and wrote down their names. The
man at the battered old desk, who was twice Art's age
and badly needed a shave, was Emil Duross, proprietor of
the business conducted in that room—Duross Specialties,
a mail-order concern dealing in gimcrack jewelry. The
younger man, small, dark and neat, seated on a chair
squeezed in between the desk and shelves stacked with
cardboard boxes, was H. E. Koenig, adjuster, according to
a card he had proffered, for the Apex Insurance Company.
The girl, who had pale watery eyes and a stringy neck,
stood backed up to a pile of cartons the height of her
shoulder. She had on a dark brown felt hat and a lighter
brown woolen coat that had lost a button. Her name was
Helen Lauro, and it could have been not rheum in her
eyes but the remains of tears.

Because Art Hipple was thorough it took him twenty
minutes to get the story to his own satisfaction. Then he
returned his notebook to his pocket, looked at Duross, at
Koenig, and last at the girl. He wanted to tell her to wipe
her eyes, but what if she didn't have a handkerchief?

He spoke to Duross, "Stop me if I'm wrong," he said.
"You bought the ring a week ago to give to your wife for
Christmas and paid sixty-two dollars for it. You put it
there in a desk drawer after showing it to Miss Lauro.
Why did you show it to Miss Lauro?"

Duross turned his palms up. "Just a natural thing. She
works for me, she's a woman, and it's a beautiful ring."

"Okay. Today you work with her—filling orders, addressing packages, and putting postage on. You send her
to the post office with a bag of the packages. Why didn't
she take all of them?"

"She did."

"Then what are those?" Art pointed to a pile of little
boxes, addressed and stamped, on the end of a table.

"Orders that came in the afternoon mail. I did them
while she was gone to the post office."

Art nodded. "And also while she was gone you looked in the drawer to get the ring to take home for Christmas, and it wasn't there. You know it was there this morning because Miss Lauro asked if she could look at it again, and you showed it to her and let her put it on her finger, and then you put it back in the drawer. But this afternoon it was gone, and you couldn't have taken it yourself because you haven't left this room. Miss Lauro went out and got sandwiches for your lunch. So you decided she took the ring, and you phoned the insurance company, and Mr. Koenig came and advised you to call the police, and—"

"Only his stock is insured," Koenig put in. "The ring was not a stock item and is not covered."

"Just a legality," Duross declared scornfully. "Insurance companies can't hide behind legalities. It hurts their reputation."

Koenig smiled politely but noncommittally.

Art turned to the girl. "Why don't you sit down?" he asked her. "There's a chair we men are not using."

"I will never sit down in this room again," she declared in a thin tight voice.

"Okay." Art scowled at her. She was certainly not comely. "If you did take the ring you might—"

"I didn't!"

"Very well. But if you did you might as well tell me where it is because you won't ever dare to wear it or sell it."

"Of course I wouldn't. I knew I wouldn't. That's why I didn't take it."

"Oh? You thought of taking it?"

"Of course I did. It was a beautiful ring." She stopped to swallow. "Maybe my life isn't much, but what it is, I'd give it for a ring like that, and a girl like me, I could live a hundred years and never have one. Of course I thought of taking it—but I knew I couldn't ever wear it."

"You see?" Duross appealed to the law. "She's foxy, that girl. She's slick."

Art downed an impulse to cut it short, get out, return to the station house, and write a report. Nobody here deserved anything, not even justice—especially not justice.

Writing a brief report was all it rated, and all, ninety-nine
times out of a hundred, it would have got. But instead of
breaking it off, Art sat and thought it over through a long
silence, with the three pairs of eyes on him. Finally he
spoke to Duross:

"Get me the orders that came in the afternoon mail."

Duross was startled. "Why?"

"I want to check them with that pile of boxes you addressed and stamped."

Duross shook his head. "I don't need a cop to check
my orders and shipments. Is this a gag?"

"No. Get me the orders."

"I will not!"

"Then I'll have to open all the boxes." Art arose and
headed for the table. Duross bounced up and got in front
of him and they were chest to chest.

"You don't touch those boxes," Duross told him. "You
got no search warrant. You don't touch anything!"

"That's just another legality." Art backed off a foot to
avoid contact. "And since I guessed right, what's a little legality? I'm going to open the boxes here and now, but I'll
count ten first to give you a chance to pick it out and hand
it to me and save both of us a lot of bother. One, two,
three—"

"I'll phone the station house!"

"Go ahead. Four, five, six, seven, eight, nine . . ."

Art stopped at nine because Duross had moved to the
table and was fingering the boxes. As he drew away with
one in his hand Art demanded, "Gimme." Duross hesitated but passed the box over, and after a glance at the
address Art ripped the tape off, opened the flap of the
box, took out a wad of tissue paper, and then a ring box.
From that he removed a ring, yellow gold, with a large
greenish stone. Helen Lauro made a noise in her throat.
Koenig let out a grunt, evidently meant for applause. Duross made a grab, not for the ring but for the box on which
he had put an address, and missed.

"It stuck out as plain as your nose," Art told him, "but
of course my going for the boxes was just a good guess.
Did you pay sixty-two bucks for this?"

Duross's lips parted, but no words came. Apparently he had none. He nodded, not vigorously.

Art turned to the girl. "Look, Miss Lauro. You say you're through here. You ought to have something to remember it by. You could make some trouble for Mr. Duross for the dirty trick he tried to play on you, and if you lay off I expect he'd like to show his appreciation by giving you this ring. Wouldn't you, Mr. Duross?"

Duross managed to get it out. "Sure I would."

"Shall I give it to her for you?"

"Sure." Duross's jaw worked. "Go ahead."

Art held out the ring and the girl took it, but not looking at it because she was gazing incredulously at him. It was a gaze so intense as to disconcert him, and he covered up by turning to Duross and proffering the box with an address on it.

"Here," he said, "you can have this. Next time you cook up a plan for getting credit with your wife for buying her a ring, and collecting from the insurance company for its cost, and sending the ring to a girl friend—all in one neat little operation—don't do it. And don't forget you gave Miss Lauro that ring before witnesses."

Duross gulped and nodded.

Koenig spoke. "Your name is not Hipple, officer, it's Santa Claus. You have given her the ring she would have given her life for, you have given him an out on a charge of attempted fraud, and you have given me a crossoff on a claim. That's the ticket! That's the old yuletide spirit! Merry Christmas!"

"Nuts," Art said contemptuously, and turned and marched from the room, down the stairs, and out to the sidewalk. As he headed in the direction of the station house he decided that he would tone it down a little in his report. Getting a name for being tough was okay, but not too damn tough. That insurance guy sure was dumb, calling him Santa Claus—him, Art Hipple, feeling as he did about Christmas.

Which reminded him, Christmas Eve would be a swell time for the murder.

WHO KILLED
FATHER CHRISTMAS?

BY PATRICIA MOYES

"Good morning, Mr. Borrowdale. Nippy out, isn't it? You're in early, I see." Little Miss MacArthur spoke with her usual brisk brightness, which failed to conceal both envy and dislike. She was unpacking a consignment of stout Teddy bears in the stockroom behind the toy department at Barnum and Thrums, the London store. "Smart as ever, Mr. Borrowdale," she added, jealously.

I laid down my curly-brimmed bowler hat and cane and took off my British warm overcoat. I don't mind admitting that I do take pains to dress as well as I can, and for some reason it seems to infuriate the Miss MacArthurs of the world.

She prattled on. "Nice looking, these Teddies, don't you think? Very reasonable, too. Made in Hong Kong, that'll be why. I think I'll take one for my sister's youngest."

The toy department at Barnum's has little to recommend it to anyone over the age of twelve, and normally it is tranquil and little populated. However, at Christmastime it briefly becomes the bustling heart of the great shop, and also provides useful vacation jobs for chaps like me who wish to earn some money during the weeks before the university term begins in January. Gone, I fear, are the days when undergraduates were the gilded youth of

184

England. We all have to work our passages these days, and sometimes it means selling toys.

One advantage of the job is that employees—even temporaries like me—are allowed to buy goods at a considerable discount, which helps with the Christmas gift problem. As a matter of fact, I had already decided to buy a Teddy bear for one of my nephews, and I mentioned as much.

"Well, you'd better take it right away," remarked Miss MacArthur, "because I heard Mr. Harrington say he was taking two, and I think Disaster has her eye on one." Disaster was the unfortunate but inevitable nickname of Miss Aster, who had been with the store for thirty-one years but still made mistakes with her stockbook. I felt sorry for the old girl. I had overheard a conversation between Mr. Harrington, the department manager, and Mr. Andrews, the deputy store manager, and so I knew—but Disaster didn't—that she would be getting the sack as soon as the Christmas rush was over.

Meanwhile, Miss MacArthur was arranging the bears on a shelf. They sat there in grinning rows, brown and woolly, with boot-button eyes and red ribbons round their necks.

It was then that Father Christmas came in. He'd been in the cloakroom changing into his costume—white beard, red nose, and all. His name was Bert Denman. He was a cheery soul who got on well with the kids, and he'd had the Father Christmas job at Barnum's each of the three years I'd been selling there. Now he was carrying his sack, which he filled every morning from the cheap items in the stockroom. A visit to Father Christmas cost 50 pence, so naturally the gift that was fished out of the sack couldn't be worth more than 20 pence. However, to my surprise, he went straight over to the row of Teddy bears and picked one off the shelf. For some reason, he chose the only one with a blue instead of a red ribbon.

Miss MacArthur was on to him in an instant. "What d'you think you're doing, Mr. Denman? Those Teddies aren't in your line at all—much too dear. One pound ninety, they are."

Father Christmas did not answer, and suddenly I realized that it was not Bert Denman under the red robe.

"Wait a minute," I said. "Who are you? You're not our Father Christmas."

He turned to face me, the Teddy bear in his hand. "That's all right," he said. "Charlie Burrows is my name. I live in the same lodging house with Bert Denman. He was taken poorly last night, and I'm standing in for him."

"Well," said Miss MacArthur. "How very odd. Does Mr. Harrington know?"

"Of course he does," said Father Christmas.

As if on cue, Mr. Harrington himself came hurrying into the stockroom. He always hurried everywhere, preceded by his small black mustache. He said, "Ah, there you are, Burrows. Fill up your sack, and I'll explain the job to you. Denman told you about the Teddy bear, did he?"

"Yes, Mr. Harrington."

"Father Christmas can't give away an expensive bear like that, Mr. Harrington," Miss MacArthur objected.

"Now, now, Miss MacArthur, it's all arranged," said Harrington fussily. "A customer came in yesterday and made a special request that Father Christmas should give his small daughter a Teddy bear this morning. I knew this consignment was due on the shelves, so I promised him one. It's been paid for. The important thing, Burrows, is to remember the child's name. It's ... er ... I have it written down somewhere."

"Annabel Whitworth," said Father Christmas. "Four years old, fair hair, will be brought in by her mother."

"I see that Denman briefed you well," said Mr. Harrington, with an icy smile. "Well, now, I'll collect two bears for myself—one for my son and one for my neighbor's boy—and then I'll show you the booth."

Miss Aster arrived just then. She and Miss MacArthur finished uncrating the bears and took one out to put on display next to a female doll that, among other endearing traits, actually wet its diaper. Mr. Harrington led our surrogate Father Christmas to his small canvas booth, and the rest of us busied and braced ourselves for the moment when the great glass doors opened and the floodtide was let in. The toy department of a big store on December 23 is no place for weaklings.

It is curious that even such an apparently random stream of humanity as Christmas shoppers displays a pattern of behavior. The earliest arrivals in the toy department are office workers on their way to their jobs. The actual toddlers, bent on an interview with Father Christmas, do not appear until their mothers have had time to wash up breakfast, have a bit of a go around the house, and catch the bus from Kensington or the tube from Uxbridge.

On that particular morning it was just twenty-eight minutes past ten when I saw Disaster, who was sitting in a decorated cash desk labeled "The Elfin Grove," take 50 pence from the first parent to usher her child into Santa's booth. For about two minutes the mother waited, chatting quietly with Disaster. Then a loudly wailing infant emerged from the booth.

The mother snatched her up, and—with that sixth sense that mothers everywhere seem to develop—interpreted the incoherent screams. "She says that Father Christmas won't talk to her. She says he's asleep."

It was clearly an emergency, even if a minor one, and Disaster was already showing signs of panic. I excused myself from my customer—a middle-aged gentleman who was playing with an electric train set—and went over to see what I could do. By then, the mother was indignant.

"Fifty pence and the old man sound asleep and drunk as like as not, and at half-past ten in the morning. Disgraceful, I call it. And here's poor little Poppy what had been looking forward to—"

I rushed into Father Christmas's booth. The man who called himself Charlie Burrows was slumped forward in his chair, looking for all the world as if he were asleep; but when I shook him, his head lolled horribly, and it was obvious that he was more than sleeping. The red robe concealed the blood until it made my hand sticky. Father Christmas had been stabbed in the back, and he was certainly dead.

I acted as fast as I could. First of all, I told Disaster to put up the CLOSED sign outside Santa's booth. Then I smoothed down Poppy's mother by leading her to a counter where I told her she could select any toy up to one pound and have it free. Under pretext of keeping records, I got her name and address. Finally I cornered Mr. Harrington in his office and told him the news.

I thought he was going to faint. "Dead? Murdered? Are you sure, Mr. Borrowdale?"

"Quite sure, I'm afraid. You'd better telephone the police, Mr. Harrington."

"The police! In Barnum's! What a terrible thing! I'll telephone the deputy store manager first and *then* the police."

As a matter of fact, the police were surprisingly quick and discreet. A plainclothes detective superintendent and his sergeant, a photographer, and the police doctor arrived, not in a posse, but as individuals, unnoticed among the crowd. They assembled in the booth, where the deputy manager—Mr. Andrews—and Mr. Harrington and I were waiting for them.

The superintendent introduced himself—his name was Armitage—and inspected the body with an expression of cold fury on his face that I couldn't quite understand, although the reason became clear later. He said very little. After some tedious formalities Armitage indicated that the body might be removed.

"What's the least conspicuous way to do it?" he asked.

"You can take him out through the back of the booth," I said. "The canvas overlaps right behind Santa's chair. The door to the staff quarters and the stockroom is just opposite, and from there you can take the service lift to the goods entrance in the mews."

The doctor and the photographer between them carried off their grim burden on a collapsible stretcher, and Superintendent Armitage began asking questions about the arrangements in the Father Christmas booth. I did the explaining, since Mr. Harrington seemed to be verging on hysteria.

Customers paid their 50 pence to Disaster in the Elfin Grove, and then the child—usually alone—was propelled through the door of the booth and into the presence of Father Christmas, who sat in his canvas-backed director's chair on a small dais facing the entrance, with his sack of toys beside him. The child climbed onto his knee, whispered its Christmas wishes, and was rewarded with a few friendly words and a small gift from Santa's sack.

What was not obvious to the clientele was the back entrance to the booth, which enabled Father Christmas to slip in and out unobserved. He usually had his coffee break at about 11:15, unless there was a very heavy rush of business. Disaster would pick a moment when custom seemed slow, put up the CLOSED NOTICE, and inform Bert that he could take a few minutes off. When he returned, he pressed a button by his chair that rang a buzzer in the cashier's booth. Down would come the notice, and Santa was in business again.

Before Superintendent Armitage could comment on my remarks, Mr. Harrington broke into a sort of despairing wait, "It must have been one of the customers!" he cried.

"I don't think so, sir," said Armitage. "This is an inside job. He was stabbed in the back with a long thin blade of some sort. The murderer must have opened the back flap and stabbed him clean through the canvas back of his chair. That must have been someone who knew the exact arrangements. The murderer then used the back way to enter the booth—"

"I don't see how you can say that!" Harrington's voice was rising dangerously. "If the man was stabbed from outside, what makes you think anybody came into the booth?"

"I'll explain that in a minute, sir."

Ignoring Armitage, Harrington went on. "In any case, he wasn't our regular Father Christmas! None of us had ever seen him before. Why on earth would anybody kill a man that nobody knew?"

Armitage and the deputy manager exchanged glances. Then Armitage said, "I knew him, sir. Very well. Charlie Burrows was one of our finest plainclothes narcotics officers."

Mr. Harrington had gone green. "You mean—he was a policeman?"

"Exactly, sir. I'd better explain. A little time ago we got a tipoff from an informer that an important consignment of high-grade heroin was to be smuggled in from Hong Kong in a consignment of Christmas toys. Teddy bears, in fact. The drug was to be in the Barnum and Thrums carton, hidden inside a particular Teddy bear, which would be distinguished by having a blue ribbon around its neck instead of a red one."

"Surely," I said, "you couldn't get what you call an important consignment inside one Teddy bear, even a big one."

Armitage sighed. "Shows you aren't familiar with the drug scene, sir," he said. "Why, half a pound of pure high-grade heroin is worth a fortune on the streets."

With a show of bluster Harrington said, "If you knew this, Superintendent, why didn't you simply intercept the consignment and confiscate the drug? Look at the trouble that's been—"

Armitage interrupted him. "'If you'd just hear me out, sir. What I've told you was the sum total of our information. We didn't know who in Barnum's was going to pick up the heroin, or how or where it was to be disposed of. We're more interested in getting the people—the pushers—than confiscating the cargo. So I had a word with Mr. Andrews here, and he kindly agreed to let Charlie take on the Father Christmas job. And Charlie set a little trap. Unfortunately, he paid for it with his life." There was an awkward silence.

He went on. "Mr. Andrews told us that the consignment had arrived and was to be unpacked today. We know that staff get first pick, as it were, at new stock, and we were naturally interested to see who would select the bear with the blue ribbon. It was Charlie's own idea to concoct a story about a special present for a little girl—"

"You mean, that wasn't true?" Harrington was outraged. "But I spoke to the customer myself!"

"Yes, sir. That's to say, you spoke to another of our people, who was posing as the little girl's father."

"You're very thorough," Harrington said.

"Yes, sir. Thank you, sir. Well, as I was saying, Charlie made a point of selecting the bear with the blue ribbon and taking it off in his sack. He knew that whoever was picking up the drop would have to come and get it—or try to. You see, if we'd just allowed one of the staff to select it, that person could simply have said that it was pure coincidence—blue was such a pretty color. Difficult to prove criminal knowledge. You understand?"

Nobody said anything. With quite a sense of dramatic effect Armitage reached down into Santa's sack and pulled out a Teddy bear. It had a blue ribbon round its neck.

In a voice tense with strain Mr. Andrews said, "So the murderer didn't get away with the heroin. I thought you said—"

Superintendent Armitage produced a knife from his pocket. "We'll see," he said. "With your permission, I'm going to open this bear."

"Of course."

The knife ripped through the nobbly brown fabric, and a lot of stuffing fell out. Nothing else. Armitage made a good job of it. By the time he had finished, the bear was in shreds: and nothing had emerged from its interior except kapok.

Armitage surveyed the wreckage with a sort of bleak satisfaction. Suddenly brisk, he said, "Now. Which staff members took bears from the stockroom this morning?"

"I did," I said at once.

"Anybody else?"

There was a silence. I said, "I believe you took two, didn't you, Mr. Harrington?"

"I ... em ... yes, now that you mention it."

"Miss MacArthur took one," I said. "It was she who unpacked the carton. She said that Dis—Miss Aster—was going to take one."

"I see." Armitage was making notes. "I presume you each signed for your purchases, and that the bears are now with your things in the staff cloakroom." Without waiting for an answer he turned to me. "How many of these people saw Burrows select the bear with the blue ribbon?"

"All of us," I said. "Isn't that so, Mr. Harrington?"

Harrington just nodded. He looked sick.

"Well, then," said Armitage, "I shall have to inspect all the bears that you people removed from the stockroom."

There was an element of black humor in the parade of the Teddies, with their inane grins and knowing, beady eyes: but as one after the other was dismembered, nothing more sensational was revealed than a growing pile of kapok. The next step was to check the stockbook numbers—and sure enough, one bear was missing.

It was actually Armitage's Sergeant who found it. It had been ripped open and shoved behind a pile of boxes in the stockroom in a hasty attempt at concealment. There was no ribbon round its neck, and it was constructed very differently from the others. The kapok merely served as a thin layer of stuffing between the fabric skin and a spherical womb of pink plastic in the toy's center. This plastic had been cut open and was empty. It was abundantly clear what it must have contained.

"Well," said the Superintendent, "it's obvious what happened. The murderer stabbed Burrows, slipped into the booth, and substituted an innocent Teddy bear for the loaded one, at the same time changing the neck ribbon, But he—or she—didn't dare try walking out of the store with the bear, not after a murder. So, before Charlie's body was found, the murderer dismembered the bear, took out the heroin, and hid it." He sighed again. "I'm afraid this means a body search. I'll call the Yard for a police matron for the ladies."

It was all highly undignified and tedious, and poor old Disaster nearly had a seizure, despite the fact that the police matron seemed a thoroughly nice and kind woman. When it was all over, however, and our persons and clothing had been practically turned inside out, still nothing had been found. The four of us were required to wait in the staff restroom while exhaustive searches were made for both the heroin and the weapon.

Disaster was in tears, Miss MacArthur was loudly indignant and threatened to sue the police for false arrest, and Mr. Harrington developed what he called a nervous stomach, on account, he said, of the way the toy department was being left understaffed and unsupervised on one of the busiest days of the year.

At long last Superintendent Armitage came in. He said,

"Nothing. Abso-bloody-lutely nothing. Well, I can't keep you people here indefinitely. I suggest you all go out and get yourselves some lunch." He sounded very tired and cross and almost human.

With considerable relief we prepared to leave the staffroom. Only Mr. Harrington announced that he felt too ill to eat anything, and that he would remain in the department. The Misses MacArthur and Aster left together. I put on my coat and took the escalator down to the ground floor, among the burdened, chattering crowd.

I was out in the brisk air of the street when I heard Armitage's voice behind me.

"Just one moment, if you please, Mr. Borrowdale."

I turned. "Yes, Superintendent. Can I help you?"

"You're up at the university, aren't you, sir? Just taken a temporary job at Barnum's for the vacation?"

"That's right."

"Do quite a bit of fencing, don't you?"

He had my cane out of my hand before I knew what was happening. The sergeant, an extraordinarily tough and unattractive character, showed surprising dexterity and speed in getting an arm grip on me. Armitage had unscrewed the top of the cane, and was whistling in a quiet, appreciative manner. "Very nice. Very nice little sword stick. Something like a stiletto. I don't suppose Charlie felt a thing."

"Now, look here," I said. "You can't make insinuations like that. Just because I'm known as a bit of dandy, and carry a sword stick, that's no reason—"

"A dandy, eh?" said Armitage thoughtfully. He looked me up and down in a curious manner, as if he thought something was missing.

It was at that moment that Miss MacArthur suddenly appeared round the corner of the building.

"Oh, Mr. Borrowdale, look what I found! Lying down in the mews by the goods entrance! It must have fallen out of the staffroom window! Lucky I've got sharp eyes— it was behind a rubbish bin, I might easily have missed it!" And she handed me my bowler hat.

That is to say, she would have done if Armitage hadn't

intercepted it. It didn't take him more than five seconds to find the packages of white powder hidden between the hard shell of the hat and the oiled-silk lining.

Armitage said, "So you were going to peddle this stuff to young men and women at the university, were you? Charming, I must say. Now you can come back to the Yard and tell us all about your employers—if you want a chance at saving your own neck, that is."

Miss MacArthur was goggling at me. "Oh, Mr. Borrowdale!" she squeaked. "Have I gone and done something wrong?"

I never did like Miss MacArthur.

'TWIXT THE CUP
AND THE LIP

BY JULIAN SYMONS

"A beautiful morning, Miss Oliphant. I shall take a short constitutional."

"Very well, Mr. Payne."

Mr. Rossiter Payne put on his good thick Melton overcoat, took his bowler hat off its peg, carefully brushed it, and put it on. He looked at himself in a small glass and nodded approvingly at what he saw.

He was a man in his early fifties, but he might have passed for ten years less, so square were his shoulders, so ruler-straight his back. Two fine wings of gray hair showed under the bowler. He looked like a retired Guards officer, although he had, in fact, no closer relationship with the Army than an uncle who had been cashiered.

At the door he paused, his eyes twinkling. "Don't let anybody steal the stock while I'm out, Miss Oliphant."

Miss Oliphant, a thin spinster of indeterminate middle-age, blushed. She adored Mr. Payne.

He had removed his hat to speak to her. Now he clapped it on his head again, cast an appreciative look at the bow window of his shop, which displayed several sets of standard authors with the discreet legend above—*Rossiter Payne, Bookseller. Specialist in First Editions and Manuscripts*—and made his way up New Bond Street toward Oxford Street.

195

At the top of New Bond Street he stopped, as he did five days a week, at the stall on the corner. The old woman put the carnation into his buttonhole.

"Fourteen shopping days to Christmas now, Mrs. Shankly. We've all got to think about it, haven't we?"

A ten shilling note changed hands instead of the usual half crown. He left her blessing him confusedly.

This was perfect December weather—crisply cold, the sun shining. Oxford Street was wearing its holiday decorations—enormous gold and silver coins from which depended ropes of pearls, diamonds, rubies, emeralds. When lighted up in the afternoon they looked pretty, although a little garish for Mr. Payne's refined taste. But still, they had a certain symbolic feeling about them, and he smiled at them.

Nothing, indeed, could disturb Mr. Payne's good temper this morning—not the jostling crowds on the pavements or the customary traffic jams which seemed, indeed, to please him. He walked along until he came to a large store that said above it, in enormous letters, ORBIN'S. These letters were picked out in colored lights, and the lights themselves were festooned with Christmas trees and holly wreaths and the figures of the Seven Dwarfs, all of which lighted up.

Orbin's department store went right round the corner into the comparatively quiet Jessiter Street. Once again Mr. Payne went through a customary ceremony. He crossed the road and went down several steps into an establishment unique of its kind—Danny's Shoe Parlor. Here, sitting on a kind of throne in this semi-basement, one saw through a small window the lower halves of passers-by. Here Danny, with two assistants almost as old as himself, had been shining shoes for almost 30 years.

Leather-faced, immensely lined, but still remarkably sharp-eyed, Danny knelt down now in front of Mr. Payne, turned up the cuffs of his trousers, and began to put an altogether superior shine on already well-polished shoes.

"Lovely morning, Mr. Payne."

"You can't see much of it from here."

"More than you think. You see the pavements, and if

they're not spotted, right off you know it isn't raining. Then there's something in the way people walk, you know what I mean, like it's Christmas in the air." Mr. Payne laughed indulgently. Now Danny was mildly reproachful. "You still haven't brought me in that pair of black shoes, sir."

Mr. Payne frowned slightly. A week ago he had been almost knocked down by a bicyclist, and the mudguard of the bicycle had scraped badly one of the shoes he was wearing, cutting the leather at one point. Danny was confident that he could repair the cut so that it wouldn't show. Mr. Payne was not so sure.

"I'll bring them along," he said vaguely.

"Sooner the better, Mr. Payne, sooner the better."

Mr. Payne did not like being reminded of the bicycle incident. He gave Danny half a crown instead of the ten shillings he had intended, crossed the road again, and walked into the side entrance of Orbin's, which called itself unequivocally "London's Greatest Department Store."

This end of the store was quiet. He walked up the stairs, past the grocery department on the ground floor, and wine and cigars on the second, to jewelry on the third. There were rarely many people in this department, but today a small crowd had gathered around a man who was making a speech. A placard at the department entrance said: "The Russian Royal Family Jewels. On display for two weeks by kind permission of the Grand Duke and Grand Duchess of Moldo-Lithuania."

These were not the Russian Crown Jewels, seized by the Bolsheviks during the Revolution, but an inferior collection brought out of Russia by the Grand Duke and Grand Duchess, who had long since become plain Mr. and Mrs. Skandorski, who lived in New Jersey, and were now on a visit to England.

Mr. Payne was not interested in Mr. and Mrs. Skandorski, nor in Sir Henry Orbin who was stumbling through a short speech. He was interested only in the jewels. When the speech was over he mingled with the crowd round the showcase that stood almost in the middle of the room.

The royal jewels lay on beds of velvet—a tiara that

looked too heavy to be worn, diamond necklaces and bracelets, a cluster of diamonds and emeralds, and a dozen other pieces, each with an elegant calligraphic description of its origin and history. Mr. Payne did not see the jewels as a romantic relic of the past, nor did he permit himself to think of them as things of beauty. He saw them as his personal Christmas present.

He walked out of the department, looking neither to left nor right, and certainly paying no attention to the spotty young clerk who rushed forward to open the door for him. He walked back to his bookshop, sniffing that sharp December air, made another little joke to Miss Oliphant, and told her she could go out to lunch. During her lunch hour he sold an American a set of a Victorian magazine called *The Jewel Box*.

It seemed a good augury.

In the past ten years Mr. Payne had engineered successfully—with the help of other, and inferior, intellects—six jewel robberies. He had remained undetected, he believed, partly because of his skill in planning, partly because he ran a perfectly legitimate book business, and partly because he broke the law only when he needed money. He had little interest in women, and his habits were generally ascetic, but he did have one vice.

Mr. Payne developed a system at roulette, an improvement on the almost infallible Frank-Konig system, and every year he went to Monte Carlo and played his system. Almost every year it failed—or rather, it revealed certain imperfections which he then tried to remedy.

It was to support his foolproof system that Mr. Payne had turned from bookselling to crime. He believed himself to be, in a quiet way, a mastermind in the modern criminal world.

Those associated with him were far from that, as he immediately would have acknowledged. He met them two evenings after he had looked at the royal jewels, in his pleasant little flat above the shop, which could be approached from a side entrance opening into an alley.

There was Stacey, who looked what he was, a thick-nosed thug; there was a thin young man in a tight suit whose name was Jack Line, and who was always called Straight or Straight Line; and there was Lester Jones, the spotty clerk in the Jewelry Department.

Stacey and Straight Line sat drinking whiskey, Mr. Payne sipped some excellent sherry, and Lester Jones drank nothing at all, while Mr. Payne in his pedantic, almost schoolmasterly manner, told them how the robbery was to be accomplished.

"You all know what the job is, but let me tell you how much it is worth. In its present form the collection is worth whatever sum you'd care to mention—a quarter of a million pounds perhaps. There is no real market value. But alas, it will have to be broken up. My friend thinks the value will be in the neighborhood of fifty thousand pounds. Not less, and not much more."

"Your friend?" the jewelry clerk said timidly.

"The fence. Lambie, isn't it?" It was Stacey who spoke. Mr. Payne nodded. "Okay, how do we split?"

"I will come to that later. Now, here are the difficulties. First of all, there are two store detectives on each floor. We must see to it that those on the third floor are not in the Jewelry Department. Next, there is a man named Davidson, an American, whose job it is to keep an eye on the jewels. He has been brought over here by a protection agency, and it is likely that he will carry a gun. Third, the jewels are in a showcase, and any attempt to open this showcase other than with the proper key will set off an alarm. The key is kept in the Manager's Office, inside the Jewelry Department."

Stacey got up, shambled over to the whiskey decanter, and poured himself another drink. "Where do you get all this from?"

Mr. Payne permitted himself a small smile. "Lester works in the department. Lester is a friend of mine."

Stacey looked at Lester with contempt. He did not like amateurs.

"Let me continue, and tell you how the obstacles can be overcome. First, the two store detectives. Supposing that a small fire bomb were planted in the Fur Department, at the other end of the third floor from Jewelry—

that would certainly occupy one detective for a few minutes. Supposing that in the department that deals with ladies' hats, which is next to Furs, a woman shopper complained that she had been robbed—this would certainly involve the other store detective. Could you arrange this, Stace? These—assistants, shall I call them?—would be paid a straight fee. They would have to carry out their diversions at a precise time, which I have fixed as ten thirty in the morning."

"Okay," said Stacey. "Consider it arranged."

"Next, Davidson. He is an American, as I said, and Lester tells me that a happy event is expected in his family any day now. He has left Mrs. Davidson behind in America, of course. Now, supposing that a call came through, apparently from an American hospital, for Mr. Davidson. Supposing that the telephone in the Jewelry Department was out of order because the cord had been cut. Davidson would be called out of the department for the few minutes, no more, that we should need."

"Who cuts the cord?" Stacey asked.

"That will be part of Lester's job."

"And who makes the phone call?"

"Again, Stace, I hoped that you might be able to provide—"

"I can do that." Stacey drained his whiskey. "But what do you do?"

Mr. Payne's lips, never full, were compressed to a disapproving line. He answered the implied criticism only by inviting them to look at two maps—one the layout of the entire third floor, the other of the Jewelry Department itself. Stacey and Straight were impressed, as the uneducated always are, by such evidence of careful planning.

"The Jewelry Department is at one end of the third floor. It has only one exit—into the Carpet Department. There is a service lift which comes straight up into the Jewelry Department. You and I, Stace, will be in that. We shall stop it between floors with the Emergency Stop button. At exactly ten thirty-two we shall go up to the third floor. Lester will give us a sign. If everything has gone well, we proceed. If not, we call the job off. Now, what I propose ..."

He told them, they listened, and they found it good. Even the ignorant, Mr. Payne was glad to see, could recognize genius. He told Straight Line his role.

"We must have a car, Straight, and a driver. What he has to do is simple, but he must stay cool. So I thought of you." Straight grinned.

"In Jessiter Street, just outside the side entrance to Orbin's, there is a parking space reserved for Orbins' customers. It is hardly ever full. But if it is full you can double park there for five minutes—cars often do that. I take it you can—acquire a car, shall I say?—for the purpose. You will face away from Oxford Street, and you will have no more than a few minutes' run to Lambie's house on Greenly Street. You will drop Stace and me, drive on a mile or two, and leave the car. We shall give the stuff to Lambie. He will pay on the nail. Then we all split."

From that point they went on to argue about the split. The argument was warm, but not really heated. They settled that Stacey would get 25 per cent of the total, Straight and Lester 12½ per cent each, and that half would go to the mastermind. Mr. Payne agreed to provide out of his share the £150 that Stacey said would cover the three diversions.

The job was fixed six days ahead—for Tuesday of the following week.

Stacey had two faults which had prevented him from rising high in his profession. One was that he drank too much, the other that he was stupid. He made an effort to keep his drinking under control, knowing that when he drank he talked. So he did not even tell his wife about the job, although she was safe enough.

But he could not resist cheating about the money, which Payne had given to him in full.

The fire bomb was easy. Stacey got hold of a little man named Shrimp Bateson, and fixed it with him. There was no risk, and Shrimp thought himself well paid with twenty-five quid. The bomb itself cost only a fiver, from a friend who dealt in hardware. It was guaranteed to cause just a little fire, nothing serious.

For the telephone call Stacey used a Canadian who was grubbing a living at a striptease club. It didn't seem to either of them that the job was worth more than a tenner, but the Canadian asked for twenty and got fifteen.

The woman was a different matter, for she had to be a bit of an actress, and she might be in for trouble since she actually had to cause a disturbance. Stacey hired an eighteen-stone Irish woman named Lucy O'Malley, who had once been a female wrestler, and had very little in the way of a record—nothing more than a couple of drunk and disorderlies. She refused to take anything less than £50, realizing, as the others hadn't, that Stacey must have something big on.

The whole lot came to less than £100, so that there was cash to spare. Stacey paid them all half their money in advance, put the rest of the £100 aside, and went on a roaring drunk for a couple of days, during which he somehow managed to keep his mouth buttoned and his nose clean.

When he reported on Monday night to Mr. Payne he seemed to have everything fixed, including himself.

Straight Line was a reliable character, a young man who kept himself to himself. He pinched the car on Monday afternoon, took it along to the semilegitimate garage run by his father-in-law, and put new license plates on it. There was no time for a respray job, but he roughed the car up a little so that the owner would be unlikely to recognize it if by an unlucky chance he should be passing outside Orbin's on Tuesday morning. During this whole operation, of course, Straight wore gloves.

He also reported to Mr. Payne on Monday night.

Lester's name was not really Lester—it was Leonard. His mother and his friends in Balham, where he had been born and brought up, called him Lenny. He detested this, as he detested his surname and the pimples that, in spite of his assiduous efforts with ointment, appeared on his face every couple of months. There was nothing he could do about the name of Jones, because it was on his National Insurance card, but Lester for Leonard was a gesture toward emancipation.

Another gesture was made when he left home and mother for a one-room flat in Notting Hill Gate. A third gesture—and the most important one—was his friendship with Lucille, whom he had met in a jazz club called The Whizz Fizz.

Lucille called herself an actress, but the only evidence of it was that she occasionally sang in the club. Her voice was tuneless but loud. After she sang, Lester always bought her a drink, and the drink was always whiskey.

"So what's new?" she said. "Lester-boy, what's new?"

"I sold a diamond necklace today. Two hundred and fifty pounds. Mr. Marston was very pleased." Mr. Marston was the manager of the Jewelry Department.

"So Mr. Marston was pleased. Big deal." Lucille looked round restlessly, tapping her foot.

"He might give me a raise."

"Another ten bob a week and a pension for your fallen arches."

"Lucille, won't you—"

"No." The peak of emancipation for Lester, a dream beyond which his thoughts really could not reach, was that one day Lucille would come to live with him. Far from that, she had not even slept with him yet. "Look, Lester-boy, I know what I want, and let's face it, you haven't got it."

He was incautious enough to ask, "What?"

"Money, moolah, the green folding stuff. Without it you're nothing, with it they can't hurt you."

Lester was drinking whiskey too, although he didn't really like it. Perhaps, but for the whiskey, he would never have said, "Supposing I had money?"

"What money? Where would you get it—draw it out of the Savings Bank?"

"I mean a lot of money."

"Lester-boy, I don't think in penny numbers. I'm talking about real money."

The room was thick with smoke; the Whizz Fizz Kids were playing. Lester leaned back and said deliberately, "Next week I'll have money—thousands of pounds."

Lucille was about to laugh. Then she said, "It's my turn to buy a drink, I'm feeling generous. Hey, Joe. Two more of the same."

Later that night they lay on the bed in his one-room flat. She had let him make love to her, and he had told her everything.

"So the stuff's going to a man called Lambie in Greenly Street?"

Lester had never before drunk so much in one evening. Was it six whiskies or seven? He felt ill, and alarmed. "Lucille, you won't say anything? I mean, I wasn't supposed to tell—"

"Relax. What do you take me for?" She touched his cheek with red-tipped nails. "Besides, we shouldn't have secrets, should we?"

He watched her as she got off the bed and began to dress. "Won't you stay? I mean, it would be all right with the landlady."

"No can do, Lester-boy. See you at the club, though. Tomorrow night. Promise."

"Promise." When she had gone he turned over on to his side and groaned. He feared that he was going to be sick, and he was. Afterwards, he felt better.

Lucille went home to her flat in Earl's Court which she shared with a man named Jim Baxter. He had been sent to Borstal for a robbery from a confectioner's which had involved considerable violence. Since then he had done two short stretches. He listened to what she had to say, then asked, "What's this Lester like?"

"A creep."

"Has he got the nerve to kid you, or do you think it's on the level, what he's told you?"

"He wouldn't kid me. He wants me to live with him when he's got the money. I said I might."

Jim showed her what he thought of that idea. Then he said, "Tuesday morning, eh. Until then, you play along with this creep. Any change in plans I want to know about it. You can do it, can't you, baby?"

She looked up at him. He had a scar on the left side of his face which she thought made him look immensely attractive. "I can do it. And Jim?"

"Yes?"

"What about afterwards?"

"Afterwards, baby? Well, for spending money there's no place like London. Unless it's Paris."

Lester Jones also reported on Monday night. Lucille was being very kind to him, so he no longer felt uneasy.

Mr. Payne gave them all a final briefing and stressed that timing, in this as in every similar affair, was the vital element.

Mr. Rossiter Payne rose on Tuesday morning at his usual time, just after eight o'clock. He bathed and shaved with care and precision, and ate his usual breakfast of one soft-boiled egg, two pieces of toast, and one cup of unsugared coffee. When Miss Oliphant arrived he was already in the shop.

"My dear Miss Oliphant. Are you, as they say, ready to cope this morning?"

"Of course, Mr. Payne. Do you have to go out?"

"I do. Something quite unexpected. An American collector named—but I mustn't tell his name even to you, he doesn't want it known—is in London, and he has asked me to see him. He wants to try to buy the manuscripts of—but there again I'm sworn to secrecy, although if I weren't I should surprise you. I am calling on him, so I shall leave things in your care until—" Mr. Payne looked at his expensive watch—"not later than midday. I shall certainly be back by then. In the meantime, Miss Oliphant, I entrust my ware to you."

She giggled. "I won't let anyone steal the stock, Mr. Payne."

Mr. Payne went upstairs again to his flat where, laid out on his bed, was a very different set of clothes from that which he normally wore. He emerged later from the little side entrance looking quite unlike the dapper, retired Guards officer known to Miss Oliphant.

His clothes were of the shabby nondescript ready-to-wear kind that might be worn by a City clerk very much down on his luck—the sleeve and trouser cuffs distinctly frayed, the tie a piece of dirty string. Curling strands of rather disgustingly gingery hair strayed from beneath his stained gray trilby hat and his face was gray too—gray and much lined, the face of a man of sixty who has been defeated by life.

Mr. Payne had bright blue eyes, but the man who came out of the side entrance had, thanks to contact lenses, brown ones. This man shuffled off down the alley with shoulders bent, carrying a rather dingy suitcase. He was quite unrecognizable as the upright Rossiter Payne.

Indeed, if there was a criticism to be made of him, it was that he looked almost too much the "little man." Long, long ago, Mr. Payne had been an actor, and although his dramatic abilities were extremely limited, he had always loved and been extremely good at make-up.

He took with him a realistic-looking gun that, in fact, fired nothing more lethal than caps. He was a man who disliked violence, and thought it unnecessary.

After he left Mr. Payne on Monday night, Stacey had been unable to resist having a few drinks. The alarm clock wakened him to a smell of frizzling bacon. His wife sensed that he had a job on, and she came into the bedroom as he was taking the Smith and Wesson out of the cupboard.

"Bill." He turned round. "Do you need that?"

"What do you think?"

"Don't take it."

"Ah, don't be stupid."

"Bill, please. I get frightened."

Stacey put the gun into his hip pocket. "Won't use it. Just makes me feel a bit more comfortable, see?"

He ate his breakfast with a good appetite and then telephoned Shrimp Bateson, Lucy O'Malley, and the Canadian, to make sure they were ready. They were. His wife watched him fearfully. Then he came to say goodbye.

"Bill, look after yourself."

"Always do." And he was gone.

Lucille had spent Monday night with Lester. This was much against her wish, but Jim had insisted on it, saying that he must know of any possible last-minute change.

Lester had no appetite at all. She watched with barely concealed contempt as he drank no more than half a cup of coffee and pushed aside his toast. When he got dressed his fingers were trembling so that he could hardly button his shirt.

"Today's the day, then."

"Yes. I wish it was over."

"Don't worry."

He said eagerly, "I'll see you in the club tonight."

"Yes."

"I shall have the money then, and we could go away together. Oh, no, of course not—I've got to stay on the job."

"That's right," she said, humoring him.

As soon as he had gone, she rang Jim and reported that there were no last-minute changes.

Straight Line lived with his family. They knew he had a job on, but nobody talked about it. Only his mother stopped him at the door and said, "Good luck, son," and his father said, "Keep your nose clean."

Straight went to the garage and got out the Jag.

10:30.

Shrimp Bateson walked into the Fur Department with a brown-paper package under his arm. He strolled about pretending to look at furs, while trying to find a place to put down the little parcel. There were several shoppers and he went unnoticed.

He stopped at the point where Furs led to the stairs, moved into a window embrasure, took the little metal cylinder out of its brown-paper wrapping, pressed the switch which started the mechanism, and walked rapidly away.

He had almost reached the door when he was tapped

on the shoulder. He turned. A clerk was standing with the brown paper in his hand.

"Excuse me, sir, I think you've dropped something. I found this paper—"

"No, no," Shrimp said. "It's not mine."

There was no time to waste in arguing. Shrimp turned, and half walked, half ran, through the doors and to the staircase. The clerk followed him. People were coming up the stairs, and Shrimp, in a desperate attempt to avoid them, slipped and fell, bruising his shoulder.

The clerk was standing hesitantly at the top of the stairs when he heard the *whoosh* of sound and, turning, saw flames. He ran down the stairs then, took Shrimp firmly by the arm and said, "I think you'd better come back with me, sir."

The bomb had gone off on schedule, setting fire to the window curtains and to one end of a store counter. A few women were screaming, and other clerks were busy saving the furs. Flack, one of the store detectives, arrived on the spot quickly, and organized the use of the fire extinguishers. They got the fire completely under control in three minutes.

The clerk, full of zeal, brought Shrimp along to Flack. "Here's the man who did it."

Flack looked at him. "Firebug, eh?"

"Let me go. I had nothing to do with it."

"Let's talk to the manager, shall we?" Flack said, and led Shrimp away.

The time was now 10:39.

Lucy O'Malley looked at herself in the glass, and at the skimpy hat perched on her enormous head. Her fake-crocodile handbag, of a size to match her person, had been put down on a chair nearby.

"What do you feel, madam?" the young saleswoman asked, ready to take her cue from the customer's reaction.

"Terrible."

"Perhaps it isn't really you."

"It looks bloody awful," Lucy said. She enjoyed swearing, and saw no reason why she should restrain herself.

The salesgirl laughed perfunctorily and dutifully, and moved over again toward the hats. She indicated a black hat with a wide brim. "Perhaps something more like this?"

Lucy looked at her watch. 10:31. It was time. She went across to her handbag, opened it, and screamed.

"Is something the matter, madam?"

"I've been robbed!"

"Oh, really, I don't think that can have happened."

Lucy had a sergeant-major's voice, and she used it. "Don't tell me what can and can't have happened, young woman. My money was in here, and now it's gone. Somebody's taken it."

The salesgirl, easily intimidated, blushed. The department supervisor, elegant, eagle-nosed, blue-rinsed, moved across like an arrow and asked politely if she could help.

"My money's been stolen," Lucy shouted. "I put my bag down for a minute, twenty pounds in it, and now it's gone. That's the class of people they get in Orbin's." She addressed this last sentence to another shopper, who moved away hurriedly.

"Let's look, shall we, just to make sure." Blue Rinse took hold of the handbag, Lucy took hold of it too, and somehow the bag's contents spilled onto the carpet.

"You stupid fool," Lucy roared.

"I'm sorry, madam," Blue Rinse said icily. She picked up handkerchief, lipstick, powder compact, tissues. Certainly there was no money in the bag. "You're sure the money was in the bag?"

"Of course I'm sure. It was in my purse. I had it five minutes ago. Someone here has stolen it."

"Not so loud, please, madam."

"I shall speak as loudly as I like. Where's your store detective, or haven't you got one?"

Sidley, the other detective on the third floor, was pushing through the little crowd that had collected. "What seems to be the matter?"

"This lady says twenty pounds has been stolen from her handbag." Blue Rinse just managed to refrain from emphasizing the word "lady."

"I'm very sorry. Shall we talk about it in the office?"

"I don't budge until I get my money back." Lucy was carrying an umbrella, and she waved it threateningly. However, she allowed herself to be led along to the office. There the handbag was examined again and the salesgirl, now tearful, was interrogated. There also Lucy, having surreptitiously glanced at the time, put a hand into the capacious pocket of her coat, and discovered the purse. There was twenty pounds in it, just as she had said.

She apologized, although the apology went much against the grain for her, declined the suggestion that she should return to the hat counter, and left the store with the consciousness of a job well done.

"Well," Sidley said. "I shouldn't like to tangle with her on a dark night."

The time was now 10:40.

The clock in the Jewelry Department stood at exactly 10:33 when a girl came running in, out of breath, and said to the manager, "Oh, Mr. Marston, there's a telephone call for Mr. Davidson. It's from America."

Marston was large, and inclined to get pompous. "Put it through here, then."

"I can't. There's something wrong with the line in this department—it seems to be dead."

Davidson had heard his name mentioned, and came over to them quickly. He was a crew-cut American, tough and lean. "It'll be about my wife, she's expecting a baby. Where's the call?"

"We've got it in Administration, one floor up."

"Come on, then." Davidson started off at what was almost a run, and the girl trotted after him. Marston stared at both of them disapprovingly. He became aware that one of his clerks, Lester Jones, was looking rather odd.

"Is anything the matter, Jones? Do you feel unwell?"

Lester said that he was all right. The act of cutting the telephone cord had filled him with terror, but with the departure of Davidson he really did feel better. He thought of the money—and of Lucille.

Lucille was just saying goodbye to Jim Baxter and his friend Eddie Grain. They were equipped with an arsenal of weapons, including flick knives, bicycle chains, and brass knuckles. They did not, however, carry revolvers.

"You'll be careful," Lucille said to Jim.

"Don't worry. This is going to be like taking candy from a baby, isn't it, Eddie?"

"S'right," Eddie said. He had a limited vocabulary, and an almost perpetual smile. He was a terror with a knife.

The Canadian made the call from the striptease club. He had a girl with him. He had told her that it would be a big giggle. When he heard Davidson's voice—the time was just after ten thirty-four—he said, "Is that Mr. Davidson?"

"Yes."

"This is the James Long Foster Hospital in Chicago, Mr. Davidson, Maternity floor."

"Yes?"

"Will you speak up, please. I can't hear you very well."

"Have you got some news of my wife?" Davidson said loudly. He was in a small booth next to the store switchboard. There was no reply. "Hello? Are you there?"

The Canadian put one hand over the receiver, and ran the other up the girl's bare thigh. "Let him stew a little." The girl laughed. They could hear Davidson asking if they were still on the line. Then the Canadian spoke again.

"Hello, hello, Mr. Davidson. We seem to have a bad connection."

"I can hear you clearly. What news is there?"

"No need to worry, Mr. Davidson. Your wife is fine."

"Has she had the baby?"

The Canadian chuckled. "Now, don't be impatient. That's not the kind of thing you can hurry, you know."

"What have you got to tell me then? Why are you calling?"

The Canadian put his hand over the receiver again, said to the girl, "You say something."

"What shall I say?"

"Doesn't matter—that we've got the wires crossed or something."

The girl leaned over, picked up the telephone. "This is the operator. Who are you calling?"

In the telephone booth sweat was running off Davidson. He hammered with his fist on the wall of the booth. "Damn you, get off the line! Put me back to the Maternity Floor."

"This is the operator. Who do you want, please?"

Davidson checked himself suddenly. The girl had a Cockney voice. "Who are you? What's your game?"

The girl handed the telephone back to the Canadian, looking frightened. "He's on to me."

"Hell." The Canadian picked up the receiver again, but the girl had left it, uncovered, and Davidson had heard the girl's words. He dropped the telephone, pushed open the door of the booth, and raced for the stairs. As he ran he loosened the revolver in his hip pocket.

The time was now 10:41.

Straight Line brought the Jaguar smoothly to a stop in the space reserved for Orbin's customers, and looked at his watch. It was 10:32.

Nobody questioned him, nobody so much as gave him a glance. Beautiful, he thought, a nice smooth job, really couldn't be simpler. Then his hands tightened on the steering wheel.

He saw in the rear-view mirror, standing just a few yards behind him, a policeman. Three men were evidently asking the policeman for directions, and the copper was consulting a London place map.

Well, Straight thought, he can't see anything of me except my back, and in a couple of minutes he'll be gone. There was still plenty of time. Payne and Stacey weren't due out of the building until 10:39 or 10:40. Yes, plenty of time.

But there was a hollow feeling in Straight's stomach as he watched the policeman in his mirror.

Some minutes earlier, at 10:24, Payne and Stacey had met at the service elevator beside the Grocery Department on the ground floor. They had met this early because of the possibility that the elevator might be in use when they needed it, although from Lester's observation it was used mostly in the early morning and late afternoon.

They did not need the elevator until 10:30, and they would be very unlucky if it was permanently in use at that time. If they were that unlucky—well, Mr. Payne had said with the pseudo-philosophy of the born gambler, they would have to call the job off. But even as he said this he knew that it was not true, and that having gone so far he would not turn back.

The two men did not speak to each other, but advanced steadily toward the elevator by way of inspecting chow mein, hymettus honey, and real turtle soup. The Grocery Department was full of shoppers, and the two men were quite unnoticed. Mr. Payne reached the elevator first and pressed the button. They were in luck. The door opened.

Within seconds they were both inside. Still neither man spoke. Mr. Payne pressed the button which said 3, and then, when they had passed the second floor, the button that said Emergency Stop. Jarringly the elevator came to a stop. It was now immobilized, so far as a call from outside was concerned. It could be put back into motion only by calling in engineers who would free the Emergency Stop mechanism—or, of course, by operating the elevator from inside.

Stacey shivered a little. The elevator was designed for freight, and therefore roomy enough to hold twenty passengers; but Stacey had a slight tendency to claustrophobia which was increased by the thought that they were poised between floors. He said, "I suppose that bloody thing will work when you press the button?"

"Don't worry, my friend. Have faith in me." Mr. Payne opened the dingy suitcase, revealing as he did so that he was now wearing rubber gloves. In the suitcase were two long red cloaks, two fuzzy white wigs, two thick white beards, two pairs of outsize horn-rimmed spectacles, two red noses, and two hats with large tassels. "This may not be a perfect fit for you, but I don't think you can deny that it's a perfect disguise."

They put on the clothes, Mr. Payne with the pleasure

he always felt in dressing up, Stacey with a certain reluctance. The idea was clever, all right, he had to admit that,
and when he looked in the elevator's small mirror and saw
a Santa Claus looking back at him, he was pleased to find
himself totally unrecognizable. Deliberately he took the
Smith and Wesson out of his jacket and put it into the
pocket of the red cloak.

"You understand, Stace, there is no question of using
that weapon."

"Unless I have to."

"There is no question," Mr. Payne repeated firmly. "Violence is never necessary. It is a confession that one lacks
intelligence."

"We got to point it at them, haven't we? Show we
mean business."

Mr. Payne acknowledged that painful necessity by a
downward twitch of his mouth, undiscernible beneath the
false beard.

"Isn't it time, yet?"

Mr. Payne looked at his watch. "It is now ten twenty-
nine. We go—over the top, you might call it—at ten thirty-
two precisely. Compose yourself to wait, Stace."

Stacey grunted. He could not help admiring his companion, who stood peering into the small glass, adjusting his
beard and mustache, and settling his cloak more comfortably. When at last Mr. Payne nodded, and said, "Here we
go," and pressed the button marked 3, resentment was
added to admiration. He's all right now, but wait till we
get to the action, Stacey thought. His gloved hand on the
Smith and Wesson reassured him of strength and
efficiency.

The elevator shuddered, moved upward, stopped. The
door opened. Mr. Payne placed his suitcase in the open
elevator door so that it would stay open and keep the
elevator at the third floor. Then they stepped out.

To Lester the time that passed after Davidson's departure and before the elevator door opened was complete
and absolute torture.

The whole thing had seemed so easy when Mr. Payne

had outlined it to them. "It is simply a matter of perfect timing," he had said. "If everybody plays his part properly, Stace and I will be back in the lift within five minutes. Planning is the essence of this, as of every scientific operation. Nobody will be hurt, and nobody will suffer financially except—" and here he had looked at Lester with a twinkle in his frosty eyes—"except the insurance company. And I don't think the most tender-hearted of us will worry too much about the insurance company."

That was all very well, and Lester had done what he was supposed to do, but he hadn't really been able to believe that the rest of it would happen. He had been terrified, but with the terror was mixed a sense of unreality.

He still couldn't believe, even when Davidson went to the telephone upstairs, that the plan would go through without a hitch. He was showing some costume jewelry to a thin old woman who kept roping necklaces around her scrawny neck, and while he did so he kept looking at the elevator, above which was the department clock. The hands moved slowly, after Davidson left, from 10:31 to 10:32.

They're not coming, Lester thought. It's all off. A flood of relief, touched with regret but with relief predominating, went through him. Then the elevator door opened, and the two Santa Clauses stepped out. Lester started convulsively.

"Young man," the thin woman said severely, "it doesn't seem to me that I have your undivided attention. Haven't you anything in blue and amber?"

It had been arranged that Lester would nod to signify that Davidson had left the department, or shake his head if anything had gone wrong. He nodded now as though he had St. Vitus's Dance.

The thin woman looked at him, astonished. "Young man, is anything the matter?"

"Blue and amber," Lester said wildly, "amber and blue." He pulled out a box from under the counter and began to look through it. His hands were shaking.

Mr. Payne had been right in his assumption that no surprise would be occasioned by the appearance of two Santa Clauses in any department at this time of year. This, he liked to think, was his own characteristic touch—the touch of, not to be unduly modest about it, creative genius. There were a dozen people in the Jewelry Department, half of them looking at the Russian Royal Family Jewels, which had proved less of an attraction than Sir Henry Orbin had hoped. Three of the others were wandering about in the idle way of people who are not really intending to buy anything, and the other three were at the counters, where they were being attended to by Lester, a salesgirl whose name was Miss Glenny, and by Marston himself.

The appearance of the Santa Clauses aroused only the feeling of pleasure experienced by most people at sight of these slightly artificial figures of jollity. Even Marston barely glanced at them. There were half a dozen Santa Clauses in the store during the weeks before Christmas, and he assumed that these two were on their way to the Toy Department, which was also on the third floor, or to the Robin Hood in Sherwood Forest tableau, which was this year's display for children.

The Santa Clauses walked across the floor together as though they were in fact going into Carpets and then on to the Toy Department, but after passing Lester they diverged. Mr. Payne went to the archway that led from Jewelry to Carpets, and Stacey abruptly turned behind Lester toward the Manager's Office.

Marston, trying to sell an emerald brooch to an American who was not at all sure his wife would like it, looked up in surprise. He had a natural reluctance to make a fuss in public, and also to leave his customer; but when he saw Stacey with a hand actually on the door of his own small but sacred office he said to the American, "Excuse me a moment, sir," and said to Miss Glenny, "Look after this gentleman, please"—by which he meant that the American should not be allowed to walk out with the emerald brooch—and called out, although not so loudly that the call could be thought of as anything so vulgar as a shout,

"Just a moment, please. What are you doing there? What do you want?"

Stacey ignored him. In doing so he was carrying out Mr. Payne's specific instructions. At some point it was inevitable that the people in the department would realize that a theft was taking place, but the longer they could be kept from realizing it, Mr. Payne had said, the better. Stacey's own inclination would have been to pull out his revolver at once and terrorize anybody likely to make trouble; but he did as he was told.

The Manager's Office was not much more than a cubbyhole, with papers neatly arranged on a desk; behind the desk, half a dozen keys were hanging on the wall. The showcase key, Lester had said, was the second from the left, but for the sake of appearances Stacey took all the keys. He had just turned to go when Marston opened the door and saw the keys in Stacey's hand.

The manager was not lacking in courage. He understood at once what was happening and, without speaking, tried to grapple with the intruder. Stacey drew the Smith and Wesson from his pocket and struck Marston hard with it on the forehead. The manager dropped to the ground. A trickle of blood came from his head.

The office door was open, and there was no point in making any further attempt at deception. Stacey swung the revolver around and rasped, "Just keep quiet, and nobody else will get hurt."

Mr. Payne produced his cap pistol and said, in a voice as unlike his usual cultured tones as possible, "Stay where you are. Don't move. We shall be gone in five minutes."

Somebody said, "Well, I'm damned." But no one moved. Marston lay on the floor, groaning. Stacey went to the showcase, pretended to fumble with another key, then inserted the right one. The case opened at once. The jewels lay naked and unprotected. He dropped the other keys on the floor, stretched in his gloved hands, picked up the royal jewels, and stuffed them into his pocket.

It's going to work, Lester thought unbelievingly, it's going to work. He watched, fascinated, as the cascade of shining stuff vanished into Stacey's pocket. Then he became aware that the thin woman was pressing something into his hand. Looking down, he saw with horror that it was a large, brand-new clasp knife, with the dangerous-looking blade open.

"Bought it for my nephew," the thin woman whispered. "As he passes you, go for him."

It had been arranged that if Lester's behavior should arouse the least suspicion he should make a pretended attack on Stacey, who would give him a punch just severe enough to knock him down. Everything had gone so well, however, that this had not been necessary, but now it seemed to Lester that he had no choice.

As the two Santa Clauses backed across the room toward the service elevator, covering the people at the counters with their revolvers, one real and the other a toy, Lester launched himself feebly at Stacey, with the clasp knife demonstratively raised. At the same time Marston, on the other side of Stacey and a little behind him, rose to his feet and staggered in the direction of the elevator.

Stacey's contempt for Lester increased with the sight of the knife, which he regarded as an unnecessary bit of bravado. He shifted the revolver to his left hand, and with his right punched Lester hard in the stomach. The blow doubled Lester up. He dropped the knife and collapsed to the floor, writhing in quite genuine pain.

The delivery of the blow delayed Stacey so that Marston was almost up to him. Mr. Payne, retreating rapidly to the elevator, shouted a warning, but the manager was on Stacey, clawing at his robes. He did not succeed in pulling off the red cloak, but his other hand came away with the wig, revealing Stacey's own cropped brown hair. Stacey snatched back the wig, broke away, and fired the revolver with his left hand.

Perhaps he could hardly have said himself whether he intended to hit Marston, or simply to stop him. The bullet missed the manager and hit Lester, who was rising on one knee. Lester dropped again. Miss Glenny screamed, another woman cried out, and Marston halted.

Mr. Payne and Stacey were almost at the elevator when Davidson came charging in through the Carpet Department entrance. The American drew the revolver from his pocket and shot, all in one swift movement. Stacey fired back wildly. Then the two Santa Clauses were in the service elevator, and the door closed on them.

Davidson took one look at the empty showcase, and shouted to Marston, "Is there an emergency alarm that rings downstairs?"

The manager shook his head. "And my telephone's not working."

"They've cut the line." Davidson raced back through the Carpet Department to the passenger elevators.

Marston went over to where Lester was lying, with half a dozen people round him, including the thin woman. "We must get a doctor."

The American he had been serving said, "I am a doctor." He was bending over Lester, whose eyes were wide open.

"How is he?"

The American lowered his voice. "He got it in the abdomen."

Lester seemed to be trying to raise himself up. The thin woman helped him. He sat up, looked around, and said, "Lucille." Then blood suddenly rushed out of his mouth, and he sank back.

The doctor bent over again, then looked up. "I'm very sorry. He's dead."

The thin woman gave Lester a more generous obituary than he deserved. "He wasn't a very good clerk, but he was a brave young man."

Straight Line, outside in the stolen Jag, waited for the policeman to move. But not a bit of it. The three men with the policeman were pointing to a particular spot on the map, and the copper was laughing; they were having some sort of stupid joke together. What the hell, Straight thought, hasn't the bleeder got any work to do, doesn't he know he's not supposed to be hanging about?

Straight looked at his watch. 10:34, coming up to 10:35— and now, as the three men finally moved away, what should happen but that a teen-age girl should come up, and the copper was bending over toward her with a look of holiday good-will.

It's no good, Straight thought, I shall land them right in his lap if I stay here. He pulled away from the parking space, looked again at his watch. He was obsessed by the need to get out of the policeman's sight.

Once round the block, he thought, just once round can't take more than a minute, and I've got more than two minutes to spare. Then if the copper's still here I'll stay a few yards away from him with my engine running.

He moved down Jessiter Street and a moment after Straight had gone, the policeman, who had never even glanced at him, moved away too.

By Mr. Payne's plan they should have taken off their Santa Claus costumes in the service elevator and walked out at the bottom as the same respectable, anonymous citizens who had gone in; but as soon as they were inside the elevator Stacey said, "He hit me." A stain showed on the scarlet right arm of his robe.

Mr. Payne pressed the button to take them down. He was proud that, in this emergency, his thoughts came with clarity and logic. He spoke them aloud.

"No time to take these off. Anyway, they're just as good a disguise in the street. Straight will be waiting. We step out and into the car, take them off there. Davidson shouldn't have been back in that department for another two minutes."

"I gotta get to a doctor."

"We'll go to Lambie's first. He'll fix it." The elevator whirred downward. Almost timidly, Mr. Payne broached the subject that worried him most. "What happened to Lester?"

"He caught one." Stacey was pale.

The elevator stopped. Mr. Payne adjusted the wig on Stacey's head. "They can't possibly be waiting for us, there hasn't been time. We just walk out. Not too fast, remember. Casually, normally."

The elevator door opened and they walked the fifty feet to the Jessiter Street exit. They were delayed only by a small boy who rushed up to Mr. Payne, clung to his legs and shouted that he wanted his Christmas present. Mr. Payne gently disengaged him, whispered to his mother, "Our tea break. Back later," and moved on.

Now they were outside in the street. But there was no sign of Straight or the Jaguar.

Stacey began to curse. They crossed the road from Orbin's, stood outside Danny's Shoe Parlor for a period that seemed to both of them endless, but was, in fact, only thirty seconds. People looked at them curiously—two Santa Clauses wearing false noses—but they did not arouse great attention. They were oddities, yes, but oddities were in keeping with the time of year and Oxford Street's festive decorations.

"We've got to get away," Stacey said. "We're sitting ducks."

"Don't be a fool. We wouldn't get a hundred yards."

"Planning," Stacey said bitterly. "Fine bloody planning. If you ask me—"

"Here he is."

The Jag drew up beside them, and in a moment they were in and down Jessiter Street, away from Orbin's. Davidson was on the spot less than a minute later, but by the time he had found passers-by who had seen the two Santa Clauses get into the car, they were half a mile away.

Straight Line began to explain what had happened, Stacey swore at him, and Mr. Payne cut them both short.

"No time for that. Get these clothes off, talk later."

"You got the rocks?"

"Yes, but Stace has been hit. By the American detective. I don't think it's bad, though."

"Whatsisname, Lester, he okay?"

"There was trouble. Stace caught him with a bullet."

Straight said nothing more. He was not one to complain about something that couldn't be helped. His feelings showed only in the controlled savagery with which he maneuvered the Jag.

While Straight drove, Mr. Payne was taking off his own

Santa Claus outfit and helping Stacey off with his. He stuffed them, with the wigs and beards and noses, back into the suitcase. Stacey winced as the robe came over his right arm, and Mr. Payne gave him a handkerchief to hold over it. At the same time he suggested that Stacey hand over the jewels, since Mr. Payne would be doing the negotiating with the fence. It was a mark of the trust that both men still reposed in Mr. Payne that Stacey handed them over without a word, and that Straight did not object or even comment.

They turned into the quiet Georgian terrace where Lambie lived. "Number Fifteen, right-hand side," Mr. Payne said.

Jim Baxter and Eddie Grain had been hanging about in the street for several minutes. Lucille had learned from Lester what car Straight was driving. They recognized the Jag immediately, and strolled toward it. They had just reached the car when it came to a stop in front of Lambie's house. Stacey and Mr. Payne got out.

Jim and Eddie were not, after all, too experienced. They made an elementary mistake in not waiting until Straight had driven away. Jim had his flick knife out and was pointing it at Mr. Payne's stomach.

"Come on now, Dad, give us the stuff and you won't get hurt," he said.

On the other side of the car Eddie Grain, less subtle, swung at Stacey with a shortened length of bicycle chain. Stacey, hit round the head, went down, and Eddie was on top of him, kicking, punching, searching.

Mr. Payne hated violence, but he was capable of defending himself. He stepped aside, kicked upward, and knocked the knife flying from Jim's hand. Then he rang the doorbell of Lambie's house. At the same time Straight got out of the car and felled Eddie Grain with a vicious rabbit punch.

During the next few minutes several things happened simultaneously. At the end of the road a police whistle was blown, loudly and insistently, by an old lady who had seen what was going on. Lambie, who also saw what was going on and wanted no part of it, told his manservant on no account to answer the doorbell or open the door.

Stacey, kicked and beaten by Eddie Grain, drew his revolver and fired four shots. One of them struck Eddie in the chest, and another hit Jim Baxter in the leg. Eddie scuttled down the street holding his chest, turned the corner, and ran slap into the arms of two policemen hurrying to the scene.

Straight, who did not care for shooting, got back into the Jag and drove away. He abandoned the Jag as soon as he could, and went home.

When the police arrived, with a bleating Eddie in tow, they found Stacey and Jim Baxter on the ground, and several neighbors only too ready to tell confusing stories about the great gang fight that had just taken place. They interrogated Lambie, of course, but he had not seen or heard anything at all.

And Mr. Payne? With a general melee taking place, and Lambie clearly not intending to answer his doorbell, he had walked away down the road. When he turned the corner he found a cab, which he took to within a couple of hundred yards of his shop. Then, an anonymous man carrying a shabby suitcase, he went in through the little side entrance.

Things had gone badly, he reflected as he again became Mr. Rossiter Payne the antiquarian bookseller, mistakes had been made. But happily they were not his mistakes. The jewels would be hot, no doubt; they would have to be kept for a while, but all was not lost.

Stace and Straight were professionals—they would never talk. And although Mr. Payne did not, of course, know that Lester was dead, he realized that the young man would be able to pose as a wounded hero and was not likely to be subjected to severe questioning.

So Mr. Payne was whistling *There's a Silver Lining* as he went down to greet Miss Oliphant.

"Oh, Mr. Payne," she trilled. "You're back before you said. It's not half-past eleven."

Could that be true? Yes, it was.

"Did the American collector—I mean, will you be able to sell him the manuscripts?"

"I hope so. Negotiations are proceeding, Miss Oliphant. They may take some time, but I hope they will reach a successful conclusion."

The time passed uneventfully until 2:30 in the afternoon when Miss Oliphant entered his little private office. "Mr. Payne, there are two gentlemen to see you. They won't say what it's about, but they look—well, rather funny."

As soon as Mr. Payne saw them and even before they produced their warrant cards, he knew that there was nothing funny about them. He took them up to the flat and tried to talk his way out of it, but he knew it was no use. They hadn't yet got search warrants, the Inspector said, but they would be taking Mr. Payne along anyway. It would save them some trouble if he would care to show them—

Mr. Payne showed them. He gave them the jewels and the Santa Claus disguises. Then he sighed at the weakness of subordinates. "Somebody squealed, I suppose."

"Oh, no. I'm afraid the truth is you were a bit careless."

"*I* was careless." Mr. Payne was genuinely scandalized.

"Yes. You were recognized."

"Impossible!"

"Not at all. When you left Orbin's and got out into the street, there was a bit of a mixup so that you had to wait. Isn't that right?"

"Yes, but I was completely disguised."

"Danny the shoeshine man knows you by name, doesn't he?"

"Yes, but he couldn't possibly have seen me."

"He didn't need to. Danny can't see any faces from his basement, as you know, but he did see something, and he came to tell us about it. He saw two pairs of legs, and the bottoms of some sort of red robes. And he saw the shoes. He recognized one pair of shoes, Mr. Payne. Not those you're wearing now, but that pair on the floor over there."

Mr. Payne looked across the room at the black shoes— shoes so perfectly appropriate to the role of shabby little clerk that he had been playing, and at the decisive, fatally recognizable sharp cut made by the bicycle mudguard in the black leather.

AUGGIE WREN'S CHRISTMAS STORY

BY PAUL AUSTER

I heard this story from Auggie Wren. Since Auggie
doesn't come off too well in it, at least not as well as he'd
like to, he's asked me not to use his real name. Other than
that, the whole business about the lost wallet and the blind
woman and the Christmas dinner is just as he told it to me.

Auggie and I have known each other for close to eleven
years now. He works behind the counter of a cigar store
on Court Street in downtown Brooklyn, and since it's the
only store that carries the little Dutch cigars I like to
smoke, I go in there fairly often. For a long time I didn't
give much thought to Auggie Wren. He was the strange
little man who wore a hooded blue sweatshirt and sold me
cigars and magazines, the impish, wisecracking character
who always had something funny to say about the weather
or the Mets or the politicians in Washington, and that was
the extent of it.

But then one day several years ago he happened to be
looking through a magazine in the store, and he stumbled
across a review of one of my books. He knew it was me
because a photograph accompanied the review, and after
that things changed between us. I was no longer just another customer to Auggie, I had become a distinguished
person. Most people couldn't care less about books and

writers, but it turned out that Auggie considered himself
an artist. Now that he had cracked the secret of who I
was, he embraced me as an ally, a confidant, a brother-in-
arms. To tell the truth, I found it rather embarrassing.
Then, almost inevitably, a moment came when he asked
if I would be willing to look at his photographs. Given his
enthusiasm and good will, there didn't seem to be any way
I could turn him down.

God knows what I was expecting. At the very least, it
wasn't what Auggie showed me the next day. In a small,
windowless room at the back of the store, he opened a
cardboard box and pulled out twelve identical black photo
albums. This was his life's work, he said, and it didn't take
him more than five minutes a day to do it. Every morning
for the past twelve years, he had stood at the corner of
Atlantic Avenue and Clinton Street at precisely 7 o'clock
and had taken a single color photograph of precisely the
same view. The project now ran to more than four thousand photographs. Each album represented a different
year, and all the pictures were laid out in sequence from
January 1 to December 31, with the dates carefully re-
corded under each one.

As I flipped through the albums and began to study
Auggie's work, I didn't know what to think. My first impression was that it was the oddest, most bewildering thing
I had ever seen. All the pictures were the same. The whole
project was a numbing onslaught of repetition, the same
street and the same buildings over and over again, an unre-
lenting delirium of redundant images. I couldn't think of
anything to say to Auggie, so I continued turning pages,
nodding my head in feigned appreciation. Auggie himself
seemed unperturbed, watching me with a broad smile on
his face, but after I'd been at it for several minutes, he
suddenly interrupted me and said, "You're going too fast.
You'll never get it if you don't slow down."

He was right, of course. If you don't take the time to
look, you'll never manage to see anything. I picked up
another album and forced myself to go more deliberately.
I paid closer attention to details, took note of shifts in the

weather, watched for the changing angles of light as the seasons advanced. Eventually, I was able to detect subtle differences in the traffic flow, to anticipate the rhythm of the different days (the commotion of workday mornings, the relative stillness of weekends, the contrast between Saturdays and Sundays). And then, little by little, I began to recognize the faces of the people in the background, the passersby on their way to work, the same people in the same spot every morning, living an instant of their lives in the field of Auggie's camera.

Once I got to know them, I began to study their postures, the way they carried themselves from one morning to the next, trying to discover their moods from these surface indications, as if I could imagine stories for them, as if I could penetrate the invisible dramas locked inside their bodies. I picked up another album. I was no longer bored, no longer puzzled as I had been at first. Auggie was photographing time, I realized, both natural time and human time, and he was doing it by planting himself in one tiny corner of the world and willing it to be his own by standing guard in the space he had chosen for himself. As he watched me pore over his work, Auggie continued to smile with pleasure. Then, almost as if he had been reading my thoughts, he began to recite a line from Shakespeare. "Tomorrow and tomorrow and tomorrow," he muttered under his breath, "time creeps on its petty pace." I understood then that he knew exactly what he was doing.

That was more than two thousand pictures ago. Since that day, Auggie and I have discussed his work many times, but it was only last week that I learned how he acquired his camera and started taking pictures in the first place. That was the subject of the story he told me, and I'm still struggling to make sense of it.

Earlier that same week, a man from *The New York Times* called me and asked if I would be willing to write a short story that would appear in the paper on Christmas morning. My first impulse was to say no, but the man was very charming and persistent, and by the end of the conversation I told him I would give it a try. The moment

I hung up the phone, however, I fell into a deep panic. What did I know about Christmas? I asked myself. What did I know about writing short stories on commission?

I spent the next several days in despair, warring with the ghosts of Dickens, O. Henry, and other masters of the Yuletide spirit. The very phrase "Christmas story" had unpleasant associations for me, evoking dreadful out-pourings of hypocritical mush and treacle. Even at their best, Christmas stories were no more than wish-fulfillment dreams, fairy tales for adults, and I'd be damned if I'd ever allowed myself to write something like that. And yet, how could anyone propose to write an unsentimental Christmas story? It was a contradiction in terms, an impos-sibility, an out-and-out conundrum. One might just as well try to imagine a racehorse without legs, or a sparrow with-out wings.

I got nowhere. On Thursday I went out for a long walk, hoping the air would clear my head. Just past noon, I stopped in at the cigar store to replenish my supply, and there was Auggie, standing behind the counter as always. He asked me how I was. Without really meaning to, I found myself unburdening my troubles to him. "A Christ-mas story?" he said after I had finished. "Is that all? If you buy me lunch, my friend, I'll tell you the best Christ-mas story you ever heard. And I guarantee that every word of it is true."

We walked down the block to Jack's, a cramped and boisterous delicatessen with good pastrami sandwiches and photographs of old Dodgers teams hanging on the walls. We found a table at the back, ordered our food, and then Auggie launched into his story.

"It was the summer of '72," he said. "A kid came in one morning and started stealing things from the store. He must have been about nineteen or twenty, and I don't think I've ever seen a more pathetic shoplifter in my life. He's standing by the rack of paperbacks along the far wall and stuffing books into the pockets of his raincoat. It was crowded around the counter just then, so I didn't notice him at first. But once I noticed what he was up to, I started to shout. He took off like a jackrabbit, and by the time I managed to get out from behind the counter, he was already tearing down Atlantic Avenue. I chased after him for about half a block, and then I gave up. He'd dropped something along the way, and since I didn't feel like running anymore, I bent down to see what it was.

"It turned out to be his wallet. There wasn't any money inside, but his driver's license was there along with three or four snapshots. I suppose I could have called the cops and had him arrested. I had his name and address from the license, but I felt kind of sorry for him. He was just a measly little punk, and once I looked at those pictures in his wallet, I couldn't bring myself to feel very angry at him. Robert Goodwin. That was his name. In one of the pictures, I remember, he was standing with his arm around his mother or grandmother. In another one, he was sitting there at age nine or ten dressed in a baseball uniform with a big smile on his face. I just didn't have the heart. He was probably on dope now, I figured. A poor kid from Brooklyn without much going for him, and who cared about a couple of trashy paperbacks anyway?

"So I held on to the wallet. Every once in a while I'd get a little urge to send it back to him, but I kept delaying and never did anything about it. Then Christmas rolls around and I'm stuck with nothing to do. The boss usually invites me over to his house to spend the day, but that year he and his family were down in Florida visiting relatives. So I'm sitting in my apartment that morning, feeling a little sorry for myself, and then I see Robert Goodwin's wallet lying on a shelf in the kitchen. I figure what the hell, why not do something nice for once, and I put on my coat and go out to return the wallet in person.

"The address was over in Boerum Hill, somewhere in the projects. It was freezing out that day, and I remember getting lost a few times trying to find the building. Everything looks the same in that place, and you keep going over the same ground thinking you're somewhere else. Anyway, I finally get to the apartment I'm looking for and ring the bell. Nothing happens. I assume no one's there, but I try again just to make sure. I wait a little longer and just when I'm about to give up, I hear someone shuffling

to the door. An old woman's voice asks who's there, and
I say I'm looking for Robert Goodwin. 'Is that you, Robert?' the old woman says, and then she undoes about fifteen locks and opens the door.

"She has to be at least eighty, maybe ninety, years old,
and the first thing I notice about her is that she's blind. 'I
knew you'd come, Robert,' she says. 'I knew you wouldn't
forget your Granny Ethel on Christmas.' And then she
opens her arms as if she's about to hug me.

"I didn't have much time to think, you understand. I
had to say something real fast, and before I knew what
was happening, I could hear the words coming out of my
mouth. 'That's right, Granny Ethel,' I said. 'I came back
to see you on Christmas.' Don't ask me why I did it. I
don't have any idea. Maybe I didn't want to disappoint
her or something, I don't know. It just came out that way,
and then this old woman was suddenly hugging me there
in front of the door, and I was hugging her back.

"I didn't exactly say that I was her grandson. Not in so
many words, at least, but that was the implication. I wasn't
trying to trick her, though. It was like a game we'd both
decided to play—without having to discuss the rules. I
mean, that woman *knew* I wasn't her grandson Robert.
She was old and dotty, but she wasn't so far gone that she
couldn't tell the difference between a stranger and her own
flesh and blood. But it made her happy to pretend, and
since I had nothing better to do anyway, I was happy to
go along with her.

"So we went into the apartment and spent the day together. The place was a real dump, I might add, but what
else can you expect from a blind woman who does her
own housekeeping? Every time she asked me a question
about how I was, I would lie to her. I told her I'd found
a good job working in a candy store, I told her I was about
to get married, I told her a hundred pretty stories, and
she made like she believed every one of them. 'That's fine,
Robert,' she would say, nodding her head and smiling. 'I
always knew things would work out for you.'

"After a while, I started getting pretty hungry. There
didn't seem to be much food in the house, so I went out

to a store in the neighborhood and brought back a mess of stuff. A precooked chicken, vegetable soup, a bucket of potato salad, a chocolate cake, all kinds of things. Ethel had a couple of bottles of wine stashed in her bedroom, and so between us we managed to put together a fairly decent Christmas dinner. We both got a little tipsy from the wine, I remember, and after the meal was over we went out to sit in the living room, where the chairs were more comfortable. I had to take a pee, so I excused myself and went to the bathroom down the hall. That's where things took yet another turn. It was ditsy enough doing my little jig as Ethel's grandson, but what I did next was positively crazy, and I've never forgiven myself for it.

"I go into the bathroom, and stacked up against the wall next to the shower, I see a pile of six or seven cameras. Brand-new 35 millimeter cameras, still in their boxes, top-quality merchandise. I figure this is the work of the real Robert, a storage-place for one of his recent hauls. I've never taken a picture in my life, and I've certainly never stolen anything, but the moment I see those cameras sitting in the bathroom, I decide I want one for myself. Just like that. And without even stopping to think about it, I tuck one of the boxes under my arm and go back to the living room.

"I couldn't have been gone for more than three minutes, but in that time Granny Ethel had fallen asleep in her chair. Too much Chianti, I suppose. I went into the kitchen to wash the dishes, and she slept on through the whole racket, snoring like a baby. There didn't seem to be any point in disturbing her, so I decided to leave. I couldn't even write a note to say goodbye, seeing that she was blind and all, and so I just left. I put her grandson's wallet on the table, picked up the camera again, and walked out of the apartment. And that's the end of the story."

"Did you ever go back to see her?" I asked.

"Once," he said. "About three or four months later. I felt so bad about stealing the camera, I hadn't even used it yet. I finally made up my mind to return it, but Ethel wasn't there anymore. I don't know what happened to her, but someone else had moved into the apartment, and he couldn't tell me where she was."

"She probably died."

"Yeah, probably."

"Which means that she spent her last Christmas with you."

"I guess so. I never thought of it that way."

"It was a good deed, Auggie. It was a nice thing you did for her."

"I lied to her, and then I stole from her. I don't see how you can call that a good deed."

"You made her happy. And the camera was stolen anyway. It's not as if the person you took it from really owned it."

"Anything for art, eh, Paul?"

"I wouldn't say that. But at least you've put the camera to good use."

"And now you've got your Christmas story, don't you?"

"Yes," I said, "I suppose I do."

I paused for a moment, studying Auggie as a wicked grin spread across his face. I couldn't be sure, but the look in his eyes at that moment was so mysterious, so fraught with the glow of some inner delight, that it suddenly occurred to me that he had made the whole thing up. I was about to ask him if he'd been putting me on, but then I realized he would never tell. I had been tricked into believing him, and that was the only thing that mattered. As long as there's one person to believe it, there's no story that can't be true.

"You're an ace, Auggie," I said. "Thanks for being so helpful."

"Any time," he answered, still looking at me with that maniacal light in his eyes. "After all, if you can't share your secrets with your friends, what kind of a friend are you?"

"I guess I owe you one."

"No you don't. Just put it down the way I told you, and you don't owe me a thing."

"Except the lunch."

"That's right. Except the lunch."

I returned Auggie's smile with a smile of my own, and then I called out to the waiter and asked for the check.

MURDER AT CHRISTMAS

BY C. M. CHAN

There were eight days till Christmas. That meant there were six days till Phillip Bethancourt would be called to gather round the family hearth and join in the exchanging of good cheer and discussions of the principle that, although one might be independently wealthy, this did not eliminate the need for doing something useful with one's life and why couldn't he have become a barrister like his cousin Robert? Or head up a charity like his sister? If he was so interested in criminal investigation, why didn't he get a job with the CID? Bethancourt always smiled and said he wanted to be a writer, a notion that was just barely borne out by the publishing of three or four of his articles.

Eight days till Christmas also meant five days till he would be required to place before Marla, his girlfriend, a present both expensive and spectacular. This was only their second Christmas together, but Marla's attitude toward presents was clear to anyone who had known her a week, and Bethancourt knew better than to disappoint her.

Bethancourt, proceeding down Bond Street towards Asprey's, caught sight of a stocky figure in a tweed overcoat just crossing the street. This bore a strong resemblance to Detective Sergeant Jack Gibbons, a great friend of Bethancourt's and his chief source for the practicing of his amateur detective hobby. Bethancourt sprinted forward to catch him up at the corner.

"Phillip!" grinned Gibbons. "I was going to call you when I got back to the office."

"Christmas shopping, I see," said Bethancourt, eyeing the three bulging shopping bags in Gibbons' chapped red hand.

Gibbons made a face. "It may be the last chance I'll get," he said. "There's been a murder off in Dorset. I was sent back this morning to get the postmortem and interview one or two people, but I thought I'd better get some Christmas shopping done while I was still in town."

Bethancourt's eyes brightened behind his glasses. "Were you going to call me just to say happy holidays, or is the murder particularly interesting?"

Gibbons laughed. "Well, it's an odd one, certainly." He shifted the packages in his hands. "There's an elderly widow, quite well off, living alone now in a huge Victorian monstrosity where she brought up five children."

"Sounds normal so far," observed Bethancourt. "Children, I take it, live in London or other equally faraway places."

"Yes, yes," said Gibbons. "I haven't come to the odd bit yet. It's the murder itself that's so bizarre."

"Well, who was murdered?"

"We don't know."

"You don't?"

"No. If you'd just be quiet for a bit, I could tell this in an orderly fashion."

"Very well."

"Mrs. Bainbridge got a Christmas tree in a couple of days ago and went up to the attic to bring down the ornaments. Well, she opens the attic door and a truly awful stench greets her. It's so dreadful, she's nearly sick on the spot—"

"Jack, you can't mean—"

"Oh, yes, I can. Her Christmas ornaments were scattered all over the place and in the old steamer trunk where she usually stores them, there was a dead man—several months gone, we think."

"My God," said Bethancourt, fascinated. "What a shock for the old girl."

"Oh, she didn't discover the body herself," said Gibbons. "The smell alarmed her enough so that she went back downstairs and called a neighbor. He and his wife came over, and he was the one who went up and opened the trunk—and he *was* sick. It was rather a pity that he'd just finished lunch," added Gibbons reflectively.

"You can't blame him," said Bethancourt with feeling. "It must have been perfectly foul."

"Oh, certainly," agreed Gibbons cheerfully. "Well, it's all quite a mystery at the moment. Mrs. Bainbridge hadn't been up in the attic since she put the ornaments away last Christmas, and she doesn't think anyone else has been, but the place has been simply overrun by children and grandchildren. Once we find out who the dead man was and when he was killed, it may all become a lot clearer."

"It's a lovely puzzle as it stands," said Bethancourt, an eager look in his eyes. "I say, Jack, you wouldn't want a lift back to Dorset tomorrow or anything, would you?"

Gibbons laughed at him. "Well, I don't know if tomorrow will suit," he said slyly. "I've got to interview two grandchildren first, and if I don't find them in this afternoon—"

"You devil," said Bethancourt. "I will pay for the taxis and even carry one of your bags if you will let me come with you."

"*And* drive me to Dorset tomorrow?"

"Yes, damn you."

"Very well," said Gibbons, holding out a shopping bag. "I knew you'd find this one interesting, Phillip."

The postmortem was waiting for Gibbons when they returned to New Scotland Yard to drop off the packages.

"Well," said Gibbons, frowning at it, "he apparently met his fate sometime in August, or possibly early September."

"Lord," said Bethancourt, pushing his glasses more firmly onto his nose and peering over Gibbons' shoulder. "You'd think the whole house would have smelt of it by now."

"The third story did a bit," said Gibbons. "But that's the old servants' quarters, and of course nobody goes up there nowadays. Mrs. Bainbridge's daily goes up to clean once a year in the spring, but that's all."

"Stabbed, eh?"

"So they think, but you can see how vague they are. A stiletto or a whacking great kitchen knife: it could have been anything. There were bloodstains in the trunk, but the scene-of-the-crime men didn't find them anywhere else. So it's likely he was killed elsewhere."

"Well, of course. You don't lure people to attics to kill them."

"You could," said Gibbons. "I don't see why not. No, don't start, Phillip—we've got to get over to the university and find Mrs. Bainbridge's granddaughter."

Maureen Bainbridge, emerging from a chemistry class, was a truly lovely creature of about twenty. There was something kittenlike about her, how she held her head and brushed her dark hair aside, and it made a fascinating contrast to her open, straightforward manner. She was tall and slender, with the famous English peaches and cream complexion.

Even Bethancourt, who had a high standard of female beauty, gave a low whistle when the student they approached pointed her out. They extracted her from her classmates, introduced themselves and explained their presence, and then followed her to an empty classroom where they could talk.

"It's incredible, isn't it?" she said, sitting down on one of the desks. "I really can't quite believe it."

"I'm sure it's a shock," said Gibbons. "Can you tell us, please: when was the last time you were at your grandmother's house?"

"In the summer," she replied promptly. "We were all there during the Bank Holiday."

"All of you?"

"The whole family," she said expansively, and then hastily amended, "All my aunts and uncles, I mean. Only one of my cousins showed up. Oh, and Dad brought one of his business partner's sons. Grandmother was annoyed about that because it meant an extra bedroom, but there he was, you know."

Gibbons pulled a notebook from his pocket and consulted a page. "That would be Renaud Fibrier," he said.

"Yes," she nodded. "He was just a little older than me, so my cousin Daniel and I did our best to entertain him. But, of course, there were a lot of family demands, and I'm afraid Renaud must have gotten bored. He left Monday morning, at any rate, instead of staying on till Tuesday."

"He sounds a rather tedious houseguest," said Gibbons.

"I didn't mean that," Maureen said. "Renaud was really rather charming. I only thought he must have been bored because he left early."

"I see," said Gibbons. "We haven't spoken with Mr. Fibrier yet; your grandmother didn't have his address."

"Neither do I," she replied promptly, "but Dad should know."

"Yes, we should be speaking to him soon," said Gibbons. He glanced down at his notebook again. "So the houseparty consisted of Paul and Clarissa North, Bill and Bernice Clayton, Michael and—"

"Oh, no," she interrupted. "Uncle Michael wasn't there; he lives in America. But Aunt Cathy was visiting from Australia. None of us had seen her in years, so there was a sort of family reunion. Most of them were only there for the weekend. My parents and I stayed for a week—we always do during the summer. Oh!" She put a hand to her mouth in what Bethancourt could not help but feel was a very becoming gesture.

"What is it?" asked Gibbons.

"I've just remembered. I was at Grandmother's house for a weekend in November. I was a bit behind here and I just wanted a quiet place to study and Grandmother said I was welcome. She always does."

"Did you go up to the attic or the third floor while you were there?" asked Gibbons.

"No. The last time I was in the attic was last year when I helped Grandmother with the Christmas things."

"Do you remember whether anyone else went up there during the August visit?"

Maureen wrinkled her brow thoughtfully. "I don't know," she said after a moment. "I don't remember anything like that, but there were so many people . . . it was awfully busy."

"That's understandable," said Gibbons. "Now, can you tell me when you were last at the house before the August visit?"

She paused again. "I think in April," she said at last. "There was the vacation and I went up then, I know. I don't think I was there again until August."

"You were alone with your grandmother in April?"

"Yes—no, Aunt Clarissa came up and spent a night, I think."

"Don't you have brothers or sisters?" asked Bethancourt. "Or did they not go to your grandmother's in August?"

She grinned at him. "I'm an only child," she said, "and the youngest of my cousins. Dad married late."

"Really?" said Bethancourt. "Did you know that only children are often very high achievers?"

"Great," she answered. "Maybe I'll win the Nobel prize someday, then. I'm studying physics."

"Well," said Gibbons, rising, "you've been very helpful, Miss Bainbridge. Here's my card; please call me if you think of anything else. Right now, we have an appointment to keep with Daniel North. I believe he was the cousin you mentioned who was also at the August reunion?"

"That's right. Say hello to him for me."

"We will," promised Bethancourt. Outside, he added, "Quite something, isn't she?"

"She's too young for you, Phillip."

"Much too young," Bethancourt agreed. "But I could always wait for her to grow up."

"Incorrigible," muttered Gibbons.

Daniel North was a goodlooking man of about thirty, conservatively dressed as befitted a junior member of a prominent solicitor's office. He received them with a quick smile and asked them to be seated. He denied having been in his grandmother's attic since he was a child, and he had certainly not gone up there in August, which was the last time he had been at the house. Asked who else had been there at that time, his list tallied with Maureen's, with one exception.

"I thought," said Gibbons, "that Maureen's father had brought a business associate?"

"Oh, him," said North. "I'd forgotten. Yes, he was there. I can't think why Uncle David brought him—I never cared for the fellow myself. Unsavory type, if you ask me. Anyway, if you want someone who's been in the attic recently, you should talk to my mother."

Gibbons looked up. "She's been up there?"

"I don't know," answered North, "but she often visits my grandmother—much more frequently than the rest of us. If anyone's been in the attic, it would be she. In fact, I think she's in Dorset now."

"Yes," said Gibbons. "The chief inspector was going to see her this morning. Well, thank you very much for your time, Mr. North."

North ushered them to the door, where the clerk appeared to escort them from the premises.

"Well," said Gibbons, shrugging into his coat in the vestibule, "that's done with."

"It hasn't got you much further."

"No one really thought it would. But you never can tell," added Gibbons cheerfully. "One of them might have been up there near the crucial times."

"Look here," said Bethancourt, leading the way out into the street, "why don't you come round to dinner tonight and we can go over it?"

"Where are you dining?" asked Gibbons suspiciously. He had previously accepted dinner invitations from Bethancourt and found himself eating in restaurants that he could ill afford on his salary.

"I'm meeting Marla at eight thirty at Joe's Cafe," answered Bethancourt, confirming Gibbons' worst fears.

"Well, I don't know, Phillip—"

"Don't be a spoilsport, Jack. I'm sure there's heaps of things about this case you haven't told me yet."

Gibbons had an inspiration. "How would it be if I met you there for a drink before dinner?"

"If that's the best you can do, I suppose I'll have to be happy with it. Eight thirty, then, in the bar."

"We could make it earlier, so that when Marla comes—"

"She'll be late."

"So will you."

Bethancourt assumed a solemn expression. "I give you my word, Jack, tonight I shall be punctual."

"Oh, very well. Half eight then."

The bar at Joe's Cafe was crowded. Gibbons ordered a whisky and positioned himself in view of the door. He did not bother to search for Bethancourt among the other patrons, having less than no faith in his friend's promise to be on time.

He was pleasantly surprised, therefore, when Bethancourt made his way through the door at eight thirty-five, beaming triumphantly.

"I told you I'd be here," he said happily. "Here, let's move down a bit. We can just fit in over there. Now then, Jack," said Bethancourt, having obtained a drink and wedged himself firmly between Gibbons and a rather large man in evening dress, "let's start from the beginning."

"And what do you mean by the beginning?"

"The murdered man, of course," replied Bethancourt promptly.

"You saw the p.m.," said Gibbons, shrugging and sipping his drink.

"Yes. A man of about thirty, stabbed in the back sometime in August or early September and considerably decomposed. But what was he wearing? Was he dark or light?"

"Dark hair," answered Gibbons. "Open-necked shirt and linen pants and black loafers. And if that tells you anything—"

"It tells me he wasn't chopping wood when he was killed," retorted Bethancourt.

"Yes, but what we really need to know is who he was. And that will have to wait until we've finished comparing his description with the missing persons list. Until we find out who knew him, and where he might have been, we're working in a void. He might have been killed anywhere, anytime, by anybody, and put into the attic anytime subsequently."

"He didn't belong to the village, I suppose?"

"No. That was the first thing we checked. None of the villagers in the immediate area is missing anyone. But one of the villagers, or else one of Mrs. Bainbridge's family, must be the murderer."

"Because, you mean, of knowing Mrs. Bainbridge's habits. You don't suspect her?"

Gibbons shrugged. "She's a very elderly woman. She hasn't been to the top of the house in a year because it's hard for her to climb the stairs. I really can't imagine her carting a man's body up three flights."

"No, I suppose not."

There was a slight disturbance in the bar. The various conversations paused momentarily as people's attentions were caught. In a moment the cause of this became evident as several gentlemen shifted their position to allow a spectacularly beautiful woman to pass through. She walked down the aisle they made for her as if it were her right, head crowned with copper hair held high, jade green eyes passing them over until she found the one for whom she searched. And then she smiled, and her slender figure moved quickly forward.

"Marla!" said Bethancourt, glancing hastily at his watch. "It's not even nine o'clock yet."

"You said half eight," she reminded him, kissing him lightly. "Hello, Jack. Phillip didn't tell me you were joining us."

"I'm not really," denied Gibbons hastily. "Just a drink."

"Come now," said Bethancourt firmly: "You simply can't refuse to join us. Now that Marla's come, we can get a table and be comfortable. I'll just speak to the maitre d'."

And he moved off while Gibbons was explaining that he really couldn't.

"Why not?" asked Marla, smiling. "Have another date?"

"No," said Gibbons uncomfortably. "It's just that, well, I did all my Christmas shopping today and I'm feeling a little low on funds."

"That is not a good excuse," said Marla firmly. "Besides, I expect Phillip will pay."

"I expect so, but I don't like him to."

"That's just one of those male things," replied Marla, hunting in her bag for a cigarette. "If you were a woman, you wouldn't mind at all." Gibbons was spared from answering by the return of Bethancourt, who herded them without further ado towards the dining room. He sighed resignedly.

When they had put the menus aside and had ordered the wine, Bethancourt said casually, "I'll have to get up early tomorrow, Marla. I told Jack I'd drive him back to Dorset."

"Dorset?" asked Marla. "Whatever are you doing out there? I thought your people lived in Suffolk?"

"They do," answered Gibbons. "I'm working in Dorset."

"Oh, God," said Marla. "Not another murder investigation." She glared accusingly at Bethancourt.

Marla did not like her boyfriend's hobby. She found murders an unpleasant and unhealthy topic and, moreover, felt that investigating them took an inordinate amount of time and thought. Time and thought which could far more pleasantly be devoted to herself.

"Well, yes," admitted Bethancourt. "But it's only a little one, Marla, and will probably be cleared up by the time we get there."

"Hmpf," said Marla, or something very much like it.

"Actually," went on Bethancourt, unperturbed, "it's a rather unusual case."

"Is it?" she asked frostily.

"Yes," said Bethancourt firmly. "There's this old woman, you see, a widow—"

"Excuse me," said Marla, rising. "I have to go to the w.c."

This was a tactical error on her part. By the time she returned, Bethancourt and Gibbons were deep in a discussion of Mrs. Bainbridge's progeny and the possibility of their having visited the attic.

"Chris O'Leary is interviewing the ones in Northants," Gibbons was saying. "That's Bill and Bernice Clayton."

"Bernice is Mrs. Bainbridge's second daughter?" asked Bethancourt.

"That's right. Clarissa North, Daniel's mother, is the eldest. Next is Bernice Clayton, and after her is Maureen's father, David. There's another son living in America who hasn't been to England in some time, and then the youngest is Cathy Dresler, who now lives in Australia and was the cause of the August reunion."

"I suppose none of them is missing?"

"No. No, I'm afraid not."

Bethancourt filled Marla's wine glass, lit her cigarette, and considered.

"And has Mrs. Bainbridge had any visitors other than her children and grandchildren?"

"She says not."

"What on earth does it matter whether she has or not?" asked Marla impatiently.

"Because, my love, the murdered man was a stranger to the village. Either one of Mrs. Bainbridge's family ran into him unexpectedly in August, when most of them were there, killed him, and hid him in the attic, or else they killed him somewhere else, at some other time, and transported the body to Dorset, thinking that the best hiding place. Incidentally, Jack, it would be interesting to find out which of Mrs. Bainbridge's relatives visited her by car."

"It sounds very farfetched to me," said Marla.

"True," agreed Bethancourt. "Which is why it is more likely to be one of the villagers. One of them either has a visitor or goes to meet the victim. In a moment of passion, he kills him. He's left with the body, all in a panic, when suddenly he remembers Mrs. Bainbridge, all alone in a huge house and slightly deaf. It's late at night and he knows she doesn't lock her doors. So he pushes the body along and carries it up to the attic."

"Lovely," said Gibbons dryly, "but Mrs. Bainbridge is *not* slightly deaf. And how do you know he was killed late at night?"

"This theory," went on Bethancourt, unheeding, "also explains why the body was never moved. One of the family would most likely not desire their mother or grandmother to discover a rotting corpse in her attic. Moreover, they will naturally fall under some suspicion, as they are connected with the house. Whereas one of the villagers has no real connection to the house and may be less considerate of Mrs. Bainbridge's feelings."

"It's possible," allowed Gibbons. "But it is also very possible that Cathy Dresler is the murderess and did not have the opportunity to retrieve the body before she had to leave for Australia."

"Anything's possible," said Marla. "It's quite possible that Phillip killed this man himself, just to give himself something foolproof to investigate."

"Now, Marla—"

"Here come the starters," she said sweetly. "Shall I stay and eat them with you, or go elsewhere?"

"Sorry, darling," said Bethancourt. "Jack and I will keep off murder while we're eating."

"Of course," agreed Gibbons hastily, knowing Marla to be perfectly capable of dumping the starters over their heads if they did not desist. "Not an appropriate dinner topic in any case."

This rule was adhered to during the rest of the meal, for which Bethancourt insisted on paying. Gibbons excused himself soon afterward, saying he still had his notes to put in order before returning to Dorset the next day.

"All right," said Bethancourt. "I'll see you in the morning, then."

"Nine o'clock, don't forget," said Gibbons.

"I won't. Goodnight, Jack."

"Goodnight," chimed in Marla, and, just to show there were no hard feelings, kissed his cheek.

Chief Inspector Wallace Carmichael made his way down the stairs from his room and stood in the doorway, surveying the clientele of the Lion's Head pub in Dorset. He was a tall, ruddy-faced man with bristling brown mustaches and sharp blue eyes. He glanced at his watch, swore vehemently under his breath, and marched to a corner table from which he could keep the door in view. Where the hell was Gibbons, anyway? He had rung up last night to say he would be back this morning and here it was, wanting only a few minutes to twelve, and no Gibbons. Carmichael felt himself to be a lenient man with his subordinates; he gave them every opportunity to follow up their own leads and express their opinions. After all, he wasn't going to be at the Yard forever, and there were the chief inspectors of tomorrow to think of. But he didn't think much of sleeping in when there was a job to be done, and young Gibbons was going to get a piece of his mind on the subject. If he ever showed up.

Carmichael had procured himself a pint of bitter and a ploughman's lunch and was just sitting down to it when Gibbons entered, closely followed by a tall, slender young man with fair hair, horn-rimmed glasses, and a large Russian wolfhound. Carmichael heaved a great sigh.

"I have only one thing to say," he pronounced when Gibbons reached the table. "I am always pleased to have Bethancourt here give us any help he likes, but he is not a member of the force, he therefore cannot be disciplined by us, and if he can't get up in the morning, *do not*, in future, accept rides with him."

"I really am most awfully sorry, chief inspector," said Bethancourt while Gibbons murmured, "Yes, sir," and glared at his friend.

Carmichael held up a hand. "No more to be said. Just bear it in mind next time. Now, get yourselves some food and drink and make a report."

"I'll get everything," offered Bethancourt. "You sit down, Jack, and don't waste any more time."

Gibbons shot him another glare, sat down, and began digging in his briefcase for the postmortem report.

Carmichael looked it over and listened to Gibbons' recitation of the two interviews he had conducted. Bethancourt, having procured the viands, sat silent and alert, giving his best impression of the good schoolboy.

"Nothing yet on his clothes or from missing persons?" asked Carmichael when Gibbons was gone.

"No, sir. Not yet."

"Well, there's been a development or two here." Carmichael sipped his beer and wiped his mustache carefully. "I've spoken to Mrs. Dresler in Australia. She says she was in the attic sometime at the beginning of her visit here. She can't pin it down exactly, but it was certainly prior to the Bank Holiday weekend. Nothing was out of place when she was there—at any rate, the Christmas ornaments were not scattered about."

"Does Mrs. Bainbridge corroborate her statement?"

Carmichael shrugged. "She's not sure. Mrs. Dresler says she was looking for an old book of her father's. A first edition of Dickens it was. Mrs. Bainbridge remembers her daughter asking after it and later finding it. She herself was under the impression the book was still in the library, although she admits that she did pack up some of her husband's books at one time, and moved some others to different parts of the house. There is a box of books in the attic, so Mrs. Dresler's story may be quite true."

"What about fingerprints?"

"The attic's filled with them. The Australian police are taking a copy of Mrs. Dresler's and sending them along." Carmichael pulled a cigar from his breast pocket and lit it carefully.

"O'Leary's rung up from Northants," he went on, puffing, "but he hasn't got much more than you, Gibbons. In fact, we've got just about the whole family covered, but no one's been in the attic in donkey's years, or so they claim."

"Who haven't we talked to, sir?"

"David Bainbridge—he's on business over in France and his wife doesn't know when he'll be returning. He was called there rather unexpectedly, I gather. And we haven't talked to Renaud Fibrier."

"That was David Bainbridge's business partner?" asked Bethancourt.

"Actually, his partner's son. I haven't really made much of an attempt to get hold of him yet—it seems unlikely he would have gone to the attic unless he accompanied one of the others. In any case, it may be a bit of a job finding him, since we don't know whether he lives here or in France. Mrs. Bainbridge—David's wife, not the old lady—says she was under the impression that he was living in England in August but had no idea if that was a permanent or temporary situation."

"Probably Mr. Bainbridge will know, when he gets back," said Gibbons.

"That's what I've been counting on." Carmichael drained the last of his pint. "Well, if you're finished, boys, we best get on with it. There's a whole village out there that may know something. I assume you're coming with us, Bethancourt?"

"Actually, I think I'd better beg off," said that young man. "Since you two are occupying the only two rooms this pub has to offer, I have to find someplace to stay. And somewhere to leave Cerberus." He indicated the dog at his feet. "But I'll catch you up later, if I may."

"Certainly, certainly," answered Carmichael heartily. He was a broadminded man, and even if Bethancourt's father had not been thick as thieves with the chief commissioner of New Scotland Yard, well, he had to say Bethancourt had never gotten in the way yet. And he could be very helpful when he chose, although Carmichael couldn't help thinking that if Phillip was so interested in detection, he should get himself a proper job doing it.

Bethancourt, once they had gone, moved over to the bar and ordered another pint. Cerberus came and lay patiently at his feet. From his overcoat pocket, he produced a book entitled *Where to Stay in England,* and began leafing through the Dorset section.

"Sorry I can't put you up," said the publican, noticing this.

"That's all right," replied Bethancourt amiably. "If you've only got two guest rooms, well, there it is."

"That's a fact, sir. Or should I say inspector?"

"No, no," said Bethancourt, sampling his beer. "I'm not a policeman."

"Oh," said the publican, taken aback. "Excuse me, sir, but I saw you with the chief inspector and the sergeant there, and I just assumed. . . ."

"I'm just a friend," explained Bethancourt. "I sometimes push round and give the police a hand, if I'm wanted. My name's Bethancourt."

"Sam Heathcote, at your service, Mr. Bethancourt."

The two men shook hands.

"Perhaps you could help me," said Bethancourt, referring to his book. "Do you happen to know a Mrs. Tyzack?"

Heathcote chuckled. "There's not many folk I don't know hereabouts. Mrs. Tyzack's place is just outside the village, on the same road as Mrs. Bainbridge, and she'll do you proud. Nice rooms she has, and a good cook into the bargain. If you don't mind a bit of chat, her place is as good as they come."

"A bit of a talker, is she?"

"Lor', sir. To be frank, she'd talk the hind leg off a donkey. But she's a good sort—don't misunderstand me."

"Lived here long?"

"Ever since she was married. She started the bed and breakfast after old Tyzack passed on. Just between you and me, he left her decently provided for—she just likes the company."

"I see," said Bethancourt. "Just one more thing—what about the dog?" He indicated Cerberus, who had apparently fallen asleep.

"That's a fine animal, sir. Well, Mrs. Tyzack has a dog of her own—a Yorkshire terrier, he is. If you think your dog wouldn't mind that. . . ."

"Oh, Cerberus is a friendly sort," Bethancourt assured him. "So long as the terrier is friendly, too, there shouldn't be a problem. Perhaps I might use your phone to see if Mrs. Tyzack has a room free?"

"You can take it from me she does. There's not much call for that sort of thing at this time of year. She doesn't have a guest in the place."

"Well, then," said Bethancourt, finishing his beer, "I'll just pop round and fix it up with her. Thank you very much, Mr. Heathcote."

Mrs. Tyzack was a short, plump woman of sixty who was delighted to give Bethancourt a room and thought Cerberus a lovely dog. This opinion was given after Cerberus had put down his nose to sniff at the terrier doubtfully, and then proceeded to ignore him. The terrier, puzzled by this attitude, butted him playfully; Cerberus looked round dispassionately, carefully moved his hindquarters out of the terrier's reach, and then turned back with the air of having settled something. This did not deter the terrier, however, and the performance was repeated several times on the way upstairs.

"This is the nicest room," said Mrs. Tyzack, opening a door. "Looks down on the garden, as you can see, and, being on the corner of the house, it has an extra window. Makes it ever so airy, I always think. Oh, yes, thank you, I did do it up myself, although I had someone in to help with the wallpaper. I'm glad you like it. There's the bathroom just down the hall on the right—it's the second door down, you can't miss it. And your towels are here, as you can see. There's no one else in the house at the moment, so you can leave them in the bathroom if you'd rather. Well, I suppose I'd best let you get settled. Would you like some tea or anything?"

"That would be lovely," said Bethancourt. "I'll be down in a few minutes."

"Take your time," she replied cheerfully. "Oh, and when you do come down, Mr. Bethancourt, would you sign the register for me? I always like to have a little record of the people who visit. It's fun to look through and see where they all come from."

Bethancourt promised to sign the register, and with that she left him.

He was not very long in following her down, and the

tea had not yet appeared in the sitting room. He went
back to the entrance hall and found the register spread
open on a little table. He wrote his name and address
beneath a signature dated in late November, and then
turned back the pages to the August entries. These were
plentiful; apparently Mrs. Tyzack did brisk business during
the summer months. Unfortunately, it was impossible to
tell who had been traveling alone and who had not, since
everyone except the married couples signed their names
on a separate line. Still, if Carmichael was looking for
strangers to the village, here was a large list of them. Bethancourt wondered if Mrs. Tyzack had seen all of them
leave, luggage in hand.

"There you are, Mr. Bethancourt. I've got the tea all
set up now."

"I'm just coming, Mrs. Tyzack."

"You've been signing the book, I see," she went on,
leading the way back to the sitting room.

"Yes. You haven't had anybody in lately."

"No, it's not the season for it, you see. People mostly
come in the summer—by the end of October we're down
to a trickle. And it's *very* unusual to get anyone this close
to Christmas." She looked at him curiously.

"I'm here to work with the police," supplied Bethancourt.

"Oh, about poor Mrs. Bainbridge's body," said Mrs. Tyzack with eager interest. She seated herself and began to
pour out the tea. "Wasn't it just awful? Who would have
left it there for the poor woman to find I just can't imagine.
People have no consideration for the elderly these days
at all."

"I suppose you know her quite well?"

"Oh, yes. The family was living here when I married
George. Louisa Bainbridge is older than I am, but she had
her Cathy just about the same time I had my Ken, and
we got quite chummy over the baby prams. She's not had
a very easy time of it, poor woman, and now to have this
happen in her old age—well, it's just too bad."

"Not an easy time?" asked Bethancourt cautiously, hoping this was not a reference to childbirth. "But I under-

stood she was in easy circumstances, and her family seems to be very close."

"They are now," said Mrs. Tyzack with emphasis. "But it was a long time coming, I can tell you. It was her husband, you see. Very strict he was, with a nasty temper, *and* an awful snob. I'm afraid they didn't get on very well, though she never complained except to say once she'd been married too young. I know you won't believe this, but when the third child died—just a baby, it was, and born before its time, too—and Mrs. Connelly said to him how sorry she was, he said it didn't matter much, it had only been another girl, anyhow."

"That," said Bethancourt with distaste, "is unpardonable."

"Just so," said Mrs. Tyzack, nodding. "Although he changed his mind in the end, when he found out what a bother boys can be. Louisa had two boys in a row after that, but it was the last child, Cathy, who was always his favorite. Not that he didn't end by alienating her, just as he had all the rest."

"He didn't get on with his children, then?"

"Far from it," said Mrs. Tyzack. "Everything was more or less fine when they were little, but when they began to grow up! Well, there were fireworks. He positively tormented the oldest boy, David. Nothing the child did was good enough. He's been a sore trial to his mother over the years, and it's my belief that it was all his father's doing. He wouldn't let the boy marry the girl he wanted to—threatened to cut him off without a penny if he went ahead with the wedding. Didn't think she was good enough for his son, although she was a decent, well-brought-up girl even if she wasn't no more than the baker's daughter. He forced David to join the navy, though he didn't want to and didn't stick it for very long. He tried to make his second son, Michael, join too, but Michael always had more spirit than David and he flat refused. Ran off to America, he did. But poor David was so muddled, he didn't know what to do. He was very devoted to little Cathy, too, and it's my belief he stuck it out so's not to be separated from her."

"He must have been sad when she married and moved to Australia," said Bethancourt, pouring more tea for them both.

"Why, thank you, dear, that's kind of you. David wasn't just sad when she went, he nearly went out of his mind. He accused his father of driving her away, which was true enough. I'm not saying she doesn't have a happy marriage, because to the best of my knowledge she does, but she told her mother at the time that she was going to get away from her father. And then she slipped off one night, without him knowing. And they weren't married until they got to Melbourne. Mr. Bainbridge had old fashioned ideas about that sort of thing, and he refused ever to speak to her or have her in his house again. He said he would disinherit David for accusing him of driving her away, but he never did. I expect it was because David was the only one left, really. The two older girls were married and didn't come home much, and if they wrote, it was to their mother. Michael was off in America, and Cathy in Australia. Anyway, they had a lot of trouble with David from then on. He started drinking too much and lost a couple of jobs because of it. Was taken up for being drunk and disorderly, and for fighting once, too. It went on for years. Then all at once he ran off—no news of him at all for more than a year—and when he turned up again, he was sober, hardly drinking at all, and had married a French girl. Mr. Bainbridge didn't take to that much, but there wasn't a thing he could do. David's wife was already pregnant, and once the baby was born, David never looked back. He dotes on that child to this day, and so did his father."

"That's a very interesting history," said Bethancourt. "When did Mr. Bainbridge die?"

"Oh, about ten years back. And things have been fine ever since. All the children come to visit their mother now, and she is so pleased to see them. They'll be here for Christmas—all except for Michael and Cathy—and all the grandchildren, too. That's why it's such a pity their nice time has to be ruined by this dreadful body."

"It is indeed," agreed Bethancourt. "Do your children come to you, too?"

"No, no. I go up to Ken's home in Bristol, ever since they had the baby."

Mrs. Tyzack chatted on about her grandchild for a few minutes, and then Bethancourt excused himself, saying he had better get back to the police.

Bethancourt found Scotland Yard back at the pub, having a well-deserved pint before proceeding to Mrs. Bainbridge's.

"I want to get that in before supper," said Carmichael, "because most of the old lady's family hasn't been here since August and if we can get their movements over that weekend clear, we may be able to eliminate the whole lot."

But the interview with Mrs. Bainbridge and her daughter, Clarissa North, was uncomfortable and unprofitable. Both women were alarmed, despite Carmichael's reassurances, at having their family's movements investigated, nor could they remember very accurately what had occurred. Gibbons took notes furiously, occasionally getting muddled among the different names and relationships. It seemed, once they had at last finished, that it would have been virtually impossible for anyone to sneak a body up to the attic at any time except at night when everyone was asleep. At night, it was perfectly possible since everyone had slept on the second floor, with the exception of the French boy, who had slept in a little room off the kitchen. Unfortunately, both Mrs. Bainbridge and her daughter were early risers and could shed no light on how late the others might have stayed up on any given night. They suggested that Maureen Bainbridge or her cousin Daniel North might know better.

"And night is about the only time any of them could have committed the murder," said Gibbons afterward in the pub, with his notes strewn about him. "None of them seems to have been alone for any appreciable time over the entire weekend. Although," he added apologetically, "it was awfully hard to keep track."

"I can see that it was," said Carmichael. "I've a large family myself, but at least they don't all mill about together over weekends, killing people. Well, never mind. We'll just have to interview the family members to see if their accounts tally with what we've got here."

"It *would* be useful to know at what time people were getting to bed," said Bethancourt. "If Mrs. Bainbridge and Mrs. North were rising between seven and eight every morning, and the younger members of the family were going to bed at four in the morning, well, it doesn't leave much time."

"On the other hand," put in Gibbons, "if they were going to bed virtuously before midnight, eight hours is plenty of time for any killer."

"It'll have to be checked into," sighed Carmichael. "And may have no bearing on the case at all, once we find out who the dead man was. Well, I'm for bed and start again tomorrow."

"Wake up, Phillip."

Bethancourt opened a bleary eye and reached for his glasses. "What time is it?"

"Quarter past eight," replied Gibbons.

Bethancourt groaned and sat up slowly. "Why don't you start without me?"

"I couldn't possibly. You're driving me to Brighton. Here." Gibbons picked up the dressing gown from the foot of the bed and threw it at his friend. "Mrs. Tyzack is bringing up early tea—you'd better put something on." He grinned. "I gathered you'd told her to give breakfast a miss."

"Yes, I did," said Bethancourt, flinging on his robe. "I loathe food first thing in the morning. Good morning, Cerberus."

Cerberus thumped his tail on the carpet, and Gibbons knelt to rub his chest.

"I am going to brush my teeth," announced Bethancourt. "When I return, I hope you will have devised a suitable explanation for your ill-considered phrase, 'driving to Brighton.' "

Bethancourt took some time in the bathroom, and the tea had arrived by the time he emerged. He took the cup Gibbons poured for him and sipped cautiously at it. "Now then, Jack," he said.

"We are going to Brighton because we've had word that David Bainbridge has returned from France and I've been told to see him."

"When you put it like that," said Bethancourt, "it seems more reasonable. I don't suppose it's more than a couple of hours anyway."

"That's right," said Gibbons. "I will even volunteer to drive there, if you will drive back. Now, do put on your clothes, there's a good chap."

They arrived at the offices of David Bainbridge's import-export business shortly before lunchtime and were shown into his office by a youthful, if severe, secretary. Bainbridge himself was a sober-faced man with dark circles beneath his eyes, dressed conservatively in a blue suit and unobtrusive tie. He greeted them quietly and offered them seats and coffee.

"My wife told me the news last night," he said. "It's an appalling thing for my mother."

"It is indeed," agreed Gibbons, "but she seems to be bearing up well. Your sister, Mrs. North, is with her."

"That's good," he said. "One can always count on Clarissa. Well, how may I help you gentlemen?"

"First of all, Mr. Bainbridge, we'd like to know of any visit you've made to your mother's house since August."

Bainbridge grimaced. "Only one," he answered. "I usually go up more frequently, but various business emergencies have prevented me this fall. In fact, I planned to be there a week ago, to help with Christmas things, but just when I was ready to go, I got another call from France." He sighed. "Well, let me see. I was there for the Bank Holiday in August, and then again about a month later."

"Were your family with you in September?"

"No. No, I was alone that weekend."

"Did you go up to the third floor or attic on either of those occasions?"

"Oh, I see," said Bainbridge. "No, I'm afraid I didn't. I can't remember the last time I was up there, in fact."

"That's all right, sir, no one else can either. Now, if you'd be so good as to go over with us how you spent the holiday weekend."

Bainbridge looked startled. "The holiday weekend?" he repeated. "Was that when—"

"We're not certain, sir," replied Gibbons implacably, "but it is a possibility at this time."

Bainbridge's account of the weekend did not measurably differ from his mother's.

"One last thing," said Gibbons when he had done, "we'd appreciate it if you could give us Renaud Fibrier's address."

"I'm afraid I can't do that, sergeant. I don't know it."

"Well then, the name and address of your partner."

"That I can give you, but I'm afraid he'll be no help. You see, Renaud and his family are estranged."

Gibbons was surprised. "And yet you took him to your family reunion?" he said.

"Oh, yes. I can explain that. You see, Renaud is his father's eldest son, but I'm afraid they've never got on very well together. I've always found the boy most charming myself. Very polite and so on. Anyway, about a year or more ago, Renaud got himself into some scrape or another, and his father absolutely refused to help him again. Renaud ran off and ceased to communicate with his family at all. His father was very upset. Then last August I was in London and happened to run into him. It wasn't the most congenial meeting—he wasn't disposed to trust me at first, even though I had some sympathy for him." Bainbridge smiled. "I had some differences with my own father in my youth, so I wasn't prepared to lay quite *all* the blame at Renaud's door. At any rate, I managed to make sure he was all right for money and to get his phone number, although he wouldn't tell me where he was staying. I called his father, and it was he who suggested I invite Renaud to our family gathering. He hoped, I suppose, that seeing how happily my own situation had turned out would influence Renaud. But I'm afraid it didn't."

"It was not a success?"

Bainbridge sighed and rubbed his chin. "No," he answered. "Family life bored Renaud. He was very pleasant, but he insisted on taking the first train on Monday morning, even though I had understood that he would stay until Tuesday. I had to get up to drive him, at some inconvenience to myself—no one else was even up yet. Still, I thought it better that he leave if he wished to. You can't force family feeling on people."

"That's true, sir." Gibbons nodded and slowly closed his notebook. "Well, thank you very much, sir. That's quite clear. We may call on you again once we discover who this unfortunate man was."

"Certainly, sergeant. I hope you clear it up quickly."

They took their leave and made their way back to the car where Cerberus waited for them with a doleful look on his face.

"It's all right, boy," murmured Bethancourt a little absently.

"Well," said Gibbons, settling himself into his seat while Bethancourt maneuvered out of the parking space, "that was a fat lot of help. I wish to God they'd hurry up and identify the body. At this rate, I'm going to miss my Christmas Holidays altogether."

"There's still a week to go, Jack. Who knows? Maybe there'll be good news waiting for us when we get back to Dorset."

Gibbons grunted disconsolately, and they drove on in silence. In a few minutes, Gibbons roused himself to point out that Bethancourt had made a wrong turn.

"You should have stayed on the A27," he said.

"Actually," said Bethancourt, "I thought we'd run up to London."

"What on earth for?"

"I thought we'd see Maureen again. David Bainbridge was no help at all as to when they all went to bed over the weekend."

"Phillip, it's perfectly likely that the body was put there after the weekend."

"If it was, that exonerates the family."

"Except for Cathy Dresler in Australia. We've only her word for it that there was no body there before the weekend."

"Yes, but it seems unlikely that she would have any motive. She's been living in Australia for years. Why should she go around murdering people in England?"

"Maybe our corpse was Australian."

They wrangled comfortably over this point as the car shot northward to London.

When they arrived, Maureen Bainbridge, to Bethancourt's disappointment, had just begun a two hour lecture, so they sought out Daniel North instead. He seemed pleased at this distraction from his normal duties and insisted on giving them tea. Then he leaned his elbows on his desk and frowned in an effort to recall the Bank Holiday weekend.

"Well, let's see," he said. "I went down on Friday with Dad—Mother was already there. We got a late start and were the last to arrive. There was dinner, of course . . . yes, and we all went up early, except for Maureen and Renaud. They stayed up talking for a bit, but it couldn't have been long because I heard her come up just as I was turning out my light."

"They got on well, then?" asked Gibbons.

North looked offended. "Renaud is certainly the type that women are attracted to," he said, "but Maureen is hardly that superficial. She wouldn't take up with someone like him."

"Perhaps," suggested Bethancourt tactfully, "their late chat was rather onesided?"

North smiled, appeased. "I expect so," he said.

"You seem to have known Renaud prior to that weekend," said Gibbons, "but the rest of the family had never met him before. How is that?"

"Met him one evening at a club," North said. "A friend of mine knew someone in his party, and after some talk, Renaud and I discovered our connection. He seemed quite pleasant at first, but I didn't care for the whole crowd. I'm sure they were doing drugs, and their behavior, well, it left much to be desired."

"Then you wouldn't know anything about his present whereabouts?"

"Certainly not." North was affronted again. "Uncle David should know, if that's what you want."

"Unfortunately," said Gibbons, "he doesn't."

"Oh." North paused thoughtfully. "Wait a moment," he said slowly, "I believe Renaud did say something about where he was staying. Yes, Camden Town, I think it was. North London, anyhow."

Gibbons jotted "Camden?" in his notebook. "Thank you," he said, "that may be helpful. Now, sir, if you could go on with your description of the weekend?"

"Yes, of course. Where was I up to? Saturday? Everyone was up quite late that night. It was well past two by the time the last of us went to bed. I think the last up were Uncle David, Aunt Cathy, Maureen, Renaud, and myself."

"That brings us to Sunday."

"Yes, let's see. Oh, Sunday was the night we went to the pub. Just Maureen, Renaud, and I. We ran into a couple there that Renaud knew from London." A look of distaste came over North's face. "Not the sort of people I usually associate with."

"Of course not," said Bethancourt, his voice full of false sympathy. He was beginning to think North was a bit of a prig.

"Could you describe them for us, sir?" asked Gibbons, ignoring his friend.

"Well, the man—Dick was his name—was all right. He was about my age, I suppose, dark-haired and wearing a leather jacket. I think he said he was a mechanic. The girl was called Penny. Bleached hair and too much eye makeup, and wearing a dress that kept slipping off her shoulder. Way off."

Bethancourt made a "tsk-tsk" sound, and Gibbons glared at him.

"You stayed at the pub how long?" he asked.

"Maureen and I left first," said North. "Renaud was behaving quite badly. He'd spent most of the weekend chatting up Maureen, but now he'd switched to Penny. Naturally I didn't mind that, and Maureen didn't seem to care, but after all, Penny was with another man. I didn't think Penny was very happy with his attentions, but when I got up to go to the men's room, I saw his hand on her leg. No," he corrected himself, "not on her leg. He'd pushed her dress up and had his hand on the inside of her thigh."

"No!" exclaimed Bethancourt, feigning shock. Gibbons kicked him surreptitiously.

"I can quite see how you felt," he said.

"Yes," said North, gratified by this display of sympathy. "Well, you can imagine that I came back from the w.c. and took Maureen right off."

"Of course," said Gibbons. "Was everyone else still up when you got back?"

North took a moment to put aside righteous indignation. "No," he said. "Not everyone. Just, let's see, Aunt Cathy, and my father and Aunt Bernice. But they went off to bed twenty minutes or so after we got back. Maureen and I stayed up a bit. It must have been about midnight—perhaps a little after—when I said goodnight and Maureen went to get a glass of milk to take to bed with her."

"And Renaud hadn't yet returned?"

"No. Well, if he had, he didn't come into the living room." He paused and scratched his chin. "That brings us to Monday. Most of us left that evening so as to be at work on Tuesday. Mother stayed on, and so did Maureen and her parents—they always take a week in the summer to visit Grandmother."

"Yes," said Gibbons, consulting his notes. "They all stayed until Thursday, except for David Bainbridge, who was called away on business Tuesday." He looked up. "Well, that's very clear, Mr. North, thank you. You heard nothing, I suppose, during any of the nights you spent there?"

"Not me," replied North. "I'm a heavy sleeper."

Gibbons thanked him and rose to leave.

Outside, Bethancourt walked Cerberus round the block while Gibbons phoned Carmichael in Dorset to say they were starting back. Having supplied themselves with sandwiches and coffee for the drive back, they threaded their way out of London and were soon spinning along the M3 under heavy skies.

"It's going to rain," observed Gibbons.

"Or snow," said Bethancourt. "Dorset should look very pretty in the snow. Very Christmaslike and all that."

"Don't be silly," answered Gibbons. "It's not cold enough to snow." Then he went on, rather abruptly, "I wonder if we shouldn't make more of an effort to find Renaud Fibrier than we have been doing. The only members of the family who knew anything about him confirm the bad reputation his own father gave him. Supposing he and that other chap fought over the girl after North and Maureen had left. Fibrier might have killed him and put the body in the attic after everyone else was in bed. It certainly fits with his wanting to leave first thing in the morning."

Bethancourt nodded. "That's true, Jack. I think it would be very interesting to find out what sort of trouble he was in in France."

"Very interesting," agreed Gibbons. "We'll run it by Carmichael and see if he doesn't want to put in a call to France this afternoon."

Chief Inspector Carmichael did. They found him at the local police station, where he informed them that missing persons was no further along with connecting the body to anyone on their lists. He was considerably cheered, however, by the thought of Renaud Fibrier as murderer and Dick the mechanic as victim.

"We'll have to check all the hotels and B&B's in the area," he said. "If we can find their last names, it should be easy enough to trace them in London. If we start now," he added wistfully, "we might even be able to go back to town tonight. I'll just ring the Sûreté and then we can have some supper and get on with it."

"I'll meet you at the pub," said Bethancourt. "I want a change of clothes. It won't take me long."

Mrs. Tyzack's house was quiet as Bethancourt let himself in. There was a light burning in the front hall, and he paused by the registry book lying open on the hall table. Pulling off his gloves, he turned the pages back once again to the late August entries and was pleased to find that Dick Tottle and Penny Cranston had conformed to custom and inscribed their names and addresses.

Turning away, he had another thought and, bypassing the stairs, headed for the back of the house and the sitting room, where Cerberus was greeted with joyful barks by the terrier.

"Hello," said Mrs. Tyzack. "I didn't hear you come in. Can I get you anything?"

Bethancourt smiled and dropped into the easy chair opposite her. "What I really need is information," he said. "Can you think back to the August Bank Holiday weekend and a couple of guests you had then?"

The names meant nothing to her, but once he had described the couple and placed the weekend in her mind by mentioning the Bainbridge reunion, she began to remember.

"Yes," she said slowly. "Yes, I think they came on the Saturday. Here, let me just fetch the reservation book—"

Bethancourt politely performed this service for her. She pored over the entries for a moment and then looked up and beamed at him.

"Here it is," she said. "They came on the Saturday evening, booked through till Monday. I remember them now—they had the room across the hall from yours and were rather quiet. Spent a lot of time at the pub, I believe."

"That's splendid," said Bethancourt warmly. "Now, what I really need to know is: did you see them returning from the pub on Sunday or leaving Monday morning?"

She thought for a moment. "No," she said at last. "No, I shouldn't have seen them Sunday night—oh, yes, of course. Look, it's here in the book as well. They paid up on Sunday afternoon, saying they'd be off on the first train on Monday. Yes, the girl explained she had to work Monday, although I don't remember now what she said she did. I asked if they'd want breakfast, but they said no, it would be too early, they'd just get up and leave. So I had a nice lie-in because the other guests didn't want breakfast till nine. They were gone by the time I got up—I remember I checked their room to make sure."

She smiled up at him, pleased with her success. "Is that what you wanted?" she asked. "Is it important?"

"It's very important," answered Bethancourt, beaming back at her. "Mrs. Tyzack, you're a marvel."

Carmichael and Gibbons were equally pleased when Bethancourt joined them at the Lion's Head.

"That's pure jam," said Carmichael with satisfaction. "We might as well start back directly after supper then. Thank you, Bethancourt." He fished in his pocket for a train schedule, pulling out a whole sheaf of papers in the process.

"I can drive you back, sir," offered Bethancourt.

"Why, thank you again," responded the chief inspector. "I—oh, damme." He was gazing at a slip of paper in dismay. "Bethancourt, I forgot. When I talked to the Yard earlier, they said several urgent messages had been left for you. I do apologize for not telling you sooner."

"Urgent?" asked Gibbons, startled.

"From a young lady. Name of Marla Tate."

Gibbons laughed heartily while Bethancourt said, "Oh, my God," and Carmichael raised a bushy eyebrow.

"It's Phillip's girlfriend," explained Gibbons. "And it's hardly likely to be urgent."

"To Marla it is," said Bethancourt glumly. "I'd better go outside and ring her before I eat."

He returned while the others were in the midst of their meal and breathed a sigh of relief as he sat down.

"Disaster has been averted," he announced. "There's a Christmas party tonight that I forgot, but I promised her I'd be back in time for it." He looked at his watch. "Can we be ready to leave in forty-five minutes?"

"Yes, by all means," answered Carmichael. "Mustn't keep a pretty young lady waiting," he added with a wink. "I assume she is pretty, Bethancourt?"

Gibbons guffawed, thinking of Marla's flawless beauty, while Bethancourt replied modestly that he found her so.

                              *   *   *

"Hello, Phillip," said Gibbons cheerfully. "Did I wake you?"

"Yes," answered Bethancourt tartly, shifting the phone to light a cigarette. "It's only nine thirty, and that party went on till all hours."

"I thought you'd want to hear the latest."

Bethancourt sighed. "I suppose I do," he answered. "I take it by the tone of your voice it's good news?"

"It is," Gibbons assured him. "Dick Tottle's no longer at that address you got from Mrs. Tyzack—in fact, no one is. The building was razed to make way for a new block of flats last October. But Penny Cranston is listed in the phone directory. We haven't talked to her yet—she's out, but it's only a matter of time. Best of all, Carmichael heard from the Sûreté this morning. Renaud Fibrier was involved in several brawls, was convicted of petty larceny, and was involved in another brawl just before he disappeared. Unofficially, the police in his hometown say that he was once accused of rape but no charges were ever brought, and that he stole from his parents as well, who naturally never pressed charges. They're sure the latter is true, but unsure about the first, the source of the accusation being somewhat unreliable."

Bethancourt gave a low whistle. "Not a very good record," he observed. "I wonder how much of that David Bainbridge knew."

"Probably not very much," said Gibbons cheerfully. "He was likely just told that Renaud was 'in trouble' from time to time. I believe that's the usual conversational refuge of parents with problem children. Anyway, Fibrier could well be our man, Phillip. We're trying to track him down. Carmichael's sent out a bulletin on him, and I'm to start trying to find out where he was staying in London."

"Starting in Camden?"

"Starting in Camden. Do you want to come?"

"And spend all day knocking on one door after another? No, thank you. I'm going back to my nice warm bed with my nice warm girlfriend."

"Fine. You'll be sorry when I find the place myself."

"I'll join you tomorrow. Plenty of doors left for then."

"Ha! You don't know how lucky I'm feeling."

"Well, I'm not feeling lucky at all, and I wouldn't want to ruin your day," retorted Bethancourt. "Call me when you get back to the Yard."

"Very well," said Gibbons. "But you'll be sorry." He rang off and contemplated the long list in front of him. It consisted of all the hotels and bed and breakfasts in Camden and had been compiled by himself with the help of the London telephone directory. Bethancourt was right, of course: he couldn't possibly get through all of them in one day. Moreover, there was no guarantee that Fibrier hadn't been staying with friends. But that line of inquiry would have to wait until the Sûreté had done their best to find some of Fibrier's acquaintances and had discovered, if they could, any English connections.

He sighed, wishing he had been able to persuade Bethancourt to accompany him, and went forth to do his job.

His feeling of luck soon evaporated in the cold, damp day and, indeed, he met with no success. It was well after dark and he was chilled to the bone when he decided to stop for the day. He found a public call box and rang Penny Cranston's number as he had at intervals throughout the day, but once again there was no answer. Sighing, he turned away toward the underground to return to the Yard and report to Chief Inspector Carmichael.

The next morning Bethancourt consented to accompany his friend on his cheerless rounds of lodgings in Camden Town, with the proviso that they stop at Bond Street first.

"What on earth for?" asked Gibbons.

"Marla's Christmas present, of course," replied Bethancourt. "She is furious with me for letting this investigation interfere with the holiday festivities, and she will get still angrier before we're done."

"Oh, very well," said Gibbons. "But it had better not take long."

"It won't," Bethancourt assured him. "It need only be handsome, very extravagant, and green."

Indeed, Bethancourt accomplished his goal as swiftly as

the Christmas crowds permitted, but Gibbons was horrified at the cost of the emerald and diamond bracelet.

"Surely that's a bit much," he said in a low voice.

"You forget how annoyed she is with me," replied Bethancourt. "This will put her right in a minute."

"It bloody well ought to," muttered Gibbons.

From Asprey's, they proceeded to Camden Town, but success did not crown their efforts. Moreover, it was a slow, painstaking business, asking people to remember a young Frenchman who might have stayed with them last August and then to look up past records. It was the kind of thing Bethancourt hated, and Gibbons soon found him more hindrance than help, for he amused himself by trying to charm the innkeepers senseless or, when that palled, by poking about shamelessly in everything he could find while Gibbons conducted the interview.

They lunched solidly at a pub, Bethancourt drinking several pints of Old Peculiar to fortify himself, and then went back to it under increasingly threatening skies.

"It's going to rain again," said Bethancourt at about four o'clock as they tramped down Anson Road.

"Probably," agreed Gibbons.

"Must we do very many more? In all probability he was staying with friends."

"We'll stop at five," said Gibbons consolingly.

"And get caught in rush hour? Thanks very much."

"Here's the next," said Gibbons. "And do try to behave, Phillip."

A middle-aged woman greeted them pleasantly and announced that she wasn't taking any boarders over the holidays.

"Goodness!" she said once Gibbons had explained their purpose. "Last August, you say? Now that's difficult to remember. I'll have to pull out the books for that."

"We are fairly certain he would have checked out in late August," said Bethancourt with a smile. "But unfortunately, we're not at all sure when he would have arrived. We're working on the assumption at the moment that he arrived no earlier than the beginning of July."

"Well," she answered, setting a heavy book down on

the counter with a thump, "I haven't had anyone staying that long. A two month stay I would have remembered. There was that American family—they stayed three weeks." She opened the book and began flipping through the pages. "And I did have a whole group of Frenchmen in, but they only stayed a day or two. And that was earlier on, I think. Half a mo'!" She looked up at them suddenly. "There *was* a young man that stayed a fortnight or so. Only I thought he was Swiss."

"Swiss?" asked Gibbons.

"Yes," she answered, going back to the book and rapidly turning the leaves. "There was a group—I'm sure the couple were Swiss. There was another man, too, I think. They all stayed a few days and then, when the others left, one stayed on and I switched him to a single." She bent over the book, running her finger down the page. "I *think* it was August," she muttered. "Yes, here we are: 11 August, two doubles. The others left on the sixteenth, and the one that was left changed rooms. Here he is: Renaud Fibrier. Wasn't that the name you mentioned?"

Bethancourt gave a loud whoop of triumph and, leaning over the counter, kissed her soundly on the cheek. "That's it, adorable woman," he said, "that's it! We've found him, Jack!"

Gibbons was grinning broadly. "When did he check out?"

"On the twenty-ninth," she answered, consulting the book. "The Tuesday after Bank Holiday."

"That fits," said Gibbons to Bethancourt. "He returns from the murder, packs up, and clears off. He's probably been back on the Continent for months."

They thanked her for her help and left, well pleased with themselves.

There was a call box on the corner and here Gibbons stopped, fishing in his pocket for change.

"I'm going to try Penny Cranston again," he said.

Bethancourt looked surprised. "You did that half an hour ago," he said mildly.

Gibbons grinned at him. "I'm feeling lucky," he said.

His luck held true. In a moment he emerged, his grin broader than ever.

"She's home," he announced. "We can go straight over. Let's grab a taxi—it's not far."

Penny Cranston's bedsitter was small and rather dirty. There was a pile of clothes on the single armchair, the carpet had seen better days and had faded to a pinky-brown, and the kitchen sink was crowded with unwashed dishes.

Penny herself had a slatternly appearance; her hair was bleached an incredible shade of yellow, revealing almost an inch of dark brown at the roots. She was thin, but not elegantly so; rather, she gave the impression of being scrawny except for her breasts, which were large and swung freely beneath a shiny purple shirt. She seemed suspicious of them, despite Gibbons' reassurances and Bethancourt's scrupulous politeness. Indeed, the latter appeared to make her uneasy and, as if in reaction, she did not offer them seats, but only leaned against the little breakfast table, planted squarely in the center of the worn carpet.

However, she was willing enough, once their mission was explained, to discuss Renaud Fibrier.

"That one," she said, and snorted to show her opinion of him. "I haven't seen him in months, nor want to, neither."

"We're particularly interested in the August Bank Holiday weekend," said Gibbons, and waited, a little anxiously, for her reaction.

But the mention of it did not appear to stir any deep feelings. "That was when I gave him the shove-off," she nodded. "Down in that nowhere place in the country."

"Just so," said Gibbons, a little disappointed, but still hoping. "You went down with your boyfriend?" She looked blank, so he added, "Dick Tottle?"

"Oh." She giggled. "Dick's not my boyfriend. He's just a friend."

Gibbons apologized for misunderstanding. "Anyway, you ran into Renaud Fibrier?"

"Not exactly ran into. We were supposed to meet him there."

"I see."

Bit by bit the story emerged. She had met Renaud Fibrier in a nightclub a fortnight or so before that weekend and they had had, she stated defiantly, a good time. Then he had told her he was going to Dorset for the holiday weekend and suggested she come along. It would be awfully dull, he said, but between the two of them, they might liven it up a bit and he could use the free meal ticket. He couldn't invite her to stay with him, but she could stay cheaply in a B&B. They could appear to run into each other by accident.

"I couldn't get away till Saturday evening," she said. "I was scheduled to work the restaurant, see? So we fixed up to meet at the village pub on Saturday night. Renaud said he might have to wait until after dinner to slip out, but I should just sit tight at the pub. Only then I didn't fancy the idea of waiting for hours in some dead and gone pub, and besides, when I rung the B&B, it was more than we'd thought. So I asked Dick if he'd like to come with me. I told him what was up," she added. "He knew it was Renaud I was going to see."

"So you met Renaud on Saturday?"

Her eyes flashed. "That's just what we didn't do," she said. "We went to the pub for dinner and stayed till closing, but he never showed. I was mad, I can tell you. I wanted to go straight to London, but Dick pointed out that we'd reserved the room for Sunday and the B&B lady would probably make us pay for it anyway. So we stayed. I was sure glad I'd thought of asking Dick along—I'd've gone out of my mind in that place otherwise. We went back to the pub the next night—there wasn't no place else—and lo and behold, in comes Renaud. And then I see why he didn't show the night before because he's got a real snooty looker on his arm. So I says to Dick, 'Let's get out of here,' only before we get the chance, Renaud comes over and is introducing us, and everybody's sitting down. I didn't want to make a fuss in front of that girl, so I sat tight for a bit. And you know what that nogooder does next?"

"He—er—started chatting you up?" ventured Bethancourt.

"Chatting up's not the half of it," she replied fiercely. "He started feeling my leg underneath the table, just as if everything was fine. I tried to brush him off, but he was back in a flash. Like I said, I didn't want to make a fuss, but was I ever glad when that girl and her cousin took off. I gave him a piece of my mind then, I did."

"And well-deserved, too."

"I told him just what I thought of him and his fancy bit, and then I said he could just tear up my phone number because I wouldn't be answering calls from him no more. And then I took Dick and left."

"Did he follow you?"

She sniffed. "Not him. I meant what I said and he knew it."

Gibbons and Bethancourt exchanged glances, hope waning. If Dick Tottle had left Dorset hale and hearty . . .

"And you and Dick left by the first train on Monday?"

"That's right. I had early shift at the restaurant, you see."

"Yes," said Gibbons, disappointed. "I take it, in view of what you've said, that Renaud didn't ride back to town with you?"

"Of course not," she replied, amazed at his stupidity.

"You didn't see him on the station platform?" asked Bethancourt.

"No. There wasn't anybody there. Dick and I were early and had to wait a bit and we didn't see a soul except for one man who drove into the car park right when the train arrived."

"He didn't let anybody off?"

"We didn't see. We were busy boarding. A blue Ford Escort, it was. I remember because Dick's a mechanic and he was laughing at me trying to make out the makes of cars, but I knew that one because my sister's got an Escort." She looked curious. "Did you think Renaud had taken the same train as us?"

"Yes," answered Gibbons, dispiritedly. "We did."

"Well, maybe he did come on at the last minute. We were waiting, like I said, and got on right away."

"That's certainly possible," said Bethancourt. "Thank you very much, Miss Cranston. You've been an enormous help."

Gibbons paused in the act of picking up his coat. "I expect you still keep in touch with Dick Tottle?" he asked.

"Oh, yes. Saw him last night, in fact."

"Could you let us have his address and phone number?"

She gave them the information from memory and they bade her goodbye, making their way down the narrow stairs in silence.

"You don't think she was lying?" asked Gibbons hopelessly.

"No," answered Bethancourt. "Anyway, if she was, you'll soon know when you see Tottle."

"Aren't you coming with me?" asked Gibbons in surprise.

Bethancourt shook his head. "Another Christmas party," he said. "I've got to dress and meet Marla. It's getting late."

He swung open the front door, and they stepped out into the chill drizzle.

"I'll call you tomorrow. Don't look so down, Jack. We were wrong, that's all. Tomorrow we'll come up with a better theory."

"Yes, all right. Tomorrow, then, Phillip."

Gibbons turned away from his friend, in search of a call box and Dick Tottle, desperately wishing he was the one going to a Christmas party. Then it occurred to him that there was no reason he should not partake of some holiday cheer himself, at least after he had interviewed Tottle. Accordingly, he put through two calls instead of one and, with his plans for the evening made, went off to see Dick Tottle in a better frame of mind.

Marla was annoyed with him again, but Bethancourt would hardly have noticed if she hadn't announced the fact. He had, she said, been preoccupied during the whole of the cocktail party they had attended, and he was to stop thinking of his silly case and rouse himself for dinner, which was to be eaten with two other couples. Bethancourt meekly agreed to this on the condition that he could phone Gibbons from the restaurant. Gibbons was not home, however, and it was not long before Bethancourt dropped out of the conversation and began to smoke abstractedly. Marla nudged him with a steely look in her green eyes.

"Darling," she said, "do you want any more of those escargots or can the waiter clear?"

"What?" Bethancourt became aware that everyone else had long since finished their first course. "Oh, no, have him take them away."

He lit another cigarette and leaned back out of the waiter's way. Something had occurred to him during the cocktail party, triggered by a chance remark, and he was desperate to get hold of Gibbons and check it out. It was such a simple solution that he couldn't help but feel that there must be something against it or they would have thought of it earlier.

"You're not very lively tonight, Phillip," said Shelley.

"Late party last night," he replied absently. Then he stubbed out his cigarette and rose. "Will you excuse me a minute? I've just remembered something."

Marla looked daggers at him, but the others all murmured politely and went on with their conversation.

Gibbons was still not home. Annoyed, Bethancourt tapped his fingers impatiently against the receiver. He felt it was quite unreasonable of his friend to be out on the town just when he was wanted.

Bethancourt returned to the table and, after being kicked sharply on the ankle by Marla, managed to enter into the conversation with some animation. He was halfway through his entree when another thought struck him. He turned it over in his mind for a few minutes, and then bolted the rest of his dinner and asked to be excused again.

Once more there was no answer at Gibbons', but with this new idea in his brain, Bethancourt was in no mood to sit through the rest of dinner. Returning to the dining room, he announced he had been called away and dashed off, thinking to himself it was lucky he had come up to scratch on Marla's Christmas present because otherwise she would never forgive him.

Outside, it was beginning to rain again. Bethancourt hailed a taxi and gave Gibbons' address. He was determined to plant himself on the doorstep and wait even if Gibbons stayed out until three in the morning. In reality, however, he soon grew cold and went round the corner to wait in the nearest pub. Bursting with his news, the minutes dragged by like hours until at last Gibbons answered his call—the fifth in half an hour.

"I'm round the corner," announced Bethancourt. "I'll be up directly." And he rang off before Gibbons could protest.

Gibbons had not yet undressed. He felt it was unreasonable of Bethancourt to desert him for the evening and then to come tramping up to his flat at a quarter past eleven when he was trying to have an early night. Resignedly, he poured himself a scotch.

"I've got the answer!" Bethancourt announced dramatically as soon as Gibbons opened the door.

Gibbons eyed him as he stood flushed with the cold, eyes bright behind his glasses, grinning happily.

"You've been drinking," he said.

"Of course I've been drinking," replied Bethancourt, pushing past him and shedding his overcoat. "I've just come from cocktails and dinner. At least I'm not still drinking," he added, seeing the glass in Gibbons' hand. Then he rounded on his friend and asked abruptly, "Did Dick Tottle confirm Penny's story?"

"In every particular," answered Gibbons, getting another glass and filling it. He handed the drink to Bethancourt who took it mechanically and sat down. "Now, what's this idea of yours?"

"It's not an idea," retorted Bethancourt, "it's the solution to the whole puzzle. Who the dead man is and who killed him."

"Well, who?"

"The dead man was Renaud Fibrier."

"I thought we'd just decided he was the murderer."

"We were wrong. Think about it, Jack—he's everything we want in a victim. The right age, the right looks, and he disappeared late on Sunday night or early Monday morning."

Gibbons thought about it. "So you're casting David Bainbridge as the murderer?"

"Why not? After all, Renaud spent the weekend chatting up his daughter, on whom he dotes. Who knows, maybe she even succumbed. Or maybe Renaud was blackmailing him—he sounds the sort of chap who wouldn't balk at a little extortion. And we've only Bainbridge's word for it that Fibrier left for London early Monday. Penny and Dick never saw him."

"Well, yes," said Gibbons reflectively, "but wait a minute, Phillip. We know Renaud checked out of his lodgings on Tuesday. He could hardly do that if he was murdered on Sunday night."

Bethancourt waved a hand airily. "That's because when we talked to Mrs. Whatsis at his lodgings, we were expecting to hear that he had checked out on Monday or Tuesday. We didn't ask her the right questions. If I hadn't pressed Mrs. Tyzack when I was inquiring after Penny and Dick, she would just have said that they left on Monday, not that they paid up on Sunday afternoon and she hadn't seen them since."

"That's true," said Gibbons.

"And, Jack, I've remembered something else. You know what Penny said about a Ford Escort? Well, there was a blue one parked outside Bainbridge's office when we went to see him."

"Was there?" said Gibbons, more confused by this piece of information than enlightened.

"Yes!" said Bethancourt triumphantly. "If Bainbridge killed Renaud during the night, then he had to substantiate his story about taking him to the train in the morning, you know."

"Of course," said Gibbons, the light dawning. "He had his wife with him. He'd have to get up early and what better way to lend verisimilitude to an otherwise—"

"Just so."

"That's more promising," said Gibbons. "You could be right, Phillip. Look here, we'll go round to Fibrier's lodgings again first thing in the morning, and if that turns out right, I'll put it up to Carmichael. If the dead man *is* Fibrier, it should be easy enough to confirm through the Sûreté. Then we can go on from there. It's going to be tricky, though, getting evidence."

"Bah!" said Bethancourt, finishing off his drink. "His own words damn him. If Fibrier was dead in the attic on Monday morning, the best barrister in the world is going to find it difficult to explain why Bainbridge claims to have driven him to the station."

"Well, perhaps," said Gibbons, grinning. He raised his glass. "You may well have it, Phillip. Congratulations."

They interrupted Renaud's landlady during her first cup of coffee the next morning. She poured coffee for them while they explained what they wanted and then went to consult her registration book.

"Look here," she said, returning with the book. "I remember now. I've even made a note in the book, but I missed it yesterday somehow." She set the volume down and took up her coffee. "Renaud came to me," she said slowly, as if trying to get the memory clear in her head, "and said he'd been invited to the country for the weekend but would be back on the Monday night. I said I could probably rent the room for the weekend, it being the holiday and all, but if I didn't he'd have to pay for it. So he moved his things out and I put them in the closet. I did rent the room for the weekend, you can see by the book, but he never came back."

"So his things are still here?"

She shook her head. "No. On the Tuesday another man came and said Renaud had to leave in a hurry—his father had fallen ill, I think. Anyway, he paid me up to Tuesday and returned the key Renaud had gone off with and took his things away."

"Would you recognize this man again?" asked Gibbons eagerly.

She looked doubtful. "I might," she said, "and then

again I might not. He was older, I remember, and looked respectable.''

Gibbons described David Bainbridge. "Could that have been the man?'' he asked.

"It could be,'' she agreed, "there's nothing against it to my recollection. But I wouldn't know until I saw him, and even then I'm not sure I'd recognize him.''

They thanked her profusely for her help, warned her they might call again, and left on swift, jubilant feet for Scotland Yard.

Carmichael was enormously pleased with both of them. He put through a call to the Sûreté and then sat puffing out his mustaches at them.

"Well done,'' he said several times. "That's a champion bit of work, lads.''

In an hour or two, the copy of Renaud Fibrier's dental records arrived and were matched by forensics with those of the previously unidentified body. An air of satisfaction pervaded Carmichael's office.

"I'll just ring down to Brighton and have Bainbridge detained,'' he said. "Then we'd better drive down ourselves. Bethancourt, would you care to accompany us?''

Bethancourt accepted this offer, and Carmichael smiled and nodded while he dialed the Brighton station. He made his request, and in seconds all the light had gone out of the room. The two young men watched Carmichael anxiously, but they could make little of the few monosyllables he spoke. At last he rang off and sighed.

"We're too late,'' he announced. "Bainbridge committed suicide yesterday.''

"What?'' exclaimed Gibbons.

"He must have realized,'' said Bethancourt, "that it was only a matter of time before we identified the body.''

"Did he leave a note?''

"Yes,'' answered Carmichael, "but it's hardly a confession. It asks his wife to forgive him and says it will be better this way. Then he says she knows he's always been a weak man, and that he's glad to have found the strength to do this.''

"Well,'' said Gibbons dully, "that's that.''

                    *   *   *

It was raining again and the evening air was chill. Bethancourt paused for a moment in the vestibule while Cerberus shook himself dry. Then he firmly pressed the bell.

She was surprised to see him. Her eyes were red with weeping and she looked tired, but she invited him in politely.

"I didn't expect the police again," she said.

"I'm not the police, Maureen," said Bethancourt gently, divesting himself of his overcoat. "I came to satisfy a personal curiosity. There is no reason for you to talk to me if you don't want to. But if you do, it will be between you and me."

"I don't mind," she said. "But I don't know if I can tell you anything more."

"Your father either wrote or called you before he died," said Bethancourt simply.

Her eyes widened a little. "How do you know that?" she asked.

"The note that he left was addressed only to your mother, yet you were very dear to him. I've been thinking it all over, and my guess is that you know what happened that night, the night Renaud Fibrier died, that you knew before you heard from your father. You know because you were there."

She did not look at him, nor did she speak.

"Did Renaud rape you?" Bethancourt asked softly.

She flung her head up in surprise and pain, and tears started in her eyes. "Yes!" she said, almost defiantly. "'If that's what you came to find out: yes, he did. He held a knife to my throat and threatened to kill me if I didn't do what he said. I was terrified. . . .'"

"I'm sorry," said Bethancourt. "I'm truly sorry."

She had begun to cry again, and she wiped the tears furiously from her face. "How did you know?"

"He raped another girl once, in France," answered Bethancourt. "I couldn't think why your father would have killed him. After all, he knew he was a bad sort long before that weekend. But it wasn't until tonight, when I realized your father had communicated with you separately, that I thought of the answer." He paused. "Your father must have come down to the kitchen for something and found you."

"Yes. He couldn't sleep and came down for some milk."

"There was the knife," continued Bethancourt, "the one Renaud had used to threaten you, still lying where he cast it aside afterward. Anyway, when your father came down, you were in shock. He must have taken you upstairs and then come back down. The attic must have seemed a good temporary hiding place. What I can't understand is why he didn't remove the body later."

"He tried," she answered, "when he went back in September. But he couldn't bring himself to do it. I expect it was pretty awful by then, and he lost his nerve. That's what he said, anyway. He knew he'd have to do it before Christmas, but then he was called away, and Grandmother went up to the attic early. . . ."

"I see," said Bethancourt. "Of course, you knew nothing of that. He would have been careful to keep it from you."

She nodded slowly. "He wrote me about it before he—before he killed himself."

Bethancourt sighed. "Then there's only one thing more," he said. "That night, after your father took you upstairs and then came back down, what did he do?"

She stared at him uncomprehendingly.

"Did he confront Renaud and stab him? Or did he merely remove the knife that was already there and hide the body, so that no one would ever know what his beloved daughter had done or what had happened to her to make her do it."

There was a long pause. Maureen raised her eyes to gaze at him levelly, the tears still wet on her face. Then she lifted her chin, and said, "I loved my father very much. He died so that this murder would never be connected with me. I will not make his sacrifice useless. He killed Renaud Fibrier. Renaud raped me, and my father killed him for it. That is what happened."

"I understand," said Bethancourt. "Thank you for talking with me." He rose and reached for his overcoat. In silence, she accompanied him to the door. He paused there for a moment, thoughtfully drawing on his gloves.

"Does your mother know you were raped?" he asked.

She shook her head violently. "No one knows."

"It's a horrible thing," he said. "Sometimes it can be very difficult to deal with. If you ever need to talk about it, well, my number's in the phone directory."

"Thank you," she said. "Thank you very much."

Outside it was still raining. Cerberus stepped over a puddle and bent to sniff the base of the lamp post. Bethancourt stood for a moment, watching the rainfall in the light from the street lamp. Then he sighed and looked at his watch.

"A bad business, old thing," he said to the dog. "Sometimes I wonder what I do it for. Come on then, Cerberus, it's time to meet Marla and give her Christmas present to her."

FATHER CRUMLISH CELEBRATES CHRISTMAS

BY ALICE SCANLAN REACH

"Eat that and you'll be up all night with one of your stomach gas attacks." Emma Catt's voice boomed out from the doorway of what she considered to be her personal sanctuary—the kitchen of St. Brigid's rectory.

Caught in the act of his surreptitious mission, Father Francis Xavier Crumlish hastily withdrew the arthritic fingers of his right hand which had been poised to enfold one of several dozen cookies cooling on the wide, old-fashioned table.

"I—I was just thinking to myself that a crumb or two would do no harm," he murmured, conscious of the guilty flush seeping into the seams, tucks, and gussets of his face.

"It would seem to me that a man of the cloth would be the first to put temptation behind him," Emma observed tartly as she strode across the worn linoleum flooring. "Particularly a man of your age," she added, giving him a meaningful look.

The pastor swallowed a heavy sigh. After Emma had arrived to take charge of St. Brigid's household chores some 22 years ago, he had soon learned to his sorrow that her culinary feats were largely confined to bland puddings, poached prunes, and a concoction which she called "Irish Stew" and which was no more than a feeble attempt to disguise the past week's leftovers.

So he was most agreeably surprised one day when Emma miraculously produced a batch of cookies of such flavorful taste and texture that the priest mentally forgave her all her venial sins. And since it was Father Crumlish's nature to share his few simple pleasures with others, he promptly issued instructions that, once a year, Emma should bake as many of the cookies as the parish's meager budget would allow. As a result, although St. Brigid's pastor and his housekeeper were on extra-short rations from Thanksgiving until Christmas Eve, many a parishioner's otherwise cheerless Christmas Day was brightened by a bag of the sugar-and-spice delicacies.

Now, today, as the priest quickly left the kitchen area to avoid any further allusions to his ailments and his advancing years, the ringing of the telephone was entirely welcome. He hurried down the hallway to his office and picked up the receiver.

"St. Brigid's."

"It's Tom, Father."

Father Crumlish recognized the voice of Lieutenant Thomas Patrick "Big Tom" Madigan of Lake City's police force and realized, from the urgency in the policeman's tone, that his call was not a social one.

"I'm at the Liberty Office Building," Madigan said in a rush. "A guy's sitting on a ledge outside the top-story window. Says he's going to jump. If I send a car for you—"

"I'll be waiting at the curb, Tom," Father interrupted and hung up the phone.

"Big Tom" Madigan was waiting outside the elderly office building when Father Crumlish arrived some minutes later. Quickly he ushered the priest through the emergency police and fire details and the crowd of curious onlookers who were gazing in awe at the scarecrow figure perched on a ledge high above the street.

"Do you know the man, Tom?" Father asked. He followed the broad-shouldered policeman into the building lobby and, together, they entered a self-service elevator.

"And so do you, Father," Madigan said as he pressed the elevator button. "He's one of your people. Charley Abbott."

"God bless us!" the pastor exclaimed. "What do you suppose set Charley off this time?" He sighed. "The poor lad's been in and out of sanitariums half a dozen times in his thirty years. But this is the first time he's ever tried to do away with himself."

"This may not be just one of Abbott's loony notions," Madigan replied grimly. "Maybe he's got a good reason for wanting to jump off that ledge."

"What do you mean, Tom?"

"Last week a man named John Everett was found murdered in his old farmhouse out in Lake City Heights. He was a bachelor, lived alone, no relative—"

"I read about it," Father interrupted impatiently. "What's that got to do—"

"We haven't been able to come up with a single clue," Madigan broke in, "until half an hour ago. One of my detectives, Dennis Casey, took an anonymous phone call from a man who said that if we wanted to nab Everett's murderer we should pick up the daytime porter at the Liberty Office Building."

"That's Charley," Father nodded, frowning. "I myself put in a good word for him for the job."

"Casey came over here on a routine check," Madigan went on as the elevator came to a halt and he and the priest stepped out into the corridor. "He showed Abbott his badge, said he was investigating Everett's murder, and wanted to ask a few questions. Abbott turned pale— looked as if he was going to faint, Casey says. Then he made a dash for the elevator, rode it up to the top floor, and climbed out the corridor window onto the ledge."

"But surely now, Tom," Father protested, "you can't be imagining that Charley Abbott had a hand in that killing? Why, you know as well as I that, for all his peculiar ways, Charley's gentle as a lamb."

"All I know," Madigan replied harshly, "is that when

we tried to ask him a few questions, he bolted." He ran a hand over his crisp, curly brown hair. "And I know that innocent men don't run."

"Innocent or guilty," Father Crumlish said, "the man's in trouble. Take me to him, Tom."

When Father Crumlish entered the priesthood more than forty years before, he never imagined that he was destined to spend most of those years in St. Brigid's parish—that weary bedraggled section of Lake City's waterfront where destitution and despair, avarice and evil, walked hand in hand. And although, on the occasions when he lost a battle with the Devil, he too sometimes teetered on the brink of despair, he unfailingly rearmed himself with his intimate, hard-won knowledge of his people.

But now, as the old priest leaned out the window and caught sight of the man seated on the building's ledge, his confidence was momentarily shaken. Charley Abbott had the appearance and demeanor of a stranger. The man's usually slumped, flaccid shoulders were rigid with purpose; his slack mouth and chin were set in taut hard lines; and in place of his normal attitude of wavering indecision, there was an aura about him of implacable determination.

There was not a doubt in Father Crumlish's mind that Abbott intended to take the fatal plunge into eternity. The priest took a deep breath and silently said a prayer.

"Charley," he then called out mildly, "it's Father Crumlish. I'm right here close to you, lad. At the window."

Abbott gave no indication that he'd heard his pastor's voice.

"Can you hear me, Charley?"

No response.

"I came up here to remind you that we have been through a lot of bad times together," Father continued conversationally. "And together we'll get through whatever it is that's troubling you now."

The priest waited for a moment, hoping to elicit some indication that Abbott was aware of his presence. But the man remained silent and motionless, staring into space. Father decided to try another approach.

"I've always been proud of you, Charley," Father said. "And never more so than when you were just a tyke and ran in the fifty-yard dash in our Annual Field Day Festival." He sighed audibly. "Ah, but that's so many years ago, and my memory plays leprechaun's tricks. I can't recall for the life of me, lad—did you come in second or third?"

Again Father waited, holding his breath. Actually he remembered the occasion clearly. The outcome had been a major triumph in his attempts to bring a small spark of reality into his young parishioner's dreamy, listless life.

Suddenly Abbott's long legs, which were dangling aimlessly over the perilous ledge, stiffened, twitched. Slowly he turned his head and focused his bleak eyes on the priest.

"I—I won!" he said, in the reproachful, defensive voice of a small child.

"I can't hear you, Charley," Father said untruthfully, striving to keep the tremor of relief from his voice. "Could you speak a little louder? Or come a bit closer?"

To Father Crumlish it seemed an eternity before Abbott's shoulders relaxed a trifle, before his deathlike grip on the narrow slab of concrete and steel diminished, before slowly, ever so slowly, the man began to inch his way along the ledge until he came within an arm's reach of the window and the priest. Then he paused and leaned tiredly against the building's brick wall.

"I won," he repeated, this time in a louder and firmer tone.

"I remember now," Father said, never taking his dark blue eyes from his parishioner's pale, distraught face. "So can you tell me why a fellow like yourself, with a fine pair of racing legs, would be hanging them out there in the breeze?"

The knuckles of Charley's hands grasping the ledge whitened. "The cops are going to say I murdered Mr. Everett—" He broke off in agitation.

"Go on, Charley."

"They're going to arrest me. Put me away." Abbott's voice rose hysterically. "And this time it'll be forever. I can't stand that, Father." Abruptly he turned his head away from the priest and made a move as if to rise to his feet. "I'll kill myself first."

"Stay where you are!" Father Crumlish commanded. "You'll not take your life in the sight of God, with me standing by to have it on my conscience that I wasn't able to save you."

Cowed by Father's forcefulness, Abbott subsided and once more turned his stricken gaze on the pastor's face.

"I want you to look me straight in the eye, Charley," Father said, "and answer my question: as God is your Judge, did you kill the man?"

"No, Father. No!" The man's slight form swayed dangerously. "But nobody will believe me."

Father Crumlish stared fixedly into Abbott's pale blue eyes which were dazed now and dark with desperation. But the pastor also saw in them his parishioner's inherent bewilderment, fear—and his childlike innocence. Poor lad, he though compassionately. Poor befuddled lad.

"*I* believe you, Charley," he said in a strong voice. "And I give you my word that you'll not be punished for a crime you didn't commit." With an effort the priest leaned further out the window and extended his hand. "Now come with me."

Hesitatingly Abbott glanced down at the priest's outstretched, gnarled fingers.

"My word, Charley."

Abbott sat motionless, doubt and indecision etched on his thin face.

"Give me your hand, lad," Father said gently.

Once again the man raised his eyes until they met the priest's.

"Give me your hand!"

It was a long excruciating moment before Charley released his grip on the ledge, extended a nailbitten, trembling hand, and permitted the pastor's firm warm clasp to lead him to safety.

*   *   *

It was Father Crumlish's custom to read the *Lake City Times* sports page while consuming his usual breakfast of coddled egg, dry toast and tea. But this morning he delayed learning how his beloved Giants, and in particular Willie Mays, were faring until he'd read every word of the running story on John Everett's murder.

Considerable space had been devoted to the newest angle on the case—Charley Abbott's threatened suicide after the police had received an anonymous telephone tip and had sought to question him. Abbott, according to the story, had been taken to Lake City Hospital for observation. Meanwhile, the police were continuing their investigation, based on the few facts at their disposal.

To date, John Everett still remained a "mystery man." With the exception of his lawyer, banker, and the representative of a large real estate management concern—and his dealings with all three had been largely conducted by mail or telephone—apparently only a handful of people in Lake City were even aware of the man's existence. As a result, his murder might not have come to light for some time had it not been for two youngsters playing in the wooded area which surrounded Everett's isolated farmhouse. Prankishly peering in a window, they saw his body sprawled on the sparsely furnished living-room floor and notified the police. According to the Medical Examiner, Everett had been dead less than 24 hours. Death was the result of a bullet wound from a .25 automatic.

Although from all appearances Everett was a man of modest means, the story continued, investigation showed that in fact he was extremely wealthy—the "hidden owner" of an impressive amount of real estate in Lake City. Included in his holdings was the Liberty Office Building where Charley Abbott had almost committed suicide.

Frowning, Father Crumlish put down the newspaper and was about to pour himself another cup of tea when the telephone rang. Once again it was Big Tom Madigan—and Father was not surprised. It was a rare day when Madigan failed to "check in" with his pastor—a habit formed years ago when he'd been one of the worst hooligans in the parish and the priest had intervened to save him from reform school. And in circumstances like the present, where one of St. Brigid's parishioners was involved in a crime, the policeman always made sure that Father Crumlish was acquainted with the latest developments.

"I've got bad news, Father," Madigan said, his voice heavy with fatigue.

The priest braced himself.

"Seems Everett decided to demolish quite a few old buildings that he owned. Turn the properties into parking lots. I've got a list of the ones that were going to be torn down and the Liberty is on it." Madigan paused a moment. "In other words, Charley Abbott was going to lose his job. Not for some months, of course, but—"

"Are you trying to tell me that any man would commit murder just because he was going to lose his job?" Father was incredulous.

"Not *any* man. *Charley*. You know that he didn't think his porter's job was menial. To him it was a 'position,' a Big Deal, the most important thing that ever happened to him."

Father Crumlish silently accepted the truth of what Big Tom had said. And yet . . . "But I still can't believe that Charley is capable of murder," he said firmly. "There's something more to all this, Tom."

"You're right, Father, there is," Madigan said. "Abbott lived in the rooming house run by his sister and brother-in-law, Annie and Steve Swanson."

"That I know."

"Casey—the detective who tried to question Charley yesterday—went over to the house to do a routine check on Charley's room. Hidden under the carpet, beneath the radiator, he found a recently fired .25 automatic."

The priest caught his breath.

"Casey also found a man's wallet. Empty—except for a driver's license issued to John Everett."

"What will happen to poor Charley now, Tom?" Father finally managed to ask.

"In view of the evidence I'll have to book him on suspicion of murder."

After hanging up the phone, the priest sat, disconsolate

and staring into space, until Emma Catt burst into the room, interrupting his troubled thoughts.

"I just went over to church to put some fresh greens on the roof of the crib," Emma reported. "Some of the statuettes have been stolen again."

Wincing at her choice of the word, the pastor brushed at his still-thick, snow-white hair, leaned back in his desk chair, and closed his eyes.

In observance of the Christmas season St. Brigid's church traditionally displayed a miniature crib, or manger, simulating the scene of the Nativity. Statuettes representing the participants in the momentous event were grouped strategically in the stable. And to enhance the setting, boughs of fir, pine, and holly were placed around the simple structure.

So while Father Crumlish was pleased by Emma's attention to the crib's appearance, he also understood the full meaning of her report. It was sad but true that each year, on more than one occasion, some of the statuettes would be missing. But unlike Emma, Father refused to think of the deed as "stealing." From past experience (sometimes from a sobbing whisper in the Confessional), he knew that some curious child had knelt in front of the crib, stretched out an eager hand, perhaps to caress the Infant, and then . . .

"What's missing this time," the priest asked tiredly.

"The Infant, the First Wise Man, and a lamb."

"Well, no harm done. I'll step around to Herbie's and buy some more."

"It would be cheaper if you preached a sermon on stealing."

" 'They know not what they do'," the old priest murmured as he adjusted his collar and his bifocals, shrugged himself into his shabby overcoat, quietly closed the rectory door behind him, and walked out into the gently falling snow.

Minutes later he opened the door of Herbie's Doll House, a toy and novelty store which had occupied the street floor of an aged three-story frame building on Broad Street as long as the pastor could remember. As usual at this time of the year, the store was alive with the shrill voices of excited youngsters as they examined trains, wagons, flaxen-haired dolls, and every imaginable type of Christmas decoration. Presiding over the din was the proprietor, Herbie Morris, a shy, slight man in his late sixties.

Father Crumlish began to wend his way through the crowd, reflecting sadly that most of his young parishioners would be doomed to disappointment on Christmas Day. But in a moment Herbie Morris caught sight of the priest, quickly elbowed a path to his side, and eagerly shook Father's outstretched hand.

"I can see that the Christmas spirit has caught hold of you again this year," Father Crumlish said with a chuckle. "You're a changed man." It was quite true. Herbie Morris' normally pale cheeks were rosy with excitement and his usually dull eyes were shining.

"I know you and all the store-keepers in the parish think I'm a fool to let the kids take over in here like this every Christmas," Herbie said sheepishly but smiling broadly. "You think they rob me blind." He sighed. "You're right. But it's worth it just to see them enjoying themselves—" He broke off, and a momentary shadow crossed his face. "When you have no one—no real home to go to—it gets lonely—" his voice faltered. "Especially at Christmas."

Father Crumlish put an arm around the man's thin shoulder. "It's time you had a paying customer," he said heartily. "I need a few replacements for the crib."

Nodding, Morris drew him aside to a counter filled with statuettes for the manger and Father quickly made his selections. The priest was about to leave when Herbie clasped his arm.

"Father," he said, "I've been hearing a lot about Charley Abbott's trouble. I room with the Swansons."

"I know you do," Father said. "I'm on my way now to see Annie and Steve."

"George says Charley had been acting funny lately."

"George?"

"George Floss. He rooms there too."

"The same fellow who's the superintendent of the Liberty Office Building?" Father was surprised.

"That's him. Charley's boss."

Thoughtfully the priest tucked the box of statuettes under his arm and departed. Although his destination was only a few minutes' walk, it was all of half an hour before he arrived. He'd been detained on the way in order to halt a fist fight or two, admire a new engagement ring, console a recently bereaved widow, and steer homeward a parishioner who'd been trying to drain dry the beer tap in McCaffery's Tavern. But finally he mounted the steps of a battered house with a sign on the door reading: *Rooms.*

He had little relish for his task. Annie and Steve were a disagreeable, quarrelsome pair, and the pastor knew very well that they considered his interest in Charley's welfare all through the years as "meddling." Therefore he wasn't surprised at the look of annoyance on Steve's face when he opened the door.

"Oh, it's you, Father," Steve said ungraciously. "C'mon in. Annie's in the kitchen."

Silently Father followed the short, barrel-chested man, who was clad in winter underwear and a pair of soiled trousers, down a musty hallway. Annie was seated at the kitchen table peeling potatoes. She was a scrawny, pallid-complexioned woman who, Father knew, was only in her mid-forties. But stringy gray hair and deep lines of discontent crisscrossing her face made her appear to be much older. Now, seeing her visitor, she started to wipe her hands on her stained apron and get to her feet. A word from the pastor deterred her.

"I suppose you've come about Charley," she said sulkily.

"Ain't nothing you can do for him this time, Father," Steve said with a smirk. "This time they got him for good—and good riddance."

"Shut up," Annie snapped, shooting her husband a baleful glance.

"First time the crazy fool ever had a decent-paying job," Steve continued, ignoring her. "And what does he do?" He cocked his thumb and forefinger. "Gets a gun and—"

"Shut up, I said!" Annie's face flamed angrily.

"Hiya, Father," a jovial voice interrupted from the doorway. "You here to referee?"

Father turned and saw that the tall burly man entering the kitchen was one of the stray lambs in his flock—George Floss. Murmuring a greeting, the priest noticed that Floss was attired in a bathrobe and slippers.

"It's my day off," George volunteered, aware of Father's scrutiny. He yawned widely before his heavy-jowled face settled into a grin. "So I went out on the town last night."

"That explains your high color," Father remarked dryly. He turned back to the table where Annie and Steve sat glowering at each other. "Now if you can spare a moment from your bickering," he suggested, "maybe you can tell me what happened to set Charley off again."

Steve pointed a finger at Floss. "He'll tell you."

"Charley was doing fine," George said as he poured a cup of coffee from a pot on the stove. "Didn't even seem to take it too hard—at least, not at first—when I told him he was going to be out of a job."

"*You* told him?" the priest said sharply.

"Why, sure," Floss replied with an important air. "I'm the Super at the Liberty building. Soon as I knew the old dump was going to be torn down, I told everybody on the maintenance crew that they'd be getting the ax. Me too." He scowled and his face darkened. "A stinking break. There aren't too many good Super jobs around town."

He gulped some coffee and then brightened. "Of course it won't be for some time yet. That's what I kept telling Charley. But I guess it didn't sink in. He started worrying and acting funny—" He broke off with a shrug.

"You haven't heard the latest, George," Steve said. "That cop—Casey—was here nosing around Charley's room. Found a gun and the Everett guy's wallet."

"No kidding!" Floss's eyes widened in surprise. He shook his head and whistled.

"Gun, wallet, no matter what that cop found," Annie shrilled, waving the paring knife in her hand for emphasis, "I don't believe it. Charley may be a little feeble-minded, but he's no murderer—"

The air was suddenly pierced by a loud and penetrating wail. In an upstairs bedroom a child was crying.

"Now see what you've done," Steve said disgustedly. "Started the brat bawling."

Annie gave a potato a vicious stab with her knife. "Go on up and quiet her."

"Not me," Steve retorted with a defiant shake of his balding head. "That's your job."

"I've got enough jobs, cooking and cleaning around here. It won't kill you to take care of the kid once in a while."

Father Crumlish had stood in shocked silence during the stormy scene. But now he found his tongue.

"It's ashamed you should be," he said harshly, turning his indignant dark blue eyes first on Annie, then on Steve. "When I baptized your little Mary Ann four years ago, I told both of you that you were blessed to have a child at your age and after so many years. Is this disgraceful behavior the way you give thanks to the good Lord? And is this home life the best you can offer the poor innocent babe?"

He took a deep breath to cool his temper. Annie and Steve sat sullen and wordless. The only sound in the silence was the child's crying.

"I'll go and see what's eating her," George offered, obviously glad to escape from the scene.

"I've an errand to do," Father told the Swansons. "But mind you," he held up a warning finger, "I'll be back before long to have another word or two with you."

Turning on his heel, he crossed the kitchen floor, walked down the hallway, and let himself out the door. But before he was halfway down the steps to the street, he heard Annie's and Steve's strident voices raised in anger again. And above the din he was painfully aware of the plaintive, persistent sound of the crying child.

Lieutenant Madigan was seated at his desk engrossed in a sheaf of papers when Father Crumlish walked into headquarters.

"Sit down, Father," Big Tom said sympathetically. "You look tired. And worried."

Irritated, the pastor clicked his tongue against his upper plate. He disliked being told that he looked tired and worried; he knew very well that he *was* tired and worried, and that was trouble enough. He considered remaining on his feet, stating his business succinctly, and then being on his way. But the chair next to Madigan's desk looked too inviting. He eased himself into it, suppressing a sigh of relief.

"I know all this is rough on you, Father," Madigan continued in a kind tone. "But facts are facts." He paused, extracted one of the papers in front of him, and handed it to the priest.

Father Crumlish read it slowly. It was a report on the bullet which had killed John Everett; the bullet definitely had been fired from the gun found in Charley Abbott's room. Silently the pastor placed the report on Big Tom's desk.

"This is one of those cases that are cut and dried," the policeman said. "One obvious suspect, one obvious motive." He shifted his gaze away from the bleak look on Father's face. "But you know that with his mental record Charley will never go to prison."

Abruptly Father Crumlish got to his feet.

"Can you tell me where I'll find Detective Dennis Casey?" he asked.

Madigan stared in astonishment. "Third door down the hall. But why—?"

Father Crumlish had already slipped out the door, closed it behind him, and a moment later he was seated beside Detective Casey's desk. Then, in response to the priest's request, Casey selected a manila folder from his files.

"Here's my report on the anonymous phone call, Father," he said obligingly. "Not much to it, as you can see."

A glance at the typed form confirmed that the report contained little information that Father didn't already have.

"I was hoping there might be more," the pastor said disappointedly. "I know you've been on this case since the beginning and I thought to myself that maybe there was something that might have struck you about the phone call. Something odd in the man's words, perhaps." Father paused and sighed. "Well then, maybe you can tell me about your talk with Charley. Exactly what you said to him—"

"Wait a minute, Father," Casey interrupted. He ran a hand through his carrot-hued hair. "Now that you mention it, I *do* remember something odd about that call. I remember hearing a funny sound. Just before the guy hung up."

"Yes?" Father waited hopefully for the detective to continue.

Casey's brows drew together as he tried to recall.

"It was a sort of whining. A cry, maybe." Suddenly his eyes lit up. "Yeah, that's it! It sounded like a baby—a kid—crying."

As Father Crumlish wearily started up the steps to the rectory door, his left foot brushed against a small patch of ice buried beneath the new-fallen snow. He felt himself slipping, sliding, and he stretched out a hand to grasp the old wrought-iron railing and steady himself. As he did, the package of statuettes, which he'd been carrying all these long hours, fell from under his arm and tumbled to the sidewalk.

"Hellfire!"

Gingerly Father bent down to retrieve the package. At that moment St. Brigid's chimes rang out. Six o'clock! Only two hours before Evening Devotions, the priest realized in dismay as he straightened and stood erect. And in even less time his parishioners would be arriving at church to kneel down at the crib, light their candles, and say their prayers.

Well, Father thought, he would have to see to it that they wouldn't be disappointed, that there would be nothing amiss in the scene of the Nativity. Moments later he stood in front of the crib and unwrapped the package. To his chagrin he discovered that the tumble to the sidewalk had caused one of the lambs to lose its head and one leg. But Herbie Morris could easily repair it, Father told himself as he stuffed the broken lamb into his pocket and proceeded to put his replacements in position. First, in the center of the crib, the Infant. Next, to the left, the First Wise Man. And then, close to the Babe, another unbroken lamb that he'd purchased.

Satisfied with his handiwork, Father knelt down and gazed at the peaceful tableau before him. Ordinarily the scene would have evoked a sense of serenity. But the priest's heart was heavy. He couldn't help but think that it was going to be a sad Christmas for Charley Abbott. And that the man's prospects for the future were even worse. Moreover, Father couldn't erase the memory of what he'd seen and heard at the Swansons—the anger, bitterness, selfishness, and, yes, even the cruelty.

Hoping to dispel his disquieting thoughts, the pastor started to close his eyes. But a slight movement in the crib distracted him. He stared in astonishment as he saw that a drop of moisture had appeared on the face of the Infant and had begun to trickle slowly down the pink waxen cheeks.

Even as he watched, fascinated, another drop appeared—and then the priest quickly understood the reason for the seeming phenomenon. The greens that Emma had placed on the roof of the stable had begun to lose their resilience in the steam heat of the church. The fir, pine, and holly boughs were drooping, shedding moisture on the face of the Child . . .

In the flickering rosy glow of the nearby vigil lights it struck the priest that the scene seemed almost real—as if the Child were alive and crying. As if He were weeping for all the people in the world. All the poor, lonely, homeless—

Father Crumlish stiffened. A startled expression swept over his face. For some time he knelt, alert and deep in thought, while his expression changed from astonishment to realization and, finally, to sadness. Then he rose from his knees, made his way to the rectory office, and dialed police headquarters.

"Could you read me that list you have of the buildings that John Everett was going to have torn down?" Father said when Madigan's voice came on the wire. The policeman complied.

"That's enough, Tom," the priest interrupted after a moment. "Now tell me, lad, will you be coming to Devotions tonight? I've a call to make and I thought, with this snow, you might give me a lift."

"Glad to, Father." Suspicion crept into Madigan's voice. "But if you're up to something—"

The pastor brought the conversation to an abrupt end by hanging up.

Herbie Morris was on the verge of locking up The Doll House when Father Crumlish and Big Tom walked in.

"Can you give this a bit of glue, Herbie?" Father asked as he handed the storekeeper the broken lamb.

"Forget it, Father," Herbie said, shrugging. "Help yourself to a new one."

"No need. I'm sure you can fix this one and it'll do fine."

Then, as Herbie began to administer to the statuette, the pastor walked over to a display of flaxen-haired dolls and leaned across the counter to select one. But the doll eluded his grasp and toppled over. The motion caused it to close its eyes, open its mouth, and emit the realistic sound of a child crying.

"I see your telephone is close by," Father said, pointing to the instrument a counter across the aisle. "So it's little wonder that Detective Casey thought he heard a real child crying while you were on the phone with him at headquarters. One of these dolls must have fallen over just as you were telling him to arrest Charley Abbott for John Everett's murder."

The priest was aware of Madigan's startled exclamation and the sound of something splintering. Herbie stood staring down at his hands which had convulsively gripped the lamb he'd been holding and broken it beyond repair.

"I know that you were notified that this building is going to be torn down, Herbie," Father said, "and I know these four walls are your whole life. But were you so bitter that you were driven to commit murder to get revenge?"

"I didn't want revenge," Herbie burst our passionately.

"I just wanted to keep my store. That's all!" He wrung his hands despairingly. "I pleaded with Everett for two months, but he wouldn't listen. Said he wanted this land for a parking lot." Morris' shoulders sagged and he began to weep.

Madigan moved to the man's side. "Go on," he said in a hard voice.

"When I went to his house that night, I took the gun just to frighten him. But he still wouldn't change his mind. I went crazy, I guess, and—" He halted and looked pleadingly at the priest. "I didn't really mean to kill him, Father. Honest!"

"What about his wallet?" Madigan prodded him.

"It fell out of his pocket. There was a lot of money in it—almost a thousand dollars. I—I just took it."

"And then hid it along with the gun in the room of a poor innocent man," Father Crumlish said, trying to contain his anger. "And to make sure that Charley would be charged with your crime, you called the police."

"But the police would have come after *me*," Herbie protested, as if to justify his actions. "I read in the papers that they were checking Everett's properties and all his tenants. I was afraid—" The look on Father's face caused Herbie's voice to trail away.

"Not half as afraid as Charley when you kept warning him that the police would accuse him because of his mental record, because he worked in the Liberty Building and was going to lose his job. That's what you did, didn't you?" Father asked in a voice like thunder. "You deliberately put fear into his befuddled mind, told him he'd be put away—"

The priest halted and gazed at the little storekeeper's bald bowed head. There were many more harsh words on the tip of his tongue that he might have said. But, as a priest, he knew that he must forego the saying of them.

Instead he murmured, "God have mercy on you."

Then he turned away and walked out into the night. It had begun to snow again—soft, gentle flakes. They fell on

Father Crumlish's cheeks and mingled with a few drops of moisture that were already there.

It was almost midnight before Big Tom Madigan rang St. Brigid's doorbell. Under the circumstances Father wasn't surprised by the policeman's late visit.

"How did you know, Father?" Madigan asked as he sank into a chair.

Wearily Father related the incident at the crib. "After what I heard at the Swansons and what Casey told me, a crying child was on my mind. And then, when I saw what looked like tears on the Infant's face, I got to thinking about all the homeless—" He paused for a long moment.

"Only a few hours before, Herbie had told me how hard it was, particularly at Christmas, to be lonely and without a real home. Charley was suspected of murder because he was going to lose his job. But wasn't it more reasonable to suspect a man who was going to lose his life's work? His whole world?" Father sighed. "I knew Herbie never could have opened another store in a new location. He would have had to pay much higher rent, and he was barely making ends meet where he was."

It was some moments before Father spoke again.

"Tom," he said brightly, sitting upright in his chair. "I happen to know that the kitchen table is loaded down with Christmas cookies."

The policeman chuckled. "And I happen to know that Emma Catt counts every one of 'em. So don't think you can sneak a few."

"Follow me, lad," Father said confidently as he got to his feet. "You're on the list for a dozen for Christmas. Is there any law against my giving you your present now?"

"Not that I know of, Father," Madigan replied, grinning.

"And in the true Christmas spirit, Tom," Father Crumlish's eyes twinkled merrily, "I'm sure you'll want to share and share alike."

Father Crumlish's Christmas Cookies

3 tablespoons butter
½ cup sugar
½ cup heavy cream
⅓ cup sifted flour
1¼ cup very finely
  chopped blanched
  almonds

¾ cup very finely chopped
  candied fruit and peels
¼ teaspoon ground cloves
¼ teaspoon ground
  nutmeg
¼ teaspoon ground
  cinnamon

(1) Preheat oven to 350 degrees.
(2) Combine butter, sugar, and cream in a saucepan and bring to a boil. Remove from the heat.
(3) Stir in other ingredients to form a batter.
(4) Drop batter by spoonfuls onto a greased baking sheet, spacing them about three inches apart.
(5) Bake ten minutes or until cookies begin to brown around the edges. Cool and then remove to a flat surface. If desired, while cookies are still warm, drizzle melted chocolate over tops.

YIELD: About 24 cookies

—Courtesy of the author

THE PLOT AGAINST SANTA CLAUS

BY JAMES POWELL

Rory Bigtoes, Santa's Security Chief, was tall for an elf, measuring almost seven inches from the curly tips of his shoes to the top of his fedora. But he had to stride to keep abreast of Garth Hardnoggin, the quick little Director General of the Toyworks, as they hurried, beards streaming back over their shoulders, through the racket and bustle of Shop Number 5, one of the many vaulted caverns honeycombing the undiscovered island beneath the Polar icecap.

Director General Hardnoggin wasn't pleased. He slapped his megaphone, the symbol of his office (for as a member of the Board he spoke directly to Santa Claus), against his thigh. "A bomb in the Board Room on Christmas Eve!" he muttered with angry disbelief.

"I'll admit that Security doesn't look good," said Bigtoes.

Hardnoggin gave a snort and stopped at a construction site for Dick and Jane Doll dollhouses. Elf carpenters and painters were hard at work, pipes in their jaws and beards tucked into their belts. A foreman darted over to show Hardnoggin the wallpaper samples for the dining room.

"See this unit, Bigtoes?" said Hardnoggin. "Split-level ranch type. Wall-to-wall carpeting. Breakfast nook. Your choice of Early American or French Provincial furnishings. They said I couldn't build it for the price. But I did. And how did I do it?"

"Cardboard," said a passing elf, an old carpenter with a plank over his shoulder.

"And what's wrong with cardboard? Good substantial cardboard for the interior walls!" shouted the Director General striding off again. "Let them bellyache, Bigtoes. I'm not out to win any popularity contests. But I do my job. Let's see you do yours. Find Dirk Crouchback and find him fast."

At the automotive section the new Lazaretto sports cars ($\frac{1}{32}$ scale) were coming off the assembly line. Hardnoggin stopped to slam one of the car doors. "You left out the *kachunk*," he told an elf engineer in white cover-alls.

"Nobody gets a tin door to go *kachunk*," said the engineer.

"Detroit does. So can we," said Hardnoggin, moving on. "You think I don't miss the good old days, Bigtoes?" he said. "I was a spinner. And a damn good one. Nobody made a top that could spin as long and smooth as Garth Hardnoggin's."

"I was a jacksmith myself," said Bigtoes. Satisfying work, building each jack-in-the-box from the ground up, carpentering the box, rigging the spring mechanism, making the funny head, spreading each careful coat of paint.

"How many could you make in a week?" asked Director General Hardnoggin.

"Three, with overtime," said Security Chief Bigtoes.

Hardnoggin nodded. "And how many children had empty stockings on Christmas morning because we couldn't handcraft enough stuff to go around? That's where your Ghengis Khans, your Hitlers, and your Stalins come from, Bigtoes—children who through no fault of their own didn't get any toys for Christmas. So Santa had to make a policy decision: quality or quantity? He opted for quantity."

Crouchback, at that time one of Santa's righthand elves, had blamed the decision on Hardnoggin's sinister influence. By way of protest he had placed a bomb in the new plastic machine. The explosion had coated three elves with a thick layer of plastic which had to be chipped off with hammers and chisels. Of course they lost their beards. Santa, who was particularly sensitive about beards, sentenced Crouchback to two years in the cooler, as the elves called it. This meant he was assigned to a refrigerator (one in Ottawa, Canada, as it happened) with the responsibility of turning the light on and off as the door was opened or closed.

But after a month Crouchback had failed to answer the daily roll call which Security made by means of a two-way intercom system. He had fled the refrigerator and become a renegade elf. Then suddenly, three years later, Crouchback had reappeared at the North Pole, a shadowy fugitive figure, editor of a clandestine newspaper, *The Midnight Elf,* which made violent attacks on Director General Hardnoggin and his policies. More recently, Crouchback had become the leader of SHAFT—Santa's Helpers Against Flimsy Toys—an organization of dissident groups including the Anti-Plastic League, the Sons and Daughters of the Good Old Days, the Ban the Toy-Bomb people and the Hippie Elves for Peace . . .

"Santa opted for quantity," repeated Hardnoggin. "And I carried out his decision. Just between the two of us it hasn't always been easy." Hardnoggin waved his megaphone at the Pacification and Rehabilitation section where thousands of toy bacteriological warfare kits (JiffyPox) were being converted to civilian use (The Freckle Machine). After years of pondering Santa had finally ordered a halt to war-toy production. His decision was considered a victory for SHAFT and a defeat for Hardnoggin.

"Unilateral disarmament is a mistake, Bigtoes," said Hardnoggin grimly as they passed through a door marked *Santa's Executive Helpers Only* and into the carpeted world of the front office. "Mark my words, right now the tanks and planes are rolling off the assembly lines at Acme Toy and into the department stores." (Acme Toy, the international consortium of toymakers, was the elves' greatest bugbear.) "So the rich kids will have war toys, while the poor kids won't even have a popgun. That's not democratic."

Bigtoes stopped at a door marked *Security*. Hardnoggin strode on without slackening his pace. "Sticks-and-stones session at five o'clock," he said over his shoulder. "Don't be late. And do your job. Find Crouchback!"

Dejected, Bigtoes slumped down at his desk, receiving a sympathetic smile from Charity Nosegay, his little blonde blue-eyed secretary. Charity was a recent acquisition and Bigtoes had intended to make a play for her once the Sticks-and-Stones paperwork was out of the way. (Security had to prepare a report for Santa on each alleged naughty boy and girl.) Now that play would have to wait.

Bigtoes sighed. Security looked bad. Bigtoes had even been warned. The night before, a battered and broken elf had crawled into his office, gasped, "He's going to kill Santa," and died. It was Darby Shortribs who had once been a brilliant doll designer. But then one day he had decided that if war toys encouraged little boys to become soldiers when they grew up, then dolls encouraged little girls to become mothers, contributing to overpopulation. So Shortribs had joined SHAFT and risen to membership on its Central Committee.

The trail of Shortribs' blood had led to the Quality Control lab and the Endurance Machine which simulated the brutal punishment, the bashing, crushing, and kicking that a toy receives at the hands of a four-year-old (or two two-year-olds). A hell of a way for an elf to die!

After Shortribs' warning, Bigtoes had alerted his Security elves and sent a flying squad after Crouchback. But the SHAFT leader had disappeared. The next morning a bomb had exploded in the Board Room.

On the top of Bigtoes' desk were the remains of that bomb. Small enough to fit into an elf's briefcase, it had been placed under the Board Room table, just at Santa's feet. If Owen Brassbottom, Santa's Traffic Manager, hadn't chosen just that moment to usher the jolly old man into the Map Room to pinpoint the spot where, with the permission and blessing of the Strategic Air Command,

Santa's sleigh and reindeer were to penetrate the DEW Line, there wouldn't have been much left of Santa from the waist down. Seconds before the bomb went off, Director General Hardnoggin had been called from the room to take a private phone call. Fergus Bandylegs, Vice-President of Santa Enterprises, Inc., had just gone down to the other end of the table to discuss something with Tom Thumbskin, Santa's Creative Head, and escaped the blast. But Thumbskin had to be sent to the hospital with a concussion when his chair—the elves sat on high chairs with ladders up the side like those used by lifeguards—was knocked over backward by the explosion.

All this was important, for the room had been searched before the meeting and found safe. So the bomb must have been brought in by a member of the Board. It certainly hadn't been Traffic Manager Brassbottom who had saved Santa, and probably not Thumbskin. That left Director General Hardnoggin and Vice-President Bandylegs . . .

"Any luck checking out that personal phone call Hardnoggin received just before the bomb went off?" asked Bigtoes.

Charity shook her golden locks. "The switchboard operator fainted right after she took the call. She's still out cold."

Leaving the Toyworks, Bigtoes walked quickly down a corridor lined with expensive boutiques and fashionable restaurants. On one wall of Mademoiselle Fanny's Salon of Haute Couture some SHAFT elf had written: *Santa, Si! Hardnoggin, No!* On one wall of the Hotel St. Nicholas some Hardnoggin backer had written: *Support Your Local Director General!* Bigtoes was no philosopher and the social unrest that was racking the North Pole confused him. Once, in disguise, he had attended a SHAFT rally in The Underwood, that vast and forbidding cavern of phosphorescent stinkhorn and hanging roots. Gathered beneath an immense picture of Santa were hippie elves with their beards tied in outlandish knots, matron-lady elves in sensible shoes, tweedy elves and green-collar elves.

Crouchback himself had made a surprise appearance,

coming out of hiding to deliver his now famous "Plastic Lives!" speech. "Hardnoggin says plastic is inanimate. But I say that plastic lives! Plastic infects all it touches and spreads like crab grass in the innocent souls of little children. Plastic toys make plastic girls and boys!" Crouchback drew himself up to his full six inches. "I say: quality—quality now!" The crowd roared his words back at him. The meeting closed with all the elves joining hands and singing "We Shall Overcome." It had been a moving experience . . .

As he expected, Bigtoes found Bandylegs at the Hotel St. Nicholas bar, staring morosely down into a thimble-mug of ale. Fergus Bandylegs was a dapper, fast-talking elf with a chestnut beard which he scented with lavender. As Vice-President of Santa Enterprises, Inc., he was in charge of financing the entire Toyworks operation by arranging for Santa to appear in advertising campaigns, by collecting royalties on the use of the jolly old man's name, and by leasing Santa suits to department stores.

Bandylegs ordered a drink for the Security Chief. Their friendship went back to Rory Bigtoes' jacksmith days when Bandylegs had been a master sledwright. "These are topsy-turvy times, Rory," said Bandylegs. "First there's that bomb and now Santa's turned down the Jolly Roger cigarette account. For years now they've had this ad campaign showing Santa slipping a carton of Jolly Rogers into Christmas stockings. But not any more. 'Smoking may be hazardous to your health,' says Santa."

"Santa knows best," said Bigtoes.

"Granted," said Bandylegs. "But counting television residuals, that's a cool two million sugar plums thrown out the window." (At the current rate of exchange there are 4.27 sugar plums to the U.S. dollar.) "Hardnoggin's already on my back to make up the loss. Nothing must interfere with his grand plan for automating the Toyworks. So it's off to Madison Avenue again. Sure I'll stay at the Plaza and eat at the Chambord, but I'll still get homesick."

The Vice-President smiled sadly. "Do you know what I used to do? There's this guy who stands outside Grand Central Station selling those little mechanical men you wind up and they march around. I used to march around with them. It made me feel better somehow. But now they remind me of Hardnoggin. He's a machine, Rory, and he wants to make all of us into machines."

"What about the bomb?" asked Bigtoes.

Bandylegs shrugged. "Acme Toy, I suppose."

Bigtoes shook his head. Acme Toy hadn't slipped an elf spy into the North Pole for months. "What about Crouchback?"

"No," said Bandylegs firmly. "I'll level with you, Rory. I had a get-together with Crouchback just last week. He wanted to get my thoughts on the quality-versus-quantity question and on the future of the Toyworks. Maybe I'm wrong, but I got the impression that a top-level shake-up is in the works with Crouchback slated to become the new Director General. In any event I found him a very perceptive and understanding elf."

Bandylegs smiled and went on, "Darby Shortribs was there, prattling on against dolls. As I left, Crouchback shook my hand and whispered, 'Every movement needs its lunatic fringe, Bandylegs. Shortribs is ours.' " Bandylegs lowered his voice. "I'm tired of the grown-up ratrace, Rory. I want to get back to the sled shed and make Blue Streaks and High Flyers again. I'll never get there with Hardnoggin and his modern ideas at the helm."

Bigtoes pulled at his beard. It was common knowledge that Crouchback had an elf spy on the Board. The reports on the meetings in *The Midnight Elf* were just too complete. Was it his friend Bandylegs? But would Bandylegs try to kill Santa?

That brought Bigtoes back to Hardnoggin again. But cautiously. As Security Chief, Bigtoes had to be objective. Yet he yearned to prove Hardnoggin the villain. This, as he knew, was because of the beautiful Carlotta Peachfuzz, beloved by children all around the world. As the voice of the Peachy Pippin Doll, Carlotta was the most envied female at the North Pole, next to Mr. Santa. Girl elves followed her glamorous exploits in the press. Male elves had Peachy Pippin Dolls propped beside their beds so they could fall asleep with Carlotta's sultry voice saying: "Hello,

I'm your talking Peachy Pippin Doll. I love you. I love
you. I love you ..."

But once it had just been Rory and Carlotta, Charlotta
and Rory—until the day Bigtoes had introduced her to
Hardnoggin. "You have a beautiful voice, Miss Peachfuzz,"
the Director General had said. "Have you ever considered
being in the talkies?" So Carlotta had dropped Bigtoes for
Hardnoggin and risen to stardom in the talking-doll industry. But her liaison with Director General Hardnoggin had
become so notorious that a dutiful Santa—with Mrs. Santa
present—had had to read the riot act about executive
hanky-panky. Hardnoggin had broken off the relationship.
Disgruntled, Carlotta had become active with SHAFT,
only to leave after a violent argument with Shortribs over
his anti-doll position.

Today Bigtoes couldn't care less about Carlotta. But he
still had that old score to settle with the Director General.

Leaving the fashionable section behind, Bigtoes turned
down Apple Alley, a residential corridor of modest, old-
fashioned houses with thatched roofs and carved beams.
Here the mushrooms were in full bloom—the stropharia,
inocybe, and chanterelle—dotting the corridor with indigo,
vermilion, and many yellows. Elf householders were out
troweling in their gardens. Elf wives gossiped over hedges
of gypsy pholiota. Somewhere an old elf was singing one
of the ancient work songs, accompanying himself on a con-
certina. Until Director General Hardnoggin discovered
that it slowed down production, the elves had always sung
while they worked, beating out the time with their hammers; now the foremen passed out song sheets and led
them in song twice a day. But it wasn't the same thing.

Elf gardeners looked up, took their pipes from their
mouths, and watched Bigtoes pass. They regarded all
front-office people with suspicion—even this big elf with
the candy-strip rosette of the Order of Santa, First Class,
in his buttonhole.

Bigtoes had won the decoration many years ago when
he was a young Security elf, still wet behind his pointed
ears. Somehow on that fateful day, Billy Roy Scoggins,

President of Acme Toy, had found the secret entrance to the North Pole and appeared suddenly in parka and snowshoes, demanding to see Santa Claus. Santa arrived, jolly and smiling, surrounded by Bigtoes and the other Security elves. Scoggins announced he had a proposition "from one hard-headed businessman to another."

Pointing out the foolishness of competition, the intruder had offered Santa a king's ransom to come in with Acme Toy. "Ho, ho, ho," boomed Santa with jovial firmness, "that isn't Santa's way." Scoggins—perhaps it was the "ho, ho, ho" that did it—turned purple and threw a punch that floored the jolly old man. Security sprang into action.

Four elves had died as Scoggins flayed at them, a snowshoe in one hand and a rolled up copy of *The Wall Street Journal* in the other. But Bigtoes had crawled up the outside of Scoggins' pantleg. It had taken him twelve karate chops to break the intruder's kneecap and send him crashing to the ground like a stricken tree. To this day the President of Acme Toy walks with a cane and curses Rory Bigtoes whenever it rains.

As Bigtoes passed a tavern—The Bowling Green, with a huge horse mushroom shading the door—someone inside banged down a thimblemug and shouted the famous elf toast: "My Santa, right or wrong! May he always be right, but right or wrong, my Santa!" Bigtoes sighed. Life should be so simple for elves. They all loved Santa—what did it matter that he used blueing when he washed his beard, or liked to sleep late, or hit the martinis a bit too hard—and they all wanted to do what was best for good little girls and boys. But here the agreement ended. Here the split between Hardnoggin and Crouchback—between the Establishment and the revolutionary—took over.

Beyond the tavern was a crossroads, the left corridor leading to the immense storage areas for completed toys, the right corridor to The Underwood. Bigtoes continued straight and was soon entering that intersection of corridors called Pumpkin Corners, the North Pole's bohemian quarter. Here, until his disappearance, the SHAFT leader Crouchback had lived with relative impunity, protected by the inhabitants. For this was SHAFT country. A special

edition of *The Midnight Elf* was already on the streets
denying that SHAFT was involved in the assassination attempt on Santa. A love-bead vendor, his beard tied in a
sheepshank, had *Hardnoggin Is a Dwarf* written across the
side of his pushcart. *Make love, not plastic* declared the
wall of The Electric Carrot, a popular discotheque and
hippie hangout.

The Electric Carrot was crowded with elves dancing the
latest craze, the Scalywag. Until recently, dancing hadn't
been popular with elves. They kept stepping on their
beards. The hippie knots effectively eliminated that stumbling block.

Buck Withers, leader of the Hippie Elves for Peace, was
sitting in a corner wearing a *Santa Is Love* button. Bigtoes
had once dropped a first-offense drug charge against Withers and three other elves caught nibbling on morning-glory
seeds. "Where's Crouchback, Buck?" said Bigtoes.

"Like who's asking?" said Withers. "The head of Hardnoggin's Gestapo?"

"A friend," said Bigtoes.

"Friend, like when the news broke about Shortribs, he
says 'I'm next, Buck.' Better fled than dead, and he split
for parts unknown."

"It looks bad, Buck."

"Listen, friend," said Withers, "SHAFT's the wave of
the future. Like Santa's already come over to our side on
the disarmament thing. What do we need with bombs?
That's a bad scene, friend. Violence isn't SHAFT's bag."

As Bigtoes left The Electric Carrot a voice said, "I wonder, my dear sir, if you could help an unfortunate elf."
Bigtoes turned to find a tattered derelict in a filthy button-
down shirt and greasy gray-flannel suit. His beard was mat-
ted with twigs and straw.

"Hello, Baldwin," said Bigtoes. Baldwin Redpate had
once been the head of Santa's Shipping Department. Then
came the Slugger Nolan Official Baseball Mitt Scandal.
The mitt had been a big item one year, much requested in
letters to Santa. Through some gigantic snafu in Shipping,
thousands of inflatable rubber ducks had been sent out
instead. For months afterward, Santa received letters from

indignant little boys, and though each one cut him like a
knife he never reproached Redpate. But Redpate knew he
had failed Santa. He brooded, had attacks of silent crying,
and finally took to drink, falling so much under the spell
of bee wine that Hardnoggin had to insist he resign.

"Rory, you're just the elf I'm looking for," said Redpate. "Have you ever seen an elf skulking? Well, I have."

Bigtoes was interested. Elves were straightforward creatures. They didn't skulk.

"Last night I woke up in a cold sweat and saw strange
things, Rory," said Redpate. "Comings and goings, lights,
skulking." Large tears rolled down Redpate's cheeks.
"You see, I get these nightmares, Rory. Thousands of inflatable rubber ducks come marching across my body and
their eyes are Santa's eyes when someone's let him down."
He leaned toward Bigtoes confidentially. "I may be a
washout. Occasionally I may even drink too much. But I
don't skulk!" Redpate began to cry again.

His tears looked endless. Bigtoes was due at the Sticks-
and-Stones session. He slipped Redpate ten sugar plums.
"Got to go, Baldwin."

Redpate dabbed at the tears with the dusty end of his
beard. "When you see Santa, ask him to think kindly of
old Baldy Redpate," he sniffed and headed straight for
The Good Gray Goose, the tavern across the street—making a beeline for the bee wine, as the elves would say. But
then he turned. "Strange goings-on," he called. "Storeroom Number 14, Unit 24, Row 58. Skulking."

"Hardnoggin's phone call was from Carlotta Peachfuzz,"
said Charity, looking lovelier than ever. "The switchboard
operator is a big Carlotta fan. She fainted when she recognized her voice. The thrill was just too much."

Interesting. In spite of Santa's orders, were Carlotta and
Hardnoggin back together on the sly? If so, had they con-
spired on the bomb attempt? Or had it really been Carlotta's voice? Carlotta Peachfuzz impersonations were a dime
a dozen.

"Get me the switchboard operator," said Bigtoes and

returned to stuffing Sticks-and-Stones reports into his briefease.

"No luck," said Charity, putting down the phone. "She just took another call and fainted again."

Vice-President Bandylegs looked quite pleased with himself and threw Bigtoes a wink. "Don't be surprised when I cut out of Sticks-and-Stones early, Rory," he smiled. "An affair of the heart. All of a sudden the old Bandylegs charm has come through again." He nodded down the hall at Hardnoggin, waiting impatiently at the Projection Room door. "When the cat's away, the mice will play."

The Projection Room was built like a movie theater. "Come over here beside Santa, Rory, my boy," boomed the jolly old man. So Bigtoes scrambled up into a tiny seat hooked over the back of the seat on Santa's left. On Bigtoes' left sat Traffic Manager Brassbottom, Vice-President Bandylegs, and Director General Hardnoggin. In this way Mrs. Santa, at the portable bar against the wall, could send Santa's martinis to him down an assembly line of elves.

Confident that no one would dare to try anything with Santa's Security Chief present, Bigtoes listened to the Traffic Manager, a red-lipped elf with a straw-colored beard, talk enthusiastically about the television coverage planned for Santa's trip. This year, live and in color via satellite, the North Pole would see Santa's arrival at each stop on his journey. Santa's first martini was passed from Hardnoggin to Bandylegs to Brassbottom to Bigtoes. The Security Chief grasped the stem of the glass in both hands and, avoiding the heady gin fumes as best he could, passed it to Santa.

"All right," said Santa, taking his first sip, "let's roll 'em, starting with the worst."

The lights dimmed. A film appeared on the screen. "Waldo Rogers, age five," said Bigtoes. "Mistreatment of pets, eight demerits." (The film showed a smirking little boy pulling a cat's tail.) "Not coming when he's called, ten demerits." (The film showed Waldo's mother at the screen door, shouting.) "Also, as an indication of his general bad behavior, he gets his mother to buy Sugar Gizmos but he won't eat them. He just wants the boxtops." (The camera panned a pantry shelf crowded with opened Sugar Gizmo boxes.) The elves clucked disapprovingly.

"Waldo Rogers certainly isn't Santa's idea of a nice little boy," said Santa. "What do you think, Mother?" Mrs. Santa agreed.

"Sticks-and-stones then?" asked Hardnoggin hopefully.

But the jolly old man hesitated. "Santa always likes to check the list twice before deciding," he said.

Hardnoggin groaned. Santa was always bollixing up his production schedules by going easy on bad little girls and boys.

A new film began. "Next on the list," said Bigtoes, "is Nancy Ruth Ashley, age four and a half . . ."

Two hours and seven martinis later, Santa's jolly laughter and Mrs. Santa's jolly laughter and Mrs. Santa's giggles filled the room. "She's a little dickens, that one," chuckled Santa as they watched a six-year-old fill her father's cus-tommade shoes with molasses, "but Santa will find a little something for her." Hardnoggin groaned. That was the end of the list and so far no one had been given sticks-and-stones. They rolled the film on Waldo Rogers again. "Santa understands some cats like having their tails pulled," chuckled Santa as he drained his glass. "And what the heck are Sugar Gizmos?"

Bandylegs, who had just excused himself from the meeting, paused on his way up the aisle. "They're a delicious blend of toasted oats and corn," he shouted, "with an energy-packed coating of sparkling sugar. As a matter of fact, Santa, the Gizmo people are thinking of featuring you in their new advertising campaign. It would be a great selling point if I could say that Santa had given a little boy sticks-and-stones because he wouldn't eat his Sugar Gizmos."

"Here now, Fergy," said the jolly old man, "you know that isn't Santa's way."

Bandylegs left, muttering to himself.

"Santa," protested Hardnoggin as the jolly old man

passed his glass down the line for a refill, "let's be realistic. If we can't draw the line at Waldo Rogers, where can we?"

Santa reflected for a moment. "Suppose Santa let you make the decision, Garth, my Boy. What would little Waldo Rogers find in his stocking on Christmas morning?"

Hardnoggin hesitated. Then he said, "Sticks-and-stones."

Santa looked disappointed. "So be it," he said.

The lights dimmed again as they continued their review of the list. Santa's eighth martini came down the line from elf to elf. As Bigtoes passed it to Santa, the fumes caught him—the smell of gin and something else. Bitter almonds. He struck the glass from Santa's hand.

Silent and dimly lit, Storeroom Number 14 seemed an immense, dull suburb of split-level, ranchtype Dick and Jane Doll dollhouses. Bigtoes stepped into the papier-mâché shrubbery fronting Unit 24, Row 58 as an elf watchman on a bicycle pedaled by singing "Colossal Carlotta," a current hit song. Bigtoes hoped he hadn't made a mistake by refraining from picking Hardnoggin up.

Bandylegs had left before the cyanide was put in the glass. Mrs. Santa, of course, was above suspicion. So that left Director General Hardnoggin and Traffic Manager Brassbottom. But why would Brassbottom first save Santa from the bomb only to poison him later? So that left Hardnoggin. Bigtoes had been eager to act on this logic, perhaps too eager. He wanted no one to say that Santa's Security Chief had let personal feelings color his judgment. Bigtoes would be fair.

Hardnoggin had insisted that Crouchback was the villain. All right, he would bring Crouchback in for questioning. After all, Santa was now safe, napping under a heavy guard in preparation for his all-night trip. Hardnoggin—if *he* was the villain—could do him no harm for the present.

As Bigtoes crept up the fabric lawn on all fours, the front door of the dollhouse opened and a shadowy figure came down the walk. It paused at the street, looked this way and that, then disappeared into the darkness. Redpate had been right about the skulking. But it wasn't Crouch-back—Bigtoes was sure of that.

The Security Chief climbed in through a dining-room window. In the living room were three elves, one on the couch, one in an easy chair, and, behind the bar, Dirk Crouchback, a distinguished-looking elf with a salt-and-pepper beard and graying temples. The leader of SHAFT poured himself a drink and turned. "Welcome to my little ménage-à-trois, Rory Bigtoes," he said with a surprised smile. The two other elves turned out to be Dick and Jane dolls.

"I'm taking you in, Crouchback," said the Security Chief.

The revolutionary came out from behind the bar pushing a .55mm. howitzer (1/32 scale) with his foot. "I'm sorry about this," he said. "As you know we are opposed to the use of violence. But I'd rather not fall into Hardnoggin's hands just now. Sit over there by Jane." Bigtoes obeyed. At that short range the howitzer's plastic shell could be fatal to an elf.

Crouchback sat down on the arm of Dick's easy chair. "Yes," he said, "Hardnoggin's days are numbered. But as the incidents of last night and today illustrate, the Old Order dies hard. I'd rather not be one of its victims."

Crouchback paused and took a drink. "Look at this room, Bigtoes. This is Hardnoggin's world. Wall-to-wall carpeting. Breakfast nooks. Cheap materials. Shoddy workmanship." He picked up an end table and dropped it on the floor. Two of the legs broke. "Plastic," said Crouch-back contemptuously, flinging the table through the plastic television set. "It's the whole middle-class, bourgeois, sub-urban scene." Crouchback put the heel of his hand on Dick's jaw and pushed the doll over. "Is this vapid plastic nonentity the kind of grownup we want little boys and girls to become?"

"No," said Bigtoes. "But what's your alternative?"

"Close down the Toyworks for a few years," said Crouchback earnestly. "Relearn our ancient heritage of handcrafted toys. We owe it to millions of little boys and girls as yet unborn!"

"All very idealistic," said Bigtoes, "but—"

"Practical, Bigtoes. And down to earth," said the SHAFT leader, tapping his head. "The plan's all here."

"But what about Acme Toy?" protested Bigtoes. "The rich kids would still get presents and the poor kids wouldn't."

Crouchback smiled. "I can't go into the details now. But my plan includes the elimination of Acme Toy."

"Suppose you could," said Bigtoes. "We still couldn't handcraft enough toys to keep pace with the population explosion."

"Not at first," said Crouchback. "But suppose population growth was not allowed to exceed our rate of toy production?" He tapped his head again.

"But good grief," said Bigtoes, "closing down the Toyworks means millions of children with empty stockings on Christmas. Who could be that cruel?"

"Cruel?" exclaimed Crouchback. "Bigtoes, do you know how a grownup cooks a live lobster? Some drop it into boiling water. But others say, 'How cruel!' They drop it in cold water and then bring the water to a boil slowly. No, Bigtoes, we have to bite the bullet. Granted there'll be no Christmas toys for a few years. But we'd fill children's stockings with literature explaining what's going on and with discussion-group outlines so they can get together and talk up the importance of sacrificing their Christmas toys today so the children of the future can have quality handcrafted toys. They'll understand."

Before Bigtoes could protest again, Crouchback got to his feet. "Now that I've given you some food for thought I have to go," he said. "That closet should hold you until I make my escape."

Bigtoes was in the closet for more than an hour. The door proved stronger than he had expected. Then he remembered Hardnoggin's cardboard interior walls and karate-chopped his way through the back of the closet and out into the kitchen.

Security headquarters was a flurry of excitement as Bigtoes strode in the door. "They just caught Hardnoggin trying to put a bomb on Santa's sleigh," said Charity, her voice shaking.

Bigtoes passed through to the Interrogation Room where Hardnoggin, gray and haggard, sat with his wrists between his knees. The Security elves hadn't handled him gently. One eye was swollen, his beard was in disarray, and there was a dent in his megaphone. "It was a Christmas present for that little beast, Waldo Rogers," shouted Hardnoggin.

"A bomb?" said Bigtoes.

"It was supposed to be a little fire engine," shouted the Director General, "with a bell that goes clang-clang!" Hardnoggin struggled to control himself. "I just couldn't be responsible for that little monster finding nothing in his stocking but sticks-and-stones. But a busy man hasn't time for last-minute shopping. I got a—a friend to pick something out for me."

"Who?" said Bigtoes.

Hardnoggin hung his head. "I demand to be taken to Santa Claus," he said. But Santa, under guard, had already left his apartment for the formal departure ceremony.

Bigtoes ordered Hardnoggin detained and hurried to meet Santa at the elevator. He would have enjoyed shouting up at the jolly old man that Hardnoggin was the culprit. But of course that just didn't hold water. Hardnoggin was too smart to believe he could just walk up and put a bomb on Santa's sleigh. Or—now that Bigtoes thought about it—to finger himself so obviously by waiting until Bandylegs had left the Sticks-and-Stones session before poisoning Santa's glass.

The villain now seemed to be the beautiful and glamorous Carlotta Peachfuzz. Here's the way it figured: Carlotta phones Hardnoggin just before the bomb goes off in the Board Room, thus making him a prime suspect; Carlotta makes a rendezvous with Bandylegs that causes him to leave Sticks-and-Stones, thus again making Hardnoggin Suspect Number One; then when Bigtoes fails to pick up the Director General, Carlotta talks him into giving little Waldo Rogers a present that turns out to be a bomb. Her object? To frame Hardnoggin for the murder or attempted murder of Santa. Her elf spy? Traffic Manager Brassbottom. It all worked out—or seemed to ...

Bigtoes met Santa at the elevator surrounded by a dozen Security elves. The jolly old eyes were bloodshot, his smile slightly strained. "Easy does it, Billy," said Santa to Billy Brisket, the Security elf at the elevator controls. "Santa's a bit hungover."

Bigtoes moved to the rear of the elevator. So it was Brassbottom who had planted the bomb and then deliberately taken Santa out of the room. So it was Brassbottom who had poisoned the martini with cyanide, knowing that Bigtoes would detect the smell. And it was Carlotta who had gift-wrapped the bomb. All to frame Hardnoggin. And yet ... Bigtoes sighed at his own confusion. And yet a dying Shortribs had said that someone was going to kill Santa.

As the elevator eased up into the interior of the Polar icecap, Bigtoes focused his mind on Shortribs. Suppose the dead elf had stumbled on your well-laid plan to kill Santa. Suppose you botched Shortribs' murder and therefore knew that Security had been alerted. What would you do? Stage three fake attempts on Santa's life to provide Security with a culprit, hoping to get Security to drop its guard? Possibly. But the bomb in the Board Room could have killed Santa. Why not just do it that way?

The elevator reached the surface and the first floor of the Control Tower building which was ingeniously camouflaged as an icy crag. But suppose, thought Bigtoes, it was important that you kill Santa in a certain way—say, with half the North Pole looking on?

More Security elves were waiting when the elevator doors opened. Bigtoes moved quickly among them, urging the utmost vigilance. Then Santa and his party stepped out onto the frozen runway to be greeted by thousands of cheering elves. Hippie elves from Pumpkin Corners, green-collar elves from the Toyworks, young elves and old had all gathered there to wish the jolly old man godspeed.

Santa's smile broadened and he waved to the crowd. Then everybody stood at attention and doffed their hats as the massed bands of the Mushroom Fanciers Association, Wade Snoot conducting, broke into "Santa Claus Is Coming to Town." When the music reached its stirring conclusion, Santa, escorted by a flying wedge of Security elves, made his way through the exuberant crowd and toward his sleigh.

Bigtoes' eyes kept darting everywhere, searching for a happy face that might mask a homicidal intent. His heart almost stopped when Santa paused to accept a bouquet from an elf child who stuttered through a tribute in verse to the jolly old man. It almost stopped again when Santa leaned over the Security cordon to speak to some elf in the crowd. A pat on the head from Santa and even Roger Chinwhiskers, leader of the Sons and Daughters of the Good Old Days, grinned and admitted that perhaps the world wasn't going to hell in a handbasket. A kind word from Santa and Baldwin Redpate tearfully announced—as he did every year at that time—that he was off the bee wine for good.

After what seemed an eternity to Bigtoes, they reached the sleigh. Santa got on board, gave one last wave to the crowd, and called to his eight tiny reindeer, one by one, by name. The reindeer leaned against the harness and the sleigh, with Security elves trotting alongside, and slid forward on the ice. Then four of the reindeer were airborne. Then the other four. At last the sleigh itself left the ground. Santa gained altitude, circled the runway once, and was gone. But they heard him exclaim, ere he drove out of sight: "Happy Christmas to all and to all a good night!"

The crowd dispersed quickly. Only Bigtoes remained on the wind-swept runway. He walked back and forth, head down, kicking at the snow. Santa's departure had gone off without a hitch. Had the Security Chief been wrong about the frame-up? Had Hardnoggin been trying to kill Santa after all? Bigtoes went over the three attempts again. The bomb in the Board Room. The poison. The bomb on the sleigh.

Suddenly Bigtoes broke into a run.

He had remembered Brassbottom's pretext for taking Santa into the Map Room.

Taking the steps three at a time, Bigtoes burst into the Control Room. Crouchback was standing over the remains of the radio equipment with a monkey wrench in his hand. "Too late, Bigtoes," he said triumphantly. "Santa's as good as dead."

Bigtoes grabbed the phone and ordered the operator to put through an emergency call to the Strategic Air Command in Denver, Colorado. But the telephone cable had been cut. "Baby Polar bears like to teethe on it," said the operator.

Santa Claus was doomed. There was no way to call him back or to warn the Americans.

Crouchback smiled. "In eleven minutes Santa will pass over the DEW Line. But at the wrong place, thanks to Traffic Manager Brassbottom. The American ground-to-air missiles will make short work of him."

"But why?" demanded Bigtoes.

"Nothing destroys a dissident movement like a modest success or two," said Crouchback. "Ever since Santa came out for unilateral disarmament, I've felt SHAFT coming apart in my hands. So I had to act. I've nothing against Santa personally, bourgeois sentimentalist that he is. But his death will be a great step forward in our task of forming better children for a better world. What do you think will happen when Santa is shot down by American missiles?"

Bigtoes shaded his eyes. His voice was thick with emotion. "Every good little boy and girl in the world will be up in arms. A Children's Crusade against the United States."

"And with the Americans disposed of, what nation will become the dominant force in the world?" said Crouchback.

"So that's it—you're a Marxist-Leninist elf!" shouted Bigtoes.

"No!" said Crouchback sharply. "But I'll use the Russians to achieve a better world. Who else could eliminate Acme Toy? Who else could limit world population to our rate of toy production? And they have agreed to that in writing, Bigtoes. Oh, I know the Russians are grownups too and just as corrupt as the rest of the grownups. But once the kids have had the plastic flushed out of their systems and are back on quality hand-crafted toys, I, Dirk Crouchback, the New Santa Claus, with the beautiful and beloved Carlotta Peachfuzz at my side as the New Mrs. Santa, will handle the Russians.''

"What about Brassbottom?'' asked Bigtoes contemptuously.

"Brassbottom will be Assistant New Santa,'' said Crouchback quickly, annoyed at the interruption. "Yes,'' he continued, "the New Santa Claus will speak to the children of the world and tell them one thing: Don't trust anyone over thirty inches tall. And that will be the dawning of a new era full of happy laughing children, where grownups will be irrelevant and just wither away!''

"You're mad, Crouchback. I'm taking you in,'' said Bigtoes.

"I'll offer no resistance,'' said Crouchback. "But five minutes after Santa fails to appear at his first pit stop, a special edition of *The Midnight Elf* will hit the streets announcing that he has been the victim of a conspiracy between Hardnoggin and the CIA. The same mob of angry elves that breaks into Security headquarters to tear Hardnoggin limb from limb will also free Dirk Crouchback and proclaim him their new leader. I've laid the groundwork well. A knowing smile here, an innuendo there, and now many elves inside SHAFT and out believe that on his return Santa intended to make me Director General.''

Crouchback smiled. "Ironically enough, I'd never have learned to be so devious if you Security people hadn't fouled up your own plans and assigned me to a refrigerator in the Russian Embassy in Ottawa. Ever since they found a CIA listening device in their smoked sturgeon, the Russians had been keeping a sharp eye open. They nabbed me almost at once and flew me to Moscow in a diplomatic pouch. When they thought they had me brainwashed, they trained me in deviousness and other grownup revolutionary techniques. They thought they could use me, Bigtoes. But Dirk Crouchback is going to use them!''

Bigtoes wasn't listening. Crouchback had just given him an idea—one chance in a thousand of saving Santa. He dived for the phone.

"We're in luck," said Charity, handing Bigtoes a file. "His name is Colin Tanglefoot, a stuffer in the Teddy Bear Section. Sentenced to a year in the cooler for setting another stuffer's beard on fire. Assigned to a refrigerator in the DEW Line station at Moose Landing. Sparks has got him on the intercom."

Bigtoes took the microphone. "Tanglefoot, this is Bigtoes," he said.

"Big deal," said a grumpy voice with a head cold.

"Listen, Tanglefoot," said Bigtoes, "in less than seven minutes Santa will be flying right over where you are. Warn the grownups not to shoot him down."

"Tough," said Tanglefoot petulantly. "You know, old Santa gave yours truly a pretty raw deal."

"Six minutes, Tanglefoot."

"Listen," said Tanglefoot. "Old Valentine Woody is ho-ho-hoing around with that 'jollier than thou' attitude of his, see? So as a joke I tamp my pipe with the tip of his beard. It went up like a Christmas tree."

"Tanglefoot—"

"Yours truly threw the bucket of water that saved his life," said Tanglefoot. "I should have got a medal."

"You'll get your medal!" shouted Bigtoes. "Just save Santa."

Tanglefoot sneezed four times. "Okay," he said at last. "Do or die for Santa. I know the guy on duty—Myron Smith. He's always in here raiding the cold cuts. But he's not the kind that would believe a six-inch elf with a head cold."

"Let me talk to him then," said Bigtoes. "But move—you've got only four minutes."

Tanglefoot signed off. Would the tiny elf win his race against the clock and avoid the fate of most elves who revealed themselves to grownups—being flattened with the first object that came to hand? And if he did, what would Bigtoes say to Smith? Grownups—suspicious, short of imagination, afraid—grownups were difficult enough to reason with under ideal circumstances. But what could you say to a grownup with his head stuck in a refrigerator?

An enormous squawk came out of the intercom, toppling Sparks over backward in his chair. "Hello there, Myron," said Bigtoes as calmly as he could. "My name is Rory Bigtoes. I'm one of Santa's little helpers."

Silence. The hostile silence of a grownup thinking. "Yeah? Yeah?" said Smith at last. "How do I know this isn't some Commie trick? You bug our icebox, you plant a little pinko squirt to feed me some garbage about Santa coming over and then, whammo, you slip the big one by us, nuclear warhead and all, winging its way into Heartland, U.S.A."

"Myron," pleaded Bigtoes. "We're talking about Santa Claus, the one who always brought you and the other good little boys and girls toys at Christmas."

"What's he done for me lately?" said Smith unpleasantly. "And hey! I wrote him once asking for a Slugger Nolan Official Baseball Mitt. Do you know what I got?"

"An inflatable rubber duck," said Bigtoes quickly.

Silence. The profound silence of a thunderstruck grownup. Smith's voice had an amazed belief in it. "Yeah," he said. "Yeah."

Pit Stop Number One. A December cornfield in Iowa blazing with landing lights. As thousands of elfin eyes watched on their television screens, crews of elves in cover-alls changed the runners on Santa's sleigh, packed fresh toys aboard, and chipped the ice from the reindeer antlers. The camera panned to one side where Santa stood out of the wind, sipping on a hot buttered rum. As the camera dollied in on him, the jolly old man, his beard and eyebrows caked with frost, his cheeks as red as apples, broke into a ho-ho-ho and raised his glass in a toast.

Sitting before the television at Security headquarters, a smiling Director General Hardnoggin raised his thimble-mug of ale. "My Santa, right or wrong," he said.

Security Chief Bigtoes raised his glass. He wanted to think of a new toast. Crouchback was under guard and

Carlotta and Brassbottom had fled to the Underwood. But he wanted to remind the Director General that SHAFT and the desire for something better still remained. Was automation the answer? Would machines finally free the elves to handcraft toys again? Bigtoes didn't know. He did know that times were changing. They would never be the same. He raised his glass, but the right words escaped him and he missed his turn.

Charity Nosegay raised her glass. "Yes, Virginia," she said, using the popular abbreviation for another elf toast; "yes, Virginia, there is a Santa Claus."

Hardnoggin turned and looked at her with a smile. "You have a beautiful voice, Miss Nosegay," he said. "Have you ever considered being in the talkies?"

CHRISTMAS COP

BY THOMAS LARRY ADCOCK

By the second week of December, when they light up the giant fir tree behind the statue of a golden Prometheus overlooking the ice-skating rink at Rockefeller Center, Christmas in New York has got you by the throat.

Close to five hundred street-corner Santas (temporarily sober and none too happy about it) have been ringing bells since the day after Thanksgiving; the support pillars on Macy's main selling floor have been dolled up like candy canes since Hallowe'en; the tipping season arrives in the person of your apartment-house super, all smiles and open-palmed and suddenly available to fix the leaky pipes you've complained about since July; total strangers insist not only that you have a nice day but that you be of good cheer on top of it; and your Con Ed bill says HAPPY HOLIDAYS at the top of the page in a festive red-and-green dot-matrix.

In addition, New York in December is crawling with boosters, dippers, yokers, smash-and-grabbers, bindlestiffs on the mope, aggressive pross offering special holiday rates to guys cruising around at dusk in station wagons with Jersey plates, pigeon droppers and assorted other bunco artists, purveyors of all manner of dubious gift items, and entrepreneurs of the informal branch of the pharmaceutical trade. My job is to try and prevent at least some of these fine upstanding perpetrators from scoring against at least some of their natural Yuletide prey—the seasonal hordes of out-of-towners, big-ticket shoppers along Fifth Avenue, blue-haired Wednesday matinee ladies, and wide-eyed suburban matrons lined up outside Radio City Music Hall with big, snatchable shoulder bags full of credit cards.

I'm your friendly neighborhood plainclothesman. *Very* plain clothes. The guy in the grungy overcoat and watch cap and jeans and beat-up shoes and a week's growth of black beard shambling along the street carrying something in a brown paper bag—that ubiquitous New York bum you hurry past every day while holding your breath—might be me.

The name is Neil Hockaday, but everybody calls me Hock, my fellow cops and my snitches alike. And that's no pint of muscatel in my paper bag, it's my point-to-point shortwave radio. I work out of a boroughwide outfit called Street Crimes Unit-Manhattan, which is better known as the befitting S.C.U.M. patrol.

For twelve years, I've been a cop, the last three on S.C.U.M. patrol, which is a prestige assignment despite the way we dress on the job. In three years, I've made exactly twice the collars I did in my first nine riding around in precinct squad cars taking calls from sector dispatch. It's all going to add up nicely when I go for my gold shield someday. Meanwhile, I appreciate being able to work pretty much unsupervised, which tells you I'm at least a half honest cop in a city I figure to be about three-quarters crooked.

Sometimes I do a little bellyaching about the depart-ment—and who doesn't complain along about halfway through the second cold one after shift?—but mainly I enjoy the work I do. What I like about it most is how I'm always up against the elements of chance and surprise, one way or another.

That's something you can't say about most careers these days. Not even a cop's, really. Believe it or not, you have plenty of tedium if you're a uniform sealed up in a blue-and-white all day, even in New York. But the way my job plays, I'm out there on the street mostly alone and it's an hour-by-hour proposition: fifty-eight minutes of walking around with my pores open so I don't miss anything and two minutes of surprise.

No matter what, I've got to be ready because surprise comes in several degrees of seriousness. And when it does, it comes out of absolutely nowhere.

On the twenty-fourth of December, I wasn't ready.

To me, it was a day like any other. That was wishful thinking, of course. To a holiday-crazed town, it was Christmas Eve and the big payoff was on deck—everybody out there with kids and wives and roast turkeys and plenty of money was anxious to let the rest of us know how happy they were.

Under the circumstances, it was just as well that I'd pulled duty. I wouldn't have had anyplace to go besides the corner pub, as it happened—or, if I could stand it, the easy chair in front of my old Philco for a day of *Christmas in Connecticut* followed by *Miracle on Thirty-fourth Street* followed by *A Christmas Carol* followed by *March of the Wooden Soldiers* followed by Midnight Mass live from St. Patrick's.

Every year since my divorce five years ago, I'd dropped by my ex-wife's place out in Queens for Christmas Eve. I'd bring champagne, oysters, an expensive gift, and high hopes of spending the night. But this year she'd wrecked my plans. She telephoned around the twentieth to tell me about this new boy friend of hers—some guy who wasn't a cop and whose name sounded like a respiratory disease, Flummong—and how he was taking her out to some rectangular state in the Middle West to meet his parents, who grow wheat. Swell.

So on the twenty-fourth, I got up at the crack of noon and decided that the only thing that mattered was business. Catching bad guys on the final, frantic shopping day—that was the ticket. I reheated some coffee from the day before, then poured some into a mug after I picked out something small, brown, and dead. I also ate a week-old piece of babka and said, "Bah, humbug!" right out loud.

I put on my quilted longjohns and strapped a lightweight .32 automatic Baretta Puma around my left ankle. Then I pulled on a pair of faded grey corduroys with holes in the knees, a black turtleneck sweater with bleach stains to wear over my beige bulletproof vest and my patrolman's badge on a chain, a New York Knicks navy-blue stocking cap with a red ball on top, and Army-surplus boots. The brown-paper bag for my PTP I'd saved from the past Sunday when I'd gotten bagels down on Essex Street and shaved last.

I strapped on my shoulder holster and packed away the heavy piece, my .44 Charter Arms Bulldog. Then I topped off my ensemble with an olive-drab officer's greatcoat that had seen lots of action in maybe the Korean War. One of the side pockets was slashed open. Moths and bayonet tips had made holes in other places. I dropped a pair of nickel-plated NYPD bracelets into the good pocket.

By half past the hour, I was in the Bleecker Street subway station near where I live in the East Village. I dropped a quarter into a telephone on the platform and told the desk sergeant at Midtown South to be a goody guy and check me off for the one o'clock muster. A panhandler with better clothes than mine and a neatly printed plywood sandwich sign hanging around his shoulders caught my eye. The sign read, TRYING TO RAISE $1,000,000 FOR WINE RESEARCH. I gave him a buck and caught the uptown D train.

When I got out at Broadway and Thirty-fourth Street, the weather had turned cold and clammy. The sky had a smudgy grey overcast to it. It would be the kind of afternoon when everything in Manhattan looks like a black-and-white snapshot. It wasn't very Christmaslike, which suited me fine.

Across the way, in a triangle of curbed land that breaks up the Broadway and Sixth Avenue traffic flow at the south end of Herald Square, winos stood around in a circle at the foot of a statue of Horace Greeley. Greeley's limed shoulders were mottled by frozen bird dung and one granite arm was forever pointed toward the westward promise. I thought about my ex and the Flummong guy. The winos coughed, their foul breath hanging in frosted lumps of exhaled air, and awaited a ritual opening of a large economy-sized bottle of Thunderbird. The leader broke the seal and poured a few drops on the ground, which is a gesture of respect to mates recently dead or imprisoned. Then he took a healthy swallow and passed it along.

On the other side of the statue, a couple of dozen more guys carrying the stick (living on the street, that is) reclined on benches or were curled up over heating grates. All were in proper position to protect their stash in the event of sleep: money along one side of their hat brims, one hand below as a sort of pillow. The only way they could be robbed was if someone came along and cut off their hands, which has happened.

Crowds of last-minute shoppers jammed the sidewalks everywhere. Those who had to pass the bums (and me) did so quickly, out of fear and disgust, even at this time of goodwill toward men. It's a curious thing how so many comfortable middle-class folks believe vagrants and derelicts are dangerous, especially when you consider that the only people who have caused them any serious harm have been other comfortable middle-class folks with nice suits and offices and lawyers.

Across Broadway, beyond the bottle gang around the stone Greeley, I recognized a mope I'd busted about a year ago for boosting out of a flash clothes joint on West Fourteenth street. He was a scared kid of sixteen and lucky I'd gotten to him first. The store goons would have broken his thumbs. He was an Irish kid who went by the street name Whiteboy and he had nobody. We have lots of kids like Whiteboy in New York, and other cities, too. But we don't much want to know about them.

Now he leaned against a Florsheim display window, smoking a cigarette and scoping out the straight crowd around Macy's and Gimbels. Whiteboy, so far as I knew, was a moderately successful small-fry shoplifter, purse snatcher, and pickpocket.

I decided to stay put and watch him watch the swarm of possible marks until he got up enough nerve to move on somebody he figured would give him the biggest return for the smallest risk, like any good businessman. I moved back against a wall and stuck out my hand and asked passers-by for spare change. (This is not exactly regulation, but it guarantees that nobody will look at my face and it happens to be how I cover the monthly alimony check.) A smiling young fellow in a camel topcoat, the sort of guy who might be a Jaycee from some town up in Rockland County, pressed paper on me and whispered, "Bless you, brother." I looked down and saw that he'd given me a circular from the Church of Scientology in the size, color, and shape of a dollar bill.

When I looked up again, Whiteboy was crossing Broadway. He tossed his cigarette into the street and concentrated on the ripe prospect of a mink-draped fat lady on the outside of a small mob shoving its way into Gimbels. She had a black patent-leather purse dangling from a rhinestone-studded strap clutched in her hand. Whiteboy could pluck it from her pudgy fingers so fast and gently she'd be in third-floor housewares before she noticed.

I followed after him when he passed me. Then, sure enough, he made the snatch. I started running down the Broadway bus lane toward him. Whiteboy must have lost his touch because the fat lady turned and pointed at him and hollered "Thief!" She stepped right in front of me and I banged into her and she shrieked at me, "Whyn't you sober up and get a job, you bum you?"

Whiteboy whirled around and looked at me full in the face. He made me. Then he started running, too.

He darted through the thicket of yellow taxicabs, cars, and vans and zigzagged his way toward Greeley's statue. There was nothing I could do but chase him on foot. Taking a shot in such a congestion of traffic and pedestrians would get me up on IAD charges just as sure as if I'd stolen the fat lady's purse myself.

Then a funny thing happened.

Just as I closed in on Whiteboy, all those bums lying around on the little curbed triangle suddenly got up and blocked me as neatly as a line of zone defensemen for the Jets. Eight or ten big, groggy guys fell all over me and I lost Whiteboy.

I couldn't have been more frustrated. A second collar on a guy like Whiteboy would have put him away for two years' hard time, minimum. Not to mention how it would get me a nice commendation letter for my personal file. But in this business, you can't spend too much time crying over a job that didn't come off. So I headed east on Thirty-second toward Fifth Avenue.

At mid-block, I stopped to help a young woman in a raggedy coat with four bulging shopping bags and three shivering kids. She set the bags on the damp sidewalk and rubbed her bare hands as I neared her. Two girls and a boy, the oldest maybe seven, huddled around her. "How much farther?" one of the girls asked.

I didn't hear an answer. I walked up and asked the woman, "Where you headed, lady?" She looked away, embarrassed because of the tears in her eyes. She was small and slender, with light-brown skin and black hair pulled straight back from her face and held with a rubber band. A gust of dry wind knifed through the air.

"Could you help me?" she finally asked. "I'm just going up to the hotel at the corner. These bags are cutting my hands."

She meant the Martinique. It's a big dark hulk of a hotel, possibly grand back in the days when Herald Square was nearly glamorous. Now its peeling and forbidding and full of people who have lost their way for a lot of different reasons—most of them women and children. When welfare families can't pay the rent any more and haven't anyplace to go, the city puts them up "temporarily" at the Martinique. It's a stupid deal even by New York's high standards of senselessness. The daily hotel rate amounts to a monthly tab of about two grand for one room and an illegal hotplate, which is maybe ten times the rent on the apartment the family just lost.

"What's your name?" I asked her.

She didn't hesitate, but there was a shyness to her voice. "Frances. What's yours?"

"Hock." I picked up her bags, two in each hand. "Hurry up, it's going to snow," I said. The bags were full of children's clothes, a plastic radio, some storybooks, and canned food. I hoped they wouldn't break from the sidewalk dampness.

Frances and her kids followed me and I suppose we looked like a line of shabby ducks walking along. A teenage girl in one of those second-hand men's tweed overcoats you'd never find at the Goodwill took our picture with a Nikon equipped with a telephoto lens.

I led the way into the hotel and set the bags down at the admitting desk. Frances's three kids ran off to join a bunch of other kids who were watching a couple of old coots with no teeth struggling with a skinny spruce tree at the entry of what used to be the dining room. Now it was dusty and had no tables, just a few graffiti-covered vending machines.

Frances grabbed my arm when I tried to leave her. "It's not much, I know that. But maybe you can use it all the same." She let me go, then put out a hand like she wanted to shake. I slipped off my glove and took hold of her small, bone-chilled fingers. She passed me two dimes. "Thanks, and happy Christmas."

She looked awfully brave and awfully heartsick, too. Most down-and-outers look like that, but people who eat regularly and know where their next dollar will likely come from make the mistake of thinking they're stupid and confused, or maybe shiftless or crazy.

I tried to refuse the tip, but she wouldn't have any of that. Her eyes misted up again. So I went back out to the street, where it was starting to snow.

The few hours I had left until the evening darkness were not productive. Which is not to say there wasn't enough business for me. Anyone who thinks crooks are nabbed sooner or later by us sharp-witted, hard-working cops probably also thinks there's a tooth fairy. Police files everywhere bulge with unfinished business. That's because cops are pretty much like everybody else in a world that's not especially efficient. Some days we're inattentive or lazy or hungover—or in my case on Christmas Eve, preoccupied with the thought that loneliness is all it's cracked up to be.

For about an hour after leaving Frances and the kids at the Martinique, I tailed a mope with a big canvas laundry sack, which is the ideal equipment when you're hauling off valuables from a place where nobody happens to be home. I was practically to the Hudson River before I realized the perp had made me a long time back and was just having fun giving me a walk-around on a raw, snowy day. Perps can be cocky like that sometimes. Even though I was ninety-nine percent sure he had a set of lock picks on him, I didn't have probable cause for a frisk.

I also wasted a couple of hours shadowing a guy in a very uptown cashmere coat and silk muffler. He had a set of California teeth and perfect sandy-blond hair. Most people in New York would figure him for a nice simple TV anchorman or maybe a GQ model. I had him pegged for a shoulder-bag bus dipper, which is a minor criminal art that can be learned by anyone who isn't moronic or crippled in a single afternoon. Most of its practitioners seem to be guys who are too handsome. All you have to do is hang around people waiting for buses or getting off buses, quietly reach into their bags, and pick out wallets.

I read this one pretty easily when I noticed how he passed up a half empty Madison Avenue bus opposite B. Altman's in favor of the next one, which was overloaded with chattering Lenox Hill matrons who would never in a thousand years think such a nice young man with nice hair and a dimple in his chin and so well dressed was a thief.

Back and forth I went with this character, clear up to Fifty-ninth Street, then by foot over to Fifth Avenue and back down into the low Forties. When I finally showed him my tin and spread him against the base of one of the cement lions outside the New York Public Library to pat him down, I only found cash on him. This dipper was brighter than he looked. Somewhere along the line, he'd ditched the wallets and pocketed only the bills and I never once saw the slide. I felt fairly brainless right about then and the crowd of onlookers that cheered when I let him go didn't help me any.

So I hid out in the Burger King at Fifth and Thirty-eighth for my dinner hour. There aren't too many places that could be more depressing for a holiday meal. The lighting was so oppressively even that I felt I was inside an ice cube. There was a plastic Christmas tree with plastic ornaments chained to a wall so nobody could steal it, with dummy gifts beneath it. The gifts were strung together with vinyl cord and likewise chained to the wall. I happened to be the only customer in the place, so a kid with a bad complexion and a broom decided to sweep up around my table.

To square my pad for the night, I figured I had to make some sort of bust, even a Mickey Mouse. So after my festive meal (Whopper, fries, Sprite, and a toasted thing with something hot and gummy inside it), I walked down to Thirty-third Street and collared a working girl in a white fake-fox stole, fishnet hose, and a red-leather skirt. She was all alone on stroll, a freelance, and looked like she could use a hot meal and a nice dry cell. So I took her through the drill. The paper work burned up everything but the last thirty minutes of my tour.

When I left the station house on West Thirty-fifth, the snow had become wet and heavy and most of midtown Manhattan was lost in a quiet white haze. I heard the occasional swish of a car going through a pothole puddle. Plumes of steam hissed here and there, like geysers from the subterranean. Everybody seemed to have vanished and the lights of the city had gone off, save for the gauzy red-and-green beacon at the top of the Empire State Building. It was rounding toward nine o'clock and it was Christmas Eve and New York seemed settled down for a long winter's nap.

There was just one thing wrong with the picture. And that was the sight of Whiteboy. I spotted him on Broadway again, lumbering down the mostly blackened, empty street with a big bag on his back like he was St. Nicholas himself.

I stayed out of sight and tailed him slowly back a few blocks to where I'd lost him in the first place, to the statue of Greeley. I had a clear view of him as he set down his bag on a bench and talked to the same bunch of grey, shapeless winos who'd cut me off the chase. Just as before, they passed a bottle. Only this time Whiteboy gave it to them. After everyone had a nice jolt, they talked quickly for a couple of minutes, like they had someplace important to go.

I hung back in the darkness under some scaffolding. Snow fell between the cracks of planks above me and piled on my shoulders as I stood there trying to figure out their act. It didn't take me long.

When they started moving from the statue over to Thirty-second Street, every one of them with a bag slung over his shoulder, I hung back a little. But my crisis of conscience didn't last long. I followed Whiteboy and his unlikely crew of elves—and wasn't much surprised to find the blond shoulder-bag dipper with the cashmere coat when we got to where we were all going. Which was the Martinique. By now, the spindly little spruce I'd felt sorry for that afternoon was full of bright lights and tinsel and had a star on top. The same old coots I'd seen when I helped Frances and her kids there were standing around playing with about a hundred more hungry-looking kids.

Whiteboy and his helpers went up to the tree and plopped down all the bags. The kids crowded around them. They were quiet about it, though. These were kids who didn't have much experience with Norman Rockwell Christmases, so they didn't know it was an occasion to whoop it up.

Frances saw me standing in the dimly lit doorway. I must have been a sight, covered in snow and tired from walking my post most of eight hours. "Hock!" she called merrily.

And then Whiteboy spun around like he had before and his jaw dropped open. He and the pretty guy stepped away from the crowd of kids and mothers and the few broken-down men and walked quickly over to me. The kids looked like they expected all along that their party would be busted up. Frances knew she'd done something very wrong hailing me like she had, but how could she know I was a cop?

"We're having a little Christmas party here, Hock. Anything illegal about that?" Whiteboy was a cool one. He'd grown tougher and smarter in a year and talked to me like we'd just had a lovely chat the other day. We'd have to make some sort of deal, Whiteboy and me, and we both knew it.

"Who's your partner?" I asked him. I looked at the pretty guy in cashmere who wasn't saying anything just yet.

"Call him Slick."

"I like it," I said. "Where'd you and Slick get all the stuff in the bags?"

"Everything's bought and paid for, Hock. You got nothing to worry about."

"When you're cute, you're irritating, Whiteboy. You know I can't turn around on this empty-handed."

Then Slick spoke up. "What you got on us, anyways? I've just about had my fill of police harassment today, Officer. I was cooperative earlier, but I don't intend to cooperate a second time."

I ignored him and addressed Whiteboy. "Tell your friend Slick how we all appreciate discretion and good manners on both sides of the game."

Whiteboy smiled and Slick's face grew a little red.

"Let's just say for the sake of conversation," Whiteboy suggested, "that Slick and me came by a whole lot of money some way or other we're unwilling to disclose since that would tend to incriminate us. And then let's say we used that money to buy a whole lot of stuff for those kids back of us. And let's say we got cash receipts for everything in the bags. Where's that leave us, Officer Hockaday?"

"It leaves you with one leg up, temporarily. Which can be a very uncomfortable way of standing. Let's just say that I'm likely to be hard on your butts from now on."

"Well, that's about right. Just the way I see it." He lit a cigarette, a Dunhill. Then he turned back a cuff and looked at his wristwatch, the kind of piece that cost him plenty of either nerve or money. Whiteboy was moving up well for himself.

"You're off duty now, aren't you, Hock? And wouldn't you be just about out of overtime allowance for the year?"

"Whiteboy, you better start giving me something besides lip. That is, unless you want forty-eight hours up at Riker's on suspicion. You better believe there isn't a judge in this

whole city on straight time or over time or any kind of
time tonight or tomorrow to take any bail application
from you."

Whiteboy smiled again. "Yeah, well, I figure the least I
owe you is to help you see this thing my way. Think of it
like a special tax, you know? Around this time of year, I
figure the folks who can spare something ought to be
taxed. So maybe that's what happened, see? Just taxation."

"Same scam as the one Robin Hood ran?"

"Yeah, something like that. Only Slick and me ain't
about to start living out of town in some forest."

"You owe me something more, Whiteboy."

"What?"

"From now on, you and Slick are my two newest
snitches. And I'll be expecting regular news."

There is such a thing as honor among thieves. This is
every bit as true as the honor among Congressmen you
read about in the newspapers all the time. But when enlightened self-interest rears its ugly head, it's also true that
rules of gallantry are off.

"Okay, Hock, why not?" Whiteboy shook my hand.
Slick did, too, and when he smiled his chin dimple spread
flat. Then the three of us went over to the Christmas tree
and everybody there seemed relieved.

We started pulling merchandise out of the bags and
handing things over to disbelieving kids and their parents.
Everything was the best that money could buy, too. Slick's
taste in things was top-drawer. And just like Whiteboy
said, there were sales slips for it all, which meant that this
would be a time when nobody could take anything away
from these people.

I came across a pair of ladies' black-leather gloves from
Lord & Taylor, with grey-rabbit-fur lining. These I put
aside until all the kids had something, then I gave them
to Frances before I went home for the night. She kissed
me on the cheek and wished me a happy Christmas again.

BUT ONCE A YEAR
... THANK GOD!

BY JOYCE PORTER

Nobody, with one glittering exception, ever enjoyed the Christmas party which the Totterbridge & District Conservative & Unionist Club traditionally gave every year for the children of its members. The ladies who organised and ran the party naturally hated every minute of it, while the guests (all under the age of ten) invariably professed themselves bored out of their tiny minds by the lousy tea, the lousy entertainment, and the even lousier presents. Only the Honourable Constance Morrison-Burke stood up to be counted when it came to asserting that the kiddies' Christmas party was a simply spiffing "do" and well worth all the trouble and heartbreak.

The Honourable Constance's enthusiasm might ring strange in the ears of those aware of her intense dislike of small children and her vehement objection to lavishing on them vast sums of money which might be better spent on comforts for Britain's impoverished aristocracy. The explanation is, however, quite simple: it was only at the Conservative Club's Christmas party that the Honourable Constance got the chance to play Father Christmas, all the Conservative menfolk having chickened out of this particular privilege many years ago.

The Honourable Constance (or the Hon. Con as she

was generally known in the small provincial town in which she lived) was famous for always wearing the trousers, literally and figuratively, so that yet another breeches role was in itself no great attraction for her. What did draw her irresistibly to the part were those bushy white whiskers. To tell the truth, the Hon. Con rather fancied herself in a moustache and full beard, claiming that it brought out the colour of her eyes, and she spent the fortnight before the party swaggering around her house in Upper Waxwing Drive arrayed in the complete get-up. Her ho-ho-hoing was so exuberant that Miss Jones went down daily with one of her sick headaches. Miss Jones, who also lived in the house in Upper Waxwing Drive, was the Hon. Con's dearest chum, confidante, dogsbody, doormat, better half, and who knows what else besides. It was she who had extracted a solemn promise from the Hon. Con ("see that wet, see that dry, cross my heart and hope to die") that she wouldn't wear her Santa Claus whiskers out in the street, no matter how much breaking in they required.

The Hon. Con was not of course so bedazzled that she overlooked the grimmer side of the picture. Bringing good will and Christmas cheer to a pack of some seventy-five infant savages is no joking matter, and the Hon. Con took every reasonable precaution for her own protection. She would like to have equipped herself with an electric cattle prod or a lion-tamer's whip and a kitchen chair, but she knew the Ladies' Organising Committee would never stand for that so she settled for something less exotic. Like heavy boots with reinforced toe-caps, a pair of cricket pads to protect the old shins, and a small rubber truncheon stuffed down the leg of her red trousers just in case she was obliged to move on to the offensive.

On the day of the party the Hon. Con and Miss Jones set off in good time. This was partly because the Hon. Con, arrayed in full festive rig, had trouble even getting into the Mini, never mind actually driving it, and partly because they had to attend a final briefing in the main or Margaret Thatcher Hall of the Conservative Club.

The lady helpers were all somewhat anxious and on

edge as they gathered round their leader, Mrs. Rose Johnson, Chairperson of the Ladies' Organising Committee.
Mrs. Johnson, however, rattled through the battle orders
with an air of quiet confidence which, though completely
spurious, did help to steady the troops. Indeed, some of
the ladies felt so much better that they even started grum-
bling about the allocation of duties. Mrs. Johnson sighed.
This happened every year, no matter how often she reminded them that all the various jobs were distributed
strictly by lot. She knew as well as anybody that some
posts were more, well, dangerous than others, but what
could she or anybody else do about it? Trying to keep
track of what people had done in previous years was
simply too complicated, and considerable concessions
had already been made in respect of the so-called latrine
fatigues. Nowadays only bona fide mothers were stationed
in the cloakrooms as, when it came to overexcited kids
and the undoing of buttons, a certain deftness had been
found essential if disasters were to be avoided.

Taking everything into consideration, Mrs. Johnson felt
that everybody should be reasonably satisfied with the arrangements, but it came as no very great surprise that one
person in particular wasn't. As the meeting came to an
end and the ladies, with exhortations to stand firm and
unflinching ringing in their ears, began dispersing to their
battle lines, the imposing figure of Lady Fowler could be
seen swimming doughtily against the stream. She trapped
Mrs. Johnson by the platform.

"God damn and blast it, Rose," she exclaimed—her husband had been knighted for services to the fish-paste and
tinned pilchard industry which may account for the forcefulness of her language—"you've bloody well done it
again!"

Mrs. Johnson tried, and failed, to move what was obviously going to be a bruising encounter away from the platform on which a dejected group of total strangers was
huddled, listening gloomily to every word. "Done what,
dear?"

"Given that bloody Lyonelle Lawn bitch the best god-
damn job again! That's three bloody years on the trot!"

Mrs. Johnson ruffled unhappily through her sheaf of papers. "The best job, dear? Oh, I'd hardly call being stuck by the fire exit at the end of that draughty old corridor 'the best job,' would you?"

"Compared with being stuck for two solid hours in the middle of World War Three," snarled Lady Fowler, "yes, I damned well would! Last year I was on serving bloody teas and this year I've copped marshalling the little bastards up to collect their presents—and that's in addition to being on sentry-go out here all the time the entertainment's going on. I suppose you know one of the little sods bit me last time? Why the hell don't I ever get one of these cushy jobs where—with luck—you don't even see a blasted kid from start to finish?"

"The Committee draw the names out of a hat, dear," protested Mrs. Johnson feebly, noting with chagrin that the Hon. Con and that peculiar little woman of hers had moved up and were now avidly eavesdropping on the other side. "It's all absolutely fair and aboveboard."

Lady Fowler blew heavily down her nose. "Damned funny it's always Lyonelle Lawn who comes up smelling of roses!"

Mrs. Johnson bridled. "I hope you are not accusing me of indulging in some kind of favouritism, Felicity!" she snapped. "I can't think why you should imagine that I would do Lyonelle Lawn, of all people, any favours. You know she's definitely got planning permission to build that bungalow at the bottom of their garden, in spite of our objections? It'll ruin our view of the river and knock thousands off the price of our house." Mrs. Johnson gave a bitter laugh. "Lyonelle Lawn is hardly *my* blue-eyed girl."

"Maybe you're over-compensating," suggested Lady Fowler unkindly. "You know, being especially bloody kind to the cow because you hate her so much. Understandable, but damned tough luck on your friends."

"Oh, don't be so ridiculous!" Mrs. Johnson looked round for something or somebody upon which to vent her pent-up irritation. She found it on the platform where those peculiar-looking folk were still hanging aimlessly around. Mrs. Johnson pounced on them with relief. "I say, isn't it about time you people were getting yourselves ready?" she called. "You know—make-up and costumes and things? The kiddies will be here any minute now and we don't want to start running late."

Silently, sullenly, and led, somewhat improbably, by a midget, the group began shuffling off backstage.

Lady Fowler watched them go before awarding herself the last word. "I don't know why we bother hiring outside entertainers, Rose," she observed. "Your pet, Lyonelle Lawn, is supposed to have been an actress of sorts, isn't she? I'm sure she'd be delighted to put on a show for us. Belly dancing, was it? Or striptease? Anyhow, something frightfully artistic, I'm sure. I hear they loved her in those ghastly workingmen's clubs up North."

The Hon. Con looked at her watch as Lady Fowler and Mrs. Johnson went somewhat icily their separate ways. "Oh, well, suppose it's time I went and sorted those dratted old presents out."

Miss Jones, who didn't approve of eavesdropping—at least not in such a blatant manner—thought it was more than time. She would like to have chided the Hon. Con for such ill-bred behaviour, but she knew what the answer would be so she saved her breath.

The Hon. Con, being the daughter of a peer of the realm as well as the finest private detective in Totterbridge, was naturally a law unto herself. What in common people like you and me would have been idle curiosity was in her case a serious, in-depth research project into behavioural patterns. Private detectives were by definition great students of human nature and everything was grist to their mill.

Untrammelled by the demands of husband and children, blessed with a considerable independent income and spared even from having to bother with all those time-consuming little domestic chores by the selfless devotion of Miss Jones, the Hon. Con did occasionally find it hard to fill up her day. At first she had thrown herself into charitable work, until the protests from the poor, the sick and the deprived became too vociferous to be ignored. Then she had gone in for sport, demolishing two tennis clubs, wrecking the entire local league for crown green bowling, and implanting the kiss of death on mixed hockey. Her sallies into the world of art fared little better, though the charge that she set back the cause of modern music in Totterbridge by fifty years is exaggerated.

It came, therefore, as a great relief all round (except to the police) when the Hon. Con discovered, almost by chance, that she was a natural private detective. Her progress to the very heights of her chosen profession would have been meteoric had it not been for some petty jealousy on the part of the official forces of law and order, and for the acute shortage of really juicy crimes in the Totterbridge area. Had there been even a modest sufficiency of spy rings, mass murders, kidnapings, and bank robberies to keep her going, you wouldn't have found the Hon. Con pottering around in a blooming old Santa Claus outfit, oh dear me, no! However, there wasn't so she was.

"Were that mangey crew hanging about on the stage really the entertainers?" asked the Hon. Con.

Miss Jones nodded. Although laying no claims to being either a master private detective or even a student of human nature, Miss Jones always seemed to know what was going on.

"Thought we were going to have a film show this year."

"You have to have the lights out for a film show, dear. Mrs. Johnson felt we just daren't risk it."

"What happened to that conjuror fellow?"

"He refused to come again, dear. After what they did to his rabbit."

The Hon. Con jerked her head in the direction of the stage. "So what are this lot supposed to be doing?"

"They're a kind of mini-circus, dear. You know, clowns and a juggler and a tightrope walker, I think. And that midget, of course."

"No animals?"

"They apparently have a performing dog, dear, but Mrs. Johnson thought we hadn't better tempt fate."

The Hon. Con pondered the situation and pronounced her verdict. "The kids'll eat 'em alive." She looked at her watch again. "You'd better be getting your skates on, Bones. It's only five minutes to D-day."

Miss Jones managed a brave little smile before trotting off to her post. She was on duty by the door which led from the Margaret Thatcher Hall to the corridor in which the two cloakrooms were located. It was her job to ensure that no more children at any one time passed through those portals than the facilities could cope with. It was no sinecure as almost everything seemed to get those Conservative toddlers right in the bladder.

Two o'clock struck like a death knell and the Totterbridge & District Conservative & Unionist Club's annual Christmas party got under way with both bangs and whimpers. Viewed as a whole, this year's effort was better than some but worse than most.

It was unfortunate that the proceedings opened with the professional entertainers. They were not a success and the Hon. Con, tucked away in the manager's office, listened to the howls and cat-calls coming from the Margaret Thatcher Hall with gloomy satisfaction. Her predictions were coming true and she could only hope that the little swine would have run out of steam by the time it came to distribute the presents.

The trouble was that the children, reared on a healthy diet of slick TV sex and violence, just couldn't take a real man tossing three colored balls in the air while balancing a plate on his nose. The contortionist came on, received several suggestions as to how he might enliven his act, and switched frantically into his fire-eating routine. This did cause a momentary lull but, when it became apparent that he wasn't about to set himself on fire and burn to death, the hostilities were resumed. The midget fared no better, being told by one juvenile wit that he ought to be in a preserving bottle at the Royal College of Surgeons. But it was the lady tightrope walker who really whipped things up. Her appearance was greeted by a hail of shoes, the only offensive weapons that the mites could lay their tiny paws on, thanks to the foresight of the Ladies' Organising Committee, who had frisked every child on arrival.

The lady tightrope walker, having been given the bird in better places than Totterbridge and being in any case well insulated from the slings and arrows by gin, would probably have weathered the storm if the midget hadn't tried to come to the rescue. He rushed onstage lugging a large packing case stuffed with cheap animal masks made of paper which he proceeded to fling out at the audience by the handful. It was reminiscent of some ignoble savage attempting to placate his gods, and about as successful.

True, the children ceased baying for the lady tightrope walker's blood but only in order to husband their strength for the furious internecine struggle which now flared up over items so abysmally undesirable that, in calmer times, they wouldn't even have been removed from the corn-flakes box.

Mrs. Johnson viewed the melee with resignation and a faint touch of hope that it might die down of its own accord. Only when blood began to flow and some of the smaller children had gone not so much to the wall as half-way through it did she acknowledge that the moment for desperate measures had arrived.

"Plan B, ladies!" she screamed. "Plan B! Quickly, now!"

The ladies took a deep breath, squared their shoulders, clenched their fists, and dived in.

Plan B was simple and consisted only of taking the cheap paper masks away from the little kids and giving them to the big kids, who were going to get them anyhow in the end. It merely speeded up the natural order of things and was justified only by the fact that it worked. Gradually the turmoil quietened. The circus performers had long ago beaten a cowardly retreat and so it was, as ever, to Mrs. Carmichael that Mrs. Johnson turned in her hour of need. Mrs. Carmichael was a pianist with an inexhaustible repertoire of your old favourites and mine, and the touch of a baby elephant. But she was used to soothing the savage beast and the children were ready for a change. In a matter of seconds they were gleefully bawling out highly obscene versions to the stream of popular songs which flowed from Mrs. Carmichael's leaden fingers.

Over by the door, Miss Jones put away her smelling

salts. Plan B had not involved her, of course. She was required to stick resolutely to her post at all times, but even watching the struggle to save civilisation as we know it had been alarming enough. Now that the community singing was in full swing, more children than ever were hearkening to the calls of Nature and Miss Jones had her hands full regulating the flow. Some of the tougher kids predictably began trying to buck the system but fortunately tea was announced before that appalling blond-haired boy—son of the town's leading Baptist minister—got a chance to demonstrate whether or not he was man enough to carry out the threats he'd been uttering in respect of Miss Jones's virtue.

For tea the children were herded into the adjoining Sir Winston Churchill Salon where a veritable feast had been laid out for them. Almost before the last child had been seated the walls were thick with jelly and trifle, and the sausage rolls were zooming through the air like missiles in an interplanetary war. Even the gorgeous cream cakes were deemed too good to eat and were squashed flat instead upon the heads of unsuspecting neighbours.

For the twenty minutes allotted to the pleasures of the table, Mrs. Johnson and her cohorts battled to maintain some semblance of order, but their task was made even more difficult by the animal masks that some of the children were still wearing. The masks hindered one of the most effective ploys for riot control—that of actually recognising a youngster, addressing it by name and threatening to report its unspeakable behaviour to its parents. Not that these brats gave a damn for their parents, but the experience of being publicly identified did seem to unnerve them for a moment or two.

When the tea party was over, it was time for the Hon. Con to hog the limelight. The children were driven back into the Margaret Thatcher Hall and grouped around the platform which, by means of some old army blankets and a few strips of silver paper, had now been transformed into a magic cave. In the middle, surrounded by heaps of exciting-looking parcels, sat the Hon. Con, beaming benevolently and not relaxing her guard for one second.

At the side of the platform, Mrs. Johnson read the names out from her list in alphabetical order. Each child then, theoretically, came forward in turn, shook hands with Father Christmas, received its present, and said thank you for it. In practice, any child that could break through the protective barrier of lady helpers made a dive and grabbed what it could.

Personation was rife.

"Here," demanded the Hon. Con of a rather rotund frog in striped trousers and bovver boots whom, she could swear, she'd seen twice already before, "you sure you're little Gwendoline Roberts, aged six?"

"You sure you're Father Christmas, missus?" retorted the frog, tearing the parcel wrapped in pink paper out of the Hon. Con's hands. "And not some nosy old judy called Burke?"

A sweet little girl in pigtails ducked back through the phalanx of lady helpers and thrust the battered remnants of her present into the Hon. Con's hands. "I don't want no lousy farmyard animals!" she shrilled, her blue eyes flashing. " 'Sides, they're all broke. Haven't you got a knuckle duster or a horse whip or something?"

The Hon. Con tried, but failed, to give back as good as she got. All around her the Margaret Thatcher Hall was knee-deep in discarded wrapping paper, crushed cardboard boxes and broken toys—all watered by infantile tears of rage and disappointment.

Still, all good things come to an end and four o'clock struck. Mrs. Johnson and her gallant band girded up their loins for one final effort and at five past four Lady Fowler proclaimed the glad tidings in stentorian tones.

"All right, girls!" she roared. "You can relax! I counted seventy-three of the litttle buggers in and seventy-three of them out! They've gone. It's over for another bloody year!"

The news ran round like wildfire and most of the ladies dropped where they stood. Oh, the blessed peace and quiet! Shoes were slipped off, clothing loosened, and foreheads dabbed with eau-de-cologne. But the human frame is amazingly resilient and before too long everybody was gathering in the kitchens for a cup of tea which, it was hoped, would give them enough strength to go home. Those ladies who had given up smoking cadged cigarettes off their less strong-willed sisters and before long the air was thick with tobacco smoke and recriminations.

Everybody had her complaints, but none was more vociferous than Mrs. Hinchliffe. "Somebody," she announced, trying to ease her aching back, "is going to have to do something about that cloakroom duty. It's too much."

"We did give you those fresh air sprays, dear," Mrs. Johnson reminded her.

"It's not the pong, Rose, it's the sheer hard work. Two people aren't enough. We need at least three."

"Hear, hear!" agreed the other ladies who had been relentlessly dressing and undressing children all afternoon.

Mrs. Johnson sighed. "There isn't room for three, dear. You yourself said that."

"Two on and one off!" declared Mrs. Hinchliffe. "So we can at least take a bit of a breather. Do you realise neither Clarice nor I so much as got our noses out of that damned boys' loo all afternoon?"

"Irene and I were just the same with the girls," chimed in one of her equally aggrieved colleagues. "I'd thought one of us would be able to take a break while the other held the fort, but no such luck. We were both of us slogging away the whole time."

"We'll look into it next time," promised Mrs. Johnson blandly. "Now," she looked round brightly, "is everybody here?" It was getting time for her little speech of thanks and appreciation.

The Hon. Con was reaching for the sugar bowl. "All present and correct, old fruit! I say," she addressed the company at large, "anybody see a pork pie lying around that hasn't actually been violated? I'm feeling dashed peckish."

Miss Jones, one of whose duties was to keep the Hon. Con's waist-line within bounds, endeavoured to divert the conversation from the topic of food. "Actually, Mrs. Johnson," she twittered helpfully, "I don't think we are quite all gathered together yet, are we? There's Mrs. Lawn, for example."

"Oh, she'll have sneaked off hours ago," said Lady Fowler with her usual snort. "Bloody idle cow!"

Mrs. Johnson, who'd had enough of Lady Fowler for one afternoon, pretended not to have heard and, since she had Miss Jones there, she decided she might as well make use of her. "I wonder, Miss—er . . . would you mind just popping along and seeing what's happened to her? Remind her that we're all waiting, would you? Perhaps her watch has stopped."

"Why not just leave her there to bloody rot?" enquired Lady Fowler charitably. "Serve her damned well right if she gets locked in."

But Miss Jones was already scurrying away. After long association with the Hon. Con, it was not in her nature to question orders, however dog-tired she might be.

In a remarkably short space of time she came scurrying back, ashen-faced and trembling like a leaf.

Even the Hon. Con noticed that she wasn't quite herself. "Something up, Bones?" she asked, pausing with her second vol-au-vent of the afternoon halfway to her lips.

Miss Jones had worked out how she was going to break the news. "Mrs. Lawn is sitting on her chair by the fire exit, dear," she said with chilling composure, "quite dead and with a large knife sticking out of her chest."

"Holy cats!" breathed the Hon. Con. She tossed the unconsumed portion of the vol-au-vent heedlessly aside and leaped to her feet. "Nobody move!" she bawled. "This sounds like murder, and I don't want you lot trampling all over the clues. Everybody stay here while I go and have a look!"

"Hadn't we better phone the police, Constance?"

There's always some clever devil, isn't there? Luckily, the Hon. Con's thought processes were now rattling along at the speed of light. "Better let me check first, old bean," she advised solemnly. "It may be a false alarm."

"It's no false alarm dear," moaned Miss Jones, her handkerchief pressed to her lips. "She is quite, quite dead, I do—"

The Hon. Con regarded her chum with exasperation. "Do button it, Bones!" she growled.

Still in her Father Christmas outfit, the Hon. Con strode off masterfully towards the scene of the crime. Chin up, stomach in, white whiskers fluttering importantly in the breeze of her passage, she thudded across the Margaret Thatcher Hall, through the door by which Miss Jones had stood on duty all afternoon, down the corridor past the two cloakrooms (one on either side), round the corner at the end and—"Golly!" said the Hon. Con.

Lyonelle Lawn was certainly as dead as a doornail.

The Hon. Con leaned forward for a close look. The knife sticking out of Lyonelle Lawn's chest seemed ordinary enough. Sort of kitchen knife you could get anywhere. Fingerprints? Grudgingly the Hon. Con acknowledged that that was one she'd have to leave to the boys in blue. Not much blood and it didn't seem as though she'd put up much of a fight. Taken unawares, perhaps? And robbery wasn't the motive because there was her handbag, still standing on the floor under her chair.

The Hon. Con straightened up. Bit creepy down there, actually, right at the end of the corridor and with nobody about. She turned her attention to the emergency door which Lyonelle Lawn had been guarding against anyone trying to break in or break out. They had experienced both gate-crashers and escapees in previous years. No, the door was still securely fastened. And there were no windows or—

Somebody was tiptoeing down the corridor!

The Hon. Con's hand closed round the rubber truncheon as she prepared to sell her life dearly.

"Blimey-O'Riley, Bones, I do wish you'd stop pussyfooting about!" Sheer relief that it wasn't a maniac killer with slavering jaws made the Hon. Con's tones unnecessarily sharp.

"I'm sorry, dear, but I thought you'd like to know that Lady Fowler went to phone the police."

"She-Judas!" spat the Hon. Con. "She might have given

me a few minutes. I haven't had a decent murder for months."

"Well, you're all right for the moment, dear, because somebody's disconnected the telephone and jammed up all the doors so that we can't get out. Miss Kingston thinks it's super-glue in the locks."

The Hon. Con frowned. This was getting serious. "The murderer, eh?" she mused aloud.

"More likely the children, dear," said Miss Jones with a sigh. She'd always been so fond of kiddies—before she'd been enrolled as a helper at the Totterbridge & District Conservative & Unionist Club's annual Christmas party, of course. "I left them trying to push little Mrs. Bellamy through the skylight over the front door. If she doesn't break a leg or anything, she's going to ring the police from the call box on the corner." Miss Jones glanced involuntarily at the corpse and regretted, not for the first time, that dear Constance hadn't managed to find a nicer hobby. Still, Miss Jones always felt it was up to her to take an intelligent interest. "Have you worked out any theories yet, dear?"

The Hon. Con emitted a rich chuckle. "Dozens, old girl! How does Felicity Fowler grab you, for a start?"

"Oh, Constance!"

"She was being deuced catty about Lyonelle Lawn earlier on," grunted the Hon. Con, ever ready to take any hasty word for the foulest deed. "Vicious, really. Or there's Rose Johnson."

"Mrs. Johnson is Chairperson of the Organising Committee, dear!"

"So who was in a better position to set the whole thing up? Who was it who stuck La Lawn down here all on her lonesome where she could be knocked off without anybody noticing? La Lawn's job this afternoon was precisely what Felicity Fowler was griping about, wasn't it? Well, come on, Bones, you heard her."

"Yes, I did hear her, dear," said Miss Jones with dignity, "and I think it highly improbable that Mrs. Johnson deliberately murdered Mrs. Lawn just because the extension to

Mrs. Lawn's house was going to ruin Mrs. Johnson's view of the river."

The Hon. Con scowled. "People can get jolly steamed up about that sort of thing. And then there's the depreciation in the value of the Johnsons' house. Don't forget that."

But Miss Jones was determined to take a more socially acceptable line. "Surely it's the work of an outsider, isn't it, dear? A burglar or a tramp or some sort of gibbering maniac who just happened to be passing?"

" 'Fraid that rabbit won't run, old girl," said the Hon. Con with evident relish. "No outsider could infiltrate this blooming building—you know that. We've had every door manned all afternoon to keep gate-crashers out and our dratted brats in. Nor," the Hon. Con raised a lordly hand before Miss Jones could voice the theory that the killer might have concealed himself in the Club earlier on, "is it any good you thinking of that door where Lyonelle Lawn was sitting. That's a proper emergency exit, you see. You can only open or close it from the inside with that bar thing. Well, the late lamented might possibly have opened it up and let her murderer in, but she jolly well didn't close it behind him after he'd gone out. No, we've just got to face facts, Bones. It was one of us. And my money's on Rose Johnson—with Felicity Fowler a good each-way bet."

Miss Jones was reluctant to be the hand that threw the spanner, but she had no choice. "I'm afraid it can't be one of us, dear."

"Why not?"

"There are only two ways of reaching the spot where Mrs. Lawn was killed, dear. You have demonstrated that we can forget about the emergency door. Well, that only leaves the route from the Margaret Thatcher Hall, along the corridor past the cloakrooms."

"So?"

"I was on duty on the door from the Margaret Thatcher Hall, dear, all afternoon, without a second's break. After Mrs. Lawn and the four ladies on duty in the cloakrooms went through, nobody else did—apart from the kiddies, of course."

The Hon. Con didn't look best pleased. "You prepared to swear that on a stack of Bibles, Bones?"

Miss Jones shuddered. "I should hope that wouldn't be necessary, Constance dear," she said reproachfully.

"All right," said the Hon. Con, whose thought processes under pressure frequently achieved the velocity of light, "somebody sneaked through after the party was over and you'd gone to the kitchen for a cup of tea."

Miss Jones was no slouch when it came to spiking the Hon. Con's guns. "I was the last person to arrive in the kitchen, dear. Or almost the last. Certainly both Mrs. Johnson and Lady Fowler were already there. Besides, if poor Mrs. Lawn was killed after I left my post by the door, that would mean she had only died a matter of moments before I found her." Miss Jones swallowed hard as she recalled the scene. "I don't think that was the case, dear. The blood seemed to be quite—"

The Hon. Con was growing impatient. "Then it was one of the four lassies on duty in the cloakrooms. One of them could have sloped off any old time, nipped round the corner, stuck the knife in La Lawn, and Bob's your uncle!"

Miss Jones's head was already shaking. "But you heard them yourself, dear, complaining that they'd never had a moment's relaxation and that they never left their cloakrooms all afternoon. They'll be able to give each other alibis, won't they? I mean, each couple will be able to—"

If there was anything that got right up the Hon. Con's nose it was hearing blessed amateurs using technical terms like "alibi." "There's such a thing as collusion!" she snapped. "Or conspiracy! Two of 'em could be in it together."

"Now don't be silly, dear!"

Miss Jones's reproof was feather-light and her smile indulgent, but the Hon. Con was never one to take criticism lying down. "Hope you're in the clear, Bones," she said nastily. "Because, if anybody could have slipped away during the afternoon and done Lyonelle Lawn in, it was *you!*"

The idea was so absurd that Miss Jones even managed

a little laugh, though with a fresh corpse only a few feet away laughter was neither very easy nor appropriate.

"Then it's one of the kids," said the Hon. Con indifferently, as though Miss Jones was in some way to blame for this conclusion. "It's the only answer—and it's not beyond the bounds of possibility, is it? I wouldn't put anything past those evil-minded little horrors. Do you know, I didn't get a thank you out of more than a couple of 'em all afternoon? Talk about manners! Yes, one of 'em could have come out to the cloakroom and popped round here to kill Lyonelle as easy as pie, having first nicked a knife at teatime, I shouldn't wonder. That explains why she didn't put up a struggle or anything. I mean, who expects getting knocked off by a nine-year-old, eh?"

Miss Jones had had a pretty gruelling day so far, what with the children's party and finding a dead body and everything, but it was all as nothing compared with the crisis she now faced. She would like to have fainted, but she daren't. Oh, why, oh, why hadn't she just let dear Constance pin the murder on whomever it was she wanted to pin it on in the first place? There would have been a little unpleasantness, no doubt, but it would be as nothing to the storm of fury and outrage that was going to erupt when the Hon. Con started pointing the finger of suspicion at a group of innocent children and innocent *Conservative* children, at that. Even Labor-voting parents would have been horrified, but the parents of this lot—well, running amuck and foaming at the mouth would just be for starters. Miss Jones's mind shied at the possibilities: tarring and feathering? Being ridden out of Totterbridge on a rail? Lynching?

Miss Jones moistened arid lips. "Constance, dear—"

"You know my methods, Bones," said the Hon. Con grandly. "When you've eliminated the impossible, what you've got left is it—however improbable. And you're the one," she added, turning the knife, "who did most of the eliminating for me."

"Constance, dear, you can't go around making wild accusations against some poor child who—"

"I know that, Bones! Drat it all, I haven't had more

than five minutes to get to the bottom of things, have I? I shall have to leave it to the cops to tie up a few loose ends and pinpoint the actual murderous little thug who did it. I am well used," the Hon. Con laughed bitterly, "to having my case snatched out of my hands by so-called professionals the minute I've cracked it. I gave up expecting any credit for my achievements a long time ago."

"In that case, dear," suggested Miss Jones with a cunning born of panic, "why not leave the whole thing to the police? Let them solve it themselves. Why should you help them? They never help you."

The Hon. Con thought a minute and then drew herself up proudly. She made a striking figure in her red Father Christmas suit and her flowing white whiskers. "Not in my nature to be a dog in the manger, Bones," she said modestly. "Now, while we're waiting, why don't you improve the shining hour by making a list for the cops of all the kids who went past you this afternoon on their way to the cloakrooms? Better stick 'em in chronological order with an indication of the times where you can."

"A list, dear?" bleated Miss Jones. "How can I possibly make a list? Every child at the party went out to the toilets at some time in the afternoon, and most of them more than once. You know what a shambles it was. Besides, I don't know more than a handful of them by name. How could I?"

The Hon. Con shrugged a pair of shoulders which would have looked better in the front row of a rugby scrum. "Hope the cops don't think you're trying to obstruct the course of justice," she rumbled with sham concern. " 'Praps they'll try and make you do it with photographs. You know, one of each kid so you can shuffle 'em around like a pack of cards till you get 'em in the right order."

"But, Constance," wailed Miss Jones, ever prey to her own sense of inadequacy, "half the time I didn't even see the children's faces! They were wearing those stupid animal masks. You can vouch for that, dear. Those who'd got them wore them the entire afternoon and—"

But the Hon. Con was no longer listening. Her somewhat protuberant eyes glazed over as they always did when sheer, undiluted inspiration was about to strike. "Golly!" she breathed in an awed voice. "I've got it! I've blooming well got it!"

"Got what, dear?"

"The solution, Bones! I know who done it!"

"Again, dear?" The words were unworthy, and Miss Jones was ashamed of herself for uttering them.

Luckily the Hon. Con was still up there on Cloud Nine. "It stands out a mile. It was that dwarf!"

"Dwarf, dear?"

"That midget who was with the circus entertainers. Oh, come on, Bones, rattle the old brain-box! You can't have forgotten that crummy bunch."

"I haven't forgotten, dear," said Miss Jones, who could sometimes turn the other cheek almost audibly. "It's just that—"

"He put on an animal mask and walked right past you," explained the Hon. Con jubilantly. "Twice. Both ways. Coming and going. You just took him for one of the kids and didn't give him a second thought. Deuced cunning, eh? And he was the one who dished out the animal masks in the first place, wasn't he? You all thought he'd gone potty, but it was part of his sinister plan. Premeditated, see!"

Miss Jones took one of her deep breaths. "Constance, dear—"

"Now don't start nitpicking, Bones! Because it all fits. He knew where Lyonelle Lawn was going to be on duty and that she would be tucked away all on her own because he overheard Rose Johnson and Felicity Fowler having an argy-bargy about it. Remember? He and the rest of that grotty crew were standing there lapping up every word— and there can't be many Lyonelle Lawns kicking around, can there? Oh, *heck!*" The Hon. Con's lynx-like ears had caught the distant wail of a police siren. Little Mrs. Bellamy must have made it to the phone box in spite of some fervent prayers to the contrary. "Listen, Bones, are those circus people still in the Club?"

"Oh, I shouldn't think so, dear. They must have gone

ages ago. You could check with Miss Simpson. She was on the front door and would have let them out."

"Curses!" The Hon. Con had been picturing herself tossing the miniature miscreant bodily into the arms of the Totterbridge Constabulary. That would have caused a few astounded jaws to drop, all rightie!

Miss Jones's mind meanwhile had been running on more mundane lines—such as slander and criminal libel and the bearing of false witness and what sort of damages a court might award to an outraged and injured midget against the rambunctious and wealthy daughter of a peer. Dear Constance never appeared to her best advantage in a court of law. She would keep telling the judge how to run the case and—"Constance, dear!"

The Hon. Con hitched up her Father Christmas trousers impatiently. "What now?"

Miss Jones put it as simply as she could. "Why should this midget have killed poor Mrs. Lawn!"

"Good grief, Bones, detectives don't have to prove motive. Thought everybody knew that. All you need do is establish means and opportunity. Well, that's what I've done. And I'll bet he nicked the knife from the kitchens here."

"But he must have had some reason, dear."

"The stage!" The Hon. Con's imagination always worked best under pressure. "Lyonelle Lawn used to be on the stage, didn't she? Well, so's that midget. They probably met up somewhere. You know what theatricals are like—all nerves and tension and things. There'd be a feud, I expect, or maybe she spurned his lascivious advances, or—"

But the time for leisurely speculation was past. Masculine voices and the tramp of heavy feet could be heard coming from the direction of the Margaret Thatcher Hall. The Hon. Con prepared herself for the encounter, smoothing down her scarlet tunic and fluffing up her white whiskers. "It's all a question of psychology, really," she whispered in an attempt to allay her chum's only too evident distress. "I'm deliberately leaving this motive question for the police to solve for the sake of their morale. You follow me?

It'll give them the chance to make a contribution and earn a bit of kudos—and it'll stop 'em getting too shirty over the indisputable fact that I've unravelled the mystery and tied the whole blooming case up for 'em before they even got here."

CHRISTMAS PARTY

BY MARTIN WERNER

People in the advertising business said the Christmas party at French & Saunders was the social event of the year. For it wasn't your ordinary holiday office party. Not the kind where the staff gets together for a few mild drinks out of paper cups, some sandwiches sent in from the local deli, and a long boring speech by the company president. At F&S it was all very different: just what you'd expect from New York's hottest advertising agency.

The salaries there were the highest in town, the accounts were strictly blue chip, and the awards the agency won over the years filled an entire boardroom. And the people, of course, were the best, brightest, and most creative that money could buy.

With that reputation to uphold, the French & Saunders Christmas party naturally had to be the biggest and splashiest in the entire industry.

Year after year, that's the way it was. Back in the late Seventies, when discos were all the rage, the company took over Numero Uno, the club people actually fought over to get in. Another year, F&S hired half the New York Philharmonic to provide entertainment. And in 1989, the guest bartenders were Mel Gibson, Madonna, and the cast of *L.A. Law.*

There was one serious side to the party. That's when the president reviewed the year's business, announced how much the annual bonus would be, and then named the Board's choices for People of the Year, the five lucky employees who made the most significant contributions to the agency's success during the past twelve months.

The unwritten part to this latter (although everyone knew it, anyway) was that each one of the five would receive a very special individual bonus—some said as high as $50,000 apiece.

Then French & Saunders bought fifteen floors in the tallest, shiniest new office tower on Broadway, the one that had actually been praised by the *N. Y. Times* architecture critic.

The original plan was to hold the party in the brand-new offices that were to be ready just before Christmas. A foolish idea, as it turned out, because nothing in New York is ever finished when it's promised. The delay meant the agency had to scramble and find a new party site—either that, or make do in the half finished building itself.

Amazingly—cleverly?—enough, that was the game plan the party committee decided to follow. Give the biggest, glitziest party in agency history amid half finished offices in which paneless windows looked out to the open skies, where debris and building supplies stood piled up in every corner, and where doors opened on nothing but a web of steel girders and the sidewalk seventy floors below.

Charlie Evanston, one of the company's senior vice-presidents (he had just reached the ripe old of age of fifty), was chosen to be party chairman. He couldn't have been happier. For Charlie had a deepdown feeling that this was finally going to be his year. After being passed over time and again for one of those five special Christmas bonuses, he just knew he was going to go home a winner.

Poor Charlie.

In mid-November—the plans for the party proceeding on schedule—the agency suddenly lost their multimillion-dollar Daisy Fresh Soap account, no reason given. Charlie had been the supervisor on the account for years, and although he couldn't be held personally responsible

for the loss a few people (enemies!) shook their heads
and wondered if maybe someone else, someone a little
stronger—and younger—couldn't have held on to the
business.

Two weeks later, another showpiece account—the
prestigious Maximus Computer Systems—left the
agency. Unheard of.

The trade papers gave away the reason in the one
dreaded word "kickbacks." Two French & Saunders
television producers who had worked on the account had
been skimming it for years.

Again, Charlie's name came up. Not that he had anything remotely to do with the scandal. The trouble was
that he personally had hired both offenders. And people
remembered.

There's a superstition that events like these happen in
threes, so it was only a question of time before the next
blow. And, sure enough, two weeks before Christmas, it
happened. A murder, no less. A F&S writer shot his
wife, her lover, and himself.

With that, French & Saunders moved from front-page
sidelines in the trade papers straight to screaming head-
lines in every tabloid in town. In less than a month, it
had been seriously downgraded from one of New York's
proudest enterprises to that most dreaded of advertising
fates—an agency "in trouble."

It was now a week before Christmas and every F&S
employee was carrying around his or her own personal
lump of cold, clammy fear. The telltale signs were everywhere. People making secret telephone calls to head-
hunters and getting their resumes in order. Bitter jokes
about the cold winter and selling apples on street corners told in the elevators and washrooms. Rumors that
a buyout was in the making and *nobody* was safe.

And yet, strange as it sounds, there were those who
still thought there would be a happy ending. At the
Christmas party, perhaps. A last-minute announcement
that everything was as before—the agency was in good

shape and, just like always, everyone would get that
Christmas bonus.

Charlie was one of the most optimistic. He didn't
know why. Just a gut feeling that the world was still full
of Christmas miracles and, bad times or not, he was
going to be one of F&S's five magical People of the
Year.

Poor Charlie.

A few days before the party, his phone rang. It was
the voice of J. Stewart French, president and chairman
of the board.

"Hi, Charlie. Got a minute?"

"Sure."

"I wonder if you'd mind coming up to my office. I've
got a couple of things I'd like to talk to you about."

Nothing menacing about that, thought Charlie. J probably wants to discuss the party. The food. The caterers.
The security measures that would be needed so that no
one would be in any danger in those half finished offices.

Very neatly, very efficiently, Charlie got out his files
and headed upstairs. When he arrived in the president's
office—it was the only one that had been completely
finished (vulgar but expensive, thought Charlie)—J was
on the phone, his face pale and drawn, nothing like the
way he usually looked, with that twelve-months-a-year
suntan he was so proud of. He nodded over the phone.
"Sit down, Charlie, sit down."

Charlie sank into one of the comfortable $12,000
chairs beside the desk and waited. After a minute the
conversation ended and J turned to give him his full
attention. Charlie had known J for fifteen years and had
never seen him so nervous and ill at ease.

Then he spoke.

"Charlie, they tell me you've really got the Christmas
party all together. Looks like it'll be a smash."

"We're hoping so, J."

"Well, we can certainly use some good times around
here. I don't have to tell *you* that. It's been a bad, *bad*
year."

"Things'll be better. I know it."

"Do you really think so, Charlie? Do you? I'd like to believe that, too. That's why this party means so much to me. To all of us. Morale—"

"I know."

"Well, you've certainly done your part. More than your part. That's why I called you in."

Here it comes, thought Charlie, here comes my special Christmas bonus! Ahead of time, before anyone else hears about it!

"I wanted you to be one of the first to know. The Board and I have agreed that, even with all our troubles, there'll be something extra in everybody's paycheck again this year. Nothing like before, of course, but it will be something."

"That's wonderful."

"Yeah. Wonderful. We monkeyed around with the budget and found we could come up with a few bucks. The *problem* is, we'll have to make some cuts here and there."

"Cuts?"

"Well, for one thing, I'm afraid there won't be any of those special bonuses this year, Charlie. And I'll level with you—you were down for one. After all these years, you had really earned it. I can't tell you how sorry—"

Sure, thought Charlie. "It's not the end of the world, J," he said. "Maybe next year."

"No, Charlie, that's not all. With our losses and the cost of moving—I don't know how to tell you this, but we're doing something else. We're cutting back—some of our best people. I've never had to do anything like that in my life."

You bastard, Charlie thought. "Go on, J," he said. "I think I know what you're going to say."

J looked at him miserably. "You're one of the people we'll have to lose, Charlie. Wait a minute, please hear me out—it's nothing personal. I wanted to save you. After all, we've been together fifteen years. I talked and talked, I even threatened to resign myself. But no one wanted to listen."

Sure, Charlie thought.

"They said you hadn't produced anything worthwhile in years. And there was the business of those two crazies you hired. And—"

"Is that it?" Charlie asked.

"Don't get me wrong, Charlie. Please, let's do the Christmas party as we planned, just as if nothing happened. As for leaving, take your time. I got you a year's severance. And you can use your office to make calls, look around, and—"

"No problem, J." Charlie was moving to the door. "I understand. And don't worry about the party. Everything's all taken care of."

Not even a handshake.

Many people at some time or other have fantasized about killing the boss. In Charlie's case, it was different. From the minute he heard the bad news from J, he became a changed man. Not outwardly, of course. He wasn't about to become an overnight monster, buy a gun, make a bomb, sharpen an axe. No, he would be the same Charlie Evanston. Friendly. Smiling. Efficient. But now that he knew the worst, he began piling up all the long-suppressed injustices he had collected from J for fifteen years. The conversations that stopped abruptly when he entered an executive meeting. The intimate dinners at J's that he and his wife were never invited to. The countless other little slights. And, finally, this.

December 20. Party time! Everyone agreed it was the best bash French & Saunders had ever thrown.

The day was fair and warm. The milling crowds that drifted from the well stocked bars and refreshment tables didn't even notice there wasn't a heating system. The lack of carpets, the wide-open window spaces, the empty offices—it all added to the fun.

Carefully groomed waiters in white gloves and hard hats pressed their way from room to room, carrying silver trays laden with drinks and hors d'oeuvres. A heavy metal band blared somewhere. A troupe of strolling violinists pressed in and out. From the happy faces, laughter, and noise, you'd never know the agency had a care in the world.

But Charlie Evanston knew. He pushed his way over to a small crowd pressing around J. All of them were drunk, or on the way, and J, drink in hand, was swaying slightly. His laugh was louder than anybody's whenever one of the clients told a funny story. He spotted Charlie and shouted to him. "Charlie, c'mere a minute! Folks, you all know my old pal Charlie Evanston. We've been together since this place opened its doors. He's the guy who put this whole great party together."

There were murmurs of approval as J drew Charlie into his embrace.

"J," Charlie said, "I just came to ask you to come over here and let me show you something."

"Oh, Charlie, always business. Can't it wait till next week? After the holidays?"

"No, I think it's important. Please come over here. Let me show you."

"Oh, for Chrissakes, Charlie. What *is* it?"

"Just follow me. Won't take long."

J pulled away from the group with a back-in-a-minute wave of his hand and followed Charlie down a narrow hall to a room that would one day become the heart of the agency's computer operation.

It was empty. Even the floors hadn't been finished. Just some wooden planks, a few steel beams—and the sidewalk below. J glanced around the room and turned to Charlie. "So? What's the problem?"

"Don't you get it, J? There isn't a single Keep Out sign on that outside door. The workmen even forgot to lock it. Someone could walk in here and fall straight down to Broadway!"

"Oh, come on, Charlie, this place is off the beaten path—no one's going to be coming this way. Stop worrying."

"Yes, but—"

"No buts, Charlie. Just tell one of the security guards. My God, you drag me all the way out here just to see this. Jesus Christ, I'll bet I could even *walk* across one of these steel beams. The workmen do it every day."

It was uncanny. Charlie knew that was exactly what J would say. It was part of the macho, daredevil reputation he had cultivated so carefully. "Hey, wait a minute, J," he said.

"No. Serious. Watch me walk across this beam right here. It can't be more than twenty feet long. And I'll do it with a drink in each hand."

"Come on, J, don't be crazy."

But J had already taken his first tentative step on the beam—with Charlie directly behind him.

It was all so simple. Now all Charlie had to do was give J the tiniest of shoves in the back, watch him stagger and plunge over the side, and it would be all over.

As J continued to move along the beam, he seemed to grow more confident. Charlie continued to follow a few steps behind, his right arm outstretched. It was now or never. Suddenly he made his move. But J moved a couple of quick steps faster and Charlie missed J's back by an inch. Instead, he felt himself slipping over the side. He gasped. Then all he remembered was falling.

The hospital room was so quiet you could barely hear a murmur from the corridor outside.

On the single bed there lay what looked like a dead body. Every inch was covered in a rubbery casing and yards and yards of white gauze. All you could see of what was underneath was a little round hole where the mouth was supposed to be and another opening where a bloodshot blue eye stared up at the ceiling. Charlie Evanston.

The door opened slightly, admitting J, followed by one of Charlie's doctors.

J shuddered. He always did, every time he'd visited over the past six months. He turned to the doctor. "How's he doing today?"

"About the same. He tries to talk a little now and then."

"Can he hear me yet? Can he understand?"

"We think so. But don't try and get anything out of him."

"Yes. I know," He bent over the bed. "Charlie. Charlie. It's me, J. I just wanted you to know I'm here. And I want to thank you again—I guess I'll be thanking you for the rest of my life—for reaching out and trying to save me at that damn Christmas party."

The blue eye blinked. A tear began to tremble on the edge.

"I was a fool. Only a fool would have tried to do what I did. And you tried to stop me. I felt you grab my jacket and try to hold me back. Then you took the fall for me."

The blue eye stared.

"So what I came to say—what I hope you can understand—is that no matter how long it takes you're going to get the best care we can find. Just get well. Everything's going to be okay."

The blue eye continued to look at J without blinking.

"And, Charlie, here's the best news of all. The agency's just picked up three big accounts. Over a hundred million."

A light breeze blew the curtains from the window.

"So today the Board asked me to come up here and give you a special bonus. Not a Christmas bonus—more like Purple Heart. You deserve it, Charlie. You saved the old man's life, you bastard!"

Charlie tried to nod, but it was impossible.

"And just wait till you come back," J said enthusiastically. "You're a hero, Charlie! We've got all kinds of great things waiting for you. All kinds of plans. It's going to be a whole new ballgame, Charlie! Imagine!"

Yeah, thought Charlie. Imagine.

KELSO'S CHRISTMAS

by Malcolm McClintick

Someone had murdered a Santa Claus.

The body, rotund and clad in the traditional red suit, lay in a corner behind the gift wrap section, in the basement, hidden from the view of passing customers by a counter and stacks of cardboard boxes. He still wore his long white beard and mustache, but the hat had come off and lay a foot from his head, revealing black hair with a bald spot on top.

George Kelso looked down at the body, then at Detective Sergeant Meyer. It was ten A.M., three days before Christmas, in one of the larger downtown department stores.

"Okay," Meyer said, "let's get this area cleared so the lab boys can get to work." He sounded tired. Kelso understood that it wasn't fatigue, but depression. Every year at Christmas Meyer, a small dark Jewish man, became depressed and usually withdrawn. It was no good talking to him about it, it was something Meyer had to live with and work out for himself, at least until he became willing to confide in his associates at the police department.

"I was supposed to go shopping this afternoon with Susan," Kelso said to nobody in particular. "I suppose that's out of the question now."

"I suppose it is," Meyer replied. "All right, Kelso, why don't you take the offices upstairs and I'll check with the clerks. The other guys are talking to customers to see if anybody noticed anything unusual.''

"I'll go talk to the business staff," Kelso agreed. When Meyer was in his Christmas funk, it was best to agree with whatever he said. The store's music system was playing "Winter Wonderland" over the noise and confusion of shoppers, and a few feet away, a little boy was screaming and trying to kick his mother, who looked flustered.

Kelso headed for the elevators.

Kelso himself became somewhat depressed at Christmas, but not for the same reasons as Meyer. For one thing, he found himself constantly thrown in with relatives at this time of year, and none of them especially liked him. Being unable to understand what had possessed him to seek a career as a police detective, they tended to regard him with suspicion and hostility. One of his more enlightened uncles had once referred to Kelso behind his back (but within easy hearing distance) as "that fascist," and a younger niece had often called him a pig. He had been forbidden to bring his gun to the various family dinners, though it was the last thing he would have brought, and whenever he entered a room everyone stopped talking and stared as if, he thought, expecting him to make an arrest.

For another, Christmas jarred his nerves. He had been brought up in a deeply religious family and the season had been the highlight of his year. It had seemed magical, with its aura of good cheer, its feeling of universal peace. Then he'd grown into adulthood to find all of that shattered by the reality of global conflict, mass murders, tough cynicism, and his own rapidly fading belief in anything magical. Ultimately, he'd come to view Christmas as an elaborate hoax perpetrated on a gullible public by department store managers, advertising executives, and toy manufacturers.

And now someone had killed Santa Claus.

But the dead man wasn't really Santa Claus. Kelso rode up to the eighth floor executive offices, going over the victim's particulars in his mind. Arnold Wundt, fifty-five, in charge of accounting, divorced, wife and kids on the west coast, quiet and bookish, nondrinker, nonsmoker, rarely dated, few friends. Who would want to kill such a man? Someone had wanted to.

Someone, at about nine thirty that morning, according to the coroner's man, had cornered Arnold Wundt behind the gift wrapping counter and shoved a long thin knife directly into his plump body, angling it upward from just below his ribs and penetrating his heart, killing him almost instantly. That someone had left the knife in the blood-stained corpse and was now back at work, or shopping for presents, or on a plane bound for the Bahamas. It was anybody's guess.

"May I help you, sir?"

Kelso had entered the manager's outer office and stood looking down at a receptionist's desk, suddenly realizing where he was, as if he'd awakened abruptly from a dream. He found his unlit pipe in one hand, his overcoat in the other.

"Sergeant Kelso," he said. "Police department. I wonder if I could talk to Mr. Anderson?"

"Oh, is it about the murder?" The girl was under twenty-five, blonde, cheerful, blue-eyed, slightly plump. She was the kind of healthy, well-fed girl who'd have been a cheerleader at some midwestern university. Ohio State, Kelso thought. Or Purdue.

"Yes, ma'am," he said, noticing a gold band on her ring finger.

A big, healthy smile. "Just a minute, sergeant." She got up and went through a door behind her desk, returned almost immediately with another smile. "Go right in. Mr. Anderson's out right now, but his assistant, Mr. Briggs, will help you."

"Thanks."

Mr. Briggs was short, probably five seven or so, heavy, with oversized glasses that greatly magnified his round, staring eyes, making him look like some sort of surprised bug. His wide lips were fixed in a permanent smile. A surprised, happy bug. He held a large sandwich, trying to stuff oversized bites of it into his wide mouth. There were reddish stains on the sleeves of his white shirt, and a piece of lettuce on his pants leg.

"Stupid cafeteria," he said around a mouthful, and dabbed with a napkin at his sleeve. "They always get too much ketchup on these things. I must've told them a hundred times." He swallowed, finally, and glared. "Can't finish it. Too messy." He wrapped the remains in a paper napkin and dropped it into a wastebasket, then held out a small pale hand. "Glad to meet you, Sergeant Kelsy."

"Kelso," he corrected, and sighed.

"Right. Kelso. Glad to meet you. Been shopping, sergeant? We've got some terrific deals on suits." The bug cast a critical eye at Kelso's battered corduroy suit. "Fix you right up. No? Well, I guess it's business, isn't it? Terrible about poor Wundt."

"I'd like to ask you a few questions, Mr. Briggs." Kelso took out his notebook and ballpoint, putting away his pipe and dropping his overcoat onto a chair. "Could you tell me—"

"Listen, sergeant." The bug's manner became suddenly confidential. He hurried across the office to the door, seemed to make certain it was tightly closed, and scurried back behind the polished desk. "I'd better tell you something. I don't know how much it's got to do with poor Wundt, but you'd better know about it. Sergeant—" Briggs glanced left and right in a comic imitation of some movie character about to reveal The Big Secret "—someone in this store's been embezzling money."

The words alone were normal enough; Kelso had encountered numerous embezzlers. It was the exaggerated way in which Briggs had spoken the words—his pop-eyed stare, his stage whisper, his air of a little kid confiding something about men from Mars to his best friend.

"Embezzling?" Kelso scribbled in his notebook. Fortunately Briggs couldn't see it, because Kelso had written: "Comic book character."

"Embezzling, sergeant. Somebody's been skimming money right off the top. It amounts to over a hundred thousand to date. And not only that, I think I know who it was."

Kelso allowed a theatrical pause before asking, "Who?"

Briggs leaned closer, looking immensely satisfied with himself, and whispered loudly: "Arnold Wundt."

"Wundt?" Kelso frowned, not even pretending surprise.

"Right. Listen, sergeant. Wundt was an accountant, and a good one. He was, in fact, in charge of accounting. But as the assistant manager, and I've got a degree in accounting myself—" he cleared his throat loudly "—I'm not only qualified but also duty-bound to check Wundt's work. And I caught him at it, sergeant. Now, if you ask me, someone else caught him at it, too. Someone who maybe tried to blackmail him and then, when he couldn't bleed him any more, got rid of him."

Kelso nodded slowly, as if considering what Briggs had said.

The little bug was a waste of time. It was too hot in the office and he was hungry for lunch.

"You don't happen to know where Mr. Anderson is, do you?" he asked, trying to sound polite.

"I think he was going to meet with Wundt about something," Briggs said, smiling his bug-smile. "I haven't seen him since about nine thirty, when he left to go downstairs. Come to think of it, he said he was on his way to gift wrap. Yes, I'm certain. Gift wrap. About nine thirty." Briggs seemed to emphasize the last words, and gave Kelso a meaningful look.

Suddenly Kelso realized what Briggs reminded him of. Not a bug at all, but a toy he'd gotten one year for Christmas, a rubber or plastic likeness of Froggy the Gremlin, pop eyes, leering smile. Briggs was Froggy the Gremlin with oversized glasses. And probably about as bright.

"I appreciate your help," Kelso told him, trying not to sound sarcastic. "Well, have a nice day."

"Merry Christmas, sergeant," said Froggy. "A *very* merry Christmas."

Kelso winced and left the office. The blonde cheerleader beamed at him and said, "Merry Christmas, sergeant."

"Same to you," he replied, as though returning an insult, and hurried for the elevators.

"I wasn't able to find out a damn thing," Detective Sergeant Meyer said. "As far as anybody knows, Wundt re-

ported to his office in accounting this morning at nine
sharp, as usual. He works alone. Nobody saw him or noticed him again till the gift wrap girl found his body behind
her counter at a quarter to ten, when she was coming
back from the ladies' room.'' The small detective shrugged.
"That's it. Nobody saw anything, nobody knows anything.
Everybody liked Wundt, but not very well. Nobody disliked him. He was a nothing, a zero.''

"He was a Santa Claus,'' said Kelso.

They sat in the store's cafeteria, the noon crowd chattering and munching around them. Meyer glared at his
meatloaf and said:

"Yeah, he was a Santa Claus. Why can't people make
meatloaf any more? My grandmother used to make delicious meatloaf. This stuff is still red in the center. Don't
they cook it?''

"I thought you only ate kosher.''

"Nuts. I eat anything. Jewish food happens to taste better, but that doesn't mean I can't eat what I want. I'm
enlightened.''

"Ah.'' Kelso nodded. "I wonder if Arnold Wundt's playing Santa had anything to do with his murder.''

"He was scheduled to fill in for the regular Santa this
morning,'' Meyer said. "The store's been having Santa in
a booth for the kids every morning at ten and every afternoon at two and five, each shopping day till Christmas.
What a zoo. I'm glad I don't have kids. All my friends
with kids are raising schizophrenics. All of them have split
personalities—half Jewish, half Christian. I tell you, it's
hell having a kid in this country if you're a Jew at
Christmas.''

"Schizophrenic doesn't mean split personality,'' Kelso
pointed out. "I've taken some psych courses. It means—''

"Forget what it means.'' Meyer stabbed at his meatloaf.

Over the hubbub drifted the faint sounds of "Sleigh
Ride.'' At a nearby table two little girls sang "Jingle
Bells,'' egged on by their overweight mother, who seemed
to think her mission was to entertain the other shoppers
with her offspring and their whining voices.

"Who was supposed to have been Santa this morning?" Kelso asked.

"Huh? Oh, you mean whose place did Wundt take?" Meyer thought for a moment. "The assistant manager. Guy named Briggs."

"Froggy the Gremlin," Kelso murmured.

"What?"

"Nothing. So Briggs was supposed to have been Santa Claus."

"I'm taking this meatloaf back. It's inedible. You'd think with all their peace on earth and good will they could cook a piece of meatloaf enough to make it edible." Meyer got up and carried his plate through the milling crowd to the food line, and returned a few minutes later with the same plate, scowling.

"What happened?" Kelso asked.

"They told me to eat it," he said. "They told me I ordered meatloaf and I got meatloaf. They told me Merry Christmas."

"Greetings of the season," Kelso told him.

Meyer muttered something under his breath. The two little girls sang "Deck the Halls" at the top of their lungs.

Meyer became convinced that the murderer was the gift wrap girl, a tall brunette named Claudia Collins. She stood several inches taller than Meyer, something which, Kelso knew, infuriated him; she was sullen, even while wrapping customers' gifts, which infuriated everybody; and she was the only employee who would admit to having been in or near the gift wrap area at or about the time of the murder, nine thirty that morning.

"I'm going to question her some more," Meyer announced as he and Kelso left the cafeteria. "I'm not letting some dumb broad spoil my holiday. If she stabbed that accountant, I'll get it out of her."

"By the way," Kelso said, resisting the urge to light his pipe. "When I talked to Briggs this morning, he accused Arnold Wundt of embezzling over a hundred thousand dollars from the store."

Meyer shot him a dark look. "You're kidding. How would Briggs know that?"

"He says he's got an accounting degree, and checked Wundt's work."

"Huh." Meyer's wheels turned. They stopped turning. "Claudia Collins probably found out about Wundt's embezzling. She probably tried to extort some money from him. He pulled a knife on her, and she managed to stab him with it. Well, I'm going to find her. You check around the store. Keep your eyes and ears open, and let me know if you hear anything else."

"Have a good time," Kelso said.

Meyer nodded solemnly, as though it had been a serious wish. "I will."

They parted. Kelso watched the detective shove his way into the crowd until it engulfed him; then someone grabbed his arm.

"George!"

He turned. Susan Overstreet's wide brown eyes smiled at him. She was running one hand through wavy blonde hair and using the other to hold a shopping bag crammed with packages.

"Hi."

"Isn't this hectic? I've already got five of the things on my list. Listen, go with me to the children's department, up on three, so we can find something for Peggy and Timmy. Then—"

"Hold on a minute, Susan. I can't—"

"Did you find that aftershave for your uncle? There's a sale in men's stuff. By the way, tonight we've got the eggnog party at my Aunt Eleanor's house, and she says—"

"Susan!"

"Huh? What is it?"

"I can't go shopping with you. Haven't you heard about the murder?"

"Murder! What murder?"

"One of the employees, the head of accounting. They found him this morning, stabbed, in a Santa Claus suit. I'm on duty till further notice."

"But you had the afternoon off."

"I know. But now I don't."

"Well, darn."

A tall gray-haired man in an expensive suit and tie stepped out of the crowd. "Sergeant Kelso?"

"Yes, sir?"

"I'm James Anderson, the store manager." He offered a firm hand. "Sorry I missed you this morning."

"Glad to meet you, Mr. Anderson." He glanced at Susan. "This woman's been following me around the store, but I don't think she's done anything illegal. Did you pay for those items, miss?"

Susan smiled sweetly. "This man seems to think he's a policeman, Mr. Anderson, but I've seen him following other women around the store. I think he may be dangerous. Excuse me."

Kelso smiled blandly at the manager's quizzical look. "Just a little joke, Mr. Anderson. Uh, could we talk in your office?"

"Certainly."

They took the elevator up to eight, passed the cheerleader, and entered the office where Kelso had interviewed Briggs. Anderson sat down behind the polished desk and folded his hands. "Have you come up with anything, sergeant?" He looked grave.

Kelso started to answer, then hesitated. The office door was slightly ajar. By moving a little to his left he could just see the toes of someone's shoes.

"We haven't come up with anything officially," he said.

Anderson looked interested. "But, unofficially?"

"Unofficially, Mr. Anderson, I believe we know who murdered Arnold Wundt." Kelso took out his pipe and some matches. There was an ashtray on the manager's desk. "At least, I believe *I* know who murdered him. He was to have played Santa Claus this morning, right?"

"No, I believe that would have been Mr. Briggs."

"But apparently Wundt took his place for some reason."

"Oh. Right. I remember now. Briggs had a meeting to attend. But who was it, sergeant? Who killed Wundt, and why?"

Kelso got his pipe going and puffed at it a couple of

times. "I've sent some of my men over to Headquarters to get an accountant for me. When they get back, the accountant will check some things, and then I'll make an arrest. I really don't want to name names till the accountant gets here."

"I see."

The door opened and Briggs stepped into the office, eyes popping behind his thick lenses. "Mr. Anderson—oh, excuse me, I didn't know you were with someone. Oh, hello, Sergeant Kelso."

Kelso nodded. His pipe went out.

"What is it, Briggs?"

"It's about Santa Claus this afternoon, Mr. Anderson. The customers are really upset about missing him this morning, and it's one thirty now. They're already lining up for the two P.M. Santa."

"Can't you do it, Briggs?" Anderson's tone was sharp.

"No, sir. I'm afraid not. That is, I'd very much like not to. It's occurred to me that it might be dangerous."

"What?"

"I mean, sir—suppose the killer knew I was to play Santa at ten this morning. Suppose the killer found Santa behind the gift wrap counter. Everybody looks alike in that outfit, with the pillow and whiskers and all. The killer would have assumed it was me, and stabbed him. But by now he probably knows it was the wrong person."

"Is that possible, Sergeant Kelso? Could the murderer have been after Briggs here, instead of Wundt?"

"It's possible," Kelso said, trying hard to suppress laughter. He was imagining a cold-blooded killer stalking Froggy the Gremlin.

"Well, who are we going to get? We've got to have someone."

"I've played Santa at the police Christmas party a few times," Kelso said. "I could do it."

Anderson stared, then slowly nodded. Briggs smiled his face-breaking smile, his pop eyes dancing with delight behind his glasses.

"It's not exactly in the line of duty for a police officer," Anderson said. "But we could certainly use you."

"I'd be glad to help out. I tend to put on a few pounds over the holidays." Kelso patted his stomach. "I won't even need much of a pillow."

"Good." The manager stood up, all business. "Briggs, get Sergeant Kelso a Santa suit and show him the booth. Thank you, sergeant. I won't forget this."

Kelso let himself be led away by the assistant manager. When they were out in the hall he said:

"Excuse me, is the Santa Claus outfit at the booth?"

Briggs nodded. "Yes, down on the main floor."

"I'll meet you there," Kelso said. "I've got to go the men's room."

Briggs nodded, beaming, and Kelso hurried down the hall.

The killer stood in line, waiting for Santa. With his left hand he held the hand of a little boy whom he'd talked into standing in line with him, a third grader named Kevin whose mother worked in Credit and Layaway. The killer had paid Kevin five dollars and told him he wanted to talk to Santa but, as an adult, was embarrassed to go without a child. Kevin had taken the money and agreed to help.

In front of the killer and Kevin stood a fat woman whose two small girls had just finished singing "Rudolph the Red-nosed Reindeer" in strident voices and were starting "Silent Night," encouraged by their mother. Ahead of them an attractive black woman waited her turn, whispering to a frightened little boy. Just inside a white cardboard fence surrounding a cardboard sleigh and eight cardboard reindeer, a jolly Santa sat on a red chair, holding a small girl on his knee while the girl's mother, presumably, looked on. There was so much noise in the store, with all the talking and laughter and music and the whining of the fat lady's daughters, that the killer couldn't make out what was being said by the jolly Santa and the small girl, but it didn't matter to him.

The killer's other hand was inside his suitcoat pocket, gripping the handle of a small automatic pistol, fully loaded. He smiled as if thoroughly enjoying himself and nodded once in a while at little Kevin, who kept chattering something about a Star Wars toy. He wanted to tell little Kevin that he was an obnoxious brat, but he kept smiling and pretended to be having a good time.

The killer's name was Briggs.

For over a year he'd been embezzling money from the department store, but last week that fool, Arnold Wundt, had caught him at it. Wundt had threatened to go to the police unless Briggs replaced every cent he'd taken. He'd had to kill him, of course.

And now this detective, this Kelso, seemed to have gotten wise to him. An accountant was coming. Kelso would manage to link the embezzlement to Wundt's murder. Briggs couldn't let that happen.

He hadn't planned to kill Wundt in the Santa suit; it had just happened that way. But now the cops, except Kelso, were looking for a Santa Claus connection. He'd kill Kelso in the Santa suit and add to the confusion.

His fingers tightened on the automatic as the attractive black woman stepped forward and boosted her little boy onto Santa's knee.

"Ho ho ho," said the jolly Santa in a strangely rasping voice, but Briggs wasn't fooled by the disguise.

Next in line were the two singing brats; then it would be the killer's turn.

Briggs watched little Kevin step up to the red-painted chair.

"Ho ho ho," rasped the voice.

He had to admit that the disguise was good—with the full white beard and drooping mustache, the red hat pulled low over the forehead, steel-rimmed spectacles on the nose, and the padding in the suit, the character bore little resemblance to Sergeant Kelso. But Briggs knew it was.

He stepped forward, drew the automatic from his pocket, and held it close to his chest, aimed at the Santa suit. The gun was between his body and Santa's, invisible to the waiting shoppers.

"That's enough, Kevin," Briggs said, smiling. "Get down now, and let me have my turn."

Kevin nodded, slid down, and walked away.

The eyes behind the spectacles widened slightly.

"I don't want to shoot you," Briggs said, smiling. "But I will. Believe me, I will. Take a break now. I'll tell them Santa has to take a break." He jabbed with the gun.

Santa stood up. Briggs hid the gun and turned to face the crowd.

"Ladies and gentlemen, old Santa has to take a short break, but he'll be right back." He turned. "Get moving, Kelso. We're going to the basement. If you do what I say, maybe you've got a chance."

He would kill him in the basement. No one would hear the shot over this bedlam. They walked through the crowd.

"Keep walking," he said.

It was taking too long. He couldn't shoot Kelso here in the middle of the main floor. If they didn't get to the basement before something happened, he'd have to turn and run from the store. He felt confused. The plan no longer seemed nearly as workable as when he'd first thought of it. Kelso is the only one who's sure, Briggs had thought. Get rid of Kelso and everything will be all right. But now it occurred to him that some of those women and children might remember him, remember that he'd gone off with Santa. He'd have to kill Kelso, if he could, and leave town immediately with what money he had. His chances were limited. He was sweating.

It was too late to turn back now. He'd made his move.

Briggs held one of Santa's arms, steering him around a corner and along a narrow corridor that led to a basement stairway, aiming the gun with his other hand. Briggs was short; for some reason Kelso seemed shorter than he had earlier. Just as his face went hot with the realization that something was wrong, a hand came from nowhere and gripped his wrist painfully, twisting it so that he dropped the pistol. Powerful hands grabbed him and shoved him hard against the wall of the corridor.

"You're under arrest," said George Kelso. Kelso stood in the middle of the hall in his corduroy suit, flanked by three uniformed cops with drawn revolvers. "The charges are embezzlement and murder."

Briggs stared. "Kelso! Then who the hell . . ."

The Santa person pulled the beard and mustache away and removed the hat. Briggs saw a smiling, attractive girl with blonde hair and brown eyes.

"Are you all right, Susan?" Kelso asked.

"Ho ho ho," said the girl.

Kelso, Meyer, and Susan Overstreet sat at a table in the store's cafeteria. "Silver Bells" played from the speakers, and shoppers at neighboring tables laughed and rustled their packages.

"Look at this meatloaf," said Meyer, poking at it with his fork. "Now they've practically burned it."

"Actually, mine's not too bad." Kelso took a bite. "I was starving."

"So how did you make the switch with Susan?" Meyer asked.

"I went to the men's room," Kelso said. "When I was sure nobody else was in there, I let Susan in and we put the Santa outfit on her."

"Incredible," Meyer shook his head. "You're lucky nobody walked in on you."

"I was leaning against the door."

"Sergeant Meyer?" Susan smiled at the detective. "Would you like to come over to my aunt's house tonight for some eggnog? If you wouldn't be uncomfortable. I mean, we won't sing any carols or anything, and Aunt Eleanor doesn't have a tree this year, just a few lights in the window."

"Trees are too expensive for people on fixed incomes," Kelso said, trying not to sound angry.

"So, will you come? We'd like to have you."

Meyer put down his fork and cleared his throat. "Nobody's ever invited me to have eggnog before," he said quietly. "Tell your aunt I'd like to come." He stood up. "I can't eat this stuff. I'll leave you two alone." He started away, then added: "Take the rest of the afternoon off, Kelso."

"Gee, thanks." Kelso glanced at his watch. "All forty-three minutes, huh?"

"Well," Susan said, eyeing him closely, "are you going to tell me how you knew?"

"Knew what?"

"Don't do that. How you knew it was Briggs."

"Oh." He shrugged. "Briggs made a couple of mistakes. He tried to convince me that Anderson, the store manager, had gone down to gift wrap at nine thirty. He kept emphasizing nine thirty. But why? I was the first one to question him, and only the other cops knew about the coroner's estimate of nine thirty as the time of the stabbing. But the murderer would have known. That was one thing."

"Hmm. What else?"

"He was too eager to tell me about the embezzlement, and to blame it on Arnold Wundt. If he'd been so certain, why hadn't he exposed Wundt himself, earlier? So I wondered if maybe Briggs was the embezzler, and not Wundt. Maybe Wundt had found him out, and Briggs had killed him to keep him quiet." Kelso shrugged. "Turns out I was right."

Susan blinked and folded her arms across her chest. "That's it? That's all? I put on a Santa suit and risked my life for nine thirty and some talk about an embezzlement?"

"Well, there was one other thing . . ."

"Tell me."

"Well, when I visited Briggs in Anderson's office, he was eating a sandwich of some kind. He kept dabbing at his shirtsleeve and complaining about how the cafeteria always put too much ketchup on the bread. But after I left him in the hall, I went back to the office and found his sandwich in the trash. There wasn't any ketchup on it." Kelso paused. "That stuff on his sleeve was blood."

"Yuk."

"Incidentally, can't your aunt really afford a tree this year?"

"It'd be tough. She buys a lot of presents. You're coming tonight, aren't you? Do you think Meyer will come?"

"Sergeant Kelso—" A tall, well-dressed man hurried up to their table. It was Anderson, the store manager, looking breathless. "Finally found you."

"Don't tell me something else has happened," Kelso said.

"We're supposed to have another Santa session in fifteen minutes, sergeant. With Wundt dead and Briggs in custody, there's nobody to do it. So I was wondering . . ."

It wasn't fair, he thought. He was almost off duty. He was tired. He wanted to go home and relax. He needed a bath, and he was sick to death of the chatter of mothers and children, the tinny music, the announcements of sales in this or that department.

Susan had done it once. She'd looked cute in the padded red suit and whiskers. He turned a pleading glance in her direction, trying to look desperate. She smiled, but slowly shook her head no.

"What do you say, sergeant? Will you help out? Please?"

It wasn't fair. He sighed heavily in resignation. He nodded.

"Good man," said Anderson.

"That's the Christmas spirit," Susan said.

Kelso scowled.

Kelso met Meyer at the door. Outside it was snowing. "Come in. You're late."

"I could leave," said Meyer testily.

"Nonsense. Susan's aunt wants to meet you, and there's still plenty of eggnog. You're letting in the snow."

Meyer came in dragging a small, well-shaped tree and a paper bag.

"What's this?" Kelso asked suspiciously.

"Some sort of festive plant." Meyer frowned. "Silly lights and ornaments to hang on it. Somebody killed a tree so you people could celebrate."

Kelso was moved. He stood for a moment, feeling a little of the old magic.

"Happy holidays, Meyer," he said.

Meyer nodded. "Merry Christmas, Kelso."

There was much cheer in the house that night.

THE SPY AND THE CHRISTMAS CIPHER

BY EDWARD D. HOCH

It was just a few days before the Christmas recess at the University of Reading when Rand's wife Leila said to him over dinner, "Come and speak to my class on Wednesday, Jeffrey."

"What? Are you serious?" He put down his fork and stared at her. "I know nothing about archaeology."

"You don't have to. I just want you to tell them a Christmas story of some sort. Remember last year? The Canadian writer Robertson Davies was over here on a visit and he told one of his ghost stories."

"I don't know any good ghost stories."

"Then tell them a cipher story from before you retired. Tell them about the time you worked through Christmas Eve trying to crack the St. Ives cipher."

Ivan St. Ives. Rand hadn't thought of him in years.

Yes, he supposed it was a Christmas story of sorts.

It was Christmas Eve morning in 1974, when Rand was still head of Concealed Communications, operating out of the big old building overlooking the Thames. He remembered his superior, Hastings, making the rounds of the

383

offices with an open bottle of sherry and a stack of paper cups, a tradition that no one but Hastings ever looked forward to. A cup of government sherry before noon was not something to warm the heart or put one in the Christmas spirit.

"It promises to be a quiet day," Hastings said, pouring the ritual drink. "You should be able to leave early and finish up your Christmas shopping."

"It's finished. I have no one but Leila to buy for." Rand accepted the cup and took a small sip.

"Sometimes I wish I was as well organized as you, Rand." Hastings seemed almost disappointed as he sat down in the worn leather chair opposite Rand's desk. "I was going to ask you to pick up something for me."

"On the day before Christmas? The stores will be crowded."

Hastings decided to abandon the pretense. "They say Ivan St. Ives is back in town."

"Oh? Surely you weren't planning to send him a Christmas gift?"

St. Ives was a double agent who'd worked for the British, the Russians, and anyone else willing to pay his price. There were too many like him in the modern world of espionage, where national loyalties counted for nothing against the lure of easy money.

"He's back in town and he's not working for us."

"Who, then?" Rand asked. "The Russians?"

"Perkins and Simplex, actually."

"Perkins and Simplex is a department store."

"Exactly. Ivan St. Ives has been employed over the Christmas season as their Father Christmas—red suit, white beard, and all. He holds little children on his knee and asks them what they want for Christmas."

Rand laughed. "Is the spying business in some sort of depression we don't know about? St. Ives could always pick up money from the Irish if nobody else would pay him."

"I just found out about it last evening, almost by accident. I ran into St. Ives's old girlfriend, Daphne Sollis, at the Crown and Piper. There's no love lost between the two of them and she was quite eager to tell me of his hard times."

"It's one of his ruses, Hastings. If Ivan St. Ives is sitting in Perkins and Simplex wearing a red suit and a beard it's part of some much more complex scheme."

"Maybe, maybe not. Anyway, this is his last day on the job. Why don't you drop by and take a look for yourself?"

"Is that what this business about last-minute shopping has been leading up to? What about young Parkinson—isn't this more his sort of errand?"

"Parkinson doesn't know St. Ives. You do."

There was no disputing the logic of that. Rand drank the rest of his sherry and stood up. "Do I have to sit on his lap?"

Hastings sighed. "Just find out what he's up to, Jeff."

The day was unseasonably warm, and as Rand crossed Oxford Street toward the main entrance of Perkins and Simplex he was aware that many in the lunchtime crowd had shed their coats or left them back at the office. The department store itself was a big old building that covered an entire block facing Oxford Street. It dated from Edwardian times, prior to World War I, and was a true relic of its age. Great care had been taken to maintain the exterior just as it had been, though the demands of modern merchandising had taken their toll with the interior. During the previous decade the first two floors had been gutted and transformed into a pseudo-atrium, surrounded by a balcony on which some of the store's regular departments had become little shops. The ceiling was frosted glass, lit from above by fluorescent tubes to give the appearance of daylight.

It was in this main atrium, near the escalators, that Father Christmas had been installed on his throne amidst sparkly white mountains of ersatz snow that was hardly in keeping with the outdoor temperature. The man himself was stout, but not as fat as American Santa Clauses. His white beard and the white-trimmed cowl of his red robe effectively hid his identity. It might have been Ivan St.

Ives, but Rand wasn't prepared to swear to it. He had to get much closer if he wanted to be sure.

He watched for a time from the terrace level as a line of parents and tots wound its way up the carpeted ramp to Father Christmas's chair. There he listened carefully to each child's request, sometimes boosting the smallest of them to his knee and patting their heads, handing each one a small brightly wrapped gift box from a pile at his elbow.

After observing this for ten or fifteen minutes, Rand descended to the main floor and found a young mother approaching the end of the line with her little boy. "Pardon me, ma'am," Rand said. "I wonder if I might borrow your son and take him up to see Father Christmas."

She stared at him as if she hadn't heard him correctly. "No, I can take him myself."

Rand showed his identity card. "It's official business."

The woman hesitated, then stood firm. "I'm sorry. Roger would be terrified if I left him."

"Could I come along, then, as your husband?"

She stared at the card again, as if memorizing the name. "I suppose so, if it's official business. No violence or anything, though?"

"I promise."

They stood in line together and Rand took the little boy's hand. Roger stared up at him with his big brown eyes, but his mother was there to give him confidence. "I hate shopping on Christmas Eve," she told Rand. "I always spend too much when I wait until the last minute."

"I think most of us do that." He smiled at the boy. "Are you ready, Roger? We're getting closer to Father Christmas."

In a moment the boy was on the bearded man's knee, having his head patted as he told him what he wanted to find under the tree next day. Then he received his brightly wrapped gift box and they were on their way back down the ramp.

"Thank you," Rand told the woman. "You've been a big help." He went back up to the terrace level and spent the next hour watching Ivan St. Ives, double agent, passing out gifts to a long line of little children.

*   *   *

"It's St. Ives," Rand told Hastings when he returned to the office. "No doubt of it."

"Did he recognize you?"

"I doubt it." He explained how he'd accompanied himself with the woman and child. "If he did, he might have assumed I was with my family."

"So he's just making a little extra Christmas money?"

"I'm afraid it's more than that."

"You spotted something."

"A great deal, but I don't know what it means. I watched him for more than an hour in all. After he listened to each child, he handed them a small gift. I watched one little girl opening hers. It was a clear plastic ball to hang on a Christmas tree, with figures of cartoon characters inside."

"Seems harmless enough."

"I'm sure the store wouldn't be giving out anything that wasn't. The trouble is, while I watched him I noticed a slight deviation from his routine on three different occasions. In these cases, he chose the gift box from a separate pile, and handed it to the parent rather than the child."

"Well, some of the children are quite small, I imagine."

"In those three cases, none of the boxes were opened in the store. They were stowed away in shopping bags by the mother or father. One little boy started crying for his gift, but he didn't get it."

Hastings thought about it.

"Do you think an agent would take a position as a department store Father Christmas to distribute some sort of message to his network?"

"I think we should see one of those boxes, Hastings."

"If there *is* a message, it probably says 'Merry Christmas.' "

"St. Ives has worked for some odd people in the past, including terrorists. When I left the store, there were still seven or eight boxes left on his special pile. If I went back there now with a couple of men—"

"Very well," Hastings said. "But please be discreet, Rand. It's the day before Christmas."

*   *   *

It's not easy to be discreet when seizing a suspected spy in the midst of a crowd of Christmas shoppers. Rand finally decided he wanted one of the free gifts more than he wanted the agents at this point, so he took only Parkinson with him. As they passed through the Oxford Street entrance of Perkins and Simplex, the younger man asked, "Is this case likely to run through the holidays? I was hoping to spend Christmas and Boxing Day with the family."

"I hope there won't even be a case," Rand told him. "Hastings heard Ivan St. Ives was back in the city, working as Father Christmas for the holidays. I confirmed the fact and that's why we're here."

"To steal a child's gift?"

"Not exactly steal, Parkinson. I have another idea."

They encountered a woman and child about to leave the store with the familiar square box. "Pardon me, but is that a gift from Father Christmas?" Rand asked her.

"Yes, it is."

"Then this is your lucky day. As a special holiday treat, Perkins and Simplex is paying every tenth person ten pounds for their gift." He held up a crisp new bill. "Would you like to exchange yours for a tenner?"

"I sure would!" The woman handed over the opened box and accepted the ten-pound note.

"That was easy," Parkinson commented when the woman and child were gone. "What next?"

"This might be a bit more difficult," Rand admitted. They retreated to a men's room where Rand fastened the festive paper around the gift box once more, resticking the piece of tape that held it together. "There, looks as good as new."

Parkinson got the point. "You're going to substitute this for one of the special ones."

"Exactly. And you're going to help."

They resumed Rand's earlier position on the terrace level, where he observed that the previous stack of boxes had dwindled to three. If he was right, they would be gone shortly, too. "How about that man?" Parkinson pointed out. "The one with the little boy."

"Why him?"

"He doesn't look that fatherly to me. And the boy seems a bit old to believe in Father Christmas."

"You're right," Rand said a moment later. "He's getting one of the special boxes. Come on!"

As the man and the boy came down off the ramp and mingled with the crowd, Rand moved in. The man was clutching the box just as the others had when Rand managed to jostle him. The box didn't come loose, so Rand jostled again with his elbow, this time using his other hand to yank it free. The man, in his twenties with black hair and a vaguely foreign look, muttered something in a language Rand didn't understand. There was a trace of panic in his face as he bent to retrieve the box. Rand pretended to lose his footing then, and came down on top of the man. The crowd of shoppers parted as they tumbled to the floor.

"Terribly sorry," Rand muttered, helping the man to his feet.

At the same moment, Parkinson held out the brightly wrapped package. "I believe you dropped this, sir."

Anyone else might have cursed Rand and made a scene, but this strange man merely grasped the box and hurried away without a word, the small boy trailing along behind. "Good work," Rand said, brushing off his jacket. "Let's get this back to the office."

"Aren't we going to open it?"

"Not here."

Thirty minutes later, Rand was carefully unwrapping the gift on Hastings' desk. Both Parkinson and Hastings were watching apprehensively, as if expecting a snake to spring out like a jack-in-the-box. "My money's on drugs," Parkinson said. "What else could it be?"

"Is the box exactly the same as the others?" Hastings asked.

"Just a bit heavier," Rand decided. "A few ounces."

But inside there seemed to be nothing but the same

plastic tree ornament. Rand removed the tissue paper and stared at the bottom of the box.

"Nothing," Parkinson said.

"Wait a minute. Something had to make it heavier." Rand reached in and pried up the bottom piece of cardboard with his fingernails. It was a snugly fitted false bottom. Beneath it was a thin layer of a grey puttylike substance. "Better not touch it," Hastings cautioned. "That's plastique—plastic explosive."

The man from the bomb squad explained that it was harmless without a detonator of some sort, but they were still relieved when he removed it from the office. "How much damage would that much plastic explosive do?" Rand wanted to know.

"It would make a mess of this room. That's about all."

"What about twelve or fifteen times that much?"

"Molded together into one bomb? It could take out a house or a small building."

They looked at each other glumly. "It's a pretty bizarre method for distributing explosives," Parkinson said.

"It has its advantages," Hastings said. "The bomb is of little use until enough of the explosive is gathered together. If one small box falls into government hands, as this one did, the rest is still safe. No doubt it was delivered to St. Ives only recently, and this served as the perfect method for getting it to his network—certainly better than the mails during the Christmas rush."

"Then you think it's to be reassembled into one bomb?" Rand asked.

"Of course. And it's to be used sometime soon."

"The IRA? Russians? Arabs?"

Hastings shrugged. "Take your pick. St. Ives has worked for all of them."

Rand held the box up to the light, studying the bottom. "This may be some writing, some sort of invisible ink that's beginning to become visible. Get one of the technicians up here to see if we can bring it out."

Heating the bottom of the box to bring out the message proved an easy task, but the letters that appeared were

anything but easy to read: MPPMP MBSHG OEXA-
SEWHMR AWPGG GBEBH PMBWE ALGHQ.

"A substitution cipher," Parkinson decided at once.
"We'll get to work on it."

"Forty letters," Rand observed, "in the usual five-letter
groups. There are five Ms, five Ps, and five Gs. Using letter
frequencies, one of them could be E, but in such a short
message you can't be sure."

"GHQ at the end could stand for General Headquarters," Hastings suggested.

Rand shook his head. "The entire message would be
enciphered. Chances are that's just a coincidence."

Parkinson took the message off to the deciphering room
and Rand confidently predicted he'd have the answer
within an hour.

He didn't.

"It's tougher than it looks," Parkinson told them.
"There may not be any Es at all."

"Run it through the computer," Rand suggested. "Use
a program that substitutes various frequently used letters
for the most frequently used letters in the message. See if
you hit on anything."

Hastings glanced at the clock. "It's after six and my
niece has invited me for Christmas Eve. Can you manage
without me?"

"Of course. Merry Christmas."

After he'd gone, Rand picked up the phone and told
Leila he'd be late. She was living in England now, and
he'd planned to spend the holiday with her.

"How late?" she asked.

"These things have been known to last all night."

"Oh, Jeffrey. On Christmas Eve?"

"I'll call you later if I can," Rand promised. "It might
not take that long."

He went down the hall and stood for a time watching
the computer experts work on the message. They seemed
to be having no better luck than Parkinson's people. "How
long?" he asked one.

"In the worst possible case it could take us until morning to run all the combinations."

Rand nodded. "I'll be back."

They had to know what the message said, but they also had to find Ivan St. Ives. The employment office at Perkins and Simplex would be closed now. His only chance was that pub where Hastings had spoken with Daphne Sollis. The Crown and Piper.

It was on a corner, as London pubs often are, and the night before Christmas didn't seem to have made much of a dent in the early-evening business. The bar was crowded and all the tables and booths were occupied. Rand let his eyes wander over the faces, seeking out either St. Ives or Daphne, but neither one seemed to be there. He didn't know either of them well, though he thought he would recognize St. Ives out of his Father Christmas garb. He was less certain about recognizing Daphne Sollis.

"Seen Daphne around?" he asked the bartender as he ordered a pint.

"Daphne Jenkins?"

"Daphne Sollis."

"Do I know her?"

"She was in here last night, talking to a grey-haired man wearing rimless glasses. He was probably dressed in a plaid topcoat."

"I don't—Wait a minute, you must mean Rusty. Does she have red hair?"

"Not the last time I knew her, but these things change."

"Well, if it's Rusty she comes in a couple of nights a week, usually alone. Once recently she was with a creepy-looking gent who kept laughing like Father Christmas. I sure wouldn't want *him* bringing gifts to my kids. He'd scare 'em half to death."

"Does she live around here?"

"No idea, mate." He went off to wait on another customer.

So whatever Daphne had told Hastings about her relationship with Ivan St. Ives, they were hardly enemies. He'd been with her recently in the Crown and Piper, apparently since he took on the job as Father Christmas.

Rand thought it unlikely that Daphne would visit the

pub two nights in a row, but on the other hand she might stop by if she was lonely on Christmas Eve. He decided to linger over his pint and see if she appeared. Thirty minutes later he was about to give it up and head for Leila's flat when he heard the bartender say, "Hey, Rusty! Fellow here's been askin' after you."

Rand turned and saw Daphne Sollis standing not five feet behind him, unwrapping a scarf to reveal a tousled head of red hair. "Daphne!" She looked puzzled for a moment and he identified himself. "Ivan St. Ives introduced us a year or so back. He did some work for me."

She nodded slowly as it came back to her. "Oh, yes— Mr. Rand. I remember you now. Is this some sort of setup? The other one, Hastings, was here just last night."

"No setup, but I *would* like to talk with you, away from this noise. How about the lobby of the hotel next door?"

"Well—all right."

The hotel lobby was much quieter. They sat beneath a large potted palm and no one disturbed them. "What do you want?" she asked. "What did your friend Hastings want last night?"

"It was only happenstance that he met you, though I'll admit I came to the Crown and Piper looking for you. I need to locate Ivan St. Ives."

"I told Hastings we're on the outs."

"I saw him at Perkins and Simplex earlier today."

"Then you've already located him."

"No," Rand explained. "His Christmas job would have ended today. I need to know where he's living."

"I said we're on the outs."

"You were drinking with him at the Crown and Piper just a week or two ago."

She bit her lip and stared off into space. "I don't know where he's living. He rang me up and we had a drink for old times sake. That's when he told me about the Christmas job. He talked about getting back together again, but I don't know. He works for a lot of shady people."

"Who's he working for now?"

"Just the store, so far as I know. He said he'd fallen on hard times."

Rand leaned forward. "It could be worth some money if you located him for us, told us who he's palling around with."

She seemed to consider the idea. "I could tell you plenty about who he's palled around with in the past. It wasn't just our side, you know."

"I know."

"But it would have to be after New Year's. I'm going to visit a girlfriend in Hastings, on the coast. Is your friend Hastings from there?"

"From Leeds, actually." Rand was frowning. "I need St. Ives now."

"I'm sorry, I can't help you. Perhaps the store has his address."

"I'll have to ask them." Rand stood up. "Can I buy you a pint back at the pub?"

"I'd better skip it now," she said, glancing at her watch. "I want to get home and change. I'm going to Midnight Mass with some friends."

"If you'll jot down your phone number I'd like to ring you up after New Year's."

"Fine," she agreed.

He'd intended to phone Leila after he left Daphne, but back at the Double-C office, Parkinson was in a state of dejection. "We've run every possible substitution of the letter E and there's still nothing. We're going down the letter-frequency list now, working on T, A, O, and N."

"Forty characters without a single E. Unusual, certainly."

"Any luck locating St. Ives?"

"Not yet."

Rand worked with them for a time and then dozed on his office couch. It was long after midnight when Parkinson shook him awake. "I think we've got part of it."

"Let me see."

The younger man produced long folds of computer printout. "On this one we concentrated on the first six characters—the repetitive MPPMPM. We got nowhere substituting E, T, or A, but when we tried the next letters on the frequency list, O and N, look what came up."

Rand focused his sleepy eyes and read NOONON. "Noon on?"

"Exactly. And there's another ON combination later in the message."

"Just a simple substitution cipher after all," Rand marveled. "School children make them up all the time."

"And it took us all these hours to get this far."

"St. Ives didn't worry about making the cipher too complex because he was writing it in invisible ink. It was our good luck that the box warmed enough so that some of the message began to appear."

"A terrorist network armed with plastic explosives, and St. Ives is telling them when and where to set off the bomb. Do you think we should phone Hastings?"

Rand glanced at the clock. It was almost dawn on Christmas morning. "Let's wait till we get the rest of it."

He followed Parkinson down the hall to the computer room where the others were at work. Not bothering with the machines, he went straight to the old blackboard at the far end of the room. "Look here, all of you. The group of letters following *noon on* is probably a day of the week, or a date if it's spelled out. If it's a day of the week, three of these letters have to stand for *day*."

As he worked, he became aware that someone had chalked the most common letter-frequency list down the left side of the board, starting with E, T, A, O, N, and continuing down to Q, X, Z. It was the list from David Kahn's massive 1967 book, *The Codebreakers,* which everyone in the department had on their shelves. He stared at it and noticed that M and P came together about halfway down the list. Together, just like N and O in the regular alphabet. Quickly he chalked the letters A to Z next to the frequency list. "Look here! The key is the standard letter-frequency list. ABCDE is enchipered as ETAON. There are no Ns in the message we found, so there are no Es in the plaintext."

The message became clear at once: NOONO NTHIS DAYCH ARING CROSS STATI ONTRA CKSIX.

"Noon on this day, Charing Cross Station, track six," Rand read.

"Noon on which day?" Parkinson questioned. "It was after noon yesterday before he distributed most of the boxes."

"He must mean today. Christmas Day. A Christmas Day explosion at Charing Cross Station."

"I'll phone Hastings," Parkinson decided. "We can catch them in the act."

Police and Scotland Yard detectives converged on the station shortly after dawn. Staying as unobtrusive as possible, they searched the entire area around track six. No bomb was found.

Noon came and went, and no bomb exploded.

Rand turned up at Leila's flat late that afternoon. "Only twenty-four hours late," she commented drily, holding the door open for him.

"And not in a good mood."

"You mean you didn't crack it after all this time?"

"We cracked it, but that didn't do us much good. We don't have the man who sent it, and we may be unable to prevent a terrorist bombing."

"Here in London?"

"Yes, right here in London." He knew a few police were still at Charing Cross Station, but he also knew it was quite easy to smuggle plastic explosives past the tightest security. They could be molded into any shape, and metal detectors were of no use against them.

He tried to put his mind at ease during dinner with Leila, and later when she asked if he'd be spending the night he readily agreed. But he awakened before dawn and walked restlessly to the window, looking out at the glistening streets where rain had started to fall. It would be colder today, more like winter.

The bomb hadn't gone off at Charing Cross Station yesterday. Either the time or the place was wrong.

But it hadn't gone off anywhere else in London, so he could assume the place was correct. It was the time that was off.

The time, or the day.

This day.

Noon on this day.

He went to Leila's telephone and called Parkinson at home. When he heard his sleepy voice answer, he said, "This is Rand. Meet me at the office in an hour."

"It's only six o'clock," Parkinson muttered. "And a holiday."

"I know. I'm sorry. But I'm calling Hastings, too. It's important."

He leaned over the bed to kiss Leila but left without awakening her.

An hour later, with Hastings and Parkinson seated before him in the office, Rand picked up a piece of chalk. "You see, we assumed the wrong meaning for the word 'this.' If someone wants to indicate 'today,' they say it— they don't say 'this day.' On the other hand, if I write the word 'this' on the desk in front of me—" he did so with the piece of chalk "—what am I referring to?"

"The desk," Parkinson replied.

"Right. If I wrote the word on a box, what would I be referring to?"

"The box."

"When St. Ives's message said, 'this day,' he wasn't referring to Christmas Eve or Christmas Day. He was telling them Boxing Day. Even if they were foreign, they'd know it was the day after Christmas here and a national holiday."

"That's today," Hastings said.

"Exactly. We need to get the men back to Charing Cross Station."

The station was almost deserted. The holiday travelers were at their destinations, and it was too soon for anyone to have started home yet. Rand stood near one of the newsstands looking through a paper while the detectives again searched unobtrusively around track six. It was nearly noon and time was running out.

"No luck," Hastings told him. "They can't find a thing."

"Plastique." Rand shook his head. "It could be molded

around a girder and painted most any color. We'd better keep everyone clear from now until after noon." It was six minutes to twelve.

"Are you sure about this, Rand? St. Ives is using a dozen or more people. Perhaps they all didn't understand his message."

"They had to come together to assemble the small portions of explosive into a deadly whole. Most of them would understand the message even if a few didn't. I'm sure St. Ives trained them well."

"It's not a busy day. He's not trying to kill a great many people or he'd have waited until a daily rush hour."

"No," Rand agreed. "I think he's content to—" He froze, staring toward the street entrance to the station. A man and a woman had entered and were walking toward track six. The man was Ivan St. Ives and the woman was Daphne Sollis.

Rand had forgotten that the train to Hastings left from Charing Cross Station.

He ran across the station floor, through the beams of sunlight that had suddenly brightened it from the glass-enclosed roof. "St. Ives!" he shouted.

Ivan St. Ives had just bent to give Daphne a good-bye kiss. He turned suddenly at the sound of his name and saw Rand approaching. "What *is* this?" he asked.

"Get away from him, Daphne!" Rand warned.

"He just came to see me off. I told you I was visiting—"

"Get away from him!" Rand repeated more urgently.

St. Ives met his eyes, and glanced quickly away, as if seeking a safe exit. But already the others were moving in. His eyes came back to Rand, recognizing him. "You were at the store, in line for Father Christmas! I knew I'd seen you before!"

"We broke the cipher, St. Ives. We know everything."

St. Ives turned and ran, not toward the street from where the men were coming but through the gate to track six. A police constable blew his whistle, and the sound merged with the chiming of the station clock. St. Ives had gone about fifty feet when the railway car to his left seemed to come apart with a blinding flash and roar of sound that sent waves of dust and debris billowing back toward Rand and the others. Daphne screamed and covered her face.

When the smoke cleared, Ivan St. Ives was gone. It was some time later before they found his remains among the wreckage that had been blown onto the adjoining track. By then, Rand had explained it to Hastings and Parkinson. "Ivan St. Ives was a truly evil man. When he was hired to plan and carry out a terrorist bombing in London over the Christmas holidays, he decided quite literally to kill two birds with one stone. He planned the bombing for the exact time and place where his old girlfriend Daphne Sollis would be. To make certain she didn't arrive too early or too late, he even escorted her to the station himself. She knew too much about his past associations, and he wanted her out of his life for good. I imagine one of his men must have ridden the train into Charing Cross Station and hidden the bomb on board before he left."

But he didn't tell any of this to Daphne. She only knew that they'd come to arrest St. Ives and he'd been killed by a bomb while trying to flee. A tragic coincidence, nothing more. She never knew St. Ives had tried to kill her.

In a way Rand felt it was a Christmas gift to her.

THE CAROL SINGERS

BY JOSEPHINE BELL

Old Mrs. Fairlands stepped carefully off the low chair she had pulled close to the fireplace. She was very conscious of her eighty-one years every time she performed these mild acrobatics. Conscious of it and determined to have no humiliating, potentially dangerous mishap. But obstinate, in her persistent routine of dusting her own mantelpiece, where a great many too many photographs and small ornaments daily gathered a film of greasy London dust.

Mrs. Fairlands lived in the ground floor flat of a converted house in a once fashionable row of early Victorian family homes. The house had been in her family for three generations before her, and she herself had been born and brought up there. In those faroff days of her childhood, the whole house was filled with a busy throng of people, from the top floor where the nurseries housed the noisiest and liveliest group, through the dignified, low-voiced activities of her parents and resident aunt on the first and ground floors, to the basement haunts of the domestic staff, the kitchens and the cellars.

Too many young men of the family had died in two world wars and too many young women had married and left the house to make its original use in the late 1940's any longer possible. Mrs. Fairlands, long a widow, had inherited the property when the last of her brothers died.

She had let it for a while, but even that failed. A conversion was the obvious answer. She was a vigorous seventy at the time, fully determined, since her only child, a married daughter, lived in the to her barbarous wastes of the Devon moors, to continue to live alone with her much-loved familiar possessions about her.

The conversion was a great success and was made without very much structural alteration to the house. The basement, which had an entrance by the former back door, was shut off and was let to a businessman who spent only three days a week in London and preferred not to use an hotel. The original hall remained as a common entrance to the other three flats. The ground floor provided Mrs. Fairlands with three large rooms, one of which was divided into a kitchen and bathroom. Her own front door was the original dining room door from the hall. It led now into a narrow passage, also chopped off from the room that made the bathroom and kitchen. At the end of the passage two new doors led into the former morning room, her drawing room as she liked to call it, and her bedroom, which had been the study.

This drawing room of hers was at the front of the house, overlooking the road. It had a square bay window that gave her a good view of the main front door and the steps leading up to it, the narrow front garden, now a paved forecourt, and from the opposite window of the bay, the front door and steps of the house next door, divided from her by a low wall.

Mrs. Fairlands, with characteristic obstinacy, strength of character, integrity, or whatever other description her forceful personality drew from those about her, had lived in her flat for eleven years, telling everyone that it suited her perfectly and feeling, as the years went by, progressively more lonely, more deeply bored, and more consciously apprehensive. Her daily came for four hours three times a week. It was enough to keep the place in good order. On those days the admirable woman cooked Mrs. Fairlands a good solid English dinner, which she shared, and also constructed several more main meals that could be eaten cold or warmed up. But three half days of cleaning and cooking left four whole days in each week when Mrs. Fairlands must provide for herself or go out to the High Street to a restaurant. After her eightieth birthday she became more and more reluctant to make the effort. But every week she wrote to her daughter Dorothy to say how well she felt and how much she would detest leaving London, where she had lived all her life except when she was evacuated to Wiltshire in the second war.

She was sincere in writing thus. The letters were true as far as they went, but they did not go the whole distance. They did not say that it took Mrs. Fairlands nearly an hour to wash and dress in the morning. They did not say she was sometimes too tired to bother with supper and then had to get up in the night, feeling faint and thirsty, to heat herself some milk. They did not say that although she stuck to her routine of dusting the whole flat every morning, she never mounted her low chair without a secret terror that she might fall and break her hip and perhaps be unable to reach the heavy stick she kept beside her armchair to use as a signal to the flat above.

On this particular occasion, soon after her eighty-first birthday, she had deferred the dusting until late in the day, because it was Christmas Eve and in addition to cleaning the mantelpiece she had arranged on it a pile of Christmas cards from her few remaining friends and her many younger relations.

This year, she thought sadly, there was not really much point in making the display. Dorothy and Hugh and the children could not come to her as usual, nor could she go to them. The tiresome creatures had chicken pox, in their late teens, too, except for Bobbie, the afterthought, who was only ten. They should all have had it years ago, when they first went to school. So the visit was canceled, and though she offered to go to Devon instead, they told her she might get shingles from the same infection and refused to expose her to the risk. Apart altogether from the danger to her of traveling at that particular time of the year, the weather and the holiday crowds combined, Dorothy had written.

Mrs. Fairlands turned sadly from the fireplace and

walked slowly to the window. A black Christmas this year, the wireless report had promised. As black as the prospect of two whole days of isolation at a time when the whole western world was celebrating its midwinter festival and Christians were remembering the birth of their faith.

She turned from the bleak prospect outside her window, a little chilled by the downdraft seeping through its closed edges. Near the fire she had felt almost too hot, but then she needed to keep it well stocked up for such a large room. In the old days there had been logs, but she could no longer lift or carry logs. Everyone told her she ought to have a cosy stove or even do away with solid fuel altogether, install central heating and perhaps an electric fire to make a pleasant glow. But Mrs. Fairlands considered these suggestions defeatist, an almost insulting reference to her age. Secretly she now thought of her life as a gamble with time. She was prepared to take risks for the sake of defeating them. There were few pleasures left to her. Defiance was one of them.

When she left the window, she moved to the far corner of the room, near the fireplace. Here a small table, usually covered, like the mantelpiece, with a multitude of objects, had been cleared to make room for a Christmas tree. It was mounted in a large bowl reserved for this annual purpose. The daily had set it up for her and wrapped the bowl round with crinkly red paper, fastened with safety pins. But the tree was not yet decorated.

Mrs. Fairlands got to work upon it. She knew that it would be more difficult by artificial light to tie the knots in the black cotton she used for the dangling glass balls. Dorothy had provided her with some newfangled strips of pliable metal that needed only to be threaded through the rings on the glass balls and wrapped round the branches of the tree. But she had tried these strips only once. The metal had slipped from her hands and the ball had fallen and shattered. She went back to her long practiced method with black cotton, leaving the strips in the box for her grandchildren to use, which they always did with ferocious speed and efficiency.

She sighed as she worked. It was not much fun decorating the tree by herself. No one would see it until the day after Boxing Day when the daily would be back. If only her tenants had not gone away she could have invited them in for some small celebration. But the basement man was in his own home in Essex, and the first floor couple always went to an hotel for Christmas, allowing her to use their flat for Dorothy and Hugh and the children. And this year the top floor, three girl students, had joined a college group to go skiing. So the house was quite empty. There was no one left to invite, except perhaps her next door neighbors. But that would be impossible. They had detestable children, rude, destructive, uncontrolled brats. She had already complained about broken glass and dirty sweet papers thrown into her forecourt. She could not possibly ask them to enjoy her Christmas tree with her. They might damage it. Perhaps she ought to have agreed to go to May, or let her come to her. She was one of the last of her friends, but never an intimate one. And such a chatterer. Nonstop, as Hugh would say.

By the time Mrs. Fairlands had fastened the last golden ball and draped the last glittering piece of tinsel and tied the crowning piece, the six-pronged shining silver star, to the topmost twig and fixed the candles upright in their socket clips, dusk had fallen. She had been obliged to turn on all her lights some time before she had done. Now she moved again to her windows, drew the curtains, turned off all the wall lights, and with one reading lamp beside her chair sat down near the glowing fire.

It was nearly an hour after her usual teatime, she noticed. But she was tired. Pleasantly tired, satisfied with her work, shining quietly in its dark corner, bringing back so many memories of her childhood in this house, of her brief marriage, cut off by the battle of the Marne, of Dorothy, her only child, brought up here, too, since there was nowhere for them to live except with the parents she had so recently left. Mrs. Fairlands decided to skip tea and have an early supper with a boiled egg and cake.

She dozed, snoring gently, her ancient, wrinkled hand twitching from time to time as her head lolled on and off the cushion behind it.

She woke with a start, confused, trembling. There was a ringing in her head that resolved, as full consciousness returned to her, into a ringing of bells, not only her own, just inside her front door, but those of the other two flats, shrilling and buzzing in the background.

Still trembling, her mouth dry with fright and open-mouthed sleep, she sat up, trying to think. What time was it? The clock on the mantelpiece told her it was nearly seven. Could she really have slept for two whole hours? There was silence now. Could it really have been the bell, all the bells, that had woken her? If so, it was a very good thing. She had no business to be asleep in the afternoon, in a chair of all places.

Mrs. Fairlands got to her feet, shakily. Whoever it was at the door must have given up and gone away. Standing still, she began to tremble again. For she remembered things Dorothy and Hugh and her very few remaining friends said to her from time to time. "Aren't you afraid of burglars?" "I wouldn't have the nerve to live alone!" "They ring you up, and if there is no answer, they know you're out, so they come and break in."

Well, there had been no answer to this bell ringing, so whoever it was, if ill-intentioned, might even now be forcing the door or prowling round the house, looking for an open window.

While she stood there in the middle of her drawing room, trying to build up enough courage to go round her flat pulling the rest of the curtains, fastening the other windows, Mrs. Fairlands heard sounds that instantly explained the situation. She heard, raggedly begun, out of tune, but reassuringly familiar, the strains of "Once in Royal David's City."

Carol singers! Of course. Why had she not thought of them instead of frightening herself to death with gruesome suspicions?

Mrs. Fairlands, always remembering her age, her gamble, went to the side window of the bay and, pulling back the edge of the curtain, looked out. A darkclad group stood there, six young people, four girls with scarves on their heads, two boys with woolly caps. They had a single electric torch directed onto a sheet of paper held by the central figure of the group.

Mrs. Fairlands watched them for a few seconds. Of course they had seen the light in her room, so they knew someone was in. How stupid of her to think of burglars. The light would have driven a burglar away if he was out looking for an empty house to break into. All her fears about the unanswered bell were a nonsense.

In her immense relief, and seeing the group straighten up as they finished the hymn, she tapped at the glass. They turned quickly, shining the torch in her face. Though she was a little startled by this, she smiled and nodded, trying to convey the fact that she enjoyed their performance.

"Want another, missis?" one boy shouted.

She nodded again, let the curtain slip into place, and made her way to her bureau, where she kept her handbag. Her purse in the handbag held very little silver, but she found the half crown she was looking for and took it in her hand. "The Holly and the Ivy" was in full swing outside. Mrs. Fairlands decided that these children must have been well taught in school. It was not usual for small parties to sing real carols. Two lines of "Come, All Ye Faithful," followed by loud knocking, was much more likely.

As she moved to the door with the half crown in one hand, Mrs. Fairlands put the other to her throat to pull together the folds of her cardigan before leaving her warm room for the cold passage and the outer hall door. She felt her brooch, and instantly misgiving struck her. It was a diamond brooch, a very valuable article, left to her by her mother. It would perhaps be a mistake to appear at the door offering half a crown and flaunting several hundred pounds. They might have seen it already, in the light of the torch they had shone on her.

Mrs. Fairlands slipped the half crown into her cardigan pocket, unfastened the brooch, and, moving quickly to the little Christmas tree on its table, reached up to the top and pinned the brooch to the very center of the silver tinsel star. Then, chuckling at her own cleverness, her quick wit, she went out to the front door just as the bell rang again in her flat. She opened it on a group of fresh young faces and sturdy young bodies standing on her steps.

"I'm sorry I was so slow," she said. "You must forgive me, but I am not very young."

"I'll say," remarked the younger boy, staring. He thought he had never seen anything as old as this old geyser.

"You shut up," said the girl next to him, and the tallest one said, "Don't be rude."

"You sing very nicely," said Mrs. Fairlands. "Very well indeed. Did you learn at school?"

"Mostly at the club," said the older boy, whose voice went up and down, on the verge of breaking, Mrs. Fairlands thought, remembering her brothers.

She held out the half crown. The tallest of the four girls, the one who had the piece of paper with the words of the carols on it, took the coin and smiled.

"I hope I haven't kept you too long," Mrs. Fairlands said. "You can't stay long at each house, can you, or you would never get any money worth having."

"They mostly don't give anything," one of the other girls said.

"Tell us to get the 'ell out," said the irrepressible younger boy.

"We don't do it mostly for the money," said the tallest girl. "Not for ourselves, I mean."

"Give it to the club. Oxfam collection and that," said the tall boy.

"Don't you want it for yourselves?" Mrs. Fairlands was astonished. "Do you have enough pocket money without?"

They nodded gravely.

"I got a paper round," said the older boy.

"I do babysitting now and then," the tallest girl added.

"Well, thank you for coming," Mrs. Fairlands said. She was beginning to feel cold, standing there at the open door. "I must go back into my warm room. And you must keep moving, too, or you might catch colds."

"Thank you," they said in chorus. "Thanks a lot. Bye!"

She shut and locked the door as they turned, clattered down the steps, slammed the gate of the forecourt behind

them. She went back to her drawing room. She watched
from the window as they piled up the steps of the next
house. And again she heard, more faintly because farther
away, "Once in Royal David's City." There were tears in
her old eyes as she left the window and stood for a few
minutes staring down at the dull coals of her diminishing
fire.

But very soon she rallied, took up the poker, mended
her fire, went to her kitchen, and put on the kettle. Coming
back to wait for it to boil, she looked again at her Christmas tree. The diamond brooch certainly gave an added
distinction to the star, she thought. Amused once more by
her originality, she went into her bedroom and from her
jewel box on the dressing table took her two other valuable pieces, a pearl necklace and a diamond bracelet. The
latter she had not worn for years. She wound each with a
tinsel string and hung them among the branches of the
tree.

She had just finished preparing her combined tea and
supper when the front doorbell rang again. Leaving the
tray in the kitchen, she went to her own front door and
opened it. Once again a carol floated to her, "Hark, the
Herald Angels Sing" this time. There seemed to be only
one voice singing. A lone child, she wondered, making the
rounds by himself.

She hurried to the window of her drawing room, drew
back the curtain, peeped out. No, not alone, but singing a
solo. The pure, high boy's voice was louder here. The
child, muffled up to the ears, had his head turned away
from her towards three companions, whose small figures
and pale faces were intent upon the door. They did not
seem to notice her at the window as the other group had
done, for they did not turn in her direction. They were
smaller, evidently younger, very serious. Mrs. Fairlands,
touched, willing again to defeat her loneliness in a few
minutes' talk, took another half crown from her purse and
went out to the main hall and the big door.

"Thank you, children," she said as she opened it. "That
was very—"

Her intended praise died in her throat. She gasped, tried

to back away. The children now wore black stockings over their faces. Their eyes glittered through slits; there were holes for their noses and mouths.

"That's a very silly joke," said Mrs. Fairlands in a high voice. "I shall not give you the money I brought for you. Go home. Go away."

She backed inside the door, catching at the knob to close it. But the small figures advanced upon her. One of them held the door while two others pushed her away from it. She saw the fourth, the singer, hesitate, then turn and run out into the street.

"Stop this!" Mrs. Fairlands said again in a voice that had once been commanding but now broke as she repeated the order. Silently, remorselessly, the three figures forced her back; they shut and locked the main door, they pushed her, stumbling now, terrified, bewildered, through her own front door and into her drawing room.

It was an outrage, an appalling, unheard-of challenge. Mrs. Fairlands had always met a challenge with vigor. She did so now. She tore herself from the grasp of one pair of small hands to box the ears of another short figure. She swept round at the third, pulling the stocking halfway up his face, pushing him violently against the wall so his face met it with a satisfactory smack.

"Stop it!" she panted. "Stop it or I'll call the police!"

At that they all leaped at her, pushing, punching, dragging her to an upright chair. She struggled for a few seconds, but her breath was going. When they had her sitting down, she was incapable of movement. They tied her hands and ankles to the chair and stood back. They began to talk, all at once to start with, but at a gesture from one, the other two became silent.

When Mrs. Fairlands heard the voices, she became rigid with shock and horror. Such words, such phrases, such tones, such evil loose in the world, in her house, in her quiet room. Her face grew cold, she thought she would faint. And still the persistent demand went on.

"We want the money. Where d'you keep it? Come on. Give. Where d'you keep it?"

"At my bank," she gasped.

"That's no answer. Where?"

She directed them to the bureau, where they found and rifled her handbag, taking the three pound notes and five shillings' worth of small change that was all the currency she had in the flat.

Clearly they were astonished at the small amount. They threatened, standing round her, muttering threats and curses.

"I'm *not* rich," she kept repeating. "I live chiefly on the rents of the flats and a very small private income. It's all paid into my bank. I cash a check each week, a small check to cover my food and the wages of my daily help."

"Jewelry," one of them said. "You got jewelry. Rich old cows dolled up—we seen 'em. That's why we come. You got it. Give."

She rallied a little, told them where to find her poor trinkets. Across the room her diamond brooch winked discreetly in the firelight. They were too stupid, too savage, too—horrible to think of searching the room carefully. Let them take the beads, the dress jewelry, the amber pendant. She leaned her aching head against the hard back of the chair and closed her eyes.

After what seemed a long time they came back. Their tempers were not improved. They grumbled among themselves—almost quarreling—in loud harsh tones.

"Radio's worth nil. Prehistoric. No transistor. No record player. Might lift that old clock."

"Money stashed away. Mean old bitch."

"Best get going."

Mrs. Fairlands, eyes still closed, heard a faint sound outside the window. Her doorbell rang once. More carol singers? If they knew, they could save her. If they knew—

She began to scream. She meant to scream loudly, but the noise that came from her was a feeble croak. In her own head it was a scream. To her tormentors it was derisory, but still a challenge. They refused to be challenged.

They gagged her with a strip of sticking plaster, they pulled out the flex of her telephone. They bundled the few valuables they had collected into the large pockets of their overcoats and left the flat, pulling shut the two front doors as they went. Mrs. Fairlands was alone again, but gagged and bound and quite unable to free herself.

At first she felt a profound relief in the silence, the emptiness of the room. The horror had gone, and though she was uncomfortable, she was not yet in pain. They had left the light on—all the lights, she decided. She could see through the open door of the room the lighted passage and, beyond, a streak of light from her bedroom. Had they been in the kitchen? Taken her Christmas dinner, perhaps, the chicken her daily had cooked for her? She remembered her supper and realized fully, for the first time, that she could not open her mouth and that she could not free her hands.

Even now she refused to give way to panic. She decided to rest until her strength came back and she could, by exercising it, loosen her bonds. But her strength did not come back. It ebbed as the night advanced and the fire died and the room grew cold and colder. For the first time she regretted not accepting May's suggestion that she should spend Christmas with her, occupying the flat above in place of Dorothy. Between them they could have defeated those little monsters. Or she could herself have gone to Leatherhead. She was insured for burglary.

She regretted those things that might have saved her, but she did not regret the gamble of refusing them. She recognized now that the gamble was lost. It had to be lost in the end, but she would have chosen a more dignified finish than this would be.

She cried a little in her weakness and the pain she now suffered in her wrists and ankles and back. But the tears ran down her nose and blocked it, which stopped her breathing and made her choke. She stopped crying, resigned herself, prayed a little, considered one or two sins she had never forgotten but on whose account she had never felt remorse until now. Later on she lapsed into semiconsciousness, a half-dream world of past scenes and present cares, of her mother, resplendent in low-cut green chiffon and diamonds, the diamond brooch and bracelet now decorating the tree across the room. Of Bobbie, in a fever, plagued by itching spots, of Dorothy as a little girl, blotched with measles.

Towards morning, unable any longer to breathe properly, exhausted by pain, hunger, and cold, Mrs. Fairlands died.

The milkman came along the road early on Christmas morning, anxious to finish his round and get back to his family. At Mrs. Fairlands' door he stopped. There were no milk bottles standing outside and no notice. He had seen her in person the day before when she had explained that her daughter and family were not coming this year so she would only need her usual pint that day.

"But I'll put out the bottles and the ticket for tomorrow as usual," she had said.

"You wouldn't like to order now, madam?" he had asked, thinking it would save her trouble.

"No, thank you," she had answered. "I prefer to decide in the evening, when I see what milk I have left."

But there were no bottles and no ticket and she was a very, very old lady and had had this disappointment over her family not coming.

The milkman looked at the door and then at the windows. It was still dark, and the light shone clearly behind the closed curtains. He had seen it when he went in through the gate but had thought nothing of it, being intent on his job. Besides, there were lights in a good many houses and the squeals of delighted children finding Christmas stockings bulging on the posts of their beds. But here, he reminded himself, there were no children.

He tapped on the window and listened. There was no movement in the house. Perhaps she'd forgotten, being practically senile. He left a pint bottle on the doorstep. But passing a constable on a scooter at the end of the road, he stopped to signal to him and told him about Mrs. Fairlands. "Know 'oo I mean?" he asked.

The constable nodded and thanked the milkman. No harm in making sure. He was pretty well browned off— nothing doing—empty streets—not a hooligan in sight—

layabouts mostly drunk in the cells after last night's parties—villains all at the holiday resorts, casing jobs.

He left the scooter at the curb and tried to rouse Mrs.
Fairlands. He did not succeed, so his anxiety grew. All the
lights were on in the flat, front and back as far as he
could make out. All her lights. The other flats were in
total darkness. People away. She must have had a stroke
or actually croaked, he thought. He rode on to the nearest
telephone box.

The local police station sent a sergeant and another constable to join the man on the beat. Together they managed
to open the kitchen window at the back, and when they
saw the tray with a meal prepared but untouched, one of
them climbed in. He found Mrs. Fairlands as the thieves
had left her. There was no doubt at all what had happened.

"Ambulance," said the sergeant briefly. "Get the super
first, though. We'll be wanting the whole works."

"The phone's gone," the constable said. "Pulled out."

"Bastard! Leave her like this when she couldn't phone
anyway and wouldn't be up to leaving the house till he'd
had plenty time to make six getaways. Bloody bastard!"

"Wonder how much he got?"

"Damn all, I should think. They don't keep their savings
in the mattress up this way."

The constable on the scooter rode off to report, and
before long, routine investigations were well under way.
The doctor discovered no outward injuries and decided
that death was probably due to shock, cold, and exhaustion, taking into account the victim's obviously advanced
age. Detective-Inspector Brooks of the divisional CID
found plenty of papers in the bureau to give him all the
information he needed about Mrs. Fairlands' financial position, her recent activities, and her nearest relations. Leaving the sergeant in charge at the flat while the experts in
the various branches were at work, he went back to the
local station to get in touch with Mrs. Fairlands' daughter,
Dorothy Evans.

In Devonshire the news was received with horror, indignation, and remorse. In trying to do the best for her

mother by not exposing her to possible infection, Mrs. Evans felt she had brought about her death.

"You can't think of it like that," her husband Hugh protested, trying to stem the bitter tears. "If she'd come down, she might have had an accident on the way or got pneumonia or something. Quite apart from shingles."

"But she was all alone! That's what's so frightful!"

"And it wasn't your fault. She could have had what's-her-name—Miss Bolton, the old girl who lives at Leatherhead."

"I thought May Bolton was going to have *her*. But you couldn't make Mother do a thing she hadn't thought of herself."

"Again, that wasn't your fault, was it?"

It occurred to him that his wife had inherited to some extent this characteristic of his mother-in-law, but this was no time to remind her of it.

"You'll go up at once, I suppose?" he said when she was a little calmer.

"How can I?" The tears began to fall again. "Christmas Day and Bobbie's temperature still up and his spots itching like mad. Could you cope with all that?"

"I'd try," he said. "You know I'd do anything."

"Of course you would, darling." She was genuinely grateful for the happiness of her married life and at this moment of self-reproach prepared to give him most of the credit for it. "Honestly, I don't think I could face it. There'd be identification, wouldn't there? And hearing detail—" She shuddered, covering her face.

"Okay. I'll go up," Hugh told her. He really preferred this arrangement. "I'll take the car in to Exeter and get the first through train there is. It's very early. Apparently her milkman made the discovery."

So Hugh Evans reached the flat in the early afternoon to find a constable on duty at the door and the house locked up. He was directed to the police station, where Inspector Brooks was waiting for him.

"My wife was too upset to come alone," he explained, "and we couldn't leave the family on their own. They've all got chicken pox; the youngest's quite bad with it today."

He went on to explain all the reasons why Mrs. Fairlands had been alone in the flat.

"Quite," said Brooks, who had a difficult mother-in-law himself and was inclined to be sympathetic. "Quite. Nothing to stop her going to an hotel here in London over the holiday, was there?"

"Nothing at all. She could easily afford it. She isn't—wasn't—what you call rich, but she'd reached the age when she really *couldn't* spend much."

This led to a full description of Mrs. Fairlands' circumstances, which finished with Hugh pulling out a list, hastily written by Dorothy before he left home, of all the valuables she could remember that were still in Mrs. Fairlands' possession.

"Jewelry," said the inspector thoughtfully. "Now where would she keep that?"

"Doesn't it say? In her bedroom, I believe."

"Oh, yes. A jewel box, containing—yes. Well, Mr. Evans, there was no jewel box in the flat when we searched it."

"Obviously the thief took it, then. About the only thing worth taking. She wouldn't have much cash there. She took it from the bank in weekly amounts. I know that."

There was very little more help he could give, so Inspector Brooks took him to the mortuary where Mrs. Fairlands now lay. And after the identification, which Hugh found pitiable but not otherwise distressing, they went together to the flat.

"In case you can help us to note any more objects of value you find are missing," Brooks explained.

The rooms were in the same state in which they had been found. Hugh found this more shocking, more disturbing, than the colorless, peaceful face of the very old woman who had never been close to him, who had never shown a warm affection for any of them, though with her unusual vitality she must in her youth have been capable of passion.

He went from room to room and back again. He

stopped beside the bureau. "I was thinking, on the way up," he said diffidently. "Her solicitor—that sort of thing. Insurances. I ought—can I have a look through this lot?"

"Of course, sir," Inspector Brooks answered politely. "I've had a look myself. You see, we aren't quite clear about motive."

"Not—But wasn't it a burglar? A brutal, thieving thug?"

"There is no sign whatever of breaking and entering. It appears that Mrs. Fairlands let the murderer in herself."

"But that's impossible."

"Is it? An old lady, feeling lonely perhaps. The doorbell rings. She thinks a friend has called to visit her. She goes and opens it. It's always happening."

"Yes. Yes, of course. It could have happened that way. Or a tramp asking for money—Christmas—"

"Tramps don't usually leave it as late as Christmas Eve. Generally smash a window and get put inside a day or two earlier."

"What worries you, then?"

"Just in case she had someone after her. Poor relation. Anyone who had it in for her, if she knew something damaging about him. Faked the burglary."

"But he seems to have taken her jewel box, and according to my wife, it was worth taking."

"Quite. We shall want a full description of the pieces, sir."

"She'll make it out for you. Or it may have been insured separately."

"I'm afraid not. Go ahead, though, Mr. Evans. I'll send my sergeant in, and he'll bring you back to the station with any essential papers you need for Mrs. Fairlands' solicitor.

Hugh worked at the papers for half an hour and then decided he had all the information he wanted. No steps of any kind need, or indeed could, be taken until the day after tomorrow, he knew. The solicitor could not begin to wind up Mrs. Fairlands' affairs for some time. Even the date of the inquest had not been fixed and would probably have to be adjourned.

Before leaving the flat, Hugh looked round the rooms once more, taking the sergeant with him. They paused before the mantelpiece, untouched by the thieves, a poignant reminder of the life so abruptly ended. Hugh looked at the cards and then glanced at the Christmas tree.

"Poor old thing!" he said. "We never thought she'd go like this. We ought all to have been here today. She always decorated a tree for us—" He broke off, genuinely moved for the first time.

"So I understand," the sergeant said gruffly, sharing the wave of sentiment.

"My wife—I wonder—D'you think it'd be in order to get rid of it?"

"The tree, sir?"

"Yes. Put it out at the back somewhere. Less upsetting—Mrs. Evans will be coming up the day after tomorrow. By that time the dustmen may have called."

"I understand. I don't see any harm—"

"Right."

Hurrying, in case the sergeant should change his mind, Hugh took up the bowl, and turning his face away to spare it from being pricked by the pine needles, he carried it out to the back of the house where he stood it beside the row of three dustbins. At any rate, he thought, going back to join the sergeant, Dorothy would be spared the feelings that overcame him so unexpectedly.

He was not altogether right in this. Mrs. Evans traveled to London on the day after Boxing Day. The inquest opened on this day, with a jury. Evidence was given of the finding of the body. Medical evidence gave the cause of death as cold and exhaustion and bronchial edema from partial suffocation by a plaster gag. The verdict was murder by a person or persons unknown.

After the inquest, Mrs. Fairlands' solicitor, who had supported Mrs. Evans during the ordeal in court, went with her to the flat. They arrived just as the municipal dust cart was beginning to move away. One of the older dustmen came up to them.

"You for the old lady they did Christmas Eve?" he asked, with some hesitation.

"I'm her daughter," Dorothy said, her eyes filling again, as they still did all too readily.

"What d'you want?" asked the solicitor, who was anxious to get back to his office.

"No offense," said the man, ignoring him and keeping his eyes on Dorothy's face. "It's like this 'ere, see. They put a Christmas tree outside, by the bins, see. Decorated. We didn't like to take it, seeing it's not exactly rubbish and her gone and that. Nobody about we could ask—"

Dorothy understood. The Christmas tree. Hugh's doing, obviously. Sweet of him.

"Of course you must have it, if it's any use to you now, so late. Have you got children?"

"Three, ma'am. Two younguns. I arsked the other chaps. They don't want it. They said to leave it."

"No, you take it," Dorothy told him. "I don't want to see it. I don't want to be reminded—"

"Thanks a lot, dear," the dustman said, gravely sympathetic, walking back round the house.

The solicitor took the door key from Dorothy and let her in, so she did not see the tree as the dustman emerged with it held carefully before him.

In his home that evening the tree was greeted with a mixture of joy and derision.

"As if I 'adn't enough to clear up yesterday and the day before," his wife complained, half angry, half laughing. "Where'd you get it, anyway?"

When he had finished telling her, the two children, who had listened, crept away to play with the new glittering toy. And before long Mavis, the youngest, found the brooch pinned to the star. She unfastened it carefully and held it in her hand, turning it this way and that to catch the light.

But not for long. Her brother Ernie, two years older, soon snatched it. Mavis went for him, and he ran, making for the front door to escape into the street where Mavis was forbidden to play. Though she seldom obeyed the rule, on this occasion she used it to make loud protest, setting up a howl that brought her mother to the door of the kitchen.

But Ernie had not escaped with his prize. His elder

brother Ron was on the point of entering, and when Ernie flung wide the door, Ron pushed in, shoving his little brother back.

" 'E's nicked my star," Mavis wailed. "Make 'im give me back, Ron. It's mine. Off the tree."

Ron took Ernie by the back of his collar and swung him round.

"Give!" he said firmly. Ernie clenched his right fist, betraying himself. Ron took his arm, bent his hand over forwards, and, as the brooch fell to the floor, stooped to pick it up. Ernie was now in tears.

"Where'd 'e get it?" Ron asked over the child's doubled-up, weeping form.

"The tree," Mavis repeated. "*I* found it. On the star— on the tree."

"Wot the 'ell d'she mean?" Ron asked, exasperated.

"Shut up, the lot of you!" their mother cried fiercely from the kitchen where she had retreated. "Ron, come on in to your tea. Late as usual. Why you never—"

"Okay, Mum," the boy said, unrepentant. "I never—"

He sat down, looking at the sparkling object in his hand.

"What'd Mavis mean about a tree?"

"Christmas tree. Dad brought it in. I've a good mind to put it on the fire. Nothing but argument since 'e fetched it."

"It's pretty," Ron said, meaning the brooch in his hand. "Dress jewelry, they calls it." He slipped it into his pocket.

"That's mine," Mavis insisted. "I found it pinned on that star on the tree. You give it back, Ron."

"Leave 'im alone," their mother said, smacking away the reaching hands. "Go and play with your blasted tree. Dad didn't ought t'ave brought it. Ought t'ave 'ad more sense—"

Ron sat quietly, eating his kipper and drinking his tea. When he had finished, he stacked his crockery in the sink, went upstairs, changed his shirt, put a pair of shiny dancing shoes in the pockets of his mackintosh, and went off to the club where his current girlfriend, Sally, fifteen like himself, attending the same comprehensive school, was waiting for him.

"You're late," she said over her shoulder, not leaving the group of her girlfriends.

"I've 'eard that before tonight. Mum was creating. Not my fault if Mr. Pope wants to see me about exam papers."

"You're never taking G.C.E.?"

"Why not?"

"Coo! 'Oo started that lark?"

"Mr. Pope. I just told you. D'you want to dance or don't you?"

She did and she knew Ron was not one to wait indefinitely. So she joined him, and together they went to the main hall where dancing was in progress, with a band formed by club members.

" 'Alf a mo!" Ron said as they reached the door. "I got something you'll like."

He produced the brooch.

Sally was delighted. This was no cheap store piece. It was slap-up dress jewelry, like the things you saw in the West End, in Bond Street, in the Burlington Arcade, even. She told him she'd wear it just below her left shoulder near the neck edge of her dress. When they moved on to the dance floor she was holding her head higher and swinging her hips more than ever before. She and Ron danced well together. That night many couples stood still to watch them.

About an hour later the dancing came to a sudden end with a sound of breaking glass and shouting that grew in volume and ferocity.

"Raid!" yelled the boys on the dance floor, deserting their partners and crowding to the door. "Those bloody Wingers again."

The sounds of battle led them, running swiftly, to the table-tennis and billiards room, where a shambles confronted them. Overturned tables, ripped cloth, broken glass were everywhere. Tall youths and younger lads were fighting indiscriminately. Above the din the club warden and the three voluntary workers, two of them women, raised their voices in appeal and admonishment, equally ignored. The young barrister who attended once a week to give legal advice free, as a form of social service, to those who asked for it plunged into the battle, only to be flung out again nursing a twisted arm. It was the club caretaker, old and experienced in gang warfare, who summoned the police. They arrived silently, snatched ringleaders with expert knowledge or recognition, hemmed in their captives while the battle melted, and waited while their colleagues, posted at the doors of the club, turned back all would-be escapers.

Before long complete order was restored. In the dance hall the line of prisoners stood below the platform where the band had played. They included club members as well as strangers. The rest, cowed, bunched together near the door, also included a few strangers. Murmurings against these soon added them to the row of captives.

"Now," said the sergeant, who had arrived in answer to the call, "Mr. Smith will tell me who belongs here and who doesn't."

The goats were quickly separated from the rather black sheep.

"Next, who was playing table tennis when the raid commenced?"

Six hands shot up from the line. Some disheveled girls near the door also held up their hands.

"The rest were in here dancing," the warden said. "The boys left the girls when they heard the row, I think."

"That's right," Ron said boldly. "We 'eard glass going, and we guessed it was them buggers. They been 'ere before."

"They don't learn," said the sergeant with a baleful glance at the goats, who shuffled their feet and looked sulky.

"You'll be charged at the station," the sergeant went on, "and I'll want statements from some of your lads," he told the warden. "Also from you and your assistants. These other kids can all go home. Quietly, mind," he said, raising his voice. "Show us there's some of you can behave like reasonable adults and not childish savages."

Sally ran forward to Ron as he left the row under the platform. He took her hand as they walked towards the door. But the sergeant had seen something that surprised him. He made a signal over their heads. At the door they were stopped.

"I think you're wanted. Stand aside for a minute," the constable told them.

The sergeant was the one who had been at the flat in the first part of the Fairlands case. He had been there when a second detailed examination of the flat was made in case the missing jewelry had been hidden away and had therefore escaped the thief. He had formed a very clear picture in his mind of what he was looking for from Mrs. Evans' description. As Sally passed him on her way to the door with Ron, part of the picture presented itself to his astonished eyes.

He turned to the warden.

"That pair. Can I have a word with them somewhere private?"

"Who? Ron Sharp and Sally Biggs? Two of our very nicest—"

The two were within earshot. They exchanged a look of amusement instantly damped by the sergeant, who ordered them briefly to follow him. In the warden's office, with the door shut, he said to Sally, "Where did you get that brooch you're wearing?"

The girl flushed. Ron said angrily, "I give it 'er. So what?"

"So where did you come by it?"

Ron hesitated. He didn't want to let himself down in Sally's eyes. He wanted her to think he'd bought it specially for her. He said, aggressively, "That's my business."

"I don't think so." Turning to Sally, the sergeant said, "Would you mind letting me have a look at it, miss?"

The girl was becoming frightened. Surely Ron hadn't done anything silly? He was looking upset. Perhaps—

"All right," she said, undoing the brooch and handing it over. "Poor eyesight, I suppose."

It was feeble defiance, and the sergeant ignored it. He said, "I'll have to ask you two to come down to the station. I'm not an expert, but we shall have to know a great deal more about this article, and Inspector Brooks will be particularly interested to know where it came from."

Ron remaining obstinately silent in spite of Sally's entreaty, the two found themselves presently sitting opposite Inspector Brooks, with the brooch lying on a piece of white paper before them.

"This brooch," said the inspector sternly, "is one piece of jewelry listed as missing from the flat of a Mrs. Fairlands, who was robbed and murdered on Christmas Eve or early Christmas Day."

"*Never!*" whispered Sally, aghast.

Ron said nothing. He was not a stupid boy, and he realized at once that he must now speak, whatever Sally thought of him. Also that he had a good case if he didn't say too much. So, after careful thought, he told Brooks exactly how and when he had come by the brooch and advised him to check this with his father and mother. The old lady's son had stuck the tree out by the dustbins, his mother had said, and her daughter had told his father he could have it to take home.

Inspector Brooks found the tale too fantastic to be untrue. Taking the brooch and the two subdued youngsters with him, he went to Ron's home, where more surprises awaited him. After listening to Mr. Sharp's account of the Christmas tree, which exactly tallied with Ron's, he went into the next room where the younger children were playing and Mrs. Sharp was placidly watching television.

"Which of you two found the brooch?" Brooks asked. The little girl was persuaded to agree that she had done so.

"But I got these," the boy said. He dived into his pocket and dragged out the pearl necklace and the diamond bracelet.

" 'Struth!" said the inspector, overcome. "She must've been balmy."

"No, she wasn't," Sally broke in. "She was nice. She give us two and a tanner."

"She *what?*"

Sally explained the carol singing expedition. They had been up four roads in that part, she said, and only two nicker the lot.

"Mostly it was nil," she said. "Then there was some give

a bob and this old gentleman and the woman with 'im ten bob each. We packed it in after that.''

"This means you actually went to Mrs. Fairlands' house?" Brooks said sternly to Ron.

"With the others—yes."

"Did you go inside?"

"No."

"No." Sally supported him. "She come out."

"Was she wearing the brooch?"

"No," said Ron.

"Not when she come out, she wasn't," Sally corrected him.

Ron kicked her ankle gently. The inspector noticed this.

"When did you see it?" he asked Sally.

"When she looked through the window at us. We shone the torch on 'er. It didn't 'alf shine."

"But you didn't recognize it when Ron gave it to you?"

"Why should I? I never saw it close. It was pinned on 'er dress at the neck. I didn't think of it till you said."

Brooks nodded. This seemed fair enough. He turned to face Ron.

"So you went back alone later to get it? Right?"

"I never! It's a damned lie!" the boy cried fiercely.

Mr. Sharp took a step forward. His wife bundled the younger children out of the room. Sally began to cry.

" 'Oo are you accusing?" Mr. Sharp said heavily. "You 'eard 'ow I come by the tree. My mates was there. The things was on it. I got witnesses. If Ron did that job, would 'e leave the only things worth 'aving? It says in the paper nothing of value, don't it?"

Brooks realized the force of this argument, however badly put. He'd been carried away a little. Unusual for him; he was surprised at himself. But the murder had been a particularly revolting one, and until these jewels turned up, he'd had no idea where to look. Carol singers. It might be a line and then again it mightn't.

He took careful statements from Ron, Sally, Ron's father, and the two younger children. He took the other pieces of jewelry and the Christmas tree. Carol singers. Mrs. Fairlands had opened the door to Ron's lot, having taken off her brooch if the story was true. Having hidden it very cleverly. He and his men had missed it completely. A Christmas tree decorated with flashy bits and pieces as usual. Standing back against a wall. They'd ignored it. Seen nothing but tinsel and glitter for weeks past. Of course they hadn't noticed it. The real thief or thieves hadn't noticed it, either.

Back at the station he locked away the jewels, labeled, in the safe and rang up Hugh Evans. He did not tell him where the pieces had been found.

Afterwards he had to deal with some of the hooligans who had now been charged with breaking, entering, willful damage, and making an affray. He wished he could pin Mrs. Fairlands' murder on their ringleader, a most degenerate and evil youth. Unfortunately, the whole gang had been in trouble in the West End that night; most of them had spent what remained of it in Bow Street police station. So they were out. But routine investigations now had a definite aim. To collect a list of all those who had sung carols at the house in Mrs. Fairlands' road on Christmas Eve, to question the singers about the times they had appeared there and about the houses they had visited.

It was not easy. Carol singers came from many social groups and often traveled far from their own homes. The youth clubs in the district were helpful; so were the various student bodies and hostels in the neighborhood. Brooks's manor was wide and very variously populated. In four days he had made no headway at all.

A radio message went out, appealing to carol singers to report at the police station if they were near Mrs. Fairlands' house at any time on Christmas Eve. The press took up the quest, dwelling on the pathetic aspects of the old woman's tragic death at a time of traditional peace on earth and good will towards men. All right-minded citizens must want to help the law over this revolting crime.

But the citizens maintained their attitude of apathy or caution.

Except for one, a freelance journalist, Tom Meadows, who had an easy manner with young people because he liked them. He became interested because the case seemed to involve young people. It was just up his street. So he went first to the Sharp family, gained their complete confidence, and had a long talk with Ron.

The boy was willing to help. After he had got over his indignation with the law for daring to suspect him, he had had sense enough to see how this had been inevitable. His anger was directed more truly at the unknown thugs responsible. He remembered Mrs. Fairlands with respect and pity. He was ready to do anything Tom Meadows suggested.

The journalist was convinced that the criminal or criminals must be local, with local knowledge. It was unlikely they would wander from house to house, taking a chance on finding one that might be profitable. It was far more likely that they knew already that Mrs. Fairlands lived alone, would be quite alone over Christmas and therefore defenseless. But their information had been incomplete. They had not known how little money she kept at the flat. No one had known this except her family. Or had they?

Meadows, patient and amiable, worked his way from the Sharps to the postman, the milkman, and through the latter to the daily.

"Well, of course I mentioned 'er being alone for the 'oliday. I told that detective so. In the way of conversation, I told 'im. Why shouldn't I?"

"Why indeed? But who did you tell, exactly?"

"I disremember. Anyone, I suppose. If we was comparing. I'm on me own now meself, but I go up to me brother's at the 'olidays."

"Where would that be?"

"Notting 'Ill way. 'E's on the railway. Paddington."

Bit by bit Meadows extracted a list of her friends and relations, those with whom she had talked most often during the week before Christmas. Among her various nephews and nieces was a girl who went to the same comprehensive school as Ron and his girlfriend Sally.

Ron listened to the assignment Meadows gave him.

"Sally won't like it," he said candidly.

"Bring her into it, then. Pretend it's all your own idea."

Ron grinned.

"Shirl won't like that," he said.

Tom Meadows laughed.

"Fix it any way you like," he said. "But I think this girl Shirley was with a group and did go to sing carols for Mrs. Fairlands. I know she isn't on the official list, so she hasn't reported it. I want to know why."

"I'm not shopping anymore," Ron said warily.

"I'm not asking you to. I don't imagine Shirley or her friends did Mrs. Fairlands. But it's just possible she knows or saw something and is afraid to speak up for fear of reprisals."

"Cor!" said Ron. It was like a page of his favorite magazine working out in real life. He confided in Sally, and they went to work.

The upshot was interesting. Shirley did have something to say, and she said it to Tom Meadows in her own home with her disapproving mother sitting beside her.

"I never did like the idea of Shirl going out after dark, begging at house doors. That's all it really is, isn't it? My children have very good pocket money. They've nothing to complain of."

"I'm sure they haven't," Meadows said mildly. "But there's a lot more to carol singing than asking for money. Isn't there, Shirley?"

"I'll say," the girl answered. "Mum don't understand."

"You can't stop her," the mother complained. "Self-willed. Stubborn. I don't know, I'm sure. Out after dark. My dad'd 've taken his belt to me for less."

"There were four of us," Shirley protested. "It wasn't late. Not above seven or eight."

The time was right, Meadows noted, if she was speaking of her visit to Mrs. Fairlands' road. She was. Encouraged to describe everything, she agreed that her group was working towards the house especially to entertain the old lady who was going to be alone for Christmas. She'd got that from her aunt, who worked for Mrs. Fairlands. They began at the far end of the road on the same side as the old lady. When they were about six houses away, they saw another group go up to it or to one near it. Then they were singing themselves. The next time she looked round,

she saw one child running away up the road. She did not
know where he had come from. She did not see the others.

"You did not see them go on?"

"No. They weren't in the road then, but they might have
gone right on while we were singing. There's a turning off,
isn't there?"

"Yes. Go on."

"Well, we went up to Mrs. Fairlands' and rang the bell.
I thought I'd tell her she knew my aunt and we'd come
special."

"Yes. What happened?"

"Nothing. At least—"

"Go on. Don't be frightened."

Shirley's face had gone very pale.

"There were men's voices inside. Arguing like. Nasty.
We scarpered."

Tom Meadows nodded gravely.

"That would be upsetting. *Men's* voices? Or big boys?"

"Could be either, couldn't it? Well, perhaps more like
sixth form boys, at that."

"You thought it was boys, didn't you? Boys from your
school."

Shirley was silent.

"You thought they'd know and have it in for you if you
told. Didn't you? I won't let you down, Shirley. Didn't
you?"

She whispered, "Yes," and added, "Some of our boys
got knives. I seen them."

Meadows went to Inspector Brooks. He explained how
Ron had helped him to get in touch with Shirley and the
result of that interview. The inspector, who had worked
as a routine matter on all Mrs. Fairlands' contacts with the
outer world, was too interested to feel annoyed at the
other's success.

"Men's voices?" Brooks said incredulously.

"Most probably older lads," Meadows answered. "She
agreed that was what frightened her group. They might
have looked out and recognized them as they ran away."

"There'd been no attempt at intimidations?"

"They're not all *that* stupid."

"No."

Brooks considered.

"This mustn't break in the papers yet, you understand?"

"Perfectly. But I shall stay around."

Inspector Brooks nodded, and Tom went away. Brooks took his sergeant and drove to Mrs. Fairlands' house. They still had the key of the flat, and they still had the house under observation.

The new information was disturbing, Brooks felt. Men's voices, raised in anger. Against poor Mrs. Fairlands, of course. But there were no adult fingerprints in the flat except those of the old lady herself and of her daily. Gloves had been worn, then. A professional job. But no signs whatever of breaking and entering. Therefore, Mrs. Fairlands had let them in. Why? She had peeped out at Ron's lot, to check who they were, obviously. She had not done so for Shirley's. Because she was in the power of the "men" whose voices had driven this other group away in terror.

But there had been two distinct small footprints in the dust of the outer hall and a palmprint on the outer door had been small, childsize.

Perhaps the child that Shirley had seen running down the road had been a decoy. The whole group she had noticed at Mrs. Fairlands' door might have been employed for that purpose and the men or older boys were lurking at the corner of the house, to pounce when the door opened. Possible, but not very likely. Far too risky, even on a dark evening. Shirley could not have seen distinctly. The street lamps were at longish intervals in that road. But there were always a few passersby. Even on Christmas Eve no professional group of villains would take such a risk.

Standing in the cold drawing room, now covered with a grey film of dust, Inspector Brooks decided to make another careful search for clues. He had missed the jewels. Though he felt justified in making it, his mistake was a distinct blot on his copybook. It was up to him now to retrieve his reputation. He sent the sergeant to take another look at the bedroom, with particular attention to the dressing table. He himself began to go over the drawing room with the greatest possible care.

Shirley's evidence suggested there had been more than one thief. The girl had said "voices." That meant at least two, which probably accounted for the fact, apart from her age, that neither Mrs. Fairlands nor her clothes gave any indication of a struggle. She had been overpowered immediately, it seemed. She had not been strong enough or agile enough to tear, scratch, pull off any fragment from her attackers' clothes or persons. There had been no trace of any useful material under her fingernails or elsewhere.

Brooks began methodically with the chair to which Mrs. Fairlands had been bound and worked his way outwards from that center. After the furniture, the carpet and curtains. After that the walls.

Near the door, opposite the fireplace, he found on the wall—two feet, three inches up from the floor—a small, round, brownish, greasy smear. He had not seen it before. In artificial light, he checked, it was nearly invisible. On this morning, with the first sunshine of the New Year coming into the room, the little patch was entirely obvious, slightly shiny where the light from the window caught it.

Inspector Brooks took a wooden spatula from his case of aids and carefully scraped off the substance into a small plastic box, sniffing at it as he did so.

"May I, too?" asked Tom Meadows behind him.

The inspector wheeled round with an angry exclamation. "How did you get in?" he asked.

"Told the copper in your car I wanted to speak to you."

"What about?"

"Well, about how you were getting on, really," Tom said disarmingly. "I see you are. Please let me have one sniff."

Inspector Brooks was annoyed, both by the intrusion and the fact that he had not heard it, being so concentrated on his work. So he closed his box, shut it into his black bag, and called to the sergeant in the next room.

Meadows got down on his knees, leaned towards the wall, and sniffed. It was faint, since most of it had been scraped off, but he knew the smell. His freelancing had not been confined to journalism.

He was getting to his feet as the sergeant joined Inspector Brooks. The sergeant raised his eyebrows at the interloper.

"You can't keep the press's noses out of anything," said Brooks morosely.

The other two grinned. It was very apt.

"I'm just off," Tom said. "Good luck with your specimen, inspector. I know where to go now. So will you."

"Come back!" called Brooks. The young man was a menace. He would have to be controlled.

But Meadows was away, striding down the road until he was out of sight of the police car, then running to the nearest tube station where he knew he would find the latest newspaper editions. He bought one, opened it at the entertainments column, and read down the list.

He was a certain six hours ahead of Brooks, he felt sure, possibly more. Probably he had until tomorrow morning. He skipped his lunch and set to work.

Inspector Brooks got the report from the lab that evening, and the answer to his problem came to him as completely as it had done to Tom Meadows in Mrs. Fairlands' drawing room. His first action was to ring up Olympia. This proving fruitless, he sighed. Too late now to contact the big stores; they would all be closed and the employees of every kind gone home.

But in the morning some very extensive telephone calls to managers told him where he must go. He organized his forces to cover all the exits of a big store not very far from Mrs. Fairlands' house. With his sergeant he entered modestly by way of the men's department.

They took a lift from there to the third floor, emerging among the toys. It was the tenth day of Christmas, with the school holidays in full swing and eager children, flush with Christmas money, choosing long-coveted treasures. A Father Christmas, white-bearded, in the usual red, hooded gown, rather too short for him, was moving about trying to promote a visit to the first of that day's performances of "Snowdrop and the Seven Dwarfs." As his insistence seeped into the minds of the abstracted young, they turned their heads to look at the attractive cardboard entrance of the little "theater" at the far end of the department. A gentle flow towards it began and gathered momentum. Inspector Brooks and the sergeant joined the stream.

Inside the theater there were small chairs in rows for the children. The grownups stood at the back. A gramophone played the Disney film music.

The early scenes were brief, mere tableaux with a line thrown in here and there for Snowdrop. The queen spoke the famous doggerel to her mirror.

The curtain fell and rose again on Snowdrop, surrounded by the Seven Dwarfs. Two of them had beards, real beards. Dopey rose to his feet and began to sing.

"Okay," whispered Brooks to the sergeant. "The child who sang and ran away."

The sergeant nodded. Brooks whispered again. "I'm going round the back. Get the audience here out quietly if the balloon goes up before they finish."

He tiptoed quietly away. He intended to catch the dwarfs in their dressing room immediately after the show, arrest the lot, and sort them out at the police station.

But the guilty ones had seen him move. Or rather Dopey, more guilt-laden and fearful than the rest, had noticed the two men who seemed to have no children with them, had seen their heads close together, had seen one move silently away. As Brooks disappeared, the midget's nerve broke. His song ended in a scream; he fled from the stage.

In the uproar that followed, the dwarf's scream was echoed by the frightened children. The lights went up in the theater, the shop assistants and the sergeant went into action to subdue their panic and get them out.

Inspector Brooks found himself in a maze of lathe and plaster backstage arrangements. He found three bewildered small figures, with anxious, wizened faces, trying to restrain Dopey, who was still in the grip of his hysteria. A few sharp questions proved that the three had no idea what was happening.

The queen and Snowdrop appeared, highly indignant. Brooks, now holding Dopey firmly by the collar, demanded the other three dwarfs. The two girls, subdued and totally bewildered, pointed to their dressing room. It was empty, but a tumbled heap of costumes on the floor showed what they had done. The sergeant appeared, breathless.

"Take this chap," Brooks said, thrusting the now fainting Dopey at him. "Take him down. I'm shopping him. Get onto the management to warn all departments for the others."

He was gone, darting into the crowded toy department, where children and parents stood amazed or hurried towards the lifts, where a dense crowd stood huddled, anxious to leave the frightening trouble spot.

Brooks bawled an order.

The crowd at the lift melted away from it, leaving three small figures in overcoats and felt hats, trying in vain to push once more under cover.

They bolted, bunched together, but they did not get far. Round the corner of a piled table of soft toys Father Christmas was waiting. He leaped forward, tripped up one, snatched another, hit the third as he passed and grabbed him, too, as he fell.

The tripped one struggled up and on as Brooks appeared.

"I'll hold these two," panted Tom Meadows through his white beard, which had fallen sideways.

The chase was brief. Brooks gained on the dwarf. The latter knew it was hopeless. He snatched up a mallet lying beside a display of camping equipment and, rushing to the side of the store, leaped on a counter, from there clambered up a tier of shelves, beat a hole in the window behind them, and dived through. Horrified people and police on the pavement below saw the small body turning over and over like a leaf as it fell.

"All yours," said Tom Meadows, handing his captives, too limp now to struggle, to Inspector Brooks and tearing off his Father Christmas costume. "See you later."

He was gone, to shut himself in a telephone booth on the ground floor of the store and hand his favorite editor the scoop. It had paid off, taking over from the old boy, an ex-actor like himself, who was quite willing for a fiver to write a note pleading illness and sending a substitute.

"Your reporter, Tom Meadows, dressed as Father Christmas, today captured and handed over to the police two of the three murderers of Mrs. Fairlands—"

Inspector Brooks, with three frantic midgets demanding legal aid, scrabbling at the doors of their cells, took a lengthy statement from the fourth, the one with the treble voice whose nerve had broken on the fatal night, as it had again that day. Greasepaint had betrayed the little fiends, Brooks told him, privately regretting that Meadows had been a jump ahead of him there. Greasepaint left on in the rush to get at their prey. One of the brutes must have fallen against the wall, pushed by the old woman herself perhaps. He hoped so. He hoped it was her own action that had brought these squalid killers to justice.